On the plus side, you've raised a
wonderful, strong-willed daughter.
On the minus side, she's using that
determination to find…

A Match For
MOM

Three very different stories of mothers
and daughters and heroes, from some
of your all-time favorite authors.

Relive the romance…

About the Authors

ANNE MATHER

is an international favorite; her latest bestseller, *Dangerous Temptation,* was a February MIRA release. With more than one hundred and thirty titles to her credit, she is one of Harlequin's most prolific authors. The well-traveled mother of two grown children, Anne lives with her husband in the north-east of England, where she was born.

LINDA RANDALL WISDOM

has worked in personnel, marketing and public relations, all of which gave her a wealth of experience on which to draw when creating characters. She is now a full-time writer, and the author of over fifty books. Linda knew she was destined to write romances when her first sale came on her wedding anniversary. She lives in Southern California with her husband and a houseful of pets.

VICKI LEWIS THOMPSON

began her writing career at the age of eleven with a short story in the *Auburn, Illinois Weekly* and quickly became a byline junkie. Then she discovered she could write books. In July of 1997, she will celebrate fifteen years of writing romance with a very special promotion and a wonderful Temptation novel entitled *The Heartbreaker.* She lives in Tucson, Arizona, has two grown children and a husband who inspires her to write from the heart.

A Match For MOM

Anne Mather
Linda Randall Wisdom
Vicki Lewis Thompson

Harlequin Books

TORONTO • NEW YORK • LONDON
AMSTERDAM • PARIS • SYDNEY • HAMBURG
STOCKHOLM • ATHENS • TOKYO • MILAN
MADRID • WARSAW • BUDAPEST • AUCKLAND

HARLEQUIN BOOKS

by Request—A Match for Mom

Copyright © 1997 by Harlequin Books S.A.

ISBN 0-373-20135-4

The publisher acknowledges the copyright holders
of the individual works as follows:
GUILTY
Copyright © 1992 by Anne Mather
A MAN FOR MOM
Copyright © 1993 by Linda Randall Wisdom
THE FIX-IT MAN
Copyright © 1986 by Vicki Lewis Thompson

CONTENTS

The man of Laura's dreams suddenly walked into her life, but she despised him. She didn't want him laying bare the unguarded hunger of her soul. She desperately didn't want to want him. He was too young, too rich…and he was involved with her own daughter!

GUILTY

Anne Mather

CHAPTER ONE

THE phone was ringing as Laura opened the door, and her heart sank. She had been anticipating kicking off her shoes, helping herself to a well-deserved drink, and running a nice deep bath in which to enjoy it. But all these pleasant prospects had to be put on hold while she answered the call. And as she could think of no reason why anyone should be calling her at this time of the evening, she was necessarily reticent.

After all, it was only twenty minutes since she had left the school, after a particularly arduous session with the parents of her fourteen-year-old students, and she had hoped to indulge herself for what was left of the evening. Mrs Forrest, who came in two days a week to keep the house in order, had, as she often did, left something simmering in the oven, and, although it was probably overcooked by now, the smell emanating from the kitchen was still very appetising. But someone, another parent perhaps, or a colleague—though that was less likely—or even her superior in the English department, had decreed otherwise, and she mentally squared her shoulders before going into the living-room and picking up the phone.

'Yes,' she said evenly, her low attractive voice no less sympathetic in spite of her feelings. 'Laura Fox speaking.'

'Mum?' Her daughter's voice instantly dispelled any trace of resignation in her attitude. 'Where've you been? I've been trying to reach you for hours!'

'Julie!' Laura's initial sense of relief at hearing her daughter's voice was quickly followed by concern. After all—she glanced at the slim gold watch on her wrist—it was almost ten o'clock. 'Is something wrong? Where are you? I thought you said you were going to New York this week.'

'I was.' But her daughter didn't sound concerned, and Laura sank down on to the arm of the sofa and tucked one foot behind the other. Experience had taught her that her daughter's telephone calls—though infrequent—tended to be long, and Laura prepared herself for protracted explanations. 'I told Harry I couldn't go.'

'I see.'

Laura didn't. Not really. But it seemed a suitable reply. If Julie wanted to tell her why she should have chosen to turn down a proposedly lucrative opportunity to work in the United States she would do so. Laura knew her daughter well enough to know that asking too many questions could illicit an aggressive response. Ever since she was sixteen, and old enough to make her own decisions, Julie had resisted any efforts on her mother's part to try and offer her advice. Her favourite retort, if Laura had attempted to counsel her, was that Laura was in no position to criticise her plans, when she had made such a mess of her own life. And, although the barb was hardly justified, Laura was too sensitive about her own mistakes to carry the argument.

Now, however, her daughter was speaking again, and Laura forced herself to concentrate on what she was saying. Now was not the time to indulge in rueful recollection, and there was no denying that Julie had made a success of her career.

'So,' her daughter exclaimed impatiently, 'aren't you going to ask me why I've been trying to get in touch with you? Don't you want to know why I turned down Harry's offer?'

Laura stifled a sigh. 'Well—of course,' she said, looking longingly towards the sherry decanter residing on the bureau, just too far away to reach. 'But I assumed you were about to tell me.' A twinge of anxiety gripped her. 'What's happened? You're not ill, are you?'

'No.' Julie sounded scornful. 'I've never felt better. Is that the only reason you can think of why I should want to stay in London?'

Laura lifted her shoulders wearily. Her neck was aching from looking up at people, and her spine felt numb. It had been a long day, and she wasn't really in the mood to play twenty questions.

'Have you left the agency?' she asked carefully, conscious that Julie could throw a tantrum at the least provocation, and unwilling to arouse her daughter's anger. 'Have you found a better job?'

'You could say that.' Evidently she had made the right response, and Julie's tone was considerably warmer. 'But I haven't left the agency. Not yet, anyway.'

'Oh.' Laura endeavoured to absorb the subtler connotations of this statement. 'So—it must be a man.'

There had been a lot of men during Julie's five-year sojourn in the capital, but this was the first time Laura had known her daughter give up a modelling contract for one of them.

'You got it.' Julie was apparently too eager to deliver her news to waste any more time playing games. 'It is a man. *The* man! I'm going to marry him, Mum. At least, I am if I have anything to do with it.'

Laura's lips parted. 'You're getting married!' She had never expected this. Julie had always maintained that marriage was not for her. Not after her mother's unhappy experience.

'Well, not yet,' Julie conceded swiftly. 'He hasn't asked me. But he will. I'll make sure of that. Only—well—he wants to meet you. And I wondered if we could come up for the weekend.'

'He wants to meet me?' Laura was surprised, and Julie didn't sound as if the proposition met with her approval either.

'Yes,' she said shortly. 'Silly, isn't it? But—well—I might as well tell you. He's not English. He's Italian. An Italian count, would you believe? Although he doesn't use the title these days. In any case, he's not an impoverished member of the Italian aristocracy. His family owns factories and things in Northern Italy, and he's very wealthy. What else?' Julie uttered an excited little laugh. 'I wouldn't be considering marrying him otherwise. No matter how sexy he is!'

Laura was stunned. 'But—Julie…' She licked her lips, as she endeavoured to find the right words to voice her feelings. 'I mean—why does he want to meet me? And—coming here. This is just a tiny cottage, Julie. Why, I only have *two* bedrooms!'

'So?' Julie sounded belligerent now. 'We'll only need one.'

'No.' Laura knew she was in danger of being accused of being prudish, but she couldn't help it. 'That is—if—if you come here, you and I will share my room.'

'Oh, all right.' Julie made a sound of impatience. 'I don't suppose Jake would want to sleep with me there anyway. After all, it's his idea that he introduce himself to you. That's apparently how they do things in his part of the world. Only I explained I didn't have a father.'

Julie's scornful words scraped a nerve, but Laura suppressed the urge to defend herself. It was an old argument, and Julie knew as well as her mother that she had had a father, just like anyone else. The fact that her parents had never been married was what she was referring to, a situation she had always blamed her mother for. She had maintained that Laura should have known that the man she had allowed to get her pregnant already had a wife, and no amount of justification on her mother's part could persuade her otherwise. Even though she knew Laura had been only sixteen at the time, while Keith Macfarlane had been considerably older, she had always stuck to the belief that Laura should have been more suspicious of a man who worked in Newcastle and spent most of his weekends in Edinburgh.

But Laura hadn't been like her daughter at that age. The only child of elderly parents, she had been both immature and naïve. A man like Keith Macfarlane, whom she had met at a party at a friend's house, had seemed both worldly-wise and sophisticated, and she had been flattered that someone so confident and assured should have found her so attractive. Besides, she had enjoyed a certain amount of kudos by having him pick her up from the sixth-form college, and for someone who hitherto had lived a fairly humdrum existence it had been exciting.

Of course, with hindsight, Laura could see how stupid she had been. She should have known that a man who liked women as much as Keith did was unlikely to have reached his thirtieth birthday without getting involved with someone else. But she had been young and reckless—and she had paid the price.

Looking back, she suspected Keith had never intended to get so heavily involved. Like her, he'd evidently enjoyed having a partner who was not in his own age-group, and at sixteen, Laura supposed, she had been quite attractive. She had always been tall, and in her teens she had carried more weight than she did now. In consequence, she had looked older, and probably more experienced, too, she acknowledged ruefully. So much so that Keith had expected her to know how to take care of herself, and it had come as quite a shock to him to discover she was still a virgin.

That was when their relationship had foundered. Keith had seen the dangers, and drawn back from them. Three weeks later he'd told her he had been transferred to Manchester, and she'd never heard from him again.

Tom Dalton, the father of Laura's best friend, at whose house she had first met Keith, eventually admitted the truth. He had worked with Keith, and he knew why he spent his weekends in Edinburgh. Laura wished he had seen fit to tell her sooner, but by then it was too late. Laura was pregnant, and for a while it seemed as if her whole life was ruined.

Naturally, she had dreaded telling her parents. Mr and Mrs Fox had never approved of her generation, and she was quite prepared for them to demand she get rid of the baby. But in that instance she was wrong. Instead of making it even harder for her, her father had suggested a simple solution. She should have the baby, and then go back to school. There was no point in wasting her education, and if she was going to have a child to support then she ought to ensure that she had a career to do it. And that was what she had done, leaving the baby with her mother during the day, while she'd studied for her A levels, and subsequently gained a place at the university.

It had not been an easy life, Laura recalled without rancour. Julie had not been an 'easy' baby, and when her parents had died in a car accident during her first year of teaching it had been hard. Coping with the pupils at an inner-city comprehensive during the day, and still finding the energy to cope with a fractious five-year-old at night. But Laura had managed, somehow, although at times she was so tired that she'd wondered how she was going to go on.

Of course, much later, when Julie discovered the circumstances of her own birth, other complications had arisen. As a young girl, Julie had always resented the fact that she only had one parent, and as she grew older that resentment manifested itself in rows and tantrums that often escalated out of all proportion.

But Julie had one consolation. Her features, which as a child had been fairly ordinary, blossomed in her teens into real beauty. Not for Julie the horrors of puppy-fat and acne. Her skin was smooth and unblemished, her height unmarred by extra inches. Her hair, which she had inherited from her mother, was several shades darker than Laura's, a rich, burnished copper that flowed freely about her shoulders. She became the most popular girl in her class, and, although Laura worried that she might make the same mistakes she had made, Julie was much shrewder than she had ever been.

Laura hated to admit it, but when Julie left school before she was eighteen, and took herself off to London to work, she was almost relieved. The effort of sharing an apartment with someone who was totally self-absorbed and totally selfish had been quite a strain, and for months after Julie had gone Laura revelled in her new-found freedom.

And then, not wholly unexpectedly, Julie became famous. The secretarial job she had taken had been in a photographic agency, and not unnaturally someone had noticed how photogenic Julie was. Within months, her face began appearing on the covers of catalogues and magazines, and all the bitterness of the past was buried beneath the mask of her new sophistication.

Of course, Laura had been delighted for her. The guilt she had always felt at being the unwitting cause of Julie's illegitimacy was in some part relieved by her daughter's success, and it meant she could stop worrying about her finances, and buy herself the cottage in Northumberland she had always wanted. These days she lived in a small village about fifteen miles from the city, and only commuted to Newcastle to work.

Now, pushing the memories away, and ignoring her daughter's bitterness, Laura addressed herself to the present situation. 'Do I take it you plan to come up here tomorrow evening?' she asked, mentally assessing the contents of the freezer and finding them wanting. If Julie and this man, whoever he was, were coming to stay, she would have to do some shopping tomorrow lunchtime.

'If that won't put you out,' Julie agreed offhandedly, and Laura hoped she hadn't offended her by reminding her of the differences in their current lifestyles. Julie now owned a luxurious apartment in Knightsbridge, and her visits to Burnfoot were few and far between.

'Well, of course you won't be putting me out,' Laura assured her quickly, not wanting to get the weekend off to an uncertain start. 'Um—so who is this man? What's his name? Other than Jake, that is?'

'I've told you!' exclaimed Julie irritably. 'He's an Italian businessman. His family name is Lombardi. Jake's the eldest son.'

'I see.' So—Jake Lombardi, then, thought Laura nervously. Would that be short for Giovanni? Would Julie be living in Italy, after they were married?

'Anyway, you'll be able to meet him for yourself to-morrow,' declared Julie at last. 'We'll probably drive up in his Lamborghini. Personally I'd prefer to fly, but Jake says he wants to see something of the countryside. He's interested in history—old buildings; that sort of thing.'

'Is he?'

Laura was surprised. What little she had learned about her daughter's previous boyfriends had not led her to believe that Julie would be attracted to a man who cared about anything other than material possessions. But perhaps she was maturing after all, Laura thought hopefully. Was it too much to wish that Julie had learned there was more to life than the accumulation of wealth?

'So—we'll see you some time after five,' Julie finished swiftly. 'I can't stop now, Mum. We're on our way to a party. 'Bye!'

'G'bye.'

Laura made the automatic response, and she was still holding the phone when the line went dead. Shaking her head, she replaced the receiver, and then sat looking at the instrument for a few blank moments, before getting up to pour herself the long-awaited glass of sherry.

Then, after taking a few experimental sips of the wine, she pulled herself together and walked through to the tiny kitchen at the back of the cottage. As she had expected, the casserole Mrs Forrest had left for her was a trifle over-cooked. But, although the vegetables were soggy, the chicken was still edible, and, putting it down on the pine table, she went to get herself a plate. But all her actions were instinctive, and she had the sense of doing things at arm's length. The prospect of Julie's actually getting married, of settling down at last, had left her feeling somewhat off guard, and she knew it would take some getting used to.

Nevertheless, she was not displeased at the news. On the contrary, she hoped her daughter would find real happiness. And maybe Julie would learn to forgive her mother's mistakes, now that she loved someone herself. Or at least try to understand the ideals of an impressionable girl.

Friday was always a busy day for Laura. She had no free periods, and she usually spent her lunch-hour doing some of the paperwork that being assistant head of the English department demanded. It meant she could spend Saturday relaxing, before tackling the preparation she did on Sundays.

Consequently, when she went out to the car park to get into her small Ford, Mark Leith, her opposite number in the maths department, raised surprised eyebrows at this evident break with routine.

'Got a date?' he enquired, slamming the boot of his car, and tucking the box he had taken from it under his arm. 'Don't tell me you're two-timing me!'

Laura pulled a face at him. She and Mark had an on-off relationship that never progressed beyond the occasional date for dinner or the theatre. It was Laura's decision that their friendship should never become anything more than that, and Mark, who was in his early forties, and still lived with his mother, seemed to accept the situation. Laura guessed he preferred bachelorhood really, but now and then he attempted to assert his authority.

'I'm going shopping,' she replied now, opening the door of the car, and folding herself behind the wheel. 'Julie's coming for the weekend, and bringing a friend.'

'I see.' Mark walked across the tarmac to stand beside

her window, and, suppressing a quite unwarranted sense of impatience, Laura wound it down. 'A girlfriend?'

'What?'

Laura wasn't really paying attention, and Mark's mouth turned down at the corners. 'The friend,' he reminded her pointedly. 'Is it a girlfriend?'

'Oh...' Laura put the key into the ignition, and looked up at him resignedly. 'No. No, as a matter of fact, it's a boyfriend. Well, a man, I suppose. She rang me last night, after I got home.'

'Really?' Mark arched his sandy brows again, and Laura felt her irritation return. 'Bit sudden, isn't it?'

Laura sighed, gripping the wheel with both hands. It was nothing to do with him really, and she found she resented his assumption that he could make remarks of that sort. It was probably her own fault, she thought wearily. Although she hadn't encouraged Mark's advances, she supposed she had let him think he had some influence in her life.

Now she forced a polite smile, and shrugged her slim shoulders. 'Oh—you know what young people are like!' she exclaimed dismissively. 'They don't need weeks to plan a trip. They just do it.'

'It's a bit hard on you though, isn't it?' Mark persisted, his chin jutting indignantly. 'I mean—you might have had other plans.'

Laura nearly said, 'Who? Me?' but she didn't think Mark would appreciate the irony. His sense of humour tended towards the unsubtle, and any effort on Laura's part to parody her own position would only meet with reproval. In consequence, she only shook her head, and leaned forward to start the engine.

'I was going to suggest we might try and get tickets for that revue at the Playhouse,' Mark added, as if to justify his aggravation. 'I've heard it's jolly good, and it finishes on Saturday.'

Laura squashed her own resentment, and managed a warmer expression. 'Oh, well,' she said, 'we'll have to catch it some other time. And now I really must go, or I won't have time to get everything I want.'

Mark's mouth compressed. 'You could still——'

'No, I couldn't,' declared Laura firmly, and put the car into gear. 'I'll see you later.'

He was still standing looking after the car as Laura turned out of the car park, and lifted her hand in a reluctant farewell. Really, she thought, concentrating on the traffic on the West Road, there were times when Mark could be such a pain. Surely he could understand that as Julie paid so few visits to her mother Laura couldn't possibly desert her to go to the theatre with him? Besides, it wasn't as if Julie were making a convenience of her this time. She was bringing her future husband to meet her, and, even if it was more his suggestion than hers, it might presage a new closeness in her relationship with her daughter.

But Mark and Julie had never seen eye to eye. From the beginning, he had found her spoilt, and headstrong, and on the rare occasions when they had all been together Julie had gone out of her way to be objectionable to him. So far as she was concerned, Mark was a stuffed shirt, and her comments about his bachelor lifestyle wouldn't bear repeating.

The supermarket was heaving with people doing their weekend shopping, and Laura, who generally supplied her needs from the small store in Burnfoot, gritted her teeth as yet another mother with toddlers blocked her passage. 'Excuse me,' she said, trying to edge along the aisle, and was rewarded with a smear of ice lolly all along the sleeve of her anorak.

'Oh—sorry!' exclaimed a smiling matron, drawing her child's hand away, and examining the lolly for damage. 'These aisles are so narrow, aren't they?'

Laura glanced at the sticky red confection adorning her sleeve, and then gave a resigned shrug. There was no point in getting angry. 'Yes, very narrow,' she agreed, and, unable to prevent herself from smiling at the cheeky toddler, she moved on.

It was after one by the time she had loaded her purchases into her car, and striking half-past as she turned into the school car park. One or two stragglers were still sauntering across the playground, and they gave her a knowing look, before turning to whisper to their friends. Laura could almost hear the comments about her being late as well, and she tried not to look too flustered as she strode towards the school buildings.

The afternoon seemed endless. Now that the time for Julie's arrival was approaching, Laura could feel herself getting tense, and it didn't help when her class of fourth-years started acting up. Usually she had no trouble with her pupils, and she had gained a reputation for being tough, but fair. However, today she found it difficult to keep order, and it wasn't until she apprehended how hoarse she was getting that she realised she had had to shout to make herself heard.

But at last three-thirty arrived, and after dismissing the fourth-years Laura packed what exercise books she could into her briefcase, and tucked the rest under her arm. By her reckoning, she had at least two hours left to prepare herself for Julie's arrival, and the way she was feeling she was going to need every minute of it. She didn't know why she let Julie tie her up in knots like this, but she always did, and Laura intended to have a bath and wash her hair, so that she could have confidence in her appearance, if nothing else.

Burnfoot was situated in some of the most beautiful country in Northumberland. A small community of some one thousand souls, it was surrounded by the rolling fields and hills of the border country, with the crumbling remains of Hadrian's Wall providing a natural barrier to the north. It was farming country, with tumbling streams and shady forests, and long, straight roads, unfolding towards the old Roman forts of Chesters and Housesteads.

Laura had always loved it. Even though she had been born and brought up in Newcastle, this was the area where she felt most at home, and when the opportunity to buy the cottage had presented itself she had jumped at the chance. She knew Julie had thought she was mad; a single woman, on her own, going to live in some 'God-forsaken spot' as she'd put it; but Laura had never had cause to regret her decision. The cottage had been in a poor state of repair when she'd got it, it was true, and it had taken years to get it as she wanted. But that was all behind her now. It was still small, and the ceilings were still too low, but she had had central heating installed, and on a cold winter's evening she could light the fire in the living-room, and toast her toes.

She was perfectly content, she thought, except on these occasions when Julie invaded her life, and then she was forced to see the cottage's shortcomings. Julie was adept at pointing out its disadvantages, and never once had she admired the garden Laura had worked so painstakingly to tame, or complimented her mother on providing a home that was both attractive, and full of character.

Laura had decided to prepare fish for dinner. It was a Friday, and she couldn't be sure that as an Italian, and no doubt a Roman Catholic, Julie's boyfriend would be prepared to eat meat. She had bought some plaice, and she intended to cook it in a white wine sauce. She had decided not to provide a starter, and instead she had bought a strawberry shortcake to supplement the cheese and crackers that she herself preferred. She knew Julie had a sweet tooth, and, although she was generally on some diet or another, she could be relied upon to be tempted by the dessert. It also meant she could prepare everything in advance, and leave the fish on a low heat while she took her bath.

Before she could attend to her own needs, however, there was the bed in the spare room to make up, and fresh towels to put out. She drew a pretty, chintzy cover on to the duvet, and then surveyed the room critically, trying to see it through a stranger's eyes. She couldn't imagine what a man, who evidently came from a wealthy background, would think of this tiny bedroom, with its accent on feminine tastes. The carpet was cream, the walls were a delicate shade of pink, and the curtains matched the cover on the duvet. Laura herself had made the pleated skirt that swagged the small dressing-table, and even she had to duck her head to look out of the window.

Oh, well, she thought after opening the window and inhaling the cool air of an April evening, at least the view from the window was worth looking at, even if the spring was dragging its heels in this part of the world.

The bathroom was modern anyway, she reflected some time later, soaking in a warm, scented tub. Until she had been able to afford the renovations to the plumbing system, she had had to make do with rather primitive conditions, which was probably one of the reasons why Julie had only visited the cottage once before the new bathroom was installed. But now, although again everything had had to be scaled down to fit its surroundings, the tub was satisfyingly deep, and there was even a shower above it. Of course, it wasn't a proper shower cubicle, such as Julie had in her bathroom in London. But Laura didn't mind. She was usually the only one who used it, and she realised with a pang that, apart from Julie, this would be the first time she had had anyone to stay at the cottage.

She wondered what her daughter had told... Jake...about her mother. How had she described her, for instance? As a middle-aged frump, she supposed. She knew Julie thought she didn't make the best of herself, and her daughter was always saying that Laura ought to pay more attention to her appearance. Julie said she was a woman of thirty-eight, going on fifty, and in her opinion Laura ought to shorten her skirts and take advantage of the fact that she had nice legs.

But Laura was so accustomed to living alone and pleasing herself that she seldom considered what might or might not be flattering when she bought clothes. She was happiest in jeans and sloppy shirts or sweaters, pottering about the garden at the cottage, or taking Mrs Forrest's Labrador for long walks through the countryside. She would have had a dog herself, except she didn't think it was fair, as she was out all day. But when she retired...

She smiled, soaping her arms, and enjoying the sensation of the creamy compound against her skin. It was silly to think of retirement yet. She was only thirty-eight. But the truth was, she saw no evidence for change in her life, and she had to think of the future. She might get married, of course, but apart from Mark she could think of no one who might want to marry her. In any case, it was not an option she considered seriously. Having remained single all these years, she was probably too set in her ways to adapt to anyone else's, she decided ruefully. Besides, she could think of nothing a man could offer her that she didn't already have.

Washing her hair, however, she had to acknowledge that it did need cutting. The trouble was, most days she just coiled it into its usual knot at her nape, and by the time she thought of it again she was back at the cottage. In any case, it was essentially straight, and it was probably easiest to handle in its present condition. She was not the type to go for fancy cuts or perms. At least she didn't have many grey hairs, she thought gratefully. Her hair was still that nondescript shade between honey-blonde and chestnut, and if it was also thick, and shining, she scarcely appreciated it.

She heard the car as she was drying her hair. She had been sitting on the stool, in front of the mirror in her bedroom, trying to make an objective assessment of her appearance, and when she heard the powerful engine in the lane outside she knew a moment's panic. Obviously, she had spent longer over her toilet than she had intended, and now she met her own reflected gaze with some trepidation. For heaven's sake, she wasn't even dressed, she thought frantically. And the door downstairs was locked.

There was nothing for it. She would have to go down in her dressing-gown, she decided, shedding the towel she had worn sarong-wise around her body and snatching up her towelling bathrobe. If she hurried, she might be able to unlock the door and escape upstairs again without anyone seeing her. Julie would not be pleased if she met the man her daughter was going to marry in such a state of disarray. Although her hair was dry and silky, it was simply not suitable for a woman of her age. She looked like an ageing hippy, she thought frustratedly. If only she had paid more attention to the time.

Not stopping to put on her slippers, she started down the narrow staircase, and then stopped, aghast, when the handle of the front door was tried and rattled impatiently. It was immediately below her, the cottage having only a minuscule hallway, from which the stairs mounted on the outer wall. A second door led into the living area, which Laura had enlarged by having the wall demolished between what had been the parlour and dining-room, and there was no way she could unlock the door now without being seen.

Taking a deep breath, she gave in to the inevitable. She couldn't ask them to wait while she put on some clothes. That would be foolish. Besides, if this man was going to become her son-in-law, the sooner he saw her as she really was, the better.

But, even as she was making this decision, the flap of the letterbox was lifted, and Julie called, 'Mum! Mum, are you there? Open the door, can't you? It's raining.'

'Oh! Is it?'

Without more ado, Laura hurried down the last few stairs, and hastily turned the key. The door was propelled inward almost before she had time to step out of the way, and Julie appeared in the open doorway, looking decidedly out of humour.

'What were you——? Oh, Mum!' Julie stared at her with accusing eyes. 'You're not even dressed!'

'I was taking a bath,' replied Laura levelly, trying to maintain her composure. 'Besides,' she lifted her shoulders defensively, 'you're early.'

'It is after six,' retorted Julie, pushing her way through to the living-room. 'God, what a drive! The traffic was appalling!'

Laura's lips parted, and she stared after her daughter with some confusion. What did she mean? Surely she hadn't driven herself up to Northumberland. Julie did have a Metro, she knew that, for getting about town, but the engine she had heard hadn't sounded anything like Julie's Metro. It had been low and unobtrusive, that was true, but there had been no doubting the latent power behind its restrained compulsion.

Shaking her head, she moved to the open doorway, and peered out into the rain. And, as she did so, a tall figure loomed out of the gloom, with suitcases in both hands, and Julie's Louis Vuitton vanity case tucked under one arm. He was easily six feet in height—tall for an Italian, thought Laura inconsequently—with broad shoulders encased in a soft black leather jerkin. He was also very dark; dark-skinned, dark-haired, and dark-eyed, with the kind of hard masculine features that were harsh, yet compelling. He wasn't handsome in the accepted sense of the word, but he was very attractive, and Laura knew at once why Julie had decided that he was the one.

CHAPTER TWO

THEN, realising that by hovering in the doorway she was forcing him to stand in the rain, Laura made a gesture of apology, and got out of his way. He stepped into the tiny hall with evident relief, immediately dwarfing it by his presence, and Laura backed up the stairs to give him some space.

'Hi,' he said easily, and his deep, husky tones brushed her nerves like black velvet. With apparent indifference to her hair, or her state of undress, he put down the suitcases, and allowed the vanity case to drop on top of them 'You must be Julie's mother,' he added, straightening. 'How do you do? I'm Jake Lombardi.'

He spoke English without a trace of an accent, and Laura thought how awful it was that she couldn't even greet him in his own language. 'Laura Fox,' she responded, coming down the stairs again to take the hand he held out to her. And as the damp heat of his palm closed about hers, she had the ridiculous feeling that nothing was ever going to be the same again. 'Um—welcome to Burnfoot.'

'Thanks.'

He smiled, his dark eyes crinkling at the corners, and shaded by thick lashes. For all he had shown no obvious reaction to her appearance, she had the feeling that no aspect of her attire had missed his notice, and in spite of herself, a wave of colour swept up from her neck to her face.

She wasn't used to dealing with younger men, she

thought impatiently, chiding herself for her lack of composure. And particularly not a man who displayed his masculinity so blatantly. Against her will, her eyes had strayed down over the buttons of an olive-green silk shirt, to where the buckle of a black leather belt rode low across the flat muscles of his stomach. The belt secured close-fitting black denims that clung to the strong muscles of his thighs like a second skin. The fact that Laura also noticed how they moulded his sex with equal cohesion was something she instantly rejected. For God's sake, she thought, horrified that she should even consider such a thing. What was the matter with her?

'Are you going to close that door and come in?'

Julie's peevish complaint from the living-room came as a welcome intervention, but when Laura would have stepped round Jake to attend to it, he moved aside, and allowed his own weight to propel the door into its frame.

'It's closed,' he said, still looking at Laura, and, with the panicky feeling that he had known exactly what she was thinking a few moments ago, she turned towards the stairs.

'I won't be a minute,' she said, not looking to see if he was watching her, and, without giving Julie time to lodge a protest, she ran up the stairs to her room.

Her mirror confirmed her worst fears. Her face was scarlet, and, even to her own eyes, she looked as guilty as she felt. But guilty of what? she wondered. It wasn't as if she had done anything wrong. Heavens, she was no *femme fatale*, and she was a fool if she thought he had been flattered by her attention. On the contrary, he had probably found her unwary appraisal amusing, or pitiful, or both. Right now he was probably regaling Julie with the news that her mother had been lusting after his body. Oh, God, it was embarrassing! What must he be thinking of her?

However, right now she couldn't afford to let that get to her. She was probably exaggerating the whole incident anyway, and the best way to put the matter behind her was to go down and behave as if nothing had happened. Then, if Jake Lombardi had been discussing her with Julie, it would look as if he had been imagining things, and not her.

Earlier, she had laid out the dress she had intended to wear on the bed, but now, looking at it with new eyes, she saw it was far too formal for this evening. Made of fine cream wool, it had a soft cowled collar, and long fitted sleeves, and, bearing in mind Julie's remarks about not making the best of herself, Laura had bought it at Christmas, to silence her daughter's criticisms. In the event, however, Julie had not come home at Christmas, and the dress had hung in the wardrobe ever since, a constant reminder of her extravagance.

Now, she picked it up, and thrust it back on to its hanger. The last thing she wanted was for Julie to think she was dressing up to impress her fiancé, she thought grimly. Or for him to think the same, she added, pulling out a pair of green cords, and a purple Aran sweater, that had seen better days. Whatever Julie thought, she was almost forty, and she refused to behave like a woman twenty years younger.

Her hair gave her no trouble, and she coiled it into its usual knot without difficulty. And, as the colour receded from her face, she began to feel more optimistic. She had allowed the fact that she had answered the door in her bathrobe and nothing else to upset her equilibrium, and now she had had time to gather herself she could see how silly she had been. It had probably amused Jake

Lombardi that she had been caught out. And why not? He was no doubt used to much more sophisticated surroundings, and more sophisticated women, she acknowledged drily.

She leant towards the mirror to examine her face. Should she put on some make-up? she wondered, running her fingers over her smooth skin. She had intended to, but, now that she had been seen without it, was there much point? She didn't wear much anyway, and she was lucky enough to have eyelashes that were several shades darker than her tawny hair. Golden eyes, the colour of honey, looked back at her warily, and she allowed a small smile to touch the corners of her mouth. Compared to her daughter, she was very small change indeed, she thought ruefully. So why try and pretend otherwise?

The hardest part was going downstairs again. She entered the living-room cautiously, steeling herself to meet knowing smiles and shared humour, but it didn't happen. Although Julie was stretched out in front of the fire her mother had lit when she'd come home, Jake wasn't in the room, and Laura's expression mirrored her surprise.

'He's gone to lock up the car,' remarked Julie carelessly, extending the empty glass she was holding towards her mother. In a fine suede waistcoat over a bronze silk blouse, and form-fitting black ski-pants, she was as sleek and indolent as a cat—and her attitude said she knew it. 'Get me another Scotch, will you? I'm badly in need of sustenance.'

Laura caught her lower lip between her teeth, but she took the glass obediently enough, and poured a measure of malt whisky over the ice that still rested in the bottom. Then, handing it back to her daughter, she said carefully, 'Is this wise? Drinking spirits so early in the evening?'

'What else is there to do in this God-forsaken place?'

countered Julie cynically, raising the glass to her lips, and swallowing at least half its contents at one go. She lowered the glass again, and regarded her mother through half-closed lids. 'So—what do you think of Jake? Pretty dishy, isn't he? And he tastes just as good as he looks.'

Laura couldn't help the *frisson* of distaste that crossed her face at her daughter's words, and Julie gave her an impatient look before hauling herself up in the chair. 'I hope you're not going to spend the whole weekend looking at me with that holier-than-thou expression!' she exclaimed, using the toe of one of her knee-length boots to remove the other. Then she held out the remaining boot to her mother. 'Jake is tasty. Even you must be able to see that. Even if your criterion for what might—or might not—be sexy is based on that wimp Mark Leith!'

'Mark is not a wimp,' began Laura indignantly, and then, realising she was defending herself, she broke off. 'I—gather you didn't enjoy the journey here. I believe Friday evenings are always busy.'

'Hmm.' Free of her boots, Julie moved her stockinged feet nearer the fire. 'You could say that.' She shrugged. 'I hate driving in the rain. It's so boring!'

'Even with Jake?' enquired Laura drily, unable to resist the parry, and Julie gave her a dour look from beneath curling black lashes.

'You still haven't told me what you think of him,' she retorted, returning to the offensive. And Laura wished she had kept her sarcasm to herself.

'I'm hardly in a position to voice an opinion,' she replied guardedly, escaping into the kitchen. To her relief, the fish was simmering nicely, and the strawberry shortcake had defrosted on the window ledge. At least checking the food and setting out the plates and cutlery distracted her from the more troubling aspects of her thoughts, and it was only when Julie came to prop herself against the door that Laura fumbled with a glass, and almost dropped it.

'Would you like to know how we met?' Julie asked now, making no effort to assist her mother with the preparations, and, deciding it was probably the lesser of two evils, Laura nodded. 'It was in Rome actually,' Julie went on. 'D'you remember? I told you I was going there about six weeks ago, to shoot the *Yasmina* lay-out. Well, Jake's father—Count Domenico, would you believe?—sits on the boards of various governing bodies, and this ball had been organised to benefit some children's charity or other. Harry got an invitation, of course, so we all went. It promised to be good fun, and it was.' Her lips twisted reminiscently. 'Oh—Jake wouldn't have been there if his mother hadn't raked him in to charm all the women, so that they'd get their husbands to contribute more generously than they might have done. But he was; and we met; and the rest is history, as they say.'

Laura managed a smile. 'I see.'

'Yes.' Julie studied the liquid residing in the bottom of the glass she was cradling in her hands. 'Events like that are not really his thing, you see.' She looked up again, and her eyes glittered as they met her mother's wary glance. 'I intend to change all that, naturally.'

'You do?'

Laura didn't know how else to answer her, but then the sound of the front door closing made any further response unnecessary. Julie turned back into the living-room to speak to the man who had just come in, and Laura bent to lift the casserole out of the oven.

She knew she would have to join them shortly, of course. Although she generally ate at the pine table in the kitchen, the room was scarcely big enough for two people, let alone three, which meant she would have to pull out the gatelegged table at one end of the living-room.

However, before she had summoned up the courage to leave the comparative security of the kitchen, Jake himself appeared in the doorway. He had shed his leather jerkin, somewhere between entering the house and coming to disrupt her fragile composure, and as he raised one hand to support himself against the lintel Laura was not unaware of the sleek muscles beneath the fine silk of his shirt.

'I've left the car parked behind yours beside the house,' he said, and she noticed how the drops of rain sparkled on his hair. He wore his hair longer than the men she was used to, and where it was wet it was inclined to curl. Otherwise, it was mostly straight, and just brushed his collar at the back. 'Is that OK?' he added softly, and Laura realised rather flusteredly that she hadn't answered him.

'What...? Oh—oh, yes,' she said hastily, taking a tablecloth out of a drawer, and starting towards him. Then, realising he was blocking the doorway, she halted again, and waving the cloth at him, murmured, 'If you'll excuse me...'

Jake frowned, but he didn't move out of her way. 'Can't we eat in here?' he suggested, looking about him with some appreciation. 'This is cosy.' He nodded at the begonias on the window ledge. 'Did you cultivate those?'

'Cultivate? Oh...' Laura glanced behind her, and then nodded. 'Yes. Yes, I enjoy gardening. You wouldn't notice today, of course. I think the rain has even beaten down the daffodils.'

'The rain!' Jake grimaced. 'Oh, yes, it is certainly raining. It reminds me of home.'

'Home?' Laura frowned. 'But I thought——'

'You thought that the sun always shines in Italy?' he asked, grinning. 'Oh, no. Like the fog in London, it is somewhat overrated.'

Laura felt herself smiling in return, but then, realising she was wasting time, and the meal was almost ready, she caught her lower lip between her teeth.

'Um—do you really think we could eat in here?' she ventured, not at all sure how Julie would respond to such a suggestion, and then her daughter appeared behind Jake. Sliding possessive arms around him from behind, she reached up to rest her chin on his shoulder, before arching a curious brow at her mother.

'What's going on?'

'Your mother was going to serve the meal she had prepared in the other room,' Jake interposed swiftly. 'I thought we should eat in here. I always enjoyed eating in the kitchen, when I lived at home.'

'Yes, but how big was the kitchen you used to eat in?' countered Julie, turning her head deliberately, and allowing her tongue to brush the lobe of his ear. 'Not like this rabbit hutch, I'm sure. I bet there were acres and acres of marble tiles, and dressers simply groaning under the weight of copper pans.'

'I don't think it matters how big the room is,' Jake retorted, displaying a depth of coolness she had clearly not expected. He moved so that Julie had either to move with him, which would have been clumsy, or let him go. She chose the latter, and stood looking at him with sulky eyes. 'It's the room where the cooking is done. That's what's important. The smell of good food isn't enhanced by wasted space.'

'How gallant!'

Julie grimaced, but Laura had the feeling that Jake's reaction had surprised her daughter. Evidently, he was not going to prove as easy to manipulate as Julie had expected, and, although she was probably nursing her grievances, she had decided to reassess her options before making any reckless moves.

'Well—if you're sure,' Laura murmured now, half wishing Jake had not chosen to champion her. She had no desire to be the cause of any rift between them, and, in all honesty, she would have preferred to keep the kitchen as her sanctuary. But it was too late now, and, ignoring Julie's still mutinous expression, she shook out the tablecloth.

'D'you want a drink?' asked Julie, after a few moments, apparently deciding that sulking was getting her nowhere, and to Laura's relief Jake accepted the olive branch.

'Sounds good,' he said, and when Julie backed into the living-room he followed.

Breathing a somewhat relieved sigh, Laura quickly laid the table with the silver and glassware she had prepared earlier. Then, after rescuing the plates from the warming drawer, she set the casserole dish containing the fish on a cork mat in the middle of the table. The attractive terracotta-coloured casserole looked good amid the cream plates, with their narrow gold edging, and the crystal wine glasses that had been her gift to herself last Christmas.

She had bought some wine, and, although if Mark came for a meal she had him uncork the bottle, this evening she tackled the job herself. It wasn't as if she was helpless, she thought irritably, removing a tiny speck of cork from the rim. It was only that Julie tended to intimidate her. And that was her own fault, too.

In the event, the meal was a success. The fish tasted as delicious as Laura had hoped, and, whatever Jake and her daughter had said to one another in the living-room, the atmosphere between them was definitely lighter. Evidently, Julie had been appeased, and, although Jake still didn't respond to her frequent attempts to touch him, he didn't reject them either. Instead, he spoke equally to both women, encouraging Julie to talk about her recent trip to Scandinavia, and showing an apparently genuine interest in Laura's teaching.

Although Laura was sure he was only being polite, so far as she was concerned, she was not averse to talking about her job, and only when Julie gave a rather pronounced yawn did she realise she had been lecturing. But it was so rare that she spoke to anyone at any length outside the teaching profession, and Jake's intelligent observations had inspired her to share her opinions.

When they eventually left the table, Julie asked if she could have a bath. 'I feel grubby,' she said, deliberately stretching her arms above her head, so that the perfect lines of her slim figure could be seen to advantage. She wore her hair short these days, and with its smooth curve cupping her head like a burnished cap, and her small breasts thrusting freely against the bronze silk, she was both provocative and beautiful. She cast a mocking smile in Jake's direction. 'But you won't be able to come and wash my back, darling,' she added lightly. 'Mum doesn't approve of that sort of thing, do you, Mum?'

Laura didn't know how to answer her, but as it happened she didn't have to. 'I'll be too busy helping your mother with the washing-up, anyway,' Jake returned, causing Laura no small spasm of trepidation. 'Go ahead. Take your bath, *cara*. We don't mind—do we, Laura?'

Laura turned to stare at him then, telling herself it was his attempt to link them together that disturbed her, and not her reaction to her name on his lips. But Jake wasn't aware of her scrutiny. He was looking at Julie, and for once her daughter seemed nonplussed. Laura guessed she, too, was trying to gauge exactly what Jake was implying by his remarks, and her response revealed her uncertainty.

'I—well, of course, I'll help to clear up first——' she began but she got no further.

'It's not necessary for either of you to help me. Really,' Laura retorted, her face reddening as she spoke. 'Honestly. I can manage. Please. I'd rather.'

'I wouldn't dream of it,' declared Jake, apparently indifferent to her embarrassment. 'You've been at work all day, while we've only had a rather leisurely drive from London. In addition to which, you prepared this very appetising meal, which we've all enjoyed. I suggest you go and relax, while we deal with the clearing up.'

Laura looked at Julie now, and she could tell that her daughter didn't like this turn of events at all. It was so unexpected, for one thing, and, for another, Julie wasn't used to being treated like a servant in her own home. It did not augur well for the remainder of the weekend, and Laura decided she wasn't prepared to play pig-in-the-middle any longer.

'No,' she said clearly, gathering up the coffee-cups and saucers, and bundling them on to the drainer. 'Really, Mr—er—I insist. You're my guests. I invited you here, and I wouldn't dream of allowing you to do my job.' She couldn't quite meet his gaze as she spoke, so she looked at Julie instead. 'Go along,' she continued.

'Have your bath. The water's nice and hot, and there's plenty of it.'

'Are you sure?'

Julie hesitated, looking doubtfully from Jake to her mother and back again, but Laura was adamant. 'Of course,' she said. 'Heavens, there are only a few plates to wash, when all's said and done. Hurry up. I'm sure your—er—friend would much prefer your company to mine.'

Julie frowned. It was obvious what she wanted to do, but Jake's attitude had confused her. Still, her own basic belief, that she was not being selfish by allowing her mother to have her own way, won out, and, giving them both a grateful smile, she departed. Seconds later, Laura heard the sound of her daughter's footsteps on the stairs, and, breathing a sigh of relief, she moved towards the sink.

'You're wrong, you know.'

She had almost forgotten Jake was still there, but now his quiet words caused her to glance round at him. 'I beg your pardon?'

'I said—you're wrong,' he responded. He had got up from the table when she had, and now he was leaning against the base unit behind her, his arms folded across his chest, his long legs crossed at the ankle.

'About Julie?' Laura turned her back on him again, and proceeded to fill the sink with soapy water. 'Possibly.'

'You spoil her,' he went on. 'She's perfectly capable of washing a few dishes.'

'Maybe.' Laura didn't like his assumption that he could discuss Julie with her, as if she were some racalcitrant child. 'But—I choose to do them myself.'

'No.' Jake came to stand beside her as he spoke, and

now she was forced to meet his dark gaze. 'No, you don't *choose* to do them yourself. You take the line of least resistance. Which just happens to coincide with what Julie wants to do, no?'

Laura took a deep breath. 'I don't think it's any of your business, Mr—er—Lombardi——'

'Jake will do,' he put in briefly. 'And so long as Julie and I are together, I consider it is my business.'

Laura gasped. His arrogance was amazing, but at least it served to keep her own unwilling awareness of him at bay. 'You don't understand,' she declared, depositing the newly washed glasses on the drainer. 'Julie and I don't see one another very often——'

'And whose fault is that?'

'It's nobody's fault.' But Laura couldn't help wondering if he knew exactly how infrequently Julie made the journey north. Recently, Laura had had to travel to London if she wanted to see her daughter, and as she could only do so during school holidays, and they often coincided with Julie's working trips abroad, these occasions were getting fewer.

'So—you are quite happy with the situation, hmm?' he enquired, picking up a tea-towel, and beginning to dry a glass.

'Yes.'

Laura's response was taut, and she hoped that that would be an end of it. It was bad enough being obliged to entertain him while Julie went to take her bath. A conversation of this kind tended to increase their familiarity with one another, and she would have preferred to keep their relationship on much more formal terms.

She finished the dishes in silence, but she was very much aware of him moving about the small kitchen, and the distinctive scent of his skin drifted irresistibly to her nostrils. It was a combination of the soap he used, some subtle aftershave, and the warmth of his body, and Laura had the feeling it was not something she would easily forget. It was so essentially masculine, and she resented the knowledge that he could influence her without any volition on her part.

As she was putting the dishes away, he spoke again, and as before his words commanded her attention. 'I guess you're angry with me now, aren't you?' he said, stepping into her path, as she was about to put the plates into the cupboard. It caused her to stop abruptly, to prevent herself from cannoning into him, and she pressed the plates against her chest, like some primitive form of self-protection.

'I—don't know what you mean,' she protested, and although it was scarcely true she thought it sounded convincing enough.

'Don't you?' Jake looked down at her, and, despite the fact that she had always considered herself a tall woman, he was still at least half a foot taller. 'I think you know very well. You resented my remarks about your daughter. You don't consider I have any right to criticise the way she treats you.'

Laura took a deep breath. 'All right,' she said, deciding there was no point in lying to him. It wasn't as if she wanted them to be friends, after all. If Julie married him, the greater the distance there was between them the better. 'I don't think anyone who doesn't have a child of their own can make any real assessment on how a parent ought, or ought not, to behave.'

'Ah.' Jake inclined his head, and Laura was intensely conscious of how she must appear to him. The Aran sweater was not flattering, and she was sure her face must be shining like a beacon. 'But I do have a daughter.

Not as old as yours,' he conceded, after a moment. 'She's only eight years old. But a handful, none the less.'

Laura swallowed. 'You—have a daughter?'

He could apparently tell what she was thinking, for his lean lips parted. 'But no wife,' he assured her gently. 'Isabella—that was her name—she died when our daughter was only a few months old.'

'Oh.' Laura's tongue appeared to moisten her lips. 'I—I'm sorry. I didn't know.'

'How could you?' Jake responded. 'Until tonight, we had never even met.'

'No.'

But Laura was embarrassed nevertheless. Julie should have told her, she thought impatiently. If she knew. But, of course, she must. She had the feeling it was not something Jake would try to hide.

She half stepped forward, eager to get past him now, and put the plates away, so that she could escape to the living-room. The kitchen was too small, too confining, and that awful panicky feeling she had felt in the hall earlier was attacking her nerves again. He was too close; too familiar. He might not be aware of it, but she most definitely was.

But Jake moved as she did, probably with the same thought in mind, she guessed later, and unfortunately he chose the same direction as Laura, so that they collided.

The shock jarred her, but her first instincts were to protect the plates. She clutched them to her, instead of trying to save herself, and it was left to Jake to prevent her, and her burden, from ending up on the floor. Almost instinctively, his hands grasped the yielding flesh of her upper arms, and for a brief moment she was forced to lean against him.

Afterwards, she realised that the incident couldn't

have lasted more than a few seconds. It was one of those accidents that in retrospect seemed totally avoidable. Only it hadn't happened that way. Almost as if she was moving in slow motion, Laura was compelled into Jake's arms, and for a short, but disruptive period she was close against his lean frame.

And, during those nerve-racking seconds, when the world seemed to falter around her, her body came alive to every nerve and emotion she possessed. Her skin felt raw; sensitised; as if someone had peeled away the top layer, and left her weak and open to attack. She had never experienced such a shattering explosion of feeling, and her mind reeled beneath its implications.

She jerked away from him, of course, more violently than she should have done, and one of the plates went flying. But it wasn't the sound of the china splintering on the tiles that first made her face burn, and then robbed it of all colour. It was the fact that the ball of Jake's hand brushed her breast as she rebounded, and in the sudden narrowing of his eyes she saw a reflection of her own awareness.

CHAPTER THREE

LAURA slept badly, and it wasn't just the unfamiliar experience of sharing her bed with her daughter. She was hot and restless, and although she longed for it to be morning, she was not looking forward to the day ahead.

Of course, it didn't help that Julie had appropriated at least two-thirds of the space, and every time Laura moved she was in fear of waking her. Indeed, there were times during the night when Laura half wished she had not been so adamant about the sleeping arrangements. If Julie had been sharing Jake's bed, she would not have been so conscious of him, occupying the room on the other side of the dividing wall.

As it was, her senses persistently taunted her with that awareness, and images of Jake's dark, muscled body, relaxed against the cream poplin sheets, were a constant aggravation. It was pathetic, she thought, disgusted by her thoughts. Apart from anything else, he was Julie's boyfriend, her property—if a man like Jake Lombardi could ever be regarded as any woman's possession. Somehow she sensed he was unlikely to let that happen. Nevertheless, whatever label she put on it, he was the man her daughter intended to marry, and any attraction she felt towards him was both loathsome and pitiful. For heaven's sake, she chided herself, he was probably ten years younger than she was, and, even if Julie hadn't been involved, he simply wasn't the type of man she attracted.

She was just a middle-aged school-teacher, who had

wasted any chance of happiness she might have had by getting herself pregnant, when she should have been old enough to know better. And since then, she had never felt the need for a serious relationship. Over the years, there had been one or two men who had attempted to push a casual association into something more, but Laura had always repelled invaders. Only Mark had stayed the course, and that was primarily because he made no demands on her. She had actually begun to believe that, whatever sexual urges she had once possessed, they were now extinct, and it was disturbing, to say the least, to consider that she might have been wrong.

And what was she basing this conclusion on? she asked herself contemptuously. It wasn't as if anything momentous had happened to shatter her illusions. How stupid she was to read anything into Jake's almost knocking her over, and preventing it. It was what anyone would have done in the same circumstances, man or woman, and she was fooling herself if she thought his brief awareness of her had been sexual.

But he had grabbed her, she argued doggedly. He had propelled her into his arms. It didn't matter that on his part it had been a purely impersonal reaction. She could still feel the grip of his fingers, and the taut corded muscles of his legs...

God! She turned on to her back and gazed blindly up at the ceiling. How old was she? Thirty-eight? She was reacting like a sixteen-year-old. But then, she thought bitterly, her sexual development had been arrested around that age, so what else could she expect?

She was glad Julie had known nothing about it. By the time her daughter came down from her bath, clean, and sweetly smelling of rosebuds, her slender form wrapped in a revealing silk kimono, Laura had swept the floor, and restored the kitchen—and herself—to comparative order. That disruptive moment with Jake might never have been, and she was able to excuse herself on the pretext of being tired, without revealing any of the turmoil that was churning inside her. She left them sharing the sofa in the living-room, where Jake had been sitting since she had insisted on clearing up the broken china herself.

She got up at six o'clock. She had been wide awake since five, and only the knowledge that she would have no excuse for being up any earlier had prevented her from going downstairs as soon as it was light. But six o'clock seemed reasonably acceptable, and as the others hadn't come to bed until some time after midnight Laura doubted she would disturb anyone.

Drawing the blind in the kitchen, she saw it was a much brighter morning. The sun was sparkling like diamonds on the wet grass, and the birds were setting up a noisy chatter in the trees that formed a barrier between her garden and the lane that led to Grainger's farm.

The cottage was the second of two that stood at the end of the village, the other being occupied by an elderly widow and her daughter. Laura knew that people thought she was a widow, too, and she had never bothered to correct them. In a place as small as Burnfoot, it was better not to be too non-conformist, and, while being a one-parent family was no novelty these days, people might look differently on someone of Laura's generation.

After putting the kettle on to boil, she opened the back door and stepped out into the garden. It was fresh, but not chilly, and she pushed her hands into the pockets of her dressing-gown and inhaled the clean air. The bulbs she had planted the previous autumn were beginning to flower, and the bell-shaped heads of purple hyacinths and crimson tulips were thrusting their way between the clumps of wild daffodils. The garden was starting to regain the colour it had lost over the winter months, and Laura guessed that sooner or later she would have to clear the dead leaves, and dispose of the weeds.

It was a prospect she generally looked forward to, but this morning it was hard to summon any enthusiasm for anything. She felt depressed, and out of tune with herself, and, hearing one of Ted Grainger's heifers bellowing in the top field, she thought the animal epitomised her own sense of frustration. But frustration about what? she asked herself crossly. What did she have to be frustrated about?

The kettle was beginning to boil. She could hear it. It was a comforting sound, and, abandoning her introspection, she turned back towards the house. And that was when she saw him, standing indolently in the open doorway, watching her.

He was dressed—that was the first thing she noticed about him. He was wearing the same black jeans he had been wearing the night before, but he wasn't wearing a shirt this morning; just a V-necked cream cashmere sweater, that revealed the brown skin of his throat, and a faint trace of dark body hair in the inverted apex of the triangle. Unlike herself, she was sure, he looked relaxed and rested, although his eyes were faintly shadowed, as if he hadn't slept long enough.

And why not? she thought irritably. She had still been awake when Julie had come to bed, even if she had pretended otherwise, and by her reckoning he could not have had more than five hours. Hardly enough for someone who had driven almost three hundred miles the day before, in heavy traffic, with goodness knew what hangover from the night before that.

Laura was immediately conscious of her own state of undress, and of the fact that she hadn't even brushed her hair since she'd come downstairs. It was still a tumbled mass about her shoulders, with knotted strands of nut-brown silk sticking out in all directions.

Laura's hand went automatically to her hair, and then, as if realising it was too late to do anything about it now, she clutched the neckline of her robe, and walked towards him. Pasting a polite smile on her face, she strove to hide the resentment she felt at his unwarranted intrusion, and, reaching the step, she said lightly, 'Good morning. You're an early riser.'

'So are you,' Jake countered, moving aside to let her into the house. 'Couldn't you sleep?'

Laura went to take the tea caddy out of the cupboard, and dropped three bags into the pot before answering him. The steady infusion of the water sent up a revitalising aroma from the leaves, and Laura breathed deeply, as she considered how to reply.

'I—er—I'm always up fairly early,' she said at last, putting the lid on the teapot, and having no further reason to avoid his gaze. 'Um—would you like a cup of tea? Or would you rather have coffee? I can easily make a pot, if that's what you'd prefer.'

'Whatever you're having,' he said, closing the back door, and leaning back against it. 'I'm—what do you say?—easy.'

Laura's lips twitched. 'Milk, or lemon?'

'You choose,' he essayed flatly. 'Tea is tea, whatever way you drink it.'

'I doubt if the connoisseurs would agree with you,' declared Laura, setting out three cups and saucers. 'Tea used to be regarded as quite a ritual. It still is, in other parts of the world. China, for instance.'

'Really?'

He didn't sound as if it interested him greatly, and she guessed her line in small talk was not what he was used to. He evidently enjoyed the kind of sexual innuendo Julie employed to such effect. But Laura wasn't experienced in innuendo, sexual or otherwise, and, aware of how she had monopolised the conversation at dinner the previous evening, she knew she had to guard against being boring.

Then, remembering her hair, she started towards the door. That was something that couldn't wait any longer, and she paused, uncertainly, when he asked, 'Where are you going?'

'I—won't be a minute,' she answered, loath to admit exactly where she was headed. 'Um—help yourself; and Julie, too, if you want.'

'I'll wait,' he said, leaving the door, to pull out a chair from the table, and straddle it with his long legs. 'OK.'

Laura hesitated a little bemusedly, and then nodded. 'Of—of course.'

Brushing her hair entailed going upstairs again, and as she stood at the bathroom mirror, tugging the bristles through the tangled strands, she felt a helpless sense of inevitability. The last thing she had expected was that she would have to face another one-to-one encounter with Jake so soon. Her assessment of the day ahead had already gone badly awry, and she hoped the rest of the weekend was not going to prove as traumatic.

There were men's toiletries on the glass shelf above the handbasin, she saw, with an unwelcome twinge of trepidation. No doubt they were responsible for the spicy smell of cologne that lingered in the atmosphere, the unfamiliar scents of sandalwood and cedar. There was a razor, too. Not some sophisticated electrical gadget, as she would have expected, but a common-or-garden sword-edge, with throwaway blades. The man was a contradiction, she thought, frowning, hardly aware that she was running her fingers over a dark green bottle of aftershaving lotion. He was rich, and sophisticated; he wore handmade shirts, and Armani jackets, and he drove a Lamborghini. All aspects of the lifestyle to which he was accustomed. And yet, he had seemed genuinely pleased with the simple meal she had served the night before, and he had dried the dishes afterwards, as if it was a perfectly natural thing for him to do.

She realised suddenly that she was wasting time. It was at least five minutes since she had come upstairs, and, apart from anything else, the tea would be getting cold.

The hairpins she usually used to keep her hair in place were in the bedroom, and although she wouldn't have minded waking Julie, it was going to take too much time. Instead, she found the elastic headband in the pocket of her dressing-gown that she sometimes used when she was pottering about the garden, and, sliding it up over her forehead, she decided that would have to do.

Going downstairs again was harder, but she steeled herself to behave naturally. After all, so far as Jake was concerned, she was just Julie's mother: a little eccentric, perhaps, and obviously nervous with strangers.

He was still sitting where she had left him, but he got politely to his feet when she came into the room. However, Laura gestured for him to remain seated, and he sank back on to the chair, stretching the tight jeans across his thighs.

Laura knew her eyes shouldn't have been drawn to that particular area of his abdomen, but somehow she couldn't help it. He was disturbingly physical, and her stomach quivered alarmingly as she endeavoured to pour the tea.

'W—would you like to take Julie's up?' she ventured, the spout hovering over the third cup, but when she reluctantly glanced round at her visitor Jake shook his head.

'I doubt if she'd appreciate being woken at this hour, do you?' he remarked, his dark eyes intent and wary. 'When she's not working, she considers anything short of double figures the middle of the night. But you must know that yourself.'

Not as well as you, I'm sure, Laura was tempted to retort, but she restrained herself. After all, it was really nothing to do with her how they chose to live their lives, and just because she was finding the situation a strain was no reason to blame Jake.

However, he seemed to sense her ambivalence, for as she set a cup of the strong beverage in front of him he said quietly, 'What's wrong?' and the anxieties of the last fifteen minutes coalesced.

'I—beg your pardon?'

'You don't have to be so formal, you know,' he told her, making no attempt to touch his tea. 'I asked what was wrong. Do you resent my getting up so early? Would you rather I had stayed in bed?'

Yes. *Yes!* The simple answer sang in Laura's ears, but she couldn't say it. Not out loud. Besides, she wasn't even sure she meant it. It might be reassuring to pretend she would rather avoid talking to him, and quite another to consider the reality of doing so. The truth fell somewhere in between, and she was too conscientious to deny it.

'I—I—don't mind,' she said at last, not altogether truthfully. 'Um—would you like some sugar? I—know men usually do.'

'And how would you know that?' enquired Jake, still holding her gaze, and she knew a sudden spurt of indignation.

'Why shouldn't I? Just because I'm not married, doesn't mean I haven't had any experience where men are concerned,' she retorted, resenting his implication, and then could have bitten out her tongue at the recklessness of her words. She had no idea whether Julie had told him of the circumstances of her birth. And if she hadn't...

But Jake was speaking again. 'I know about that,' he countered mildly. 'You had Julie while you were still in high school. And I didn't imagine that was an immaculate conception.'

Laura flushed then, his cool, faintly mocking tone reminding her of how inexperienced she was when it came to his kind of verbal sparring. But she refused to let him think he had disconcerted her, and, squaring her shoulders, she added crisply, 'I am almost forty, you know. Why do young people always think sex wasn't invented until they came along?'

'Is that what they think?' Jake arched one dark brow, and, wishing she had never started this, Laura nodded.

'You tell me,' she responded tautly. 'It's your generation I'm talking about.'

'My generation?' Jake pressed his left hand against his chest, his expression mirroring his amusement. '*Dio*, how old you think I am?'

'It doesn't matter how old you are,' declared Laura,

trying to steady the cup of tea in her hand. 'All I'm saying is, you shouldn't jump to what you think are obvious conclusions.'

'Did I do that?'

'Yes.' Laura drew a trembling breath. 'And I wish you'd stop answering everything I say with a question of your own. We—we hardly know one another, and I—I don't want to fall out with you.'

'Fall out with me?' Jake adopted a puzzled expression. 'What is that?'

'Argue with you—quarrel with you—oh, I'm sure you know exactly what it means,' declared Laura crossly. 'Anyway, I don't want to do it.'

'Do what?'

'Have an argument with you,' repeated Laura shortly. 'And there you go again. Making fun of me.'

'Was I doing that?' Jake grimaced. 'Oh, damn, that's another question.'

He was teasing her. Laura knew it. And, although she knew she ought to be able to take it all in good part, she couldn't. He disturbed her too much. She returned her attention to her tea, hoping he would do the same, but she didn't sit down with him. At least when she was standing, she felt she had some chance of parity, albeit in a physical sense only. And perhaps, after he had drunk his tea, he would go for a walk, she speculated. He surely didn't intend to hang about the house until Julie chose to put in an appearance.

'So,' he remarked, after a few silent moments, 'you live here alone, is that right?'

'Well, I don't have a live-in lover,' replied Laura tersely, and then, catching the humour in his eyes, she struggled to compose herself. 'I—yes, I live alone,' she conceded, putting her empty cup down on the drainer.

'But I don't mind, if that's what you're getting at. After dealing with noisy teenagers all day, it's quite a relief to come back here.'

'I can believe it.' Jake wasn't teasing now. He had folded his arms along the back of the chair, and was regarding her with a steady appraisal. 'And it's very peaceful around here, isn't it?'

'Mmm.' Laura endeavoured to relax. 'That's what I love about it. The peace and quiet. I'd hate to live in the city again.'

Jake frowned. 'You lived in London?'

'No. Newcastle.' Somehow, she didn't mind his questions now. 'I moved here just after—Julie went to London.'

'Ah.' Jake nodded.

'I work in the city, of course,' Laura added. 'It's only about fifteen miles away.'

'Newcastle.'

'Yes.'

Jake absorbed this. Then, quite obliquely, he said, 'You'd like Valle di Lupo. It's very peaceful there, too. If slightly less civilised.'

Laura hesitated. She was loath to appear too curious after the accusation she had made towards him, but she had to ask, 'What is—Valle di Lupo?'

Jake smiled, and she felt her breath catch in her throat as his lean features assumed a disturbing sensuality. 'My home,' he said simply. 'Or rather—my family's. It's in the wilds of Toscana—Tuscany. A few miles north of Firenze.'

'Florence,' ventured Laura softly, and Jake inclined his head.

'As you say—Florence,' he agreed. 'Have you been to Italy?'

'Oh, no.' Laura shook her head. 'I'm afraid not. Apart from a school skiing trip to Austria, I haven't travelled much at all. Not outside England, anyway.'

'A pity.' Jake pulled a wry face. 'I think you would like it.'

'Oh—I'm sure I would.' Laura hoped she didn't sound too eager. 'Um—is that—is that where your—daughter lives?' She moistened her lips. 'At Valle di Lupo?'

'Sometimes.' Jake was thoughtful. 'When she's not at school. And when I'm not able to take care of her.'

Laura was interested in spite of herself. 'You—don't live at Valle di Lupo?'

Jake smiled again. 'Who's asking questions now?'

Laura's face flamed. 'I'm sorry——'

'Don't be. I don't mind.' Jake shrugged his shoulders. 'I've got nothing to hide!'

Laura pressed her lips together, and glanced awkwardly about her. 'I—er—I think I'd better go and get dressed,' she murmured, and then caught her breath again, when Jake propelled himself up from the chair, and swung it round, so that it fitted back under the table.

'I thought you wanted to know where I lived?' he protested. 'Or were you just being polite?'

Laura caught her lower lip between her teeth. 'I—just wondered, that's all,' she improvised, smoothing her damp palms down the skirt of her dressing-gown. 'It's really none of my business——'

'I have an apartment in Rome, and another on the coast near Viareggio,' he told her softly. 'But my real home is at Valle di Lupo. That is where I was born.'

'Oh.'

It all sounded very extravagant to Laura. Two apartments, *and* a family home. It was the kind of lifestyle she had only read about in glossy magazines, or seen portrayed in American soap operas. It was quite amazing to meet someone who actually lived like that. It seemed a long way from Burnfoot, and the modest appointments of this cottage.

'You don't approve?' he suggested now, and Laura was guiltily aware that she had been frowning.

'Oh—no,' she murmured. 'I mean—it all sounds very beautiful. Your home, that is. I'm sure Julie is longing to see it.'

'Are you?'

Jake rested his hands on the back of the chair, and Laura's eyes were drawn to their narrow elegance. It reminded her of how they had felt the night before, and how strongly they had supported her weight...

But he was waiting for her answer, and, lifting her shoulders, she said quickly, 'Of course.' A sudden thought occurred to her, and she felt the colour invade her cheeks once again. 'Unless—unless she's already——'

'No.'

Jake was adamant about that, and Laura's eyes widened. 'No?'

'Julie isn't interested in the provincial life,' Jake informed her carelessly. 'She doesn't care for fields, and trees, and rolling vineyards. Only in what they produce.'

Laura swallowed. 'That's a little harsh——'

'Is it?' Jake's eyes were enigmatic. 'How do you know I don't feel the same?'

She didn't, of course. And on the evidence she had so far, she had little reason to believe otherwise. And yet...

'I—really think I must go and get dressed,' she insisted, moving towards the door. 'Er—if you'd like another cup of tea, help yourself. I—won't be long.'

She made her escape before he could say anything else. And, as she went up the stairs again, she realised she was trembling. For heaven's sake, she thought impatiently, what was wrong with her? It wasn't the first time she had had a conversation with a strange man, and certainly he had given her no reason to feel this consuming sense of vulnerability in his presence. It wasn't as if he'd made a pass at her or anything. He'd been a perfect gentleman, and she was behaving like a silly spinster. For God's sake, she told herself, locking the bathroom door and taking a good look at herself in the mirror, she was too old and too jaded to be attractive to a man like him. Even if Julie had not been on the scene, there were probably dozens of women like her, waiting to take her place. She was just a middle-aged housewife, with a pathetic lust for something she had never had.

CHAPTER FOUR

SO MUCH for her efforts to move quietly earlier, Laura reflected half an hour later, having made as much noise as possible as she'd got dressed. Even though she had slammed drawers, rattled hangers, and dropped a make-up bottle on to the dressing-table, Julie hadn't stirred. She was curled languorously in the middle of the bed, and nothing her mother could do would wake her.

Of course, she could always take her by the shoulders, and shake her daughter awake, Laura considered grimly. After all, Jake was Julie's guest, not hers, and she should be the one to entertain him. But that particular alternative was not appealing. The girl was probably tired, and it wasn't fair to deny her the chance to catch up on her sleep.

The reasons why Julie might be tired were less easy to contemplate. Even though she had denied them the chance to sleep together at the cottage, Laura had no doubt that Jake had slept at Julie's apartment in London. And although her experience of sexual relationships was fairly negligible, she had a more than adequate imagination.

The brush she had been using on her hair slipped out of her sweaty fingers, and landed on the carpet, and she glanced round, half apprehensively, at the bed. But Julie slumbered on, undisturbed by her mother's vapid fantasies, and, clenching her teeth, Laura wound the silky mass around her hand, and secured it on top of her head with a half dozen hairpins.

She was a fool, she told herself irritably. This simply wasn't the time to have a mid-life crisis, and the sooner she pulled herself together, and started acting her age, the better.

She went downstairs a few minutes later, slim and workmanlike, in an unfussy cotton shirt, and her oldest jeans. As soon as breakfast was over, she was going to make a start on the garden, and, if Jake Lombardi didn't like it, it was just too bad. Maybe he would have more luck in waking Julie than she had had. He was unlikely to want to spend the rest of the morning on his own, but it really wasn't her problem.

However, when she entered the kitchen, she found Jake wasn't there. The teacups had been washed and dried and left on the drainer, but there was no sign of her visitor. He had either retired to his room—and she certainly hadn't heard him come upstairs—or he had gone out. The latter seemed the most likely, but she couldn't help remembering that he had had no breakfast.

Still, it was only half-past seven, she discovered, looking at her watch. She wondered what time he usually had breakfast. Later than this, she was sure. But she wondered where he had gone all the same.

Conversely, now that she was on her own, she found she didn't know what to do. It was too early for gardening. If Mrs Langthorne, next door, saw her in the garden at this hour, she would wonder what was going on. After all, she wasn't a professional gardener, just a rather enthusiastic amateur. And enthusiastic amateurs didn't start digging up weeds at half-past seven!

She sighed, feeling definitely peevish. This was Jake's fault, she thought, needing someone to blame. If he hadn't come down so early, she would probably still be in her dressing-gown, having another cup of tea, and trying to do the previous day's crossword in the news-paper. That was what she usually did on Saturday mornings. But today, her whole schedule had been thrown off-key.

She was making a desultory inspection of the fridge, when the back door opened, and Jake came in. And with him came the delicious scent of newly baked bread.

'Miss me?' he asked incorrigibly, depositing a carrier-bag on the table, from which spilled plain and sweet rolls, scones, and a crisp French stick. 'I wasn't sure what you'd like, so I got a selection.'

Laura stared, first at the table, then at him. 'But—where——?'

'The bakery,' declared Jake, pulling a chair out from the table, and flinging himself into it.

Laura's brows drew together. 'The—village bakery?'

'Where else?'

'But—Mr Harris doesn't open until nine o'clock!'

'No?' Jake gave her a quizzical look. 'Well, I didn't steal them, if that's what you're implying.'

'Of course, I'm not implying that, but...'

Laura was lost for words, and, taking pity on her, Jake leaned forward to rest his elbows on the table. 'He was just getting his delivery,' he explained, with a disarming grin. 'And I—persuaded him to let me be his first customer. He didn't mind. I mentioned your name, and he was happy to oblige.'

Laura shook her head. 'But—I hardly know the man.'

'No. He said that, too.' Jake's eyes were warm with humour. 'You should patronise the local shops. They depend on your custom.'

'I do.' Laura was indignant. 'Well, the general stores anyway. I usually get my bread there.'

'Pre-packed, no doubt,' remarked Jake drily, and she bridled.

'It's good enough for me,' she retorted shortly, ignoring the mouth-watering smell of the warm rolls. 'I don't find food a particular fetish. I eat to live, that's all. Not the other way about. As you probably noticed last night.'

Jake's features sobered. 'Now what is that supposed to mean?'

'Nothing.' Laura refused to say anything else she might regret later, but Jake was on his feet again, and his height and the width of his shoulders dwarfed her slender frame.

'Come on,' he said, and, although his tone was pleasant, his expression was less so. 'What about last night? What am I supposed to have noticed? I said the meal was good, didn't I? What else was I supposed to say?'

'Nothing,' said Laura again, half turning away from him, and fiddling with the teapot on the drainer. 'I shouldn't have said what I did. It—it was just a defensive reaction, that's all.'

'And why do you feel the need to be defensive with me?' demanded Jake, evidently unprepared to give up so easily, and Laura sighed.

'I don't know——'

'Don't you?' Now it was her turn to look at him with unwary eyes.

'I beg your——?'

'Don't,' he said harshly. 'Don't say that again! Ever since I got up this morning, you've been on edge with me. Everything I say, you take exception to——'

'That's not true!'

Laura was indignant, but Jake simply ignored her. 'You don't like me,' he went on. 'Well, OK, I can live with that, I guess. If I have to. But what I want to know is why. What did I do to make you turn against me?'

'I didn't. I don't—— Oh, this is silly.' Laura pressed her lips together for a moment, to steady herself, and then continued evenly, 'I—don't dislike you, Mr Lombardi——'

'Jake!'

'Jake, then.' She paused a moment, after saying his name, trying to restore some sense of normality. 'I don't know you well enough to make any kind of assessment——'

'*Grazie!*'

'—and Julie cares about you. That's what matters.'

'*Scusi*, but I am not talking about Julie,' retorted Jake, and when she would have turned her back on him completely, his hand came out and took hold of her wrist. 'Don't walk out on me again.'

She was glad he hadn't touched her arm. The lean fingers coiling about her wrist were unknowingly hard, and the flesh above her elbow still ached from the night before. Even so, she couldn't prevent the spasm of pain that crossed her face, when he pulled her round to face him, and his eyes narrowed consideringly between his thick lashes.

'What is it with you?' he demanded, and she noticed how his accent was suddenly glaringly pronounced. Was that what happened when he lost his cool? she wondered dizzily. When the heat of his emotions melted the ice of his control?

But more important than that was her own reactions to his nearness. This time, his hold on her was deliberate, not the involuntary result of circumstances, and the blood his fingers were constricting rushed madly to its source. Her heart was pounding. She could hear the sound echoing hollowly in her ears. And its palpitating beat throbbed through every vein in her body, its rioting tattoo causing her temperature to soar.

'I think,' she said carefully, 'you should let me go.'

'*Come?* Oh...' He looked down at his hand curled around the fragile bones of her wrist, and his mouth twisted. 'Am I hurting you?'

'That's not the point.'

'Then what is the point?' he asked provokingly. 'I am allowed to look, but not to touch, hmm? Is that what you are saying?'

Laura couldn't look at him. She was half afraid of what he might see in her eyes. 'I—this is ridiculous——'

'I agree.'

'Then why can't you——?'

She broke off, her eyes darting towards his face and away again, and Jake's brows arched enquiringly. 'Go on. Why can't I what? Perhaps now we can get down to—how do you say it?—basics?'

Laura sighed. 'You know exactly how to say it,' she told him huskily. 'Don't think you can fool me by pretending you don't understand the language.'

'And don't you think you can fool me by persistently avoiding answering my questions,' he countered softly. 'I thought we could be friends.'

Friends! Laura swallowed. Was that what all this was about? She shook her head. God, she had to get a hold on herself.

'Please,' she said unsteadily, 'if—if you'll just let go of my wrist, perhaps we can talk about this.'

'Why?'

'Why what?' Laura was confused, and it was all she

could do to keep her eyes fixed on the hair-darkened V of his sweater.

'Why must I let go of you before we can talk?' he replied, his thumb moving almost reflexively against the fine network of veins on the inner side of her wrist, and Laura shuddered.

'I don't think you need me to tell you that,' she retorted, snatching her wrist out of his grasp, and putting the width of the table between them. 'I don't know what you think you're doing, Mr Lombardi——'

'Jake,' he corrected, and then, on a harder note, 'Perhaps I'm just trying to find out what makes you tick, *Ms Fox!*'

Laura expelled her breath in a rush. 'I think—I think you're trying to make a fool of me, Mr Lombardi,' she declared, rubbing her wrist with a nervous hand. 'Perhaps it amuses you to make fun of older women; to play games behind Julie's back. Well, I don't like it. I may seem very old-fashioned to you, but that's the way I am. Now—if you don't mind——'

'Or even if I do, hmm?' he suggested, in a dangerously bland tone. 'I'm not a boy, Laura. And you're not a grandmother—yet. Even if you do insist on acting like one.'

She had no answer to that. She was hurt. She didn't want to be; she ought not to be; but she was. His harsh words had bared her soul, and it took all her composure to gather up the bread from the table, and spread the cloth.

By the time she had set out plates and cutlery, spooned coffee into the filter and set it to perc, she had herself in control enough to ask, albeit tensely, 'What can I get you for breakfast? Would you like orange juice, or a cereal? Bacon? Eggs?'

'Nothing, thank you.'

Straightening from the lounging position he had adopted, while he'd watched her preparations for the meal, he walked to the living-room door.

'*Nothing?*'

The anxiety in Laura's voice was evident, but he was not disposed to humour her. 'I'm going out,' he told her, sauntering across the living-room and into the hall, where he had hung his leather jerkin. He appeared briefly in the living-room doorway again, as he shrugged the jacket over his shoulders. 'Tell Julie, if she manages to regain consciousness before I come back, I'll see her later.'

'But——'

Laura pressed her hands together helplessly, but Jake didn't show any sympathy. 'No buts, Laura,' he essayed smoothly. 'Later, right?' and a moment later the front door slammed behind him.

Julie eventually put in an appearance at half-past ten. She came trailing down the stairs, wearing only the satin nightshirt she had worn to sleep in, her bright hair finger-combed, but appealing. She came into the kitchen, where Laura was making a dogged effort to mix pastry, her bare toes curling on the tiled floor.

'Hi,' she said sleepily, sinking down into a chair at the table. 'Is there any coffee?'

'In the jug,' Laura pointed, her hands caked with flour and water. However, when her daughter made no attempt to help herself, she dipped her hands into the bowl of soapy water she had ready, and rinsed them clean. 'There you are,' she said, setting a cup of the dark beverage on the table, and pushing the cream jug within reach. 'It's been made about half an hour, but it shouldn't be too bad.'

'Thanks.' Julie reached for the cup and savoured its contents, before adding only the minutest touch of cream. 'Hmm, I needed this,' she added, swallowing a mouthful. 'Where's Jake?'

Laura turned back to her pastry-making. 'I—he's gone for a walk,' she said, over her shoulder, calculating that it was a fairly reasonable conclusion. He hadn't taken his car, and she didn't think he was likely to have walked to the crossroads, and picked up the local bus service.

'*God!*' Julie sounded disgusted. 'What time did he go out?'

'Oh—early,' replied Laura, flouring the board rather more liberally than was necessary. 'I—suppose he was bored. There's not much to do around here, as you know.'

'Hmm,' Julie assented. 'I suppose he was up early, too. When he's at home, I believe he likes to go riding before breakfast. Can you believe that? Leaving a perfectly good bed, to go hacking about the countryside, before it's barely light!'

Laura peeled the pastry off the rolling-pin, and wondered if she could make do with omelettes for lunch. The quiches she had intended to make were proving more of a liability than she had expected, and the cool hands she needed were continually letting her down.

'Do—er—do you want something to eat?' she asked now, hoping to divert the conversation into other channels, but Julie shook her head.

'Just another cup of coffee will do,' she said, giving her mother a wheedling look. 'Get it for me, will you Mum? I don't think I have the strength right now to get up from this chair.'

Laura resignedly rinsed her hands again, and refilled Julie's cup, before rolling the unfortunate pastry into a ball, and depositing it in the waste-bin. So much for home cooking, she thought bitterly. Perhaps she could get some ready-made quiches from Mr Harris.

Julie watched her with some surprise, and then sniffed. 'Have you been making bread?' she asked, frowning. 'It smells delici——'

'No,' Laura broke in, before Julie could pay her any unwarranted compliments. 'Your—that is—Mr Lombardi got some fresh bread from the bakery. That's what you can smell.'

'Really?' Julie grimaced. 'Before breakfast?'

'I—yes.' Laura couldn't bring herself to say that Jake hadn't had breakfast. 'D'you want some?'

'No, thanks.' Julie was tempted. 'I guess he was afraid you were going to offer him sliced bread. Italians like their bread fresh every morning.'

'Yes.' Laura had heard enough of what one particular Italian liked for one day. 'Well, now, are you going to get dressed?'

'Did Jake say where he was going?' Julie persisted, ignoring her mother's enquiry. 'How long has he been gone?'

'Oh——' Laura made a display of looking at her watch, although she knew exactly how long he had been gone '—about—a couple of hours, I suppose.'

'A couple of hours!' Julie was aghast. 'D'you think he's got lost?'

'I shouldn't think so.' Laura expunged a little of her frustration by scraping the remainder of the pastry from the board. 'He doesn't strike me as the kind of man who wouldn't know exactly what he was doing.'

'No?' Julie gave her mother a quizzical look. 'That

was said with some feeling. What's wrong? Has he been rubbing you up the wrong way?'

'Of course not.' Laura was cross with herself for allowing Julie to even suspect how she was feeling. 'I just meant—he seems—very capable.'

'Oh, he is.' Julie cupped her chin in her hands, and sighed rather smugly. 'Believe me, he is.'

Laura lifted the board to put it into the sink, but a combination of its slippery surface, and her own unsteady hands, caused it to fall heavily against the taps, and Julie's attention was diverted again.

'I thought you were baking.'

'I was.' Laura struggled to keep the resentment out of her voice. 'But I changed my mind.'

'Why?'

'Why?' Laura cast her daughter a half-impatient glance. 'Oh—no reason. I'm just not in the mood, after all.'

'Are you sure you and Jake haven't had a fight?' Julie was curious. 'It's not like you to waste perfectly good flour and water.'

Laura sighed. 'Don't be silly, Julie!' she exclaimed shortly. 'I barely know the man. What could he and I have had a fight about?'

'Me,' said Julie simply, and Laura's jaw sagged.

The realisation that her daughter's interpretation of the facts was perfectly reasonable stopped Laura in her tracks. It hadn't occurred to her that Julie might see herself as the only possible reason for her mother and her boyfriend to have words, and, although it wasn't right, it was vaguely reassuring. Of course, Julie would never think that Jake and her mother might have had a more personal exchange, Laura thought, with some relief. So far as Julie was concerned, such an idea was ludicrous.

'Well—no,' she said now. 'Really. If—if I seem on edge, it's probably just the time of the month. Anyway,' she added, realising it was probably less suspicious to talk about Jake, than to avoid doing so, 'you didn't tell me he has a family.'

'I did.' Julie frowned. 'I told you we met at that charity bash his mother had organised.'

'I don't mean his parents,' replied Laura evenly. 'I meant his daughter.'

'Oh—*Luci*!' Julie pulled a face. 'He's told you about her, has he?'

'Obviously.'

Julie shrugged. 'So?'

'So, if you marry—Jake, you'll have a ready-made daughter.'

'Stepdaughter,' amended Julie shortly, her expression losing some of its complacency. 'Don't worry. I don't intend to see a lot of her. She's a bore!'

Laura turned to look at her. 'But she is his daughter. You can't expect him to ignore his responsibilities.'

'You know nothing about it,' retorted Julie rudely. 'In any case, she's at school in Rome. She lives with Jake's parents in term-time.'

'But I thought—that is…' Laura moistened her lips before continuing, 'I understood—his parents lived in Tuscany.'

Julie's eyes grew thoughtful. 'Did you?' She paused. 'We have been having a heart-to-heart, haven't we? Has he told you about Castellombardi, too?'

Laura frowned. 'I don't think so. *Castel*—that means castle, doesn't it?'

'Something like that.' Julie was offhand. 'It's also the name of the village where the house is situated. As for its being a castle—I don't think it's any more than a rather large country house. Old, of course. And probably draughty. Though Jake did say his grandfather had spent a lot of money restoring it.'

'I see.'

'Not that we'll live there,' went on Julie carelessly. 'Jake has homes all over the place. Rome; Viareggio; *Paris*!' She sighed. 'And, of course, the Lombardis have an apartment in London.'

'Really?' Laura put the baking board away and dried her hands. 'And—and when is all this going to take place?'

'Our getting married, you mean?' Julie lifted her shoulders in a considering gesture. 'I'm not sure. Has he said anything to you?'

'To me?' Laura was taken aback, but Julie nodded.

'Yes. To you,' she repeated. 'I assumed your little tête-à-tête was Jake's way of letting you know he was able to keep me in the manner to which I've become accustomed.' Her lips twitched. 'I wish!'

Laura shook her head. 'Well—no. I mean, we did talk about you, of course, but—but——'

'You didn't ask him what his intentions were,' finished Julie shortly. 'I should have known.'

'Now, come on.' Laura had had quite enough of being accused of things she wasn't responsible for this morning. 'You can't expect me to ask questions like that!'

'Why not?'

'Why not?' Laura gasped. 'Julie, you know him better than I do, for God's sake! If you don't know what he thinks, who does?'

Julie looked sulky. 'He wanted to come here. Not me.'

'I know that.' Laura did her best to ride the pain of her daughter's indifference. 'Nevertheless it's up to—to him to speak to me. Not the other way about.'

Julie hunched her shoulders. 'If you say so.'

'I do.' Laura took a steadying breath. 'And now, I suggest you go and get dressed, before—before Jake comes back. He may want you to go for a drive or something. You could go to Alnwick, or Bamborough. And I'm sure he'd like to see the Roman wall. Or—you could always go into Newcastle. It's busy on Saturdays, but it's better than hanging about here.'

Julie sniffed. 'Didn't he say what time he'd be back?'

'No.' Laura picked up her daughter's empty cup and carried it to the sink. 'But I'm sure he won't be much longer.' She paused to gather her composure, and then added, 'After all, there isn't much to see around here.'

'Hmm.'

Julie seemed to accept this, and to her mother's relief she pushed herself to her feet. Laura waited until she had gone upstairs, before sinking weakly into the chair her daughter had vacated. Lord, she thought wearily, running her hand over her head, and then allowing it to rest at her nape. This was going to be the longest weekend of her life.

CHAPTER FIVE

'DID you have a nice weekend?'

Mark caught Laura as she was going into the school on Monday morning, and she was forced to turn and speak to him.

'Um—very nice, actually,' she lied, unprepared to confide her deeper fears in him. 'Did you?'

Mark frowned. 'It was all right, I suppose. I had the car serviced on Saturday morning, and on Sunday I took Mother over to a friend's in Carlisle. Nothing very exciting, I'm afraid.'

Laura forced a smile. 'Oh, well——'

'Did you?'

She looked confused. 'Did I what?'

'Do anything exciting?' prompted Mark impatiently. 'What was this boyfriend of Julie's like? I expect she let you run around after her, as usual.'

'That's none of your business, Mark,' returned Laura icily, glad of a reason to break off the conversation. She thrust open the glass door. 'Excuse me.'

'Aw, Laura...'

Mark came after her, but she ignored him, and as they caught up with one of the other teachers in the corridor there was no further chance for him to try and redeem himself. The staff-room, where all the teachers gathered, was not the place to try and have a private conversation, and Laura made certain they didn't leave together.

But, later on in the morning, when she had a free period, Laura couldn't prevent thoughts of the weekend from impinging on the English papers she was marking. She knew it would be a while before she could put what had happened out of her mind. It was all very well dismissing Mark's comments with a terse rejoinder. She couldn't dismiss the things Jake had said with quite the same detachment.

Not that he had said much more to her, after he'd returned from his walk on Saturday morning. To her relief, he had confined his attentions to Julie. And if her daughter·thought there was anything strange about his attitude towards her mother, she was too wrapped up in her own affairs to attribute it any consequence.

Besides, Laura thought ruefully, Julie was unlikely to entertain any worries about Jake's relationship with her mother. It simply wouldn't occur to Julie that there could be any personal contact between them. And there hadn't been, really, Laura reminded herself severely. Just a silly misunderstanding that had alienated them both.

She refused to dwell too long on what Jake might have meant by the things he had said. As she had said to him, she wasn't used to his kind of word games. And not just word games, she appended doggedly. He had played with her emotions, and made her look a fool.

Or, at least, he had tried to, she thought defensively. She didn't think she had left him in any doubts as to her disdain for his promiscuity. The way he had behaved the rest of the weekend proved he hadn't liked her lack of response. He had been polite—just—but there had been no further attempts to disconcert her.

Of course, she hadn't seen a lot of them really. By the time Jake came back from his walk, Julie had been ready and waiting. And if she hadn't got her own way about going shopping in Newcastle, because Jake wanted to see the Roman remains, the result was the same as far as Laura was concerned. They were out for the rest of the day.

Dinner on Saturday evening had been rather fraught, Laura remembered now. She had gathered the outing hadn't been an unqualified success, and none of them had done justice to the roast beef and Yorkshire pudding she had so painstakingly prepared. But at least she had been left to do the dishes in peace, and afterwards she had excused herself on the pretext of having lessons to prepare. There had been no objections; indeed, she was aware that Julie had welcomed her departure, and, if Laura had found herself speculating over what might be going on in her living-room, she had resisted the temptation to find out. The less she and Jake Lombardi had to do with one another, the better, she had decided grimly. He was not at all the kind of prospective son-in-law she had anticipated.

They had left Burnfoot the following morning. Laura had waved them off in the low, powerful sports car, that had probably attracted quite a bit of interest in the village. It was not unusual to see the odd Mercedes or BMW gliding along the High Street, and old Colonel Renfrew had an ancient Rolls-Royce. But Lamborghinis were something else again, and she was quite sure she would have to face a few pointed questions, next time she went into the village stores.

Still, she was unlikely to see either of them again for quite some time, she consoled herself, trying to concentrate on her fourth-years' interpretation of the *The Merchant of Venice*. Julie had made the usual promises that she would see her soon, and so on, but Laura privately suspected that once her daughter was married, she would see even less of her than she did now.

She shook her head, trying not to let it bother her.

After all, it wasn't a new phenomenon. She should have learned to live with it by now. She and Julie were simply not compatible, and there was no point in blaming herself for a situation over which she had no control.

The next few days were uneventful. Mark made his peace with her, catching her in the school car park one evening, and apologising for what he had said. But, although Laura accepted his apology, she didn't accept his invitation to dinner the following weekend.

'Ask me next week,' she told him, pleasantly enough, so he would know it wasn't his fault she was turning him down. She didn't want to hurt his feelings. She just couldn't cope with Mark's pedantic company at the moment.

Jess Turner, a friend from her college days, rang on Friday evening. Jess was married, and lived in Durham these days, but the two women still kept in touch.

'I wondered if you'd like to meet me for lunch tomorrow,' Jess suggested, after they had exchanged greetings. 'I'm going shopping in Newcastle, and I hoped you might like to join me.'

'Well——' Laura had planned to start on the garden the following day, but Jess was very persuasive.

'Do come,' she urged. 'It's ages since I've seen you. And—well, I've got something to tell you.'

'Oh—all right.' Laura gave in, mentally resigning her plans to weed out the winter's casualties for another week. It wasn't as if she was really in the mood for gardening, and Jess was such an undemanding companion.

They arranged to meet at Grey's Monument at half-past twelve on Saturday, and Laura spent the rest of the evening wondering what Jess had to tell her. Perhaps she and Clive were moving again, she considered pensively. As Clive was in the police force, it seemed the likeliest option.

When she went to bed, Laura hesitated a moment, and then went into the spare bedroom. She hadn't been into the bedroom since the morning of Jake's departure, when she had stripped the sheets he had used from the bed. It hadn't been a conscious avoidance, she told herself now. Just a lack of necessity to go in there. Nevertheless, she recoiled from the faint aroma of the shaving lotion he had used, though its fragrance lingered in her nostrils, long after she had closed the door.

On Saturday morning, she spent some time deciding what she was going to wear. Jess would probably expect her to turn up in jeans and a sweater, but Laura felt like dressing up, for a change. It wasn't as if she had that many opportunities to do so, she thought defensively, and after last weekend she felt like changing her image.

It was still too chilly to wear just a suit, and combining her winter coat with a suit would be far too bulky. She could always wear the cream wool dress, with the cowl collar, which she had planned to wear last weekend, she reflected positively. In fact, it might be a good idea to take the opportunity to smarten up her wardrobe. Just because she had a twenty-one-year-old daughter was no reason to behave as if she had one foot in the grave.

She refused to consider the reasons behind her sudden change of heart. She owed it to herself to dress up sometimes, she told herself firmly. She was still a comparatively young woman. Julie was right. She ought to pay more attention to her appearance.

Nevertheless, when she viewed her reflection in the mirror of the wardrobe some time later, she did have reservations. She looked smarter, it was true, but what was Jess going to think when she saw her? It was so long since she had worn dark, filmy stockings, and three-inch heels, in the daytime. And the soft folds of the woollen dress emphasised a figure she had long since ceased to admire. Breasts were not fashionable any more—particularly rather generous ones that swelled above a narrow waist.

She turned sideways, sucking in her stomach, and then allowed it to relax again. What was she doing, for heaven's sake? she asked herself irritably. She was too old to start fretting about her shape. She had lived with it for thirty-eight years, and there wasn't much she could do about it now.

The doorbell rang as she was stroking mascara on to the tawny tips of her lashes. The unexpected sound caused her hand to slip, and she only just managed to prevent the stuff from smearing her cheek. Lowering the brush to the dressing-table, she glanced impatiently towards the window. Who could it be? she wondered, frowning. It was barely ten o'clock.

Shaking her head, she cast one final look at her appearance, before going downstairs. Whoever it was was going to get a surprise when they saw her. This was definitely not the usual way she dressed on Saturday mornings.

She paused at the foot of the stairs, ran smoothing fingers over her skirt, and opened the door. Then, she almost collapsed on the spot. A man was standing on the step outside, his broad shoulders successfully blocking her view of the road. He was tall, and lean—and distractingly familiar, and her jaw sagged helplessly, as her eyes met his.

'Hi,' he said, and she thought he sounded rather tense. 'May I come in?'

Laura caught her breath. 'I——' She looked beyond him. 'Is Julie with you?'

Jake shook his head, and her heart flipped. 'She's not—I mean nothing's happened——?'

'Julie's fine,' returned Jake evenly. 'As far as I know, that is. I came alone.'

'You did?' Laura swallowed. She had the distinct feeling she was imagining this. Jake couldn't be here. He was in London, or Italy, or some other place. But not here. Not in Burnfoot. Not at her door!

'So—may I come in?' he asked again, and although she wasn't sure it was exactly wise, she stepped aside.

He looked tired, she thought, reluctantly closing the door, and following him into the living-room. There was at least one night's growth of beard on his chin, and his eyes were red-rimmed and hollow. If she didn't know better, she would have said he looked like a man who had spent the night sleeping rough, and even the jacket of the dark suit he was wearing had creases across the back.

She paused just inside the doorway, linking her fingers together, and regarding him warily. She couldn't think of any reason he might be here, unless he and Julie had had a row. That was possible, of course, but why would he come to her? What could she possibly do to help him?

Jake halted in front of the hearth. As she was going out, Laura hadn't lit the fire; but the heating system was working, and the room was pleasantly warm, even so. However, it wasn't particularly tidy. The exercise books Laura had been working on the night before, were tipped in a haphazard pile beside her chair, and various items of clothing, awaiting ironing, were draped over the back of one of the dining chairs.

Oh, well, she thought impatiently, she hadn't been

expecting a visitor, particularly not a visitor who was used to much grander surroundings than these. And if he didn't like it, no one was asking him to stay. *To stay...*

'You look nice.'

His words took her by surprise, and Laura gazed at him blankly for a few moments, before gathering her scattered wits. 'Thank you. But——'

'Are you going out?'

Laura moistened her lips. 'I—yes. Yes, I am, as it happens.' She took a steadying breath. 'Look—what's going on, Mr Lombardi? Why have you come here? I should warn you, if it's anything to do with Julie——'

'It isn't.'

'It isn't?' Laura released her fingers, to press her palms together, and realised they were sticky. 'I—but—it must be.'

'Why must it be?'

Laura's lips flattened against her teeth. 'Don't you ever answer a question?' she exclaimed. 'I want to know what's happened. Have—have you and Julie had a row?'

'No.' Jake pushed his hands into the pockets of his trousers, and as he did so his jacket fell open, revealing a bloody stain on the shirt beneath.

Laura gasped, and pressed her fingers to her lips, and Jake, realising what she had seen, pulled one hand out of his pocket to finger the ugly discolouration of the cloth. 'A small accident,' he said, his lips twisting cynically. 'I don't think I'll die of it, do you?'

Laura stared at him disbelievingly. 'You—cut yourself?'

'I didn't say that exactly.' Jake glanced behind him at the armchair. 'D'you mind if I sit down? I appear to have lost my balance.'

He sank down into the chair, as Laura rushed across the room towards him. He had gone so pale suddenly that she was half afraid he was going to lose consciousness as well. He must have lost a lot of blood, she thought, halting nervously beside the chair. But why was he here? What was going on?

'That's better,' he said, sinking back against the cushions, and gazing up at her through the thick veil of his lashes. 'Sorry about that. I guess I'm not as tough as I thought I was.'

Laura hesitated a moment longer, and then came down on her haunches beside him. 'Do you—would you like me to—to look at it?' she ventured, and his lips twitched with a trace of humour.

'Look at what?' he countered lazily, and she tore her eyes from the revealing tautness of cloth across his crotch.

'You know what I mean,' she declared, getting swiftly to her feet again. 'You're evidently hurt. I might be able to help you.'

'OK.' Jake tugged his shirt out of the waistband of his trousers, and unfastened the first couple of buttons. 'Go ahead.'

Laura didn't want to touch him. Just being near him like this was nerve-racking enough, without having to look at his bare flesh. It reminded her too much of the way she had pictured him, lying in her spare bed upstairs. He was so disturbingly male, and she simply wasn't equipped to deal with it.

Nevertheless, as she drew his silk shirt aside to reveal the brown flesh of his midriff, her reticence was quickly overtaken by concern. He had a gash, some three inches in length, and perhaps a quarter as deep, just below the curve of his rib-cage. Someone had endeavoured—not very successfully—to close the wound with adhesive sutures, but it had opened again, and was now bleeding fitfully.

Laura knew a momentary sense of panic, and then, determinedly quelling the feeling of sickness that had risen inside her, she lifted her eyes to his pale face. 'Who did this?' she exclaimed, forcing herself to speak levelly. 'Was there a fight? Is that how it happened? If so——'

'It was my fault,' Jake interrupted her wearily. 'It was a fight, but it was perfectly controlled. Or it was supposed to be. I was fencing—you understand? I wasn't giving my opponent the attention I should. Believe me, the man who did this was more upset than me.'

Laura shook her head. 'But—don't you wear protective clothing for fencing? And aren't there foils?'

'Very good.' Jake made a weak attempt to applaud her. 'Yes, you're right, of course. One is expected to take precautions. But—I didn't feel like being careful, and this is the result.'

Laura caught her lower lip between her teeth. 'You could have been killed!'

'I think not.' Jake's lips twisted. 'Believe it or not, I am usually capable of holding my own, as they say.'

Laura shook her head. 'Have you seen a doctor?'

'I don't need a doctor,' retorted Jake flatly. 'I've just lost a little blood, is all. Doctors ask too many questions. And I was not in the mood to answer them.'

Laura bit her lip, hard, and then, realising she was wasting time, she turned and hurried into the kitchen. Armed with a bowl of warm water, some antiseptic, and bandages, she returned to the living-room, and knelt down beside his chair.

'I'm afraid this is going to hurt,' she said, deciding the reasons why—and how—he was here would have to wait for the moment. Somehow she had to stop the bleeding, and then maybe she could persuade him to seek professional help.

He winced as she drew the gaping sutures away, and at once the wound began to bleed more freely. Her hands were soon wet with his blood, and the knowledge was terrifying. She just hoped she knew what she was doing, and that she wasn't making it worse.

'You should go to a hospital,' she protested, pressing a damp cloth against the gash. At least it was clean, she thought unwillingly. If she could bind it tightly enough, he might get away with just a bad headache.

'You're doing fine,' he told her, but she could see the beads of perspiration on his forehead. Whatever he said, she knew he must be in a great deal of pain, and that awareness troubled her more than it should.

'You should have had more sense,' she added crossly, spreading some antiseptic ointment on a gauze dressing, and applying it to the cut. She guessed it must have stung like crazy, but all Jake did was suck in his breath. 'I suppose what you were doing was illegal. That's why you didn't want to call a doctor.'

'Something like that.'

Jake's response was barely audible, and, although she knew he needed to rest, Laura steeled her emotions, and said, 'I'm afraid you're going to have to sit up.'

'Sit up?' Jake looked a bit sick at the prospect, but he pushed his hands down on the arms of the chair, and propelled himself forward. 'OK.'

'You'll have to take off your jacket—and your shirt,' murmured Laura awkwardly, wishing she was not so aware of him as a man. He was her daughter's property, she kept telling herself. Apart from anything else, he was too young for her. But it didn't help, and her breathing was as shallow as his as she watched him struggling to take off his jacket.

Of course, she had to help. Even coping with the knot of his tie exhausted him, and she was forced to remove his jacket, and unfasten the remaining buttons of his shirt. His skin was clammy. The result of her inexpert ministrations, she guessed. No matter how successful he was at hiding his feelings, he couldn't hide the reactions of his body.

But it made it a little easier for her. However, although the room was warm, while he was sweating he could easily catch a chill, and she applied the length of bandage with a swift and—*she hoped*—impersonal efficiency. The fact that his skin was smooth, with ridges of corded muscle beneath the flesh, and an arrowing of fine dark hair that disappeared below the waistband of his trousers, were passing observations. Nevertheless, she couldn't fail to notice how white the bandage looked against his dark skin, or help her own response to his potent sexuality.

Leaving him to put his shirt on again, as best he could, Laura carried the dish, and the dressings she had used, back into the kitchen. She tipped the bloodstained water into the sink, and watched as it curled away, out of sight. It looked worse than it was, she reassured herself, but even so, he was lucky to have reached the cottage without passing out. But how had he reached the cottage? she wondered, gnawing at her lower lip. And why had he come here? Dear God, what was Julie going to say when she found out where he'd been?

She pushed herself away from the sink, and looked around. Tea, she thought practically, refusing to consider Julie's feelings at this moment. Hot, sweet tea! Wasn't that what they always gave you in hospital? Something to warm you, and give you energy, all at the same time.

She filled the kettle, and plugged it in, and then faltered again, unsure of how to continue. Was he fit to answer questions now? she pondered uneasily. Was he fit to leave, without seeing a doctor? And could she turn him out, if he wanted to stay?

But, of course, he didn't want to stay, she told herself impatiently, marching to the door of the living-room, and then halting, her fingers clenching and unclenching frustratedly. Her questions were going to have to wait. Jake was asleep.

Or was he? Anxiety brought her to the side of his chair again, and she bent to listen to his breathing. How would she know if he was unconscious? she fretted. It wasn't as if she had any experience in these matters.

But he *seemed* to be sleeping. And he had managed to put on his shirt again, although it was just dragged across his chest, and no attempt had been made to fasten the buttons. Even so, she thought he looked a little better. There was the faintest trace of colour in his cheeks, and, with his eyes closed, their hollowness seemed less pronounced. Instead, his lashes lay like sooty fans above his cheekbones, and she knew an unholy desire to reach out and touch their softness with the tips of her fingers...

It was enough to set her back several paces. Dear lord, she thought, aghast, what on earth was she thinking of? She was behaving as if she had never seen a man sleeping before. How amused he would be, if he opened his eyes and saw her.

Swallowing her impatience, she strode across the room, and climbed the stairs to her bedroom. There were blankets, stored in the cedarwood ottoman at the foot of her bed, and, pulling out the largest, she carried it downstairs again. Then, trying not to inhale the pungent scent of sweat that still lingered on his body, she eased the blanket up to his chin. At least, it wouldn't be her fault if he caught a chill, she thought resentfully. She could do without that on her conscience as well.

The kettle was boiling, and, giving him one last, uneasy look, Laura went into the kitchen to turn it off. There was no point in making any tea yet, she reflected ruefully. He could sleep for an hour or more, and she might have to provide him with lunch. *Lunch...*

She cast a horrified look at her watch. It was after eleven o'clock already, and although she was not meeting Jess until half-past twelve, she had planned to give herself plenty of time to find somewhere to park. It wasn't always easy on Saturdays, and the traffic into the city was always heavy.

She groaned. What was she going to do? There was no point in phoning Jess's home. Her husband was unlikely to be there, and besides, Jess had said she was planning to make a day of it. There was no way she could let her friend know what had happened—even if she wanted to.

Even if she wanted to? The ambiguity of that statement caused another crisis of conscience. Of course, she wanted to tell Jess what had happened. She couldn't leave her friend, waiting around, not knowing what was going on. Why shouldn't she tell her? What did she have to hide?

What indeed? Laura gazed blankly through the window, into the back garden of the cottage. What was she afraid of? That Jess might suspect Jake had come here, because of something she had done—or said? That she might suspect Laura was *attracted* to the man? A man who was obviously years younger than she was?

Of course. She had her pride, just like anyone else, and Jake's appearance had put her in an invidious position. What could she tell anyone? How could he have done it?

Gripping the edge of the formica-topped work unit, Laura struggled to find some perspective in this. Jake must have had some other reason for coming to this part of the country, she decided. Julie had said his family was in business, hadn't she? And everyone knew that the north-east of England was an enterprise zone. He had probably come to finalise some business deal, and, because she was in the area, he had decided to look her up.

But no. That didn't hold water. For one thing, he'd said he had been fencing, and he would hardly have been doing that prior to attending some business meeting. So did that mean he had driven all the way from London, with that gash in his side? My God, she thought sickly, how could he have done it? And where had he spent last night?

The questions just went on and on, and she simply didn't have the time to find the answers. Jake was here, and, for the moment, there was nothing she could do about it. But that didn't mean she had to alter her schedule. She had made plans, and he couldn't expect her to abandon them, just because he had chosen to practically collapse on her doorstep.

She sighed. But could she go and leave him as he was? What if he was unconscious, after all? What if she was wrong, and he slipped into a coma, or something equally ghastly, in her absence? Would she ever forgive herself if something awful happened to him? If only she had explained the situation, before he'd passed out. He could sleep for hours, and there was nothing she could do.

CHAPTER SIX

'DID I hear a kettle boiling?'

The low, attractive sound of Jake's voice brought Laura round with a start. She had believed he was asleep, or worse, and seeing him, albeit swaying, in the doorway, caused a sudden surge of impatience.

'What are you doing?' she exclaimed, forgetting for the moment that seconds before she had been lamenting his unconscious state. 'You shouldn't be walking around. That wound needs time to heal.'

Jake glanced down at his stained shirt, and laid a brown hand over the area of the injury. 'It feels much better,' he assured her, lifting his eyes to hers again. 'I'm sorry for losing consciousness like that. I guess I'm more tired than I thought.'

Laura's hands clenched at her sides. 'Did you have any sleep last night?'

'Some.' Jake was non-committal.

'Where?'

He sighed. 'In a service area.'

Laura was horrified. 'In your car?'

'Does it matter? I made it, didn't I?'

'That depends.' Laura found it was too much to cope with, right at this minute. 'Well—I've got to go. I—I'm meeting someone.'

'Are you?' Jake's eyes were dark and enigmatic. 'Does that mean you'd like me to leave?'

Laura hesitated. 'Not—necessarily,' she replied, ignoring the small voice inside her, that said that was exactly what she ought to ask him to do. But how could she? she argued with herself. He wasn't fit to go anywhere!

'No?' he said softly. 'You want me to stay?'

'I didn't say I *wanted* you to stay,' Laura countered hotly. 'I—just don't think you're fit to leave. Not if you have to drive anyway.' She pressed her lips together. 'Where did you leave your car?'

Jake inclined his head, his mouth taking on a vaguely ironic slant. 'I parked near that stretch of grass, beside the church.'

'The green!' exclaimed Laura, with an inward groan. 'Why'd you park there?'

Jake's face paled alarmingly, and he gripped the frame of the door for support before replying. 'I—thought you might prefer it,' he replied unevenly. 'I didn't want to embarrass you.'

'Embarrass me?'

Laura could have laughed, but it would have been a bitter laugh at best. She could just imagine the stir his reappearance would have caused. After last weekend, she doubted there was anyone in the village who wouldn't have recognised Jake's car, if they saw it. And parking on the green...

But Jake was obviously in no state to stand here trading words with her, and, forcing herself to move forward, she took his arm. 'I think you'd better go and sit down again, before you fall down,' she told him, intensely aware of the heat of his flesh through his shirtsleeve. 'Come on. Then I'll make you some hot tea. Are you hungry?'

Jake shook his head, but he leaned on her fairly heavily as they progressed across the living-room to where the blanket was tumbled on the armchair. Without letting go of him, Laura quickly whisked the blanket away, and then supported him, as he lowered himself into the chair. He was sweating again, she noticed, with a pang; a combination of the shock he had had, and the amount of blood he had lost, she surmised. It was draining his strength.

'*Mi dispiace,*' he said, and she noticed how, in moments of stress, he was apt to lapse into his own language. 'I'm sorry. I am a nuisance, *no*?'

Laura straightened, resisting the impulse to smooth the damp strands of dark hair back from his forehead. 'It's—all right,' she said, offhandedly, glancing towards the kitchen. 'Um—here's the blanket. I'll get the tea.'

'But your—appointment?' he queried, looking up at her through his lashes, and Laura's heart palpitated wildly.

'I've got time,' she said, leaving him, and hurrying back into the kitchen. She had—just, but only if she managed to get parked at the first attempt.

At least the kettle didn't take long to boil again, and she made the tea with hands that shook a little. It was a hangover from supporting his weight on her shoulder, she told herself firmly, but she was trembling inside, too, and she had no excuse for that.

She set a tray with the necessary cup and saucer, milk, and sugar basin, and then added a plate of biscuits, just for good measure. She supposed she should have opened a tin of soup or something, but he had said he wasn't hungry, and when she came back...

She arrested her thoughts right there. She was not going to think about what might happen when she got back. He might not be here, for heaven's sake. If he drank the sweet tea, and rested for a while, he might feel well enough to drive to a hotel, at least—and that would all be for the best, she told herself severely. Least said, soonest mended: wasn't that what they said? So long as their relationship remained on this impersonal level, she had nothing to worry about.

Jake's eyes were closed again, when she went back into the living-room, but they opened when she set the tray down on an end-table she had set beside his chair.

'*Grazie*,' he said, levering himself up from the cushions, to take the cup she handed him. 'I am most grateful.'

Laura folded her hands. 'The teapot's on the tray, and I've put plenty of sugar in your cup,' she said, realising she was sounding more and more like his mother. Well, why not? she thought cynically. If Julie had her way, she'd be his mother-in-law, at least. 'I—I should be back by about half-past three,' she went on, mentally abandoning any thoughts of prolonging the outing. 'But if—if you want to go before then—which I don't advise,' she added recklessly, 'just drop the latch, and close the door.'

Jake regarded her over the rim of his cup. 'I'll stay.'

'You will?' Laura swallowed convulsively.

'If you have no objections,' he averred, grimacing at the sweetness of the tea, and Laura's breathing felt suspended.

'I—no,' she mumbled, turning away, before he could say anything else to disturb her efforts to remain objective. Nevertheless, her heart was pounding, and it took an enormous effort to walk across the floor.

Her coat and handbag were upstairs, and by the time she came down again, the warm folds of her plum-coloured cashmere coat wrapped about her, Jake was resting back against the cushions.

'Drive carefully,' he said, as she collected her car keys

from the sideboard, and, with a jerky nod, Laura let herself out of the house.

She saw the Lamborghini, as she drove through the village. As Jake had said, it was parked on the verge, beside the wall of the churchyard. Several of the village children were peering through its windows as she passed, and she hoped they wouldn't do any damage to it. In any case, she didn't have the time to move it now, even if she'd had the guts to try.

She was late meeting Jess, but only about ten minutes, and her friend accepted her explanation of not being able to find anywhere to park. The city was busy, and Laura had been lucky to find a space in one of the multi-storey car parks. Luckily, someone had been leaving, as Laura had cruised along one of the upper floors, and, although she had had to contend with some irate glares from motorists, who'd considered they had a prior claim to the space, she'd bought her parking ticket, and stuck it bravely to the windscreen.

Jess was waiting beneath the monument that had been raised to Earl Grey, one of England's earliest prime ministers, and her eyes widened when she saw her friend. She was smaller than Laura, and, although she generally wore high heels to increase her height, today she had chosen boots, and woollen trousers. In consequence, the contrast between them was quite pronounced, and she frowned as Laura crossed the square towards her.

'Did I miss something?' she asked, after Laura had made her explanations, and, aware that Jess was referring to her appearance, Laura grimaced.

'No,' she protested, but she couldn't help the wave of hot colour that ran up her cheeks at the words. Even though the way she was dressed owed nothing to Jake Lombardi's arrival, the connotations were irresistible.

'Are you sure?' Jess regarded her with some suspicion. 'We are just going shopping, you know.'

'I know.' Laura sighed. 'I just felt like making the most of myself for once. Do I usually look such a fright?'

'Of course not.' Jess shook her dark head. 'It wouldn't have anything to do with Julie, would it?'

'Julie!' Laura managed to sound indignant, but it took an effort. 'Jess!'

'Well!' Jess was unrepentant. 'You haven't seen her, then?'

Laura took the other girl's arm. 'Can we move away from here?' she asked, without answering. 'Where are we having lunch?'

'I thought we might go to Fenwicks,' replied Jess, giving her friend a studied look. 'Then we can look round the clothes department first.'

'Fine.'

Laura nodded, and they crossed the square to the swing doors of the large department store Jess had mentioned. Walking through the store, it was difficult to talk at all, and it wasn't until Jess led the way into the maternity department that Laura realised what her friend had to tell her.

'You're pregnant!' she exclaimed, and, when Jess nodded, rather sheepishly, she gave her a hug. 'How wonderful!'

'Is it?' Jess looked a little less confident now. 'I'm not so sure.'

'What do you mean?' Laura frowned. 'Don't you want a family?'

'Well, you know I do—*did*,' amended Jess, sighing. 'But, Laura, Clive and I have been married for almost *fifteen* years. I'm almost forty. You don't think I'm too old, do you?'

'Too old?' Unbidden, thoughts of Jake sprang into Laura's mind, and she had a hard time putting them aside. 'Of course you're not too old. What does Clive think?'

'Oh, he's over the moon,' said Jess glumly, examining a navy and white maternity dress, with straight, classic lines. 'But after all these years! I never imagined I'd be having my first child at my age!'

'Lots of women have their first child in their late thirties,' declared Laura staunchly. 'Women who've put their career first, and a family second.'

'Yes, but that's not me, is it?' said Jess, sighing. 'I wanted a baby when I was younger. Now, I'm not so sure.'

'Aren't you?'

Laura looked at her disbelievingly, and Jess managed a rueful smile. 'Well, all right, yes. I want this baby. But not if anything's going to go wrong.'

Laura shook her head. 'Stop being such a pessimist. If you want to look at it that way, younger women have problems, too. If you look after yourself, and do what the doctor tells you, you'll be fine. It's not such a big deal, Jess. Honestly.'

'That's easy for you to say,' Jess argued. 'You were only a kid when you had Julie. I'm an old married woman.'

'Nonsense,' said Laura firmly. 'You'll take it in your stride. So—when is the baby due? You don't look any different.'

'At the end of September,' Jess replied, running an involuntary hand over the curve of her stomach. She smiled. 'There's not much to see yet, thank goodness.'

'No.' Laura smiled. 'I'm so pleased for you. I'm sure Clive will make a marvellous father.'

'Mmm.' Jess was thoughtful. 'Well, I hope so.'

'I'm sure he will.' Laura knew a momentary sense of envy for her friend. She had never known what it was like to share those simple human emotions.

But later, as they were sitting enjoying scampi and chips in the restaurant, Jess returned to her earlier tack. 'So,' she said, 'how are things with you? Have you seen Julie recently?'

'You don't give up, do you?' Laura regarded her friend with some resignation. 'All right, yes. Julie came up last weekend. But she didn't browbeat me into doing something about my appearance, so you can stop looking so smug.'

'So who did, then?' Jess countered, and, once again, Jake's dark features swam into Laura's consciousness. She didn't want to think about him. She particularly didn't want to admit that he had had anything to do with her desire to improve her image. But she couldn't help wondering if he was all right, and if he really did intend to stay.

'I...' Realising Jess was looking at her rather curiously now, Laura endeavoured to speak casually. 'Um— no one influenced me,' she said, not altogether truthfully. 'I just felt like smartening myself up, that's all. I look all right, don't I? You're making me feel conspicuous.'

'Don't be silly. You look great, and you know it,' declared Jess warmly. 'I just wondered if—by any chance—some man——'

'No!' Laura knew her response was too vehement, but she couldn't help it. 'Honestly, Jess, just because you think marriage is the best thing since sliced bread, don't imagine everyone has to have a man in their life, before they begin to care how they look!'

Jess flushed then, and Laura felt awful. 'I didn't mean——' Jess began, but Laura broke in before she could go any further.

'No, I know you didn't!' she exclaimed, expelling her breath on a rueful sigh. 'Oh, Jess, I'm sorry. I didn't mean to blow up at you like that. I don't know what's the matter with me today.'

Didn't she?

'It doesn't matter. I shouldn't have said anything,' protested Jess hurriedly. 'Honestly. I just wondered if Mark '

'Mark?' In spite of herself, Laura's voice rose an octave. 'Oh—well, I still see him from time to time, of course. Outside school, I mean. But he's like me. He's not interested in surrendering his freedom for some precarious sexual commitment.'

Jess studied her friend doubtfully. 'At the risk of getting my head bitten off again, I don't think that's how you really feel,' she declared, and, when Laura raised her eyebrows, she went on, 'You think you're so self-sufficient, Laura. You go to school, and support yourself. You've even bought your own home. But can you honestly say you never wish you'd got married?'

Laura bent her head. 'Yes.'

'Well, I don't believe it.' Jess finished her meal, and propped her elbows on the table. 'I think you've let one bad experience sour you for a real, loving relationship. Or perhaps you've just never met a man who could turn your world upside-down.'

'Oh, Jess!' Laura fell back on sarcasm, as a means to divert her friend. 'Is this really Mrs Turner, the terror of the maths department, talking? Look out, Barbara Cartland! You've got a rival!'

'You can mock,' declared Jess imperviously. 'But I mean it. You just never go anywhere where you might meet someone.'

'I go places,' said Laura, aware that Jess's words were not as ridiculous as she would like to think. 'I go to parties, occasionally, and the theatre——'

'With Mark Leith,' put in Jess, as the waitress came to remove their plates. 'No one's going to make a pass at you, with him keeping a proprietorial hold on you.'

'Just because you don't like Mark——'

'I hardly know him,' retorted Jess. 'But I'm pretty sure he's not the man for you.'

'There you go again.' Laura wished she had never started this. 'Jess, have you ever considered that I might not be the marrying sort?'

Jess gave her an old-fashioned look. 'No.'

'Why not?'

'Will you take a look at yourself some time?' exclaimed Jess forcefully. 'You're tall, and slim——'

'Not so slim!'

'—and attractive. You've got good legs.'

'Jess, please.' Laura shook her head. 'Can we talk about something else, please? Like—what are we going to have for dessert?'

'Doesn't Julie say anything?' persisted Jess, and Laura felt as if she was lurching from one awkward topic to another.

'I—Julie's fine,' she said, hoping Jess would take the hint, but her friend looked at her over the menu, and her expression was not encouraging.

'I meant—doesn't Julie ever mention the prospect of your getting married?'

'Me?' Laura stared fixedly at the menu. 'No, of course not. Why should she? I'm her mother. I'm too old to—to——'

'To have a sex-life of your own?' suggested Jess drily. 'Yes, I can believe she thinks that.'

Laura sighed. 'Jess, please——'

'Oh, all right.' Jess capitulated. 'So—tell me about Julie. Is she all right? I gather she's not thinking of getting married any time soon either.'

Laura's head came up. 'Why do you say that?'

'You mean, she is?' Jess's eyes widened. 'Have you met him?'

'Jess!' In spite of all her efforts, Laura could feel the colour rising to her cheeks. 'You do jump to conclusions, don't you? I haven't even said she has a boyfriend. I only—wondered why——'

'Laura, you're not a very good liar.' Jess smiled. 'Now, I can tell from your face that something's going on, so you might as well tell me what it is. I don't keep any secrets from you.'

'I'm not keeping secrets!' But she was, and she was guiltily aware of it. 'As it happens—Julie did...bring a friend home with her last weekend. He's an Italian. His name's—Jake Lombardi.'

'I see.' Jess was intrigued, and looked it. 'Was he nice? Did you like him?'

Laura felt hot. And it wasn't just the fact that the restaurant was heated. It was as if she were enveloped in the steam from a Turkish bath, and it took the utmost effort not to use the menu as a fan.

'He's—very nice,' she said, grateful for the reappearance of the waitress, to ask if they wanted a dessert. 'Er—just coffee for me, please. I—couldn't eat another thing.'

'I'll have the same,' said Jess, and, after the woman had departed, she lay back in her chair. 'Is he sexy?'

'Who?'

Laura pretended not to understand, but Jess was not to be diverted. 'This—Jake Lombardi, of course,' she answered. 'What does he look like? How old is he?'

'Oh....' Laura realised she was not going to get any peace until she had told her, and, adopting what she hoped was a careless tone, she said, 'Julie seems to like him, so I suppose he must be. Sexy, I mean. He's—an Italian, as I said. What do Italians look like? He's dark, of course. Quite good-looking, I suppose. And young. No more than about twenty-eight.'

'I see.' Jess looked at her friend with knowing eyes. 'So—what's wrong?'

'Wrong?' Laura blinked. She wished she had known what was going to happen this morning before she'd accepted Jess's invitation to lunch, but it was too late now. 'Nothing's wrong.'

'No?' Jess was not convinced. 'You don't usually get so flustered when you talk about Julie's boyfriends.' She paused, and then added softly, 'You know, if it weren't so unlikely, I'd wonder if you weren't attracted to him yourself!'

It was after four o'clock when Laura started back to Burnfoot. She had intended to make some excuse, and leave directly after lunch. She hadn't been happy about leaving Jake as it was, and the fact that he had had no food since God knew when was preying on her mind incessantly. At least, that was what she told herself was preying on her mind. Anything else was not to be considered.

But she had had to abandon the idea of leaving early.

After the conversation she and Jess had had, it would not have been politic to beat such a hasty retreat. Jess might have begun to wonder why she had felt the need to curtail their outing, and if she ever found out that Jake had come back to Burnfoot...

It had been hard enough as it was, making her friend believe that she had no personal interest in her daughter's boyfriend. She had pretended it had been Julie's idea to bring him to meet her, thus fuelling Jess's speculation that their relationship was serious. And she had made a lot of their affection for one another, and maintained that she had felt like a gooseberry the whole weekend.

Of course, she hadn't been entirely honest in that respect. At no time had she actually interrupted them in what might be called a compromising position. But the fact was, she could have. And after playing on the fact of Jake's youth, and how no man was likely to look at her when Julie was around, she thought she had convinced Jess she was barking up the wrong tree.

She hoped she hadn't been too vehement in her denials, she thought now, accelerating past a slow-moving vehicle. Jess was fairly shrewd, and they had known one another too long for Laura to find lying easy. No, not lying, she corrected, her hands tightening on the steering-wheel; just prevaricating, that was all. Jess had probably felt sorry for her, she decided grimly, slamming the car into a lower gear, with a distinct disregard for the mechanism. After what she had said about marriage, it was obvious the way her mind worked.

The car splashed through the ford into Burnfoot at about five minutes to five. Laura would have been quicker—she had driven fast, if rather badly—but she had been balked since she'd left the main road, by the vicar's modest Vauxhall. There weren't many opportunities to overtake on the narrower country roads and, besides, the Reverend Mr Johnson would probably have looked askance at one of his staider parishioners, storming past him like a teenager who'd just got her licence.

The vicar waved as he turned into the vicarage gates, thus confirming Laura's suspicions that he had recognised her behind him. But her response was barely perfunctory as she passed the vicarage and drove along the village green. Her attention was arrested by the fact that the Lamborghini had gone. The verge beside the churchyard wall was deserted, the drizzle which had started as she'd left the city sending even the children home earlier than usual.

Her stomach sank. There was no other word to describe the way she felt. Jake had gone, and the steaks she had bought for their evening meal would end up in the freezer. Of course, she was later than she had said she would be. And it was obvious he couldn't stay at the cottage overnight. She should have thought of that when she was wasting so much time in the dress stores. She should have realised what he would think when she didn't return.

There were tears in her eyes as she reached her gate, and she was glad it was raining, so that she wasn't likely to encounter her next-door neighbour in the garden. She was in no mood to talk to anyone, and she turned into the narrow driveway with a heavy heart.

And then, she gasped. The Lamborghini was parked alongside the cottage, just as it had been the previous weekend. Although she didn't have a garage, there was plenty of room to stand a car beside the cottage, and her hands tightened convulsively on the wheel of the Ford. He was still here, she thought incredulously, aware that her heart was hammering wildly. He hadn't gone away. He had just moved his car.

She sat for several seconds, after switching off the engine, trying to get a hold on her emotions. For heaven's sake, she thought, screwing the heels of her hands against her damp cheeks, it wasn't as if it meant anything. He had said he would stay until she got back, and he had. And she had to pull herself together, before he got the wrong idea as well.

Eventually, of course, she had to move, and, throwing open her door, she got out and leant into the back to collect her coat and her shopping. On the pretext of needing something to wear for work, she had invested in two new blouses, a skirt, a pair of wide-legged trousers, and a fine wool sweater. All necessary stuff, she had assured Jess, dismissing the silky trousers as pure indulgence. After all, she had argued, she seldom spent money on herself. And Jess had agreed.

There was also a bag of food from Marks and Spencer. Steak, fruit and vegetables, and a cheesecake. Quite a haul, she reflected, trying to concentrate on what she was doing, and not on Jake Lombardi. But she couldn't help wondering how he was.

She was fumbling for her key on the doorstep. Her arms were full, with her coat and the carriers, and she was wishing she had had the sense to find her key before loading herself down, when the door gave inwards.

Jake stood on the step above, looking down at her with dark unreadable eyes. He had changed his clothes, she saw at once, and the snug-fitting jeans, and dark blue shirt, hid any trace of his injury. He still looked a little pale, but rested, his face clean of the designer stubble he had sported when he'd arrived.

'Hi,' he said, reaching to take the bags from her, but when he did, her brain reasserted itself.

'I—I can manage!' she exclaimed, hugging the bags close. 'You—you might hurt yourself.'

'As if,' said Jake drily, wresting the carriers from her hands. 'It was only a jab, Laura. Not a major laceration!'

He turned then, and walked into the house, and after glancing about her, as if to reassure herself that no one else had witnessed their struggle, Laura stepped inside, and closed the door. Then, draping her coat over the banister, she followed him across the living-room, and into the kitchen.

Jake had deposited all the bags on the table, and he turned when she came into the room after him. 'I don't know where you want these——' he was beginning, when he saw her face. 'Hey!' he exclaimed, and, because the kitchen was so small, he reached her with only one step. His thumb smudged an errant tear from her cheek, and then brushed her lower lip, before her instinctive withdrawal caused his hand to drop. 'What's wrong? Did I breach some feminist principle, or something? Where I come from, women do not carry heavy bags. Not if a man is there to do it for them.'

'Don't be silly.' Laura bent her head, wishing she had a tissue. 'Nothing's wrong. It's raining, or hadn't you noticed?'

'I'd noticed,' he said tautly. 'But raindrops don't usually fall into your eyes, do they? What's the matter? Are you sorry I'm still here, is that it?'

'No.' Laura sniffed, and turned aside. 'I—you moved your car.'

As soon as she had said the words, she knew she had made a mistake. Jake frowned, and then, side-stepping her, he put himself into her path. 'So what? I got the impression you weren't very happy with it where it was.'

'I wasn't.' Laura's skin tingled with uneasiness. 'It—it was too conspicuous. Everyone was looking at it——'

But Jake had sucked in his breath. 'Wait a minute,' he said, and the hand that only seconds before had grazed her cheek, moved to grip the back of her neck, imprisoning her in front of him. 'You thought I'd gone, didn't you?' he said hoarsely. '*Dio*, Laura, as if I would.'

'You're wrong,' she cried, trying to get away from him, but, instead of letting her go, he jerked her towards him.

'No. You're wrong,' he said thickly, bending his head, and, before she could even comprehend what he planned to do, his mouth covered hers.

Even then, she knew, she could have tried to stop him. He had no right to touch her; to take her in his arms; to hold her so close she could feel every ridge of the bandage she had applied earlier. Her knees bumped against his, and one powerful thigh was thrust between her legs, as he moved to keep his balance. It made her overpoweringly aware of his sex, trapped against her hip, and the warm male scent of his body, that rose irresistibly to her nostrils.

But it was his mouth that caused the most havoc, that lean sensual mouth, that she now admitted had haunted her sleep for the past week. It ravished hers with all the skill of which he was able, and her timid objections were trampled in the dust.

Her mind swam beneath the dark hunger of his kiss. Every nerve in her body was alert to the sensuous needs he was arousing. Her lips parted beneath his, and no experience she had known had prepared her for Jake's urgent assault on her senses. When his tongue invaded her mouth, its hot wet tip raking every inch of quivering flesh, her legs turned to water. She had never, ever, felt so utterly helpless, in the grip of emotions she hadn't known existed, drawn into a maelstrom of wild seductive passion.

But when his hand slid from her waist to encircle one swollen breast, a need for self-preservation fought its way to the surface. Dear God, she thought, aware that her hands were clutching his shirt for support, whatever was she doing? Apart from anything else, this was the man her daughter had told her she intended to *marry*. How could she be standing here like this, and letting him maul her? It was insane.

'No,' she gasped, and, although the word was muffled and barely distinguishable, Jake heard her.

'No?' he repeated softly, his thumb describing a sensuous circle around her nipple, tautly—and shamefully—visible, beneath the cream wool of her dress. 'Why not? It's what you want. It's what we both want——'

'No!' Laura could hardly get her breath. 'You—you're disgusting,' she choked, thrusting his hand away from her, and taking a backward step. 'How can you do this? You know that Julie——'

Jake's mouth hardened, and, although he didn't move away from her, he didn't stop her when she widened the space between them. 'Julie's not here,' he said harshly, his accent thickening his tone.

Laura clenched her fists. 'Is that all you have to say?' she cried. 'Julie's not here! My God, is that supposed to mean something?'

Jake straightened, and when he moved Laura couldn't help watching him. He had an indolent, almost feline grace, and, when he wiped his palms down the seams of his trousers, it was all she could do not to follow them with her eyes. She wanted to. She knew what she would see if she did, what she *wanted* to see, she admitted, sickened by her own duplicity. The tight jeans were no barrier to the bulging proof of his arousal.

'What do you want me to say?' he asked now, and she hated the fact that he probably knew exactly how she was feeling. 'I am not interested in Julie at this moment. I am only interested in you.' He paused. 'And I think you are interested in me, only you have some prudish notion that you shouldn't be.'

'That's not true!'

The words were hot and vehement, and, although she sensed he didn't believe her, he knew better than to argue her down. 'If you say so,' he conceded, lifting his hand as if to massage his midriff, and then, as if thinking better of it, he let it fall. 'So—I suppose you would like me to go now.'

Laura bit her lower lip. His involuntary action had served to remind her of his injury, and although she could hardly accuse him of making use of it she was guiltily aware that she had forgotten it. Had she hurt him? she wondered. When she'd clutched at his shirt, had she grazed the tender skin? She hoped not. She didn't like to think that she might be responsible for it starting to bleed again.

'I—suppose you should,' she answered at last. But when his lips twisted rather cynically, she added, 'But that doesn't mean you have to.'

Jake took a deep breath. 'No?'

'No.' Laura squared her shoulders. 'In spite of what you think of me, I'm not a complete idiot. I don't think there was a shred of decency in what happened just now, but I'm prepared to forget it, if you are.'

'Really?'

'Yes, really.' Laura held up her head. 'It was just a— a mistake, an aberration. You'd been on your own all day, and you mistook my reactions, that's all. You felt sorry for me, and—and I was flattered. It's not every day a—a young man makes a pass at an older woman like me.'

'It wasn't a pass,' said Jake flatly, but Laura was already tackling the bags on the table, sorting the one that contained the food from the others.

'Are you hungry?' she asked brightly, determined to show him that she meant what she said. 'I thought we could have steak, and roasted parsnips——'

'You're not an older woman,' persisted Jake, sliding his hands into the hip pockets of his jeans, apparently equally determined to have his say. 'How old are you? Thirty-five? Thirty-six?'

'With a twenty-one-year-old daughter?' Laura gave him a withering smile. 'I shall be thirty-nine next birthday. But thank you for the compliment.'

Jake swore. At least, she thought he did. The word he used was incomprehensible to her, but its meaning was not. 'Why are you doing this?' he demanded. 'Why are you trying to pretend you didn't want me to touch you, just as much as I wanted to do it? You're not old. You're in the prime of your life. D'you think I'm likely to be deterred by the fact that there's a handful of years between us?'

'A handful!'

Laura was proud of the scornful way she threw his words back at him, but Jake only stared at her with raw contempt. 'Yes, a handful,' he said, his mouth curling derisively. 'I'm thirty-two, Laura. I shall be thirty-three next birthday. Not exactly a boy, wouldn't you agree?'

Laura jerked her head aside. 'You're still too young. Not—not just in years, but in—in experience. You young people, you think you invented sex. I was having Julie, when you were still a schoolboy.'

Jake's eyes glittered. 'As I understand it, you were just a schoolgirl yourself at the time,' he retorted, and Laura caught her breath.

'That doesn't alter the fact that you're my daughter's friend, not mine,' she countered, forcing herself to take the steak out of the carrier, and set it on the table. 'Now—do you think we could change the subject? If you'd like to go back into the living-room, I'll start preparing dinner.'

CHAPTER SEVEN

JAKE looked as if he would have liked to have argued, but to Laura's relief he didn't. With a grim inclination of his head, he walked out of the kitchen, and it wasn't until she was left alone that Laura realised she hadn't asked him how he was.

Oh, well, she thought unsteadily, it was obvious he was feeling much better, and although it was impossible to tell if the cut was hurting him he was apparently capable of driving his car. Not to mention everything else, a small voice taunted mockingly. He might have been in dire agony, but his emotional organs weren't impaired.

Her hands were trembling, and, feeling in need of a drink, she filled the kettle and plugged it in. She would have liked a glass of the sherry she kept for special occasions, but that was in the living-room. It was always out of reach, she reflected, remembering the night, a week ago, when Julie had rung to tell her she and Jake were coming for the weekend. It had been out of reach then, too, but she definitely needed it more at this moment.

Still, a cup of coffee would do instead, she decided. And at least it would have the added advantage of not containing any alcohol. The last thing she needed right now was the soporific effects of a fortified wine. She needed to keep her wits about her.

She wondered now why she had ever invited him to stay. There was no question about it: it was madness.

She had allowed the desire to prove to him that she could dismiss what had happened without a qualm to override basic common sense. She had wanted to show him that, as she was Julie's mother, he was welcome to her hospitality; to clear the way for their continued association. It would do her no good to try and turn her daughter against him. If she tried to tell Julie what had happened, she would never believe her. She would simply have to hope Julie detected his true character, before it was too late. And turning him out—however attractive that might sound—was the right way to achieve the opposite.

It couldn't be that difficult, could it? she asked herself. If she just kept her head, and behaved naturally with him, he was bound to get the message. She would serve him dinner, ask him about his trip, bring Julie's name into the conversation as often as she dared, and then send him off to a hotel to spend the night.

Deciding she could hardly make herself a cup of coffee without offering him one, she schooled her features, and marched to the door of the living-room. 'Would you like a cup of——?' she began, in a confident tone, and then broke off abruptly, at the sight that met her eyes.

Jake already had a drink in his hand. And it wasn't her sherry either. A newly opened bottle of malt whisky resided on the table beside his chair, and Jake was in the process of lowering the glass from his lips.

'Where did you get that?'

All Laura's plans to keep their relationship cool and impersonal were banished by the accusing edge to her voice, and Jake arched a mocking brow. 'I bought it,' he said carelessly. 'At the village store. Why are you looking so outraged? Did I need your permission?'

'As a matter of fact, there's whisky in the cupboard,' declared Laura defensively, mentally imagining the gos-

sip his shopping in the local stores must have generated.
She could hear the stiffness in her voice, and endeavoured to redress her sense of balance. 'I—I was surprised,
that's all. I was going to offer you some coffee.'

'I'll pass,' said Jake smoothly, pouring another measure of whisky into his glass. 'But you can join me, if
you like,' he added, looking up. 'You look as if you
need something to give you a bit of—life.'

Laura didn't trust herself to speak. Suppressing the
angry retort that sprang to her lips, she swung on her
heel and left him. He would not make her lose her temper again, she told herself fiercely. He knew what he
was doing. When she lost control, he had her at his
mercy, and she was determined not to give him that
satisfaction. Nevertheless, as she turned on the grill, and
began seasoning the steak, she knew a helpless sense of
frustration. Whether it was a deliberate ploy on his part
or not, Jake was not going to be able to drive. If she
wanted him to spend the night at a hotel, she would have
to take him there herself.

In spite of her state of mind, the meal was not the
disaster she had been afraid of. The food was surprisingly well-cooked, and Jake ate everything she put in
front of him. Laura served the steak with asparagus,
sweetcorn, and new potatoes, and then set out the lemon
cheesecake, alongside crackers, cheese, and celery. She
had made fresh coffee, too, and she was relieved to see
that Jake drank two cups.

She hadn't served any wine with the food, but Jake
had carried his whisky glass to the table. However, she
noticed he didn't drink while he was eating, and the
whisky bottle remained in the living-room.

It was a minor victory, vastly outweighed by their lack
of communication with one another. Conversation was

confined to comments about the food, and, even then, Laura had had to take the lead. The anger she had felt earlier had dissipated to a weary resignation. And still she wasn't sure that the way she felt was Jake's fault. He shouldn't have come here, that was true, but she was to blame for how things had developed.

Laura had done most of the washing-up before the meal, so that afterwards there were only the plates to deal with. But, although Jake helped her to clear the table, he didn't offer to dry the dishes, as he had done the week before. And, when Laura had spent as long as she dared in the kitchen and went into the living-room, he was seated in his chair again, with the whisky glass in his hand.

'Um—shall I light the fire?' she asked, striving for normality. Although she hadn't lighted it that morning, she had raked the grate, and laid it ready. It would be a simple matter to set a match to the paper, and the room seemed bare without its comforting glow.

Or perhaps it was just her mood, she thought gloomily, and the fact that it was getting dark already. She had anticipated this evening with a certain amount of excitement, and now it had all gone wrong. She realised she had probably been deluding herself by imagining she and Jake could have a normal relationship. In effect, she was only compounding her guilt by letting him remain.

'Light it, if you want,' Jake replied now, and, although she would have preferred to seek the security of her armchair, Laura picked up the matches, and complied.

It was quickly done, the flames licking swiftly up over the dry kindling. It reduced the time she had to crouch before him, and after replacing the matches on the mantel she went and sat down.

Silence could be deafening, she discovered. It

stretched between them like a yawning void, and although there were things she had to say, she found it very hard to begin.

But, at last, with the crackling wood providing at least some support, she asked, 'How does the—er—injury feel this evening? I assume it's much better.'

Jake rested his head back against the striped fabric of the cushions. Reclining in her chair like that, with his long legs stretched across the hearth, and his body relaxed and dormant, he looked very much at his ease. But his eyes were far from quiescent, and when he looked at her she flinched beneath the contempt in his gaze.

'Do you really care?' he countered, and the hand hanging loosely over the chair arm moved in a dismissing gesture.

'Of course I care,' said Laura, keeping her voice neutral with an effort. 'I did do my best to attend to it. At least you don't appear to be bleeding any more.'

Jake's mouth compressed. 'No,' he said. 'Not visibly anyway.' And then, more evenly, 'No, I'm sorry. You were most—helpful; most kind. I do appreciate it, even if I haven't acknowledged it.'

Laura swallowed. 'Well—that's good,' she murmured, not prepared to debate what he might mean by the latter half of his statement. 'I still think you should see your own doctor, when you get back to London. Cuts can become infected, and there are injections you can have to avoid problems of that kind.'

'I know.' Jake inclined his head. 'Thank you for your advice.'

Laura sighed. She was fairly sure he wouldn't take it, but there was nothing more she could do. She wondered if she ought to offer to change the dressing, but she recoiled from that idea. She couldn't do it. She couldn't

touch him again, knowing, as she did, how his skin felt
beneath her trembling hands. She might tell herself he
disgusted her; that what he had done earlier this evening
had demeaned and humiliated her, and that any woman
in her right mind would have thrown him out there and
then. But to actually consider removing the bandage
from his midriff, to imagine cleaning his wound and re-
applying the gauze dressing, made a mockery of her indignation. It wasn't revulsion that kept her from doing
her Christian duty. It was the certain knowledge that she
couldn't trust herself.

There was silence again, for a while, and then, compelled to dispel her treacherous thoughts, Laura said,
'Will you be going back to London tomorrow?'

It was an innocent question, she told herself, when
Jake looked at her again, with those dark, mocking eyes.
Hooded eyes, in a face that, she admitted, unwillingly,
had a rough male beauty. He had no right to look at her
like that, she thought resentfully. He was the interloper
here. Not her.

'Perhaps,' he answered, at last. 'It depends.'

'On the reason you came north, I suppose,' said Laura
sociably, hoping she was now going to find out the real
reason why he was here. If she could just keep their
conversation on this level, she might stop feeling so on
edge.

'As you say,' Jake conceded, pouring himself more
whisky. He lifted his glass. 'Are you sure you won't join
me?'

Laura shook her head. In fact, she would have welcomed the warming influence the alcohol would have
given her, but she had to keep her head clear for driving.
The nearest decent hotel was about eight miles away.
And on narrow roads, she would need all her skill.

'I—Julie said your family was in manufacturing, is that right?' she asked politely. 'I suppose you have contacts all over England.'

'If you're implying I came north to conclude some business deal, you couldn't be more wrong,' Jake declared, shifting so that one booted foot came to rest across his knee. 'I'm sorry to disappoint you, but I have no business contacts in this area.'

Laura took a breath. 'You don't?'

It was all she could think of to say, and Jake shook his head. 'No,' he agreed, resting the hand holding his glass across his raised ankle. 'My family's interests are primarily in motor manufacturing, and wine. But, as far as I am aware, neither the Italian car industry, nor its subsidiaries, have made any great inroads in northern England. As for wine...' He shrugged. 'We are not involved in distribution.'

Laura swallowed. 'I see.'

'Do you? I wonder?' Jake's mouth flattened. 'Why don't you ask what I'm doing here? That is what you want to know, isn't it?'

Laura avoided his dark gaze, and looked at the flames leaping up the chimney. 'Your affairs are nothing to do with me,' she retorted, wondering if she had been wise to light the fire after all. The room seemed so hot suddenly, and she ran a nervous hand around the cowled neckline of her dress.

'You're wrong, you know,' Jake said softly, and it took the utmost effort for Laura to remain where she was. Her instincts were telling her to get out of there now, while she still had the chance to avoid a confrontation. Whatever he had to say, she didn't want to hear it.

'You said you'd been fencing,' she said, hurriedly,

pressing her palms down on to her knees. 'How—how interesting! Are you a—a professional?'

'Hardly.' Jake's voice was harsh. 'For your information, I do my fencing in London. At a private club.' He paused, and she saw his fingers clench around his glass. 'And usually, I am quite proficient—though not, I might add, of a professional standard. However, on Friday evening, I was—how can I say it politely?—cheesed on?'

'Off,' put in Laura automatically, and then flushed. 'Cheesed off,' she added in a low voice, wishing she hadn't said anything, when he gave her a savage look.

'Very well,' he amended, 'I was—cheesed *off*, as you say.' But she was left in no doubt that he would have preferred to use a stronger term. 'It had not been a good week for me, no? I needed—a diversion.'

'So you tried to get yourself killed! You must have been mad!'

'If that is your interpretation of my actions, then so be it,' he declared bleakly, and Laura's intentions to remain impersonal shattered.

'Well, what else can I think?' she demanded, steeling herself to meet his disparaging stare. 'Sensible people don't play with weapons, when they've only got half their mind on the job. If you wanted a diversion, why didn't you go and see your daughter? I'm sure she'd have been delighted to see you.'

'More than you, no?' he suggested drily, and Laura's throat constricted.

'I don't come into this——' she began, but now Jake's temper got the better of him.

'No,' he said, putting his glass on the table, lowering his foot to the floor, and leaning towards her, his arms along his thighs. 'Not even you are that stupid!'

His jaw compressed, and although Laura wanted to protest, his expression kept her silent.

'You know exactly why I came here,' he went on grimly, 'and it has nothing to do with your daughter, or mine, or any of the other irrelevancies you keep throwing in my face. All right. Perhaps it was a little crazy to tempt fate as I did. When I went to the club, I wanted to do something dangerous. Perhaps I hoped I'd be hurt, I don't know. I was not—how would you say it?—in my mind?'

'In your *right* mind,' corrected Laura, barely aware of what she was saying, but her interruption only angered him even more.

'*Dio*,' he swore, 'will you stop acting like a schoolmistress? I came here because I needed to see you again. Ever since last weekend, I have thought of little else. Does that answer your question? Or would you like me to draw you a picture?'

Laura took a steadying breath. 'I—don't—believe—you——'

'Why not?'

She shook her head, her eyes a little wild. 'It doesn't make sense.'

Jake's lips twisted. 'Unfortunately, it does.'

'But, Julie——'

'Forget about Julie. This has nothing to do with Julie. This is about—*us*!'

'*Us?*' Laura got up from her chair then, unable to sit still any longer, and caught her breath when he did the same. 'I—there is no *us*, Mr Lombardi. I'm afraid if you thought there was, you've had a wasted journey.'

'I don't think so.'

Jake made no move to touch her, but she was intensely aware of him, and of the fact that he was stand-

ing directly in her path. Oh, she could get past him, if
she set her mind to it, she was sure. Apart from anything
else, he was probably still suffering the after-effects of
losing so much blood, and a jab to his ribs would probably be most effective.

But, the truth was, she knew she would never hurt
him, not deliberately at least. And while she would have
preferred for them not to have had this conversation, it
was probably just as well to clear the air.

'Look,' she said, endeavouring to keep her voice cool
and even, 'I don't deny that you're an attractive man.
Any woman would think so, and—and I'm happy for
Julie, truly. Really, she thinks you're wonderful, as I'm
sure you know, and——'

'Will you stop this?'

Jake moved, and, although she would have backed
away, the chair was right behind her. His hands descended on her shoulders, his hard fingers moulding the
narrow bones he could feel beneath the fine wool. At
the same time, his thumbs brushed the underside of her
chin, forcing her to lift her face to his.

'Listen to me,' he said, and although Laura jerked her
head aside she couldn't dislodge his fingers. 'Why don't
you stop throwing me at your daughter, and accept what
I'm trying to tell you? For God's sake, if we must speak
about Julie, let's at least be honest. We both knew what
she sees in me, and it isn't just the colour of my eyes.'

'I know.' Laura held up her head. 'She thinks
you're—good-looking—and intelligent—and sexy——'

'And rich,' said Jake flatly, bending his head to touch
her earlobe with his tongue. 'Let's not forget rich!'

Laura shuddered, her whole world turning upside-
down. 'Is that important?' she choked, as he bit the tiny
gold circlet she wore through her ear, and Jake shrugged.

'It is to Julie,' he said, his accent thickening as his mouth brushed the nerve that fluttered in her throat. 'I wasn't sure before. But after last weekend——'

'You decided I was the easier option, is that it?' Laura demanded raggedly. 'Why not try the mother? She's too old to offer much resistance. Besides, she's probably so desperate to have a man——'

Jake's hands around her throat silenced her. 'Will you shut up?' he muttered angrily. 'It wasn't like that! It *isn't* like that!'

Laura swallowed. 'But, you can't deny it crossed your mind——'

'It did not cross my mind.' Jake stared down at her savagely. 'Hear what I have to say, will you? I told you this had been a bad week for me, but not why.'

'I don't want to know why!' exclaimed Laura, aware that the longer he held her, the harder it was to keep her head. She was trembling, her whole body quivering with emotions she couldn't even identify, and, hateful as it might be, she was succumbing to those feelings.

'I'm sorry about that,' Jake said now, but he didn't sound sorry. When he braced himself to resist the hands she lifted to push him away, there was no compassion in his gaze. Instead, his hands slid from her neck, down to the small of her back, curving over her hips, and propelling her against him.

Laura almost panicked. Her nose was pressed against the dark silk of his shirt, and, whether she wanted to or not, she couldn't escape the raw male scent of him. He must have taken a shower, she thought unsteadily, because his skin smelt so fresh and clean, overlaid with just the faintest trace of antiseptic, a reminder of the dressing she had applied that morning.

But even that prosaic awareness didn't detract from

the overall awareness she had of him, of his warmth, and his nearness, and the lean muscled strength of his body.

'What happened is, I spent the whole week trying to get you out of my mind,' he told her huskily, his breath fanning her heated forehead. 'I didn't want this to happen. So far, my life has gone the way I want it. Oh, when Isabella died, I was distraught, for a while, but although we were—how would you say?—compatible with one another, there was no great passion in our relationship. Our greatest achievement was in having Luci, and I do not deny that I love my daughter very deeply. But this——' he brushed her cheek with his finger '—this is something else. Something I have never experienced before. And, whatever you think of me, I do not usually want what I cannot have.'

'Well—well, you can't have me!' Laura's voice wobbled, but the words had to be said. 'Even—even if you weren't involved with—with my daughter—it just—wouldn't work.'

'Why not?' His lips brushed her ear, and she was unsteadily aware that if this continued, he would prove her a liar.

'Because—because it wouldn't,' she replied, not very convincingly. And then, on a sob, 'Oh, please—let me go! What do I have to do to prove to you that I'm not—not interested?'

His response was unexpected. Without another word, his hands fell to his sides, and he stepped back from her. He didn't say anything, however, and, although Laura told herself that this was what she had wanted, she felt unaccountably bereft.

'I—thank you,' she said, striving for sarcasm, without much success, and put a nervous hand to her hair.

Several silky strands had come loose from the coil at her nape, and she busied herself, tucking them into place again, as she struggled to regain her composure. 'I— think you'd better go now.'

Jake studied her without comment, his dark gaze lingering on the parted contours of her mouth. She pressed her lips together then, to hide their revealing tremor, but his eyes drifted down to the equally revealing tautness of her breasts. She wanted to cross her arms, and hide their blatant betrayal from him, but she rigorously restrained herself. To do so would reveal she was aware of his appraisal, and he should not have the satisfaction of knowing how much he disturbed her.

'Go?' he said, at last, his gaze returning to her flushed face, and she nodded. 'Go—where?'

'To—to a hotel, of course,' she got out jerkily. 'You—you surely didn't expect to stay here? Not—not in the circumstances.'

Jake tucked his thumbs into the back of the low belt that encircled his hips. The action strained the buttons of his shirt across his chest, and Laura couldn't help staring at the brown flesh, visible between the fastenings. She defended herself with the thought that, unlike Jake, she was not consciously looking at *his* body. He was simply drawing her attention to it, like the sexual *animal* he was.

'What circumstances are we talking about?' he asked now, and Laura had to think for a minute before she could remember what she had said.

'The—er—circumstances of you and I—spending the night together,' she declared at once. And then, realising how ambiguous her words had sounded, she hurried on, 'I mean—spending the night here—*alone*—together. I— people in Burnfoot are rather—conservative.'

'You'll be telling me next that you have your reputation to think of,' remarked Jake drily, and Laura's face burned.

'Hardly that,' she retorted, twisting her hands together. 'But someone might tell Julie that you spent the night in the village.'

'So?'

Jake sounded indifferent, and Laura sighed. 'I just think it would be—easier all round, if you stayed at a hotel,' she said firmly. 'There's one on the Corbridge road. I think it's called the Swan.'

'And how am I to get there?' enquired Jake, lifting his shoulders. 'I hesitate to say it, but I don't think I should drive.'

'I'll take you,' declared Laura swiftly.

'In my car?'

'In your car—oh!' Laura had forgotten about his car. Even if she took him to a hotel, his car was going to stand outside the cottage all night. 'I—well, no. In mine.'

'So, whatever happens, people are going to think I spent the night here.'

Laura pressed her lips together. 'Perhaps.'

'But you still want me to go?'

Her tongue circled her lips. 'I—think you should,' she agreed doggedly.

'I guess you don't trust me, then.'

'It's not that.' Laura was dismayed at her own inability to control the conversation. 'I just think——'

'Or perhaps you don't trust yourself,' he murmured provokingly, and Laura knew that she was beaten.

'That would be foolish, wouldn't it?' she said, refusing to give him the satisfaction of admitting that possibility. She assumed what she hoped was a resigned expression, and steeled herself to meet his gaze. 'All right,' she said, as if it were of extreme indifference to her, 'as you say, if your car is going to stand outside my house all night, it does seem rather pointless to turn you out.'

CHAPTER EIGHT

LAURA lay awake, in the familiar surrounds of her own bedroom, and wondered how she had got herself into such a mess.

It was all her fault. She admitted that freely. If she hadn't been so desperate to uphold appearances, Jake would have left before dinner. He had expected to go. And after what had happened, she should have insisted upon it. But instead, she had carried on this stupid charade, of pretending his lovemaking had meant nothing to her—practically inviting him to stay here, and do it again.

Only it hadn't been like that, she defended herself swiftly. At the time, all that had seemed important was restoring a sense of normality. She still hadn't been prepared to believe that what had happened was anything more than a momentary infraction; a deviation from the rules, that he regretted as much as she did.

Of course, he had come here, uninvited and unannounced, bleeding from a wound he had received while dicing with his life, and perhaps she ought to have been more wary. But things like that didn't happen to her, and the whole situation seemed totally unreal. But Jake was still here, that much was certain, and, although she hadn't locked her door, she was undoubtedly uneasy.

Yet, since he had received her permission to stay, Jake had done nothing more to disturb her. Not consciously anyway, she conceded wearily. His just being there was disruptive enough. However, he had behaved with the utmost propriety, and the uneasy alliance had lasted until bedtime.

What Julie would think about it all, Laura didn't dare to speculate. *If* she ever found out, she appended heavily. And these things had a habit of getting found out, she knew. It would probably be better if she tried to tell her. Whatever she had thought earlier, it was different now that Jake was spending the night.

But what could she say? 'Oh, by the way, Julie, Jake slept at the cottage on Saturday night. Yes, I was surprised, too, but he'd had an accident, you see, and he wanted me to deal with it.'

No! Laura shifted restlessly. No, there was no way she could drop something like that into the conversation. She could tell her daughter the truth, of course. She could describe what had happened, and allow Julie to draw her own conclusions. But would she believe her? And if Jake chose to lie, whose story was Julie likely to accept?

The answer was obvious—Jake's. *'God,'* Laura groaned. Julie might even think she had instigated the whole affair. With Julie's distorted image of her mother's life, she might imagine Laura was jealous of her. That she had deliberately come on to Jake, to humiliate her daughter.

Laura rolled on to her stomach, and punched her pillow, wishing it were Jake's head. It was all *his* fault, she decided, performing a complete about-face. If he hadn't come here, none of this would have happened. She would be happily going on with her life, and the destructive emotions he had aroused would never have been brought to life. He was probably asleep now—sound asleep in the spare bed she had made up earlier in the evening. Were all Italians like him? Didn't he have a

conscience? What perverted streak of his character had
inspired him to humiliate her?

And yet, when he wasn't tying her up in knots, he
could be so nice, she conceded, and then scorned herself
for her own gullibility. He was only nice when he was
getting his own way, she told herself grimly. Just because they had spent the rest of the evening in comparative harmony was no reason to pretend he wasn't totally
unscrupulous. He was hurting Julie. He had probably
caused a rift between herself and Julie that would take
years to heal. How could she let him stay here, when he
cared about no one but himself?

She turned on to her back again, and stared up at the
ceiling. Moonlight, through the cracks in the curtains,
cast a shadowy patchwork above her head. Somewhere,
the eerie sound of an owl, going about its nightly business, broke the silence, and the ivy outside her window
rustled against the stone.

She had never been aware of the stillness before.
Usually, when she went to bed, she was so tired that she
never had a problem sleeping. Besides, she invariably
read for a while, until her eyelids started drooping. But
tonight, she had been eager to put out her light, and
pretend to be asleep, just in case Jake went to the bathroom, and thought she was waiting for *him*. It had been
a silly idea, particularly after she had spent the latter half
of the evening marking exercise books, while Jake read
a book he had borrowed from her shelves. Nothing less
romantic could she have imagined. Except that it had
crossed her mind how companionable it had been.

She turned over again, and picked up the clock from
the table beside the bed. It was half-past one, she saw
impatiently. For goodness' sake, was she ever going to

get to sleep? She was going to look absolutely haggard in the morning.

Unwillingly, her mind drifted to the man in the next room again. She couldn't help wondering what would have happened, if she had let him make love to her. They would not now be sleeping in separate beds, she acknowledged. And sleep might be the last thing on her mind.

A wave of heat swept over her body at the thought. Her breasts, already sensitised by her constant tossing and turning, tightened in anticipation. The knowledge aggravated her, but there was nothing she could do about it. She couldn't help their reaction, any more than she could prevent the sudden moistness between her thighs. She might have thought she was past all that, but Jake was a very attractive man. And she was human, after all.

She sighed. It was so unlikely that, after all these years, she should find herself in such a dilemma. After the unhappy associations of her youth, she had begun to believe she was immune to any unwanted feelings. She had had friends, both at college, and since she'd started teaching—male, as well as female—good friends; but none of them had got close to her emotionally. Her experiences with Keith had left her unimpressed, and wary, and, although she was quite prepared to believe that other women might find happiness in marriage, she had felt no desire to try it.

Of course, she knew that her practical experience of sex was necessarily limited. If what she read in books was true, Keith had not been a very generous lover, but at the time she had been too immature to care. She had liked the way he'd kissed her; she had liked the way it had made her feel. And if the culmination of the feelings he had aroused inside her had been something of an anticlimax, she had had more immediate things to worry about.

Not least the fact that Keith had gone, and she had missed a period, she reflected, remembering how frightened she had been then. She had had no one to confide her troubles to. The idea of telling her parents had seemed an unacceptable alternative.

She knew better now, naturally. Without them, life would have been very bleak indeed. That was what was so sad about her relationship with Julie. She had wanted to be there for her, as her parents had been, when she'd needed them.

But now...

Laura combed restless hands through the tangled mass of her hair. What would her daughter think, if she could see her now? she wondered unhappily. Julie would find it hard to believe that her mother was lying awake, fretting over the man *she* intended to marry. She would never understand the circumstances that had led her to this, and, if Laura was to tell her, there would be the most almighty row. Justified, no doubt, Laura acknowledged tiredly. And Julie would know all the right words to put it in perspective.

Words like *pathetic*, or *repulsive*; *vulgar*, or *detestable*! Oh, Julie had cornered the market on ways to make her mother feel like a monster, and, with this kind of ammunition, she could destroy her self-esteem completely. The trouble was, when it came to confronting her daughter, Laura was halfway defeated before she began. She had never been allowed to forget that youthful indiscretion, and admitting she was attracted to a man who, in spite of everything else, was years younger than she was, would only reinforce Julie's opinion that she was a fool.

Well, there's no fool like an old fool, thought Laura wearily, resorting to platitudes. Her best hope was to put everything that had happened out of her mind. She couldn't be sure, of course, but she didn't think Jake would be telling his prospective fiancée that he had taken a fleeting fancy to her mother. However open their relationship might be, she didn't think a casual fling of this kind allowed confession.

Laura eventually fell asleep as it was getting light. Exhaustion had at last taken its toll, and she sank into a dreamless slumber, just as the Graingers' dairy herd was being guided into the sheds for the first milking of the day. With her hand cupped beneath her cheek, and the tumbled sheets wrapped about her, she finally found oblivion. She didn't hear the bellows of protest from the milk-laden cows, or rouse to the birds' morning chorus. She was dead to the world for a good four hours, and when she did open her eyes her room was flooded with sunlight.

She blinked unwillingly, a sense of something ominous hanging over her, causing a heavy weight of depression that gripped her as soon as she opened her eyes. It wasn't until she turned her head, and looked at the clock, that comprehension dawned. It was nearly half-past nine!

She stilled the momentary panic, that made her think, just for a second, that it was a working day. It wasn't. It was Sunday. And she had overslept. Or rather, she had slept late, she amended grudgingly, remembering the night she had spent. God, she felt as if she had been hauled through the mincer! Every nerve in her body felt

raw and abused, and a slight ache in her head promised
a migraine later.

Groaning, she rolled over on to her back, and con-
fronted the problem that still plagued her. She assumed
Jake was still there. She couldn't imagine he would have
made it easy for her, and left. Was he still in bed? she
wondered apprehensively. It was still early by his standards, no doubt. Just because he had got up early last
weekend was no reason to suppose he would repeat the
exercise. She knew Julie didn't like getting up early, and
if they usually slept together...

But thoughts like that were not conducive to initiating
a good start to the day. It was galling, but she couldn't
anticipate such a scenario without feeling slightly sick.
The picture of Jake, sharing a bed with her daughter,
caused an actual feeling of revulsion inside her. She
didn't want to think about it in those terms, but she
couldn't help it.

Something else she couldn't help was her own memory of the sensuous warmth of his mouth on hers. She
could still feel his tongue, pressing its way between her
teeth, and the throbbing heat of his arousal, hard against
her stomach. Damn, but she couldn't help wondering
how it would have been, if she had let him make love
to her. Probably no different from when Keith had taken
her innocence, she decided irritably. Men were impatient
animals. They sought their own satisfaction first.

Her hand had stuck to her cheek as she'd slept, and
although she had removed it now, she could feel the
marks where it had been. Oh, great, she thought resignedly, pushing herself up on her elbows. As if she didn't
have enough lines already.

And then, she saw the tray of tea. It was residing on
the bedside cabinet, nearest the door. Her teapot, a milk

jug and sugar basin, and a cup and saucer. Someone must have placed it there, but how long ago?

She clenched her lips. *Someone!* she chided herself impatiently. There only was one person it could have been, and that was Jake. Dear God, he had come into the room as she'd slept. What must he have thought of her? Her hair every which way, and the bedclothes a clear indication of her disturbed night!

She put out a reluctant hand, and touched the side of the teapot. It was warm, but not hot. The tea must have been there for at least an hour, she surmised. Which meant Jake could be up and gone, without her prior knowledge.

She hesitated only a moment, before sliding out of bed. She had to know if he was still here. Padding barefoot across to the bedroom window, she squinted down into the garden. The Fiesta was still where she had left it, and she could just see the tail of the other car.

The breath left her lungs on a gulp. She told herself she was disappointed he was still here, but it wasn't true. The fact was, if he had gone without telling her goodbye, she would have been shattered. So what price now her averred intention to get him out of her life?

Parting the curtains a few inches, she turned back to her dressing-table, and surveyed her appearance in the mirror. In spite of the troubled night she had spent, she didn't look as bad as she had expected. Her hair was untidy, of course, but for the first time in ages she didn't immediately reach for the brush. With her hair loose, and in the cotton nightshirt, that skimmed her hips, and exposed her slender legs, she looked amazingly young, and vulnerable. She didn't look like a woman who had a twenty-one-year-old daughter. She looked like someone who had definite possibilities.

She lifted the weight of her hair, and swept it loosely towards her face. She had seen women who wore their hair this way, but she had never considered that she might be one of them. Because her hair was straight, she tended, always, to keep it tightly confined. But now she contemplated how it would look, if it were shorter, and cut to frame her face...

She was so intent on discovering what the possibilities might be that when the knock came at her bedroom door, she called 'Come in,' without thinking. Perhaps she had thought she was at school. It was only when Jake stepped into the room that she realised what she had done.

'What—what do you think you're doing?' she exclaimed, dry-mouthed, but her outburst was barely reasonable, and she knew it.

'You invited me to come in,' remarked Jake mildly, pushing his hands into the pockets of his jeans, and she was sure his studied evaluation missed no part of her anatomy. 'Did you sleep well?'

Laura turned away from her dressing-table, allowing her hands to slide down from her hair, as if it was a perfectly natural thing for her to do. She kept telling herself that in Jake's world it was no particular novelty to see a woman in her nightgown, and as her cotton shirt could hardly be considered provocative she mustn't overreact.

'I slept—very well,' she lied, not prepared to discuss her restless night with him. 'Um—thanks for the tea. I didn't—hear you bring it in.'

'No. No, I know.' Jake's acknowledgement was accompanied by a vaguely rueful smile. 'No, you were sound asleep. It seemed a shame to wake you.'

'How kind!'

The thread of sarcasm in Laura's voice was not wholly intentional, but Jake's response showed he had noticed. 'It was,' he said, his eyes darkening sensuously. 'I might have decided to join you.'

'I don't think so.' Laura met his challenging gaze with an effort. She was trying not to sound as uptight as she felt, but it wasn't easy. 'I'm not your type.'

'You don't know anything about my type,' retorted Jake lazily, subjecting her to another thorough appraisal. 'How do you know I don't like tawny-haired women, with long legs and golden eyes, and the kind of body a man wants to bury himself in?'

'An overweight matron, right?' Laura quipped, hoping to dispel the sudden shift in the conversation, but Jake only shook his head.

'Go on,' he said. 'Put yourself down. It seems to be an occupational hazard with you.' He paused, and then went on, 'Did you know you kick the sheets off when you're sleeping? And that thing you're wearing barely covers you. You were cold, when I pulled the quilt over you.'

'You pulled——' Laura broke off abruptly, aware that she had been in danger of showing how easily he could disconcert her, and she was not going to give him that satisfaction. 'Well—thank you.'

'My pleasure.' Jake rocked on his heels. 'I guess that's why the bed's in such a state. If I didn't know better, I'd wonder if you'd had company——'

'I always sleep alone,' Laura broke in tersely. 'And I don't think it's any concern of yours what my bed looks like. Now——' she took a breath '——I think you'd better go.'

'OK.' To her relief, he turned towards the door, but he paused on the threshold, and gave her a dangerously attractive smile. 'But, just for the record, I don't think you'd have kicked me out, if I had got in beside you. In that easy time, between sleeping and waking, you'd have had no chance to think of an excuse. I'd have seen to that.'

Laura had had just about as much as she could take. 'Will you get out?' she demanded, her hands opening and closing convulsively, and with a gesture of resignation Jake closed the door behind him.

When she went downstairs some fifteen minutes later, the aromatic scent of fresh coffee and toast was filling the air. Evidently, he wasn't unused to taking care of his own needs, and, although she told herself she should resent his casual assumption of her role, there was something decidedly appealing about having her breakfast prepared for her. She wasn't used to it. Not since she'd used to live with her parents had anyone taken the trouble to wait on her, and she couldn't deny it was—nice.

For her part, she was still struggling with the need to put what had happened in perspective. Jake had spent the night at the cottage, that was true, but apart from those few minutes, when she'd got back from town the previous afternoon, she had done nothing to be ashamed of. The trouble was, the longer they were together, the harder it got to withstand his easy charm, and she was not immune to his attraction. On the contrary, it would be all too easy to believe the things he told her, and only her strength of will stood between her and certain disaster.

When she carried the tray into the kitchen however, the idea that Jake might exert any unwelcome influence over her seemed totally misplaced. With a tea-towel draped over his shoulder, he was in the process of ladling a pan of scrambled eggs on to a serving dish. A plate piled high with golden-brown toast was keeping warm on the hob, and her coffee-pot was simmering on its stand.

'I don't know if you like scrambled eggs,' he said, when she set the tray down on the drainer. 'But I thought you might like something substantial, as you barely touched your dinner last night.'

She didn't think he'd noticed, but she should have known Jake didn't miss a thing. And when she turned to put the serving dish on the table, and she met his lazy eyes, she felt the potent heat of their awareness.

'Sit down,' he said, when she stood there like an idiot, gazing at him, and, although she felt she ought to put up some opposition, she did so. 'Help yourself,' he added, setting the plate of toast in front of her. 'Go on. It won't poison you, I promise.'

Laura dragged her eyes away from his, and stared at the food. It did look inviting, certainly, and she was hungry. Ridiculously so, in the circumstances. Her whole system seemed to have been thrown off balance, but starving herself was not going to achieve anything. She needed her strength if she was going to come out of this with some semblance of dignity, and with a faint upward lift of her lips, she spooned some of the creamy eggs on to her plate.

'Good?' he asked, bringing the coffee to the table, and seating himself across from her, and she nodded.

'Very,' she said, her voice sticking in her throat, and Jake grinned as he helped himself to a generous portion.

It was difficult to remain detached with someone when you were eating the food they had prepared, and when Jake began asking her how long she had lived in the village, and what the people did hereabouts, Laura felt obliged to tell him. She found it helped to talk about impersonal things, and only now and then did the incongruity of the situation cause a corresponding ripple of unease to disrupt her uncertain stomach. But the food definitely helped, and by the time she had eaten her eggs and two triangles of toast, and drunk two cups of coffee, she was feeling decidedly less threatened.

But, when the meal was over, and Jake was lying back in his chair, regarding her through lazily narrowed eyes, Laura knew she had to address the subject that she had been avoiding for the last half-hour. Putting her coffee-cup aside, she moistened her lips, and then said evenly, 'Will you be telling Julie where you spent the weekend?'

Jake's expression didn't alter. 'Do you know, you have an incredibly sexy mouth?' he remarked softly, and Laura closed her eyes against his blatant sexuality.

'I think it would be—unwise,' she continued at last, resting her elbows on the table, and tucking her hands around the back of her neck. 'Don't you?'

'I suppose that depends on when we're going to see one another again,' Jake responded now, running a hand into the opened neckline of his shirt, and Laura wondered if everything he did was designed to disconcert her. He must know how her eyes followed his every movement, and it took the utmost effort to look down at the square of table in front of her.

'We—won't be seeing one another again,' she declared steadily, and then gulped back a startled cry, when he abruptly thrust back his chair, and got to his feet.

'What are you saying?' he demanded, coming round the table to stand over her, and Laura steeled herself to tilt back her head and look up at him.

'I said——'

'I comprehend the words you used,' he told her bleakly, his accent appearing again as he strove to keep his patience. 'What I am asking is—why are you saying this?'

'Why am I——?' Laura broke off, and, jerking her gaze from his dark exasperated face, she crumbled the corner of the last piece of toast left on the plate. 'What do you want me to say?' she demanded at last. 'I've told you how I feel about your coming here. Oh—tell Julie, if you must, but don't be surprised if she refuses to see you again——'

'And do you think I care?'

His violent response tore into every nerve in her body, and, when she lifted her horrified face to his, his mouth curled contemptuously.

'Have I shocked you?' he asked bitterly. His lips twisted. 'What kind of a man do you think I am?'

'I don't—I didn't——'

'Oh, yes, you did,' he told her thickly, and before she had time to realise his intentions he bent his head towards her. With one hand supporting himself on the back of her chair, and the other imprisoning hers to the table, he covered her mouth with his.

It wasn't a gentle kiss. There was none of the tenderness he had shown the day before; just an unleashed passion, that savaged her emotions, and laid bare the unguarded hunger of her soul. She had no more hope of resisting him than she had of resisting a whirlwind, and when his tongue thrust possessively into her mouth her head tipped back helplessly on her shoulders. Her legs felt incapable of supporting her, and when he let go of her hands, they made no move to stop his assault. Indeed, when his knuckles brushed the tender peaks of her breasts, she sagged towards him, and when he suddenly let go of her she felt a bruising sense of bereavement.

She watched him leave the room with lacklustre eyes, hardly capable of understanding what he was doing, until he appeared in the doorway again wearing his leather jacket.

'So,' he said, as she struggled to her feet to face him, 'if you will move your car, I will trouble you no longer.'

Laura blinked. 'You're leaving?'

She was unaware of the depth of feeling in her voice, and Jake's mouth took on a mocking slant. 'That is what you want, isn't it?' he queried huskily, and his sardonic words brought a belated sense of self-preservation.

'What—I—of course,' she got out unevenly, as the full awareness of what he had done swept over her in sickening detail. Her fists balled with frustration. 'I'll get the keys.'

'If that's what you really want.'

Jake's hand brushed her cheek in passing, but she flinched away from him. 'It's what I really want,' she averred, and she had the doubtful satisfaction of having the last word.

CHAPTER NINE

'MATTHEW SUTCLIFFE! What kind of shoes are you wearing?'

'These, miss?' The boy Laura had addressed lifted his foot and examined it with apparent thoroughness, much to the amusement of the rest of the class. 'They're trainers, miss.'

'I know what *kind* of shoes they are, Sutcliffe,' retorted Laura, regarding the chunky-soled sports shoes, with their thick protruding tongues and untied laces, with some disgust.

'Then what——?'

'You know you're supposed to wear proper shoes for school,' Laura interrupted him crisply. 'What's happened to those black leather ones you were wearing the first few weeks of term?'

The fifteen-year-old adopted a cheeky grin. 'I've lost them, miss.'

Laura sighed. 'You can't have lost them,' she began, and then, realising she was setting herself up for an argument, she amended it to, 'When did you lose them?'

'Last week,' said Sutcliffe at once.

Although she knew she was wasting her time, Laura persisted, 'Where?'

'On my way home from school, miss.'

'On your way home from school?' Laura gave him a sceptical look. 'Why don't I believe you?'

'I don't know, miss.'

Sutcliffe gazed at her with a look of wide-eyed innocence, but Laura was not deceived. 'I suppose you'll be telling me next that someone took them away from you,' she remarked tersely, and the youth grinned.

'How did you know?'

'Don't be insolent, Sutcliffe.'

'I'm not being insolent, miss.' Incited by the admiration in the faces of the pupils around him, he added cockily, 'Just because you're in a bad mood——'

Laura gasped, and a ripple of anticipation ran round the room. 'What did you say?' she exclaimed.

Sutcliffe shrugged, not a whit daunted by her furious expression. 'I said, just because you're in a bad mood, miss, you don't have to take it out on us.'

'Out here, Sutcliffe!'

Laura pointed to a spot directly in front of her, and the stocky teenager pushed himself resignedly up from his seat, and sauntered forward. 'Yes, miss?'

He was unrepentant, that much was obvious, but Laura was half sorry she had to send him to the headmaster to be disciplined. This class of fourth-years was one of her favourites, and she was loath to alienate any of them by over-reacting.

The trouble was, he was right. Oh, not about the shoes. She had no doubts on that score. Half the pupils in the school were wearing prohibited footwear, and picking on Matthew Sutcliffe would do no good at all. She was fairly certain the black shoes he had previously worn, as part of the school uniform, were residing in a cupboard back home. But, like the other boys, who had persuaded their parents to buy them a pair of the current craze in canvas boots, he wanted to show off in front of his friends.

No, it was the fact that she wasn't in the best of humours that now stirred her conscience. For the past two weeks, she had been living on her nerves, and, although she had done her best to carry on as normal, the frayed edges were beginning to show.

It infuriated her that this should be so. It wasn't as if anything had happened on which she could hang the blame for her impaired sensibilities. Since Jake had driven away that Sunday morning—exactly two weeks and three days ago—she hadn't heard from either him or Julie, which seemed to point to the fact that he had kept their sordid little affair to himself.

Not that it had been an affair in the usual sense of the word, she reminded herself impatiently. He had kissed her, that was all. Even if she added everything together, she couldn't get past the fact that their romance added up to very little. He had wanted her, and she had refused. That was all there was to it.

Of course, it wasn't. In her more honest moments, she had to admit that, given time, she would have succumbed to him. He had known that, as well as she did. But that was because he knew exactly how to play upon her senses, she thought defensively. She had been a tempting challenge; an older woman, with the added twist of being his girlfriend's mother!

She told herself it was perverse; that, no matter how she phrased it, he had been attracted by their relationship. Or perhaps by the fact that she was so inexperienced, she pondered. A timid, middle-aged woman, who had never really known a man...

Now, making one last attempt to rectify the present situation, she said quietly, 'If you apologise for that last remark, and give me a serious answer as to why you're wearing those unsuitable shoes, I'll overlook your behaviour this time.' She paused. 'Well? What do you say?'

But she should have known she'd be wasting her time. For the boy to back down now would be to humiliate himself in front of his cronies. At the moment, he was regarded as something of a hero, and his shoulders hunched against any retreat.

'Very well.'

Laura squared her own shoulders, as she prepared to deliver her verdict. But before she could say a word, the classroom door opened, and Janet Mason, one of the school secretaries, put her head through the gap.

'Oh, Mrs Fox,' she said, her eyes indicating that she had some news to impart. 'Could I have a word?'

Laura sighed. It had been Mr Carpenter the headmaster's idea that she should be addressed as *Mrs* Fox, but there were times when she wished she could just be herself. Still, being regarded as a married woman—or a divorcee—did have its advantages. At least, she was not continually being taunted by her unmarried status.

Now, bidding Matthew Sutcliffe to remain where he was, she stepped out into the corridor. 'Yes, Janet?' she said, trying to keep a watchful eye on the class. 'What can I do for you?'

'You're wanted on the phone,' said Janet at once, and Laura could tell from her expression that whoever was calling had aroused some curiosity in the office. For one wild moment, she wondered if it could be Jake, and her knees went weak. But Janet's, 'It's your daughter,' quickly squashed that thought, even if the news that Julie was calling her at school was something of a body-blow. What could she want? she asked herself. What could possibly be important enough to warrant interrupting her mother during lessons? The answer seemed rather obvious, and Laura's nerves clenched. Jake must have finally got round to telling her daughter about his fall from grace.

She couldn't reveal her dismay to Janet however. The other woman was quite curious enough as it was, and Laura wished Julie was not so impulsive. But it wouldn't occur to her that speaking to her mother at school might prove rather awkward. Or if it did, it was not something she would care about.

But for now, she had other matters to attend to. After assuring Janet that she would be right there, she went back into her classroom to deal with Matthew Sutcliffe.

'Saved by the bell,' she told him, well aware that her conversation with Janet would not have gone undetected. 'Sit down, please. I'll deal with you later. The rest of you, open your books at the first scene of act four. I want you to read Portia's speech about the quality of mercy while I'm away. I shan't be long, and I shall expect you to be able to tell me what Portia's definition of mercy is, when I get back.'

There was the rustle as books were opened, but Laura had no doubt that once they were alone, there would be little actual reading going on. For all they were one of her better groups, there was still a sufficiently unruly element among them to curtail any attempt by the rest of the class to work quietly. In consequence, she put her head round the door of the adjoining room, to ask one of her colleagues to keep an eye on the group while she was away. She wanted to trust them, but she had no intention of coming back and finding half the class had disappeared.

The phone she had to use was in the staff-room. Thankfully, at this time of the afternoon, there were only one or two members of staff in there, but, all the same, it wasn't very private. Nevertheless, Laura picked up the receiver with an air of confidence. There was no point in looking anxious. It was too late for that now.

'Hello?' she said, when the call had been connected. 'Julie? Is that you?'

'How many daughters have you got?' asked Julie drily. 'Yes, of course, it's me, Mum. Have I caused a problem?'

Laura moistened her lips, and exchanged a rueful smile with Mike James, who taught woodworking. 'Well, I was teaching,' she murmured, her mind racing furiously. Julie didn't sound as if she was angry, but was that any assurance?

'I guessed you would be,' Julie responded now. 'But I've got to fly to Belgium later this afternoon, and I wanted to speak to you as soon as possible.'

Laura was confused. 'You did?' She took her life into her hands. 'Why?'

'I've got an invitation for you,' said Julie flatly, and now Laura was sure this call had nothing to do with *that* weekend. 'It's from Jake's mother. She'd like you to spend a weekend at Castellombardi. Jake and I will be going in a couple of weeks and it was his suggestion that you should come with us.'

Laura spent the evening trying to prepare a worksheet on war poetry for her first-year pupils. But the words of Wilfred Owen and Rupert Brooke only danced before her eyes, and when the flickering lights of an approaching migraine forced her to put her books away she did so willingly.

But what could she expect? she asked herself despairingly. She hadn't been able to concentrate on anything since Julie's call, and her brain just kept running in circles, trying to find some way to extricate itself from the proposed invitation.

Of course, when she had attempted to make her excuses to Julie, her daughter had proved quite implacable in her determination that Laura should not let her down. 'Jake's parents want to meet you,' she'd said, in answer to her mother's wavering uncertainty. 'Don't ask me why. They do, and that's all there is to it. Besides, I should have thought you'd welcome the chance to get away for a few days. It will be half-term, won't it? I told Jake I thought it was.'

So they were still seeing one another, Laura had acknowledged unsteadily, wondering why that news didn't give her the reassurance it should. Were they still sleeping together? Of course they were. She had practically guaranteed it by her attitude.

'Well——' she'd begun, but Julie wasn't taking no for an answer.

'Don't start making up reasons why you shouldn't come!' she'd exclaimed impatiently. 'It's not as if I'm asking much. Just a few days of your time, that's all.'

After that, there wasn't a lot Laura could say, and, as if she knew she had won the day, Julie went on to tell her the exciting news, that her agent had been approached by a film producer, with a view to Julie's being offered a screen test.

'Isn't it fantastic?' she'd exclaimed, and Laura could tell by her tone that this was more important to her daughter than a weekend spent in the Tuscan countryside. 'You know how much I've always loved acting and, according to Harry, anyone can act on film. It's just a question of learning your lines, that's all.'

Laura thought she had managed to sound reasonably enthusiastic, although she couldn't honestly remember her daughter showing any particular interest in drama classes at school. Still, if that was what Julie wanted, who was she to try and stop her? Julie had rung off with the promise that she would ring again in a few days, to make the final arrangements. In the meantime, Laura should check that her passport was in order, and be ready to leave in a little over two weeks.

'And buy yourself some decent clothes,' Julie had added, as an afterthought. 'The Lombardis are bound to live in some style, and I don't want you letting me down.'

At the moment, however, Laura was convinced she would never be ready. The idea of flying to Italy with Jake and Julie, of spending a weekend in their company, parrying Jake's parents' questions, and pretending she approved of their relationship, sounded like the worst kind of nightmare. How could she *meet* Jake again, let alone behave as if nothing had happened? Dear God, could this possibly be *his* idea? A way of punishing her for repulsing him? A way of trying to make her jealous?

But she wasn't jealous, she groaned, leaving the table, where she had been working, and flinging herself on to the sofa. The unaccustomed exertion caused her aching head to throb, and she thrust restless hands into her hair, dislodging the pins, and bringing its weight down around her shoulders. She couldn't be jealous, she told herself again. Jake meant nothing to her. She was just working herself up into a state unnecessarily, making herself miserable over a man who had no compunction about betraying her daughter.

Nevertheless, in the days that followed, Laura could think of no way to avoid the coming trip. Although she might have had perfectly valid reasons for not going, they were not reasons she could voice—not unless she wanted to alienate her daughter, once and for all. Of course, there was still the possibility that Julie might find out that Jake had spent two days at the cottage, without her knowledge. But, as time went by, that was becoming less likely. Julie spent so little time at Burnfoot, and it would be something of a coincidence if anyone made such a connection. After all, she had been with him the previous weekend, and it had probably been assumed that she was with him again. Why not? It was the most obvious conclusion, when all was said and done.

Which left Laura with the problem of preparing for a trip, for which she might have no enthusiasm, but which she couldn't ignore. As Julie had so unkindly pointed out, her present wardrobe would not stretch to the kind of occasions she might be expected to attend. She didn't even possess an evening dress, and, although she had no intention of buying some entirely extravagant creation, she knew a shopping trip to Newcastle was unavoidable.

However, the idea of going alone was not appealing, and a week later she rang Jess, and asked her if she fancied repeating their previous outing. 'Something's come up,' she said, hoping Jess wouldn't expect her to go into too much detail over the phone. 'I need a suit, and maybe a couple of dresses. I'll tell you why when I see you. What do you say?'

To her relief, Jess was enthusiastic. And she didn't ask her why she needed to supplement the shirts and trousers bought on their earlier trip, though Laura sensed she was dying to. But Jess was obviously prepared to wait until Saturday to hear all about it, and, after making the necessary arrangements, Laura rang off.

She was in the bath, when her phone rang on Friday evening.

Laura guessed it was Julie. She had seen Mark earlier

in the day, and reluctantly agreed to have dinner with
him that evening, so she was fairly sure it wasn't him.
It could always be Mrs Forrest, of course. Her twice-
weekly cleaner sometimes rang to change her arrangements, but very rarely. Besides, something told her it
wasn't Mrs Forrest. Although she wasn't psychic, Laura
sensed the call was long-distance.

She sat for a moment, calculating her chances of getting out of the bath, and getting downstairs to answer it,
before it stopped ringing, and decided they were poor.
She had been caught that way before, and she was loath
to leave the warm, soapy water for an abortive spring to
the phone. Even so, when it continued to ring, long after
she had expected it to stop, her conscience pricked her.
If it was Julie, she ought to answer it. It was no use
avoiding the inevitable.

But, although she made a belated foray for the towel,
the phone stopped ringing before she had chance to leave
the bathroom. Instead, when she opened the door, just
to make sure she wasn't mistaken, the house was silent,
and with a guilty sense of aggravation she climbed back
into the bath.

But her mood of relaxation was shattered, and she
didn't spend any longer than she had to in the water.
Instead, she concentrated on getting ready for her date
with Mark, unwillingly aware that she was going to
spend the whole evening worrying about that call.

She decided to wear the cream wool dress again. Mark
hadn't seen it, and, although it aroused a disturbing
memory of the evening she had spent with Jake, she
refused to let that deter her. She couldn't afford to dis-
card the dress, just because of its associations, and by
wearing it to go out with Mark she would dispel that
particular myth.

She was making a final examination of her appearance, when the phone rang again. Her immediate reaction was one of relief, but as she went down the stairs to answer it, that was followed by an irresistible sense of apprehension. She couldn't help it. Any thought of the coming trip to Italy sent shivers of trepidation down her spine, and she knew Julie would be ringing to confirm the arrangements.

'Hello,' she said, picking up the receiver, and she was relieved to find her voice didn't sound as anxious as she felt. 'Burnfoot, two, four, seven.'

'Laura?'

She almost put the phone straight down. That dark, disturbing voice was unmistakable, and a wave of indignation swept over her. How dared he ring her here? How dared he get in touch with her at all, after what he had done?

'Come on, Laura, I know you're there.' There was just the faintest trace of impatience in his voice now. 'At least, have the decency to speak to me.'

'Me—have decency!' Laura swallowed. 'My God, I don't know how you have the nerve!'

'We all have nerves,' Jake assured her tensely. 'And you may be interested to know that mine aren't exactly undisturbed at this moment.'

'Good!'

'This has been the longest month of my life.'

'It serves you right.'

'All right.' His voice hardened, and Laura, attuned to every nuance of his tone, felt her own nerves tingle. 'You've had your fun at my expense, but now I want you to be sensible.'

'I am being sensible,' she retorted, realising she must not allow him to get the upper hand. 'I can't imagine why you're ringing me, Mr Lombardi. What's the matter? Has Julie been giving you a hard time?'

The word he used then was incomprehensible to her, but its meaning was not. Even in his own language, the ugliness of its intent was evident, and Laura wondered why she didn't just put the phone down, and be done with it.

'You have a foul mouth, do you know that?' he grated, after a moment, and Laura gasped.

'*I* do?' she countered, indignantly. 'After what you——'

'Did you understand what I said?'

Laura hesitated. 'N—o——'

'Well, I understand you, only too well,' he told her harshly, 'and, believe me, you could use a little instruction in the art of *not* saying the wrong thing!'

'I don't think it matters what I say to you, Mr Lombardi,' Laura told him, albeit a little less forcefully, and he expelled his breath on a low groan.

'Laura,' he said, his use of her name sending a shuddering wave of heat to the surface of her skin. '*Dio*, Laura, have you no pity?'

Laura could feel herself weakening. It wasn't in her nature to hurt anyone, but she wouldn't—*she couldn't*—give in.

'How—how is Julie?' she asked, deliberately bringing her daughter's name between them once again, and Jake sighed.

'She was perfectly all right when I spoke to her yesterday evening,' he replied at last, and Laura's fingers tightened around the receiver she was holding.

Closing her eyes against the images his words had evoked, she said tautly, 'Was that before—or after—you went to bed?' and waited, with a sense of dread, for his answer.

'Before—in my case,' declared Jake obliquely, and then, before she could ask him what he meant, he added, 'I wouldn't know about Julie. I'm in Rome, and she's not.'

'Rome?' Laura quivered. 'How—how long have you been in Rome?'

Jake's laugh was ironic. 'Do you really want to know?' He paused. 'I thought you weren't interested in what I was doing.'

Laura caught her breath. 'I'm not. That is—I was just being polite, that's all——'

'I know what you were being, Laura, and it wasn't polite. But we'll let it go for now.' Jake paused. 'I assume you got my mother's invitation.'

'Yes.' She could hardly deny it. 'But, I don't know——'

'Good.' Jake broke into her attempt to question its validity. 'My parents are looking forward to meeting you. And Lucia, of course.'

'Lucia?' Laura frowned.

'My daughter. Lucia—*Luci*.'

Laura tensed. 'She'll be there?'

'Of course. She's with me now, as it happens.'

'In—Rome?'

'In Rome,' he agreed, and she guessed that was why Julie wasn't with him. It put a whole new perspective on the situation.

'So,' she said tersely. 'Was that the only reason you rang? To ensure that I had received your mother's invitation?'

'Hardly.' Jake was evidently controlling his impatience with difficulty. 'I wanted to talk to you. I wanted to explain the arrangements to you. I wanted to be sure there'd be no misunderstandings. Now—a car will pick you up at your cottage at six o'clock on Saturday morning, a week from tomorrow, and transport you to Newcastle airport——'

'That's not necessary——'

'I think it is,' said Jake inflexibly. He paused a moment, and then went on, 'You will then board the shuttle to London, arriving at Heathrow at approximately ten minutes past eight.'

'Ten-past eight!' Laura was disconcerted. 'That's rather early, isn't it?'

'Unfortunately, the next flight from Newcastle is not until nearly half-past eleven,' replied Jake evenly. 'In those circumstances, we would not arrive at Castellombardi until dinnertime.'

'I can get the train——'

Jake expelled his breath heavily. 'No.'

'Why not?'

'Because that is not the way I want it to be,' he retorted wearily. 'Laura—*cara*——'

'Don't call me *cara*!'

'—just allow me to have my way, hmm?'

Laura took a steadying breath. 'And if I don't, you'll tell Julie what happened, right?'

'Wrong.' Jake sucked in his own breath, with the same intention. 'Laura, please—can't we suspend this animosity? For—for all our sakes? I want you to enjoy these few days in my home.'

Laura closed her eyes against the disturbing appeal in his voice. Just for a moment, she allowed herself to imagine what it would be like if she were going to Castellombardi, to meet Jake's parents, as his fiancée. If she, and not her daughter, were the reason for this trip.

Oh, she would still have qualms, of course. What prospective bride hadn't, when meeting her fiancé's family for the first time? But it would have all been worth it, to know that Jake loved her...

'Laura?'

The frustration in Jake's voice brought her out of her reverie, but a little of the warmth her thoughts had engendered lingered on in her tone. 'All right,' she said, unaware of how much softer her voice sounded. 'Wh—what do I do when I get to London? What time is the flight to—to——?'

'Pisa,' put in Jake swiftly, responding to her mood. 'And it's as soon as we can make it. We'll be flying to my father's——'

'We?' Laura halted him there, the anxiety reappearing in her voice. 'But—you're already in Italy.'

'I shall be flying back to London next Friday,' Jake explained, with some resignation. 'We—that is, you, Julie, and myself—will fly back together on Saturday morning.'

'I see.' Laura bit her lower lip.

'Do you? Do you, honestly?' Jake uttered a harsh sound. 'You surely don't object to my escorting you, do you?'

Laura hesitated a moment, and then realising how futile it all was, she submitted. 'I—suppose not,' she murmured, and as she did so the doorbell rang.

She guessed it was Mark, and, glancing at her watch, she discovered she had been on the phone for almost fifteen minutes. It must be costing Jake a small fortune, she thought worriedly, before the cynical realisation that he could afford it swept all other considerations aside.

'I'll have to go,' she said now. 'There's someone at the door.'

'Answer it. I can wait,' declared Jake impatiently, but Laura knew Mark wouldn't appreciate being kept waiting. Besides, it would mean having to tell him who it was—or lying.

'I can't,' she said, as the bell pealed again. 'It—it's my date.'

'Your *what*?'

There was no mistaking Jake's savagery now, and Laura had to wet her dry lips before saying, half defensively, 'My date. I—I'm going out for dinner.'

'With a man?' Jake was grim. 'You're going out with a man?'

'Yes.' Laura found she was breathing much faster than she should. 'So, you see——'

'Who is he?'

'I—just a colleague.'

'A colleague? You mean he's a schoolteacher also?'

'That's right.' The bell rang yet again, and, realising Mark had only to peer through the front windows to discover her hovering by the phone, she added, 'I must go. Really——'

'Wait!' Jake's voice constricted. 'Are you—sleeping with him?'

'That's none of your——'

'Tell me!'

'No!' Laura felt a choking sensation in her throat. 'No, I'm not,' she replied wretchedly, and, slamming down the receiver, she pressed both hands to her burning cheeks.

CHAPTER TEN

LAURA had read that the light in Tuscany was the secret of the region's magic. In the early morning—or at dusk—painters and architects had marvelled at its clarity of illumination, and, even though it was late afternoon, she could see exactly what they meant.

From the balcony of her room, she had an uninterrupted view of the valley and the surrounding hills, and the colours were quite fantastic. From the silvery radiance of the River Lupo that wound along the valley floor, to the rich dark forests of pine and cypress that coated the hills all around, she was entranced by their brilliance. In addition to which, the air was like wine—fresh, and clear, and redolent with the fragrance of the flowers that grew in such profusion in the gardens below.

'Valle di Lupo.'

Laura said the name softly to herself. It meant the Valley of the Wolf. She had looked it up in the library at school. She guessed there had once been plenty of wild animals, wolves included, sheltering in the shadowy depths of these forests. There was still a sense of primitive beauty about the place, of ancient civilisations worshipping ancient gods.

And, for Laura, there was also a sense of stepping back in time. Everything was strange, and it was not unnatural that she should feel unsure of herself, but it was the sense of feeling young again that troubled her most. Of course, it shouldn't be something she should object to, but she did. She was not supposed to be here

155

to resurrect her own youth, but as Julie's mother, meeting her daughter's proposed in-laws for the first time.

But, it hadn't been like that, and it was all Jake's fault. Or Giacomo's—as his mother chose to call him. She should have known—and been warned—when Jake had met her in London. When he'd walked into the baggage collection area at Heathrow, and casually informed her that Julie was not with him, she should have refused to go any further.

And she would have, she remembered, ruefully, if he had not gone on to explain that Julie had merely been delayed in California. Apparently, the screen test her daughter had been so excited about had materialised, and she had flown off to Los Angeles at a moment's notice, leaving Jake to explain the situation to her mother. However, she hoped to join them on Sunday, so there was absolutely no reason why Laura should feel so apprehensive.

In the hustle and bustle of Terminal One, it had seemed ridiculous to imagine that Jake might have planned the whole thing. Dressed in a dark brown suede jacket and matching jeans, a bronze collarless body shirt open at the neck, to display the brown column of his throat, he looked so cool and attractive—and *young*— that it was inconceivable that he should have any serious interest in *her*. Tall, and dark, and undoubtedly male, he attracted female eyes wherever he went, and even in her newly bought trouser-suit, with her hair trimmed and styled, so that the ends tucked under her chin, Laura knew she couldn't compete. It had amused him to show her how inexperienced—and unsophisticated—she was, despite being older, but that was all. This wasn't a game any longer. This was for real. And like it or not, she had to carry off the next few days with as much confidence as she could muster.

And the journey had been surprisingly smooth. When she stopped worrying about Jake, and accepted his companionship for what it was, she could almost enjoy herself, and there was no doubt he had gone out of his way to make it easy for her. After all, there had been so many new things to see and absorb, not least the helicopter ride from Heathrow to Gatwick airport, and boarding Jake's father's private jet for the flight to Pisa.

She had been introduced to the pilot, who had turned out to be an Englishman himself, and the pretty Italian stewardess had made sure that their every need was catered for. They had eaten lunch, as they'd crossed the Alps into Switzerland, before flying over northern Italy, and down the Gulf of Genoa, to their landing at Pisa.

There had only been one bad moment, and that was just before they'd landed, when Jake had taken it upon himself to point out any visible places of interest. This coastline, he'd told her, was known as the Riviera di Levante, with the fishing harbour of Portofino being one of the prettiest spots.

Directing her gaze to the hazy outline of Viareggio, miles below them, had entailed his leaning over her chair, and she was disturbingly aware of his muscled chest, pressing against her arm and shoulder. As he spoke, his breath fanned her cheek, and, although he did nothing to warrant the sudden quickening of her blood, she couldn't deny its wild crescendo.

In an effort to distract him, she'd asked the question that had been troubling her, ever since he'd rung eight days ago. 'Your—your stomach,' she said. 'That is—the cut: did it heal all right?'

It was only after the words were uttered that she realised how intimate they were. Reminding him of his injury could only serve to increase their awareness of one another, and he might easily think that was what she intended.

But to her relief, Jake chose not to use the question to his own advantage. Instead, as if sensing her ambivalence, he drew back into his own seat, and running a careless hand over his midriff, he replied evenly, 'It is improving, thanks to you.' And then, more obliquely, 'Much like our relationship, wouldn't you agree?'

They'd landed in Pisa shortly afterwards, and Laura had been grateful. It meant she'd had little time to wonder what Jake had meant. Instead, she'd still been exclaiming, somewhat fulsomely, over the brilliance of the sun on the old city's towers and churches that she had seen from the air, when Jake's father's chauffeur had come up to them, as they'd cleared Customs.

A stocky, middle-aged man, with friendly features, and a thick moustache, and wearing the same purple and gold uniform that the pilot and stewardess had worn, he'd greeted Jake with evident warmth and affection. The two men had spoken together in their own language, as they'd walked to where the car was waiting, and Laura had been happy to trail behind, marvelling at the warmth of the day. It was much warmer here than in England, and she'd been glad she had not succumbed to the temptation—at five o'clock that morning—to wear a heavier outfit. As it was, the brushed cotton trouser-suit had been just about right.

The drive from the airport to Castellombardi had been uneventful—inasmuch as Laura had concentrated on the scenery, and Jake had obligingly discussed soccer with their chauffeur. It had enabled Laura to absorb a little more of her surroundings, though the glimpses of handsome villas she saw, sheltering behind citrus and olive trees, as they'd left the city, had given her more than a twinge of trepidation. They'd given her some indication of what Castellombardi might be like, and the prospect had been quite unnerving.

Beyond the city's limits, the motorway signs had all seemed to lead to Firenze—Florence—but although they'd driven for a short distance along the *autostrada*, they'd soon turned off on to narrower country roads. The flat coastal plain had soon been left behind, and they'd climbed into cypress-shaded hills, where every summit revealed a hidden valley, or the gleaming walls of a medieval town. There were farms, and vineyards, and countless churches, each with its own tower, or *campanile*, as it was called. There were ruins, too, evidence of the Etruscan civilisation that had once flourished in this area. And occasionally a barren stretch of ground, whose melancholy landscape epitomised the dignity of death in ancient cultures.

And then, Jake had turned from his conversation with the chauffeur, to tell her that they were now nearing his home. This pine-scented valley, with the tumbling waters of a narrow river at its foot, was Valle di Lupo, and the crenellated towers she could see, nestling against their dark green backcloth, belonged to Castellombardi.

Laura's nerves had tightened apprehensively, and not for the first time, she had wished Julie was with them. She, Laura, should not have been here, seeing Jake's home for the first time, meeting his parents, and sharing their hospitality. That should have been Julie's prerogative. This whole trip had been arranged for Julie's benefit, not hers. If only she could stop feeling like a usurper. If only she could stop thinking about Jake altogether.

But, arriving at Castellombardi, Laura had found herself worrying more about meeting Jake's parents than coping with Jake himself. And the sprawling manorhouse had been daunting enough, without the added complications of a handful of servants, whose names she was sure she would never remember.

A little of her consternation must have shown in her face, however, for Jake had taken time out from instructing a lusty youth where Laura's bags were to be taken, to say reassuringly, 'Don't worry! They're going to love you.' And, in her hysterical state, she wasn't sure whether he meant his parents or the members of their staff.

The creeper-hung portico, with its narrow mullioned windows, gave access to a marble-floored entrance hall. The age of the building was much in evidence here, with a restored frescoed ceiling arching above tapestry-hung walls. There was a veritable arsenal of ancient weapons, forming a grim collage above a huge stone fireplace. The number of swords and daggers on display had made Laura look automatically at Jake, and his lazy grin had stirred an unwanted awareness in the pit of her stomach.

'Now, you know why I enjoy sword-play,' he murmured, for her ears only. 'Be warned, my ancestors were not known for their tolerance.'

Laura might have replied—if she could have dismissed the shiver of sentience that shivered down her spine at his words, but she was forestalled by the appearance of another woman. And not a servant, Laura surmised, noticing the rings that adorned her slender fingers. Even without her resemblance to her son, Laura would have guessed that this was Jake's mother. Although the similarities between them were more in colouring than appearance, she walked with such grace and economy of movement—just like her son, Laura had acknowledged unwillingly.

'Mama!'

Jake's greeting had confirmed what was already a certainty, and he went to greet her with an easy confidence. For a moment, he was enfolded in his mother's arms, and then, before Laura could begin to feel an outsider, he turned and beckoned her forward, to make the introductions...

And that was when her misgivings had multiplied, Laura acknowledged now, turning back into the classical beauty of the bedroom behind her. For, in introducing her to his mother, Jake hadn't mentioned Julie. Not once. He had presented her simply as Laura Fox. Not *Julie's mother*, Laura Fox, or even as Laura Fox, the mother of a friend of his. Just Laura; nothing else; as if she, and not Julie, were the reason for this visit.

The Contessa Sophia Lombardi had been especially charming, Laura conceded, even though she must have wondered why their guest was staring at her son with such consternation. Tall, like Jake, with narrow patrician features, she had welcomed Laura into her home with real cordiality, asking if she had had a good journey, and acknowledging Laura's compliments about her country. She had made Laura feel like a wanted visitor, not the intruder she believed herself to be.

Of course, Laura hadn't been able to say anything that might create any awkwardness in his mother's presence, and she had not had a chance to speak to Jake alone since his mother's appearance. Instead, the Contessa had taken charge of her well-being, suggesting that Laura might like to see her room and rest for a while before the evening meal. Like her son, she spoke in English, and Laura had felt obliged to accept her suggestion. But that hadn't stopped her from giving Jake a quelling look, as she'd followed one of the maidservants up the stairs. It had said, she would speak to him later, and he'd been left in no doubt what she meant.

But that was over an hour ago now. Since then, Laura had taken a shower, and unpacked her case, and made a tentative exploration of her apartments. Her room—rooms, she corrected herself drily—were situated in the west wing of the building, overlooking the whole sweep of the valley. But it was the rooms themselves that had first drawn her admiration, with their skilful blend of ancient and modern.

Although, perhaps modern was not an appropriate adjective, she conceded now. Obviously, much of the renovation of the building had been done in the early part of this century, when time and materials had been no object. There was an abundance of gilt and decoration, and, despite their obvious age, the silk-encrusted walls and velvet carpets still wore the patina of an earlier age.

Nevertheless, the plumbing was reassuringly efficient, and the bathroom sported all the usual accoutrements. If the claw-footed bath and pedestal basin were rather large and ungainly, their function was not impaired. On the contrary, Laura was looking forward to taking a bath. She had the feeling that when the huge porcelain tub was full only her head would show above the rim.

Between the bathroom and the bedroom, there was a spacious dressing-room, with long walk-in wardrobes. Laura's handful of outfits looked rather lost in such an excess of space, but it was quite a novelty to have so much freedom.

Beyond the bedroom, whose generously proportioned four-poster also attracted Laura's admiration, a modest sitting-room provided reading and writing facilities. All the latest magazines—regrettably, Laura saw, in Italian—were spread on a low glass-topped table, while an exquisitely carved bureau was set with writing paper and envelopes and, Laura saw to her delight, a real quill pen.

She thought of sitting at the bureau and writing to Jess, but the connotations of that exercise were more than enough to deter her. She could just imagine her friend's reaction if she wrote and told her she was spending the weekend with Jake's family, without Julie. No matter that her daughter was supposed to be arriving the following day. Jess was bound to have suspicions. Heaven knew, she had suspicions herself.

Which brought her back to the crux of her dilemma, Laura sighed heavily. What was she going to do about Jake? And Julie? The trouble was, she didn't know what Jake had told his mother about his relationship with her daughter, and she could hardly ask. And yet, what else could she do? She had to know if Julie was expected here tomorrow, or whether that had just been a lie.

But what if it had? she asked herself now, admitting the incredible thought that it might be true. What if Julie wasn't in California at all? What if she was, even now, trying to reach her mother at Burnfoot?

But no. Julie herself had told her about this trip to Italy. Julie had tendered the invitation, and just because Jake had made the final arrangements was no reason to assume her daughter wasn't involved.

She shook her head, and, walking across to the bed, she flopped down on to the embossed coverlet. The mattress gave beneath her weight, and, squeezing the edges on either side of her, she realised it wasn't the spring interior she had expected. If she was not mistaken, the mattress was stuffed with feathers, and in spite of her worries she couldn't prevent a rueful smile from tugging at the corners of her lips. God, she thought, resting back on her elbows. Jess would never believe this place!

A knock at the outer door brought her to her feet with a start. As she tentatively walked to the door of the sitting-room, her hands automatically dragged the folds of the terry robe she had found hanging on the back of the bathroom door, closer about her. But, she could do nothing about her bare legs, protruding from its hem.

However, when she called a tentative, 'Come in,' the maid, who earlier had brought her a light meal of tea and pastries, appeared to collect the tray.

'*Scusi, signora,*' she said, picking up the tray. '*Mi dispiace di disturbarsi.*'

The words were mostly unfamiliar, but their meaning was clear enough, and Laura raised a deprecating hand. '*Prego,*' she said, quite pleased with her response. But when the maid launched into a voluble stream of her own language, she wished she had not been so clever.

'*Non capisco, non capisco,*' she exclaimed, trying to stem the tide, and she was almost relieved when she heard a low mocking laugh.

'*Grazie, Maria,*' Jake said lazily, straightening from his position by the door, and the young maid flushed becomingly, as she sidled past him, and out of the room.

With the maid's departure, however, Laura was immediately aware of her state of undress. Jake had evidently bathed and changed. There were drops of moisture gleaming on his hair, and his dark trousers and jacket, and the cream silk shirt and tie, were obviously what he was going to wear this evening. Laura, meanwhile, felt quite dishevelled, but rather than give him another reason to have fun at her expense, she put her hands into the robe's pockets, and faced him bravely.

'Did you want something?' she asked, in the dismissing tone of someone whose patience was wearing thin, and Jake glanced behind him at the open door before answering quietly, 'I rather thought you wanted to speak to me.'

'Oh…' Laura was disconcerted then, not least because he was right, and for a few moments she had forgotten the ambiguity of her position. 'Um—well, yes. Yes, I did want to speak to you. But—not like this.'

She glanced pointedly down at the bathrobe, and Jake's mouth took on a decidedly sensual slant. 'Ah,' he murmured, a wealth of understanding in the sound, and, as his insolent gaze roved down her body, Laura could almost feel the heat of its passing.

'Please!' she exclaimed, unable to withstand this kind of sexual gamesmanship, and Jake's eyes came obediently back to hers.

'Anything,' he said, his tone scraping her nerves with its husky vibration. 'Shall I close the door?'

'No!'

Laura made the denial rather louder than she had intended, and Jake arched a mocking brow. 'You want the rest of the household to hear this?' he queried politely, and she turned away, running both hands under the hair at the back of her neck.

'No. I—oh, close the door. Behind you,' she mumbled wearily. 'I'll talk to you later.'

The door closed, and she expelled her breath on a heavy sigh. But when she turned around again, she found Jake was still there.

'You——' she began, her voice taut with frustration, but Jake was not prepared to argue with her.

'Yes, me,' he said, crossing the space between them, and cupping her hot face in his hands. 'You despise me,

I know.' His eyes darkened. 'But you want me just the same.'

'I don't——' she started, but his mouth silenced her. With hungry expertise, his kiss trapped her instinctive protest, his tongue sliding between her lips to make a statement of its own.

Laura's world tilted. Much as she wanted to deny what he was saying, what he was *doing*, her body betrayed her. The moist fusion of their mouths made any protest superfluous anyway. No one could respond as she was responding and still pretend she was a victim of circumstance. If she was a victim—and of that she had few doubts—it was a victim of her own needs, her own inadequacies. What Jake was doing was simply confirming all those guilty fantasies she had entertained about him.

But no fantasy had prepared her for the treacherous delight of feeling Jake's hands on her bare flesh. She was so weak, so accessible, and the terry-cloth robe parted easily beneath his purposeful hands. Not that she was aware of it—not immediately, anyway. Her own hands were too busy clinging to his lapels, in an effort to withstand the shakiness of her knees, to notice at once what he was doing. It was only when one mohair-clad leg brushed her thighs that she perceived the reason why the tips of her breasts felt so aroused. The sides of the robe had parted, and her quivering body was open to his touch.

Sanity craved that she draw back from him now, while she still could, but her mind was swimming in a haze of emotion. She wanted to be sensible. She tried to remember where she was, and what she was doing, but her feelings got in the way. And Jake didn't make it easy for her. When he released her mouth, it was only to seek the sensitive skin below her ear, and his teeth fastening on that skin, drenched her limbs with moisture.

'I knew you were beautiful,' he breathed, tipping the robe from her shoulders, his tongue finding the pulse that fluttered in her throat. His hands slid to her waist, and then moved upward until they were brushing the undersides of her breasts. '*Bella* Laura, do you have any idea how much I want you?'

'Jake——'

Laura was finding it an effort even to breathe normally, but her panting use of his name seemed to please him, and whatever protest she had intended to make was stifled by the groan he emitted. His hands closed over her breasts as his mouth sought hers again, and she was weakly aware that so long as he was touching her like this she had no will to resist him.

Her lips opened wide to the wet invasion of his tongue, and almost without her own volition her own tongue moved tentatively to touch his. A sensuous warmth was sweeping over her, and although she had never experienced such intense lovemaking before she seemed to know instinctively what to do.

Jake was biting her lips now, little nibbling kisses that caused her chest to rise and fall with the intensity of her emotions. And, in so doing, her hard nipples thrust into his palms, sensitising them to an almost unbearable extent.

Dizziness overwhelmed her, and, as if sensing her weakness, Jake swung her up into his arms, and carried her to the bed. He deposited her in the middle of the coverlet, and although the coolness at her back was briefly sobering Jake didn't allow her to escape him.

Careless of his clothes, he came down on the bed beside her, and his hands and lips drove all sane thoughts from her head. When his mouth found the creamy rise of her breasts, and trailed a searing path of wet kisses to the throbbing nipple, she reached for him. With wondering hands, she cradled his dark head against her, tangling her fingers in his hair, and raking her nails against his scalp.

There was an ache between her thighs now, an actual physical ache, that she knew only he could ease. But the means of that easement was too mind-bending to contemplate, even if at this moment he had her at his mercy.

His tongue thrust into her mouth again, its greedy possession an indication of his own diminishing control. When her eyes fluttered open she surprised a look of raw hunger on his face, and his eyes narrowed passionately as his hands slid over her naked body.

His touch was urgent, abrasive, shaping the gentle curve of her hip, before slipping down to her knees and up again, this time between the quivering flesh of her inner thighs. He caressed the skin from her knees to the apex of her legs with slow deliberation, always brushing the triangle of curls with the back of his hand, but never really touching. It was as if he was intentionally withholding something she desired with increasing urgency, and it was all Laura could do not to grab his hand, and press it between her legs.

Her trembling cravings shamed her. Jake knew exactly what he was doing, she was sure of that. And while a small corner of her mind clung to that knowledge, and taunted her with it, it was easily overwhelmed by the needs and desires he was so effortlessly promoting. She knew he wanted her aroused and clinging to him. It was the only way he could destroy her inhibitions. But that didn't stop her from bucking against his hands.

By the time he chose to cup the throbbing core of her

womanhood, Laura was almost mindless with relief. Her legs were shaking so much that she couldn't have kept them together, even if she'd wanted to, and only when Jake bent to press his face against the tight curls did she utter a choked sob of protest.

'What's wrong?' he asked huskily, lifting his head and looking at her, and she thought how unfair it was that she was so naked and vulnerable, while he was still fully dressed.

'You—you can't,' she got out unsteadily, levering herself up on her elbow, but his smile was purely possessive.

'Why not?' he demanded. 'It's what you want. It's what we both want.'

'No——'

'Yes.' He moved so that he could take her resistant hand and press it against the rigid shaft of his own arousal, tautly visible against the fine cloth of his trousers. 'Only there isn't time to please both of us. Not right now. Only you.'

'Jake——'

'I'm here.'

He moved again, slanting his mouth across hers, and bearing her back against the covers. And as he did so, his fingers slid into the silky female flesh that was wet from wanting him. With infinite skill, his tongue mimicked the movement of his hand, and Laura was swamped with longing. This was what she wanted, she conceded dizzily, as feelings she had not even known existed rioted inside her. She did want Jake to touch her, to kiss her, and make love to her. And she wanted *him* inside her, not just an imitation.

But rational thought became impossible, as Jake's expert caresses began to arouse an unfamiliar hunger. It was no longer enough just to submit passively to what he was doing to her. She started to push against his fingers, and unfamiliar needs caused her to twist and turn beneath his hands. Even Jake's breathing quickened, she noticed unsteadily, his laboured heartbeat jerking in tune with her own.

She opened her eyes again, almost disbelievingly, as her body began to strive towards some goal she was barely aware of. Certainly, her experiences with Keith Macfarlane had not led her to believe she was capable of any depth of feeling, and the fear that she might never escape this craving brought panic-stricken intensity to her expression.

But Jake knew what she was feeling. Even though his face was taut now, his forehead and temples beaded with sweat, he understood her fear. When Laura raised a trembling hand to smooth the moist hair back from his forehead, he turned his head, and pressed his mouth to her wrist, and the heat of his lips sent a searing flame along her veins.

'Easy, *cara*,' he muttered thickly, lowering his head to her breast, and taking the burning nipple into his mouth. And, as he suckled on the rosy flesh, Laura's control deserted her.

'God—oh, God,' she groaned, hardly aware that she was digging her nails into his shoulders. A blinding wave of pleasure had overwhelmed her, and with it an urgent need to share her joy. Unaware that she was doing so, she wound her arms around his neck, and pulled him down on top of her, covering his face with kisses, until the tremors slowly receded.

But Jake did not share her abandonment. With grim determination, he extracted himself from her clinging fingers, and rolled on to his back beside her. And for a few moments, there was silence in the room, broken only by the individual sounds of their breathing.

It was the coolness of the evening air, drifting in through the open balcony doors, and chilling her bare flesh, that brought Laura fully to her senses. When Jake had first moved away from her, she had lain there, too stunned, both mentally and physically, over what had happened, to do anything. But, as her blood cooled—and likewise her flesh—she gradually felt the full impact of her own wanton behaviour.

Dear lord, she fretted wretchedly, what had she done? After all she had said; after the way she had castigated Jake for taking advantage of her, she had actually allowed him to—to——

To what? To reduce her to a trembling mass of nerves and sensations, she allowed disgustedly. He had used his not inconsiderable skills to show her exactly how vulnerable she was, so far as he was concerned. He had brought her to a peak of physical pleasure she had never known before, without even availing himself of her body. Let's face it, without even taking off his clothes, she acknowledged bitterly. Damn, how he must be laughing at her now!

She turned her head, her face twisted with contempt at her own weakness. There was no way she was going to get out of this, without humiliating herself still further, but she had to try. For her own sake. For *Julie's* sake! Oh, God! *Julie!*

Jake was still lying beside her. She had half expected to find he had moved, while she was recovering her senses, but he hadn't. He was still lying on his back, one hand raised behind his head, the other resting on the coverlet between them.

However he had sensed the nervous movement of her

head, and he turned his head on the pillows to look at her. 'Better?' he enquired, a little thickly, and, although Laura was sure there must be some sarcasm in his question, his expression was free of derision.

It took her completely by surprise, however, and the words she had been prepared to say in defence of herself, stuck in her throat. 'I—this should never have happened,' she said instead, realising how feeble that sounded. Particularly after she had just betrayed everything she had thought she believed in, she added miserably. 'Um—you'd better go.'

Jake sighed then, and rolled on to his side to face her. 'Is that all you have to say?' he exclaimed, his tone harshening. 'Laura, this was not a mistake! This was for real. And believe me, my magnanimity does not extend to soothing your pretty sensibilities!'

Laura caught her breath. 'I beg your pardon?'

'I said——'

'I know what you said,' she responded, in a trembling voice. She sat up, and presented her back to him, 'I—I want to know what—what you meant by—by my pretty—sensibilities!'

'*Dio!*' Jake's oath was heartfelt, but when he would have grasped her arm she scrambled off the bed, and snatched up the discarded bathrobe. She felt a little better with its soft folds between her and Jake's scathing eyes, though she shifted a little nervously when he came up off the bed to face her.

'What do you think I meant?' he demanded grimly, and when she moved her head in a little indifferent gesture he raked back his hair with a frustrated hand. 'You don't suppose *I* enjoyed what just happened, do you?'

Laura's face flamed. She couldn't help it. It was an involuntary response to his lack of discrimination. 'I—

don't—think—we need to—to conduct a post-mortem——' she began, but his anger overruled her prim denial.

'Do you not? Do you not?' he grated, and she noticed how his accent had appeared again. '*Mama mia*, she doesn't want to talk about it! She doesn't even realise how hard it was for me to touch her!'

Laura swallowed convulsively. 'Well—if—if that was the case,' she stammered, 'why did you?'

'*Dio!*' He pressed the ball of one hand against his forehead. 'You don't even understand what I am talking about, do you?' He glared at her. 'Laura, do you honestly believe I *didn't* want to touch you? That is not what I meant. Not what I meant at all.' He groaned. 'I have told you already, I want you, Laura. I want to be a part of you. Do you know what I am talking about now? I want to lie with you. I want to slide between your thighs, and slake my thirst in your most beautiful body, but I am careful. I know I must not rush you. I know you are not ready yet to admit your feelings, so I—I pleasure you. Not myself. Only you. And you have no idea, no idea, believe me, how I am feeling at this moment!'

Laura quivered, drawing her lower lip between her teeth, as her eyes flickered down his body. They lingered on the unmistakable evidence of his frustration, and then, when he swore, rather colourfully, her gaze returned nervously to his.

'Yes,' he said harshly, dragging his hands down his thighs, as if to ease the constriction of the tight trousers. 'So now you know. I want you, Laura. And I suggest you do not look at me like that, unless you are prepared to take the consequences.' He drew a laboured breath. 'Now, I suggest you get dressed. My parents expect you to join them for drinks in the library in——' he consulted the plain gold watch on his wrist '—a little over fifteen minutes.'

Laura caught her breath. 'I can't join them now——'

'Why not?'

Jake was buttoning his jacket as he spoke, smoothing a hand that was not quite steady over his hair, checking that his tie was straight. Laura watched him, almost possessively, aware, as she did so, that she was actually beginning to believe the things he said. He did want her. That was undeniable. But what he wanted of her—that was something else again.

'Jake——'

'Get dressed, Laura,' he said flatly, walking towards the door. 'It's impolite to be late, when you're the guest of honour!'

CHAPTER ELEVEN

'PAPA!'

Lucia nudged her pony nearer her father's bay stallion, and whispered something Laura could barely hear. She knew it was about her. Her name—Lucia called her Signora Fox—figured fairly significantly in the little girl's oratory, but as she spoke in her own language Laura couldn't understand what she was saying.

Which was all par for the course, thought Laura bitterly, holding on to her mount's reins with a grimness that bordered on desperation. She didn't understand any of this, and Lucia's shy reserve was the least of her worries.

So, instead of fretting over what Jake's daughter might be saying about her, Laura stared determinedly at the view. If she could forget that she was on the back of a horse, and that the horse was standing on a ledge, some one hundred feet above the valley floor, it should be possible to appreciate the beauty of her surroundings. Jake had said the only way to see this country was on horseback, and, although Laura had never ridden before, he had insisted he would take care of her.

The trouble was, she didn't want him taking care of her. It was bad enough, knowing she was here under false pretences. She didn't want his mother and father to get the wrong impression. They had been kind to her, and she appreciated that, but she had to keep things in perspective.

Yet it had proved harder than she had ever imagined.

Dinner, the night before, for instance. When she had eventually gathered herself together, and gone downstairs, she had found her plan to explain the situation to Jake's parents had had to be shelved. Contrary to her belief, she had not been the only guest for dinner. Jake's younger brother and his wife; two actors, who were performing in the area; an artist of some note; a priest; and various other business colleagues of Jake's father, and their wives, were gathered in the library, when Laura finally found the courage to join them. She had realised there was no chance then of any private conversation, and her head was soon swimming with so many introductions.

Not least her introduction to Jake's father, she remembered ruefully. Count Domenico Lombardi—Nico, to his friends—was simply an older version of his elder son. He was handsome, and courteous, and in other circumstances, Laura was sure, she would have been charmed by him. But he was too much like Jake for her to feel completely relaxed in his presence, and the ambiguity of their relationship made her feel like a fraud.

Jake's brother, Lorenzo, was much less threatening. Smaller than the other members of his family, he had a shy, self-deprecating manner, a little like Lucia's, that endeared itself to Laura. His wife, too, was relaxed and friendly, and, like most of the Italians Laura had met, she spoke extremely good English.

Laura was grateful she had taken some trouble over her appearance, however. Even if her hands had shaken as she'd been applying her make-up, the results were quite satisfying. The sequinned jacket she had shocked Jess by buying the previous week, worn with a simple black silk vest and trousers was definitely well-chosen. She hadn't needed Jake's studied approval to know she looked good. For once in her life, she had confidence in her appearance, even if her reasons for making the effort hadn't been what she'd expected.

Nevertheless, the evening had proved to be quite a strain. Oh, everyone had been very kind, and she had been made to feel that she was a welcome visitor. But, perhaps because of that, Laura remained on edge, aware, more than anyone, of the falseness of her position.

Her meeting with Lucia had struck a happier note. Unlike any English child of her age, she had been allowed to stay up for dinner, and the little girl was naturally curious about anyone who might focus her father's attention away from herself. It was understandable, Laura supposed, bearing in mind that the child's mother was dead, but she wished she could tell her she was not who the child evidently thought her. Even though Jake had introduced them, and had said nothing to arouse her interest, Laura was sure Lucia sensed there was something between them. But not for long, Laura had wanted to cry. Just for this weekend...

Lucia had been taken off to bed, by her nursemaid, before ten o'clock, but the evening had not ended until around midnight. Laura had wished that she, and not the protesting Lucia, could have escaped so much earlier, but she was obliged to be polite, and stay until the bitter end.

Not that it had been really bitter, she acknowledged now, as the chestnut gelding shifted beneath her. Trying not to show how nervous she really was, Laura pressed her knees against the leathers, and hung on. The meal, which had been served in the vaulted dining-room, had been mouth-wateringly delicious, and had Laura not been so tense, she would have enjoyed the food immensely. Smoked ham, served with a delicate grapefruit

mousse, pasta, stuffed with meat and cheese, and a sug-
ary fruit dessert to finish, would normally have aroused
her appetite. But in the event, she had eaten very little,
relying on the wine to keep her throat from drying up
completely.

Bed, when she'd reached it, had offered few reassur-
ances. Looking at the satin bedspread, smooth now, and
neatly folded back, she had been irresistibly reminded
of what had happened on the bed before dinner. It had
been impossible to look at that soft mattress without
thinking of how her own body had betrayed her. And
yet, much as she hated to admit it, she had known a
strange exhilaration at the memory. She might tell herself she was mortified, but her skin had tingled just the
same.

Of course, she had been half afraid Jake would come
back, once his parents had retired. Long after the house
had settled down for the night, Laura had lain awake,
determined to remain on her guard. She couldn't help
remembering what he had said before he'd left her, and
she'd been fairly sure he would try to finish what he had
started.

But Jake hadn't come back. Although she had wedged
a chair beneath the handle of the sitting-room door, no
one had tried to dislodge it. She had eventually fallen
asleep, too exhausted to care any longer. Only her
dreams had disturbed her, and they were no one's fault
but her own.

But now, sitting here, on this cypress-studded hillside,
with the sun cresting the hills, and casting dark pools of
shadow between the trees, she was aware of the instinctive response her thoughts had engendered. Her mind
might be determined to resist Jake, to put him out of her
life, but her emotions were not so controllable. Even

now, a hot sweet swirl of weakness was invading her lower limbs, and the memory of how he had made her feel was not one she was likely to forget.

The chestnut snorted softly, and tossed his head, and Laura's attention was drawn back to the precariousness of her seat. Below her, the ground fell away steeply to the river, and the knowledge that only the gelding's good nature stood between her and serious injury brought a wave of perspiration to her forehead.

'Luci thinks you're holding the reins too tightly,' Jake murmured beside her, and his knee bumped hers, causing the chestnut to shift in protest.

'Don't—don't do that!' gasped Laura, paying little attention to what he had said, and Jake reached across to anchor her reins with an expert hand.

'Hey,' he said, and she could tell by his expression, he knew exactly what she was thinking. 'Don't be scared,' he added. 'Caesar won't hurt you.'

'That's easy for you to say,' retorted Laura, her throat constricted, as much by his gloved hand resting on her knee, as by her fear. 'It just seems a long way down into the valley, that's all. And—and——'

'And you don't like it?'

'I didn't say that.' In all honesty, Laura had enjoyed parts of the outing, and she knew she would store up the memory of the beauty of this valley for when she was back in Burnfoot.

'Good.'

Jake looked into her eyes, and although he said nothing else, she knew he was remembering how she had looked the last time they were alone together. There were little sparks of awareness in the night-dark depths of his eyes, and Laura suddenly understood the meaning of drowning in someone's eyes. She wanted to drown in Jake's eyes, and the knowledge was terrifying.

'*Papa! Papa! Cosa stai facendo?*'

Luci was tugging his sleeve, wanting to know what they were doing, and, tearing his gaze away from Laura, Jake turned to his daughter. '*Niente, cara*, nothing,' he assured her soothingly, gesturing for her to lead the way down the winding track. 'We were just admiring the view, that is all,' he continued in English, but slowly, so that Luci could understand what he was saying. '*Avante, cara*. We are coming.'

Luci looked doubtful, but she urged her pony forward, and Jake used his hold on the chestnut's reins to draw him away from the ledge. Then, patting the beast's flanks, he urged him past his own mount, returning the reins to Laura, as she came up beside him.

'OK?' he asked, looking at her mouth, and Laura's lips parted nervously.

'I suppose so,' she said, a little tensely, and, keeping her eyes on Caesar's neck, she let him take her down the rocky incline.

There were terraces of vines on the lower slopes, and the sharp scent of citrus trees in blossom. It was a smell that Laura knew, from now on, she would always associate with this area, and her sweating palms cooled as the ground levelled out.

Luci came back to ride with her father as their mounts trod through lush meadows, bordering the river. It meant that Laura had little chance to talk privately with Jake, but, realising that once they got back to the house, it might be even harder to get him alone, she said tautly, 'What time is Julie coming?'

Her question had evidently disconcerted him, for he glanced swiftly at his daughter, as if gauging her reaction, before giving Laura a wooden look. 'Julie,' he said at last. 'I do not know.'

Laura noticed the 'do not', rather than the more casual 'don't', and was immediately suspicious. 'She *is* coming, isn't she?'

Jake sighed, and lifted his broad shoulders in a dismissing gesture. 'Julie does not like my country—only its cities,' he responded, guiding his horse nearer the water. Then, swinging down from the bay's back, he looked at Laura's hands, clutching the thin strips of leather that controlled her mount. 'You're still holding the reins too tightly,' he said. 'Can't you feel the way Caesar is trying to get the bit between his teeth?'

'Damn Caesar!' Laura's gaze skimmed Luci's startled face, before coming to rest on that of the man standing beside her. 'That's not an answer, Jake, and you know it!'

'Perhaps it is the only answer you are going to get,' he retorted coolly. 'Shall I help you down?'

'No!' As Luci prepared to swing out of her saddle, Laura shook her head. 'I—I want to go back.'

'Back?' Jake's features hardened. 'To the *castello*?'

'No. To England,' declared Laura unsteadily. 'I should never have come.'

Jake's mouth compressed. 'Not again, Laura. Now—will you get down, or must I haul you out of that saddle?'

Laura shook her head again, jerking the reins, so that Caesar's head came up, and his ears went back in protest. The gelding shifted backwards, as if trying to escape the bite of metal against the soft inner side of his mouth, but Laura was unaware of the animal's unease. She was too intent on showing Jake that, although he

might have some precarious control over her body, he
had none over her mind.

'I'm going back,' she said again glancing over her
shoulder. The walls of the *castello* were just visible
above the trees, and although she realised she was still
some distance from the house she was determined he
should not think he could dictate what she could or could
not do. She had ridden out here, hadn't she? Why
shouldn't she ride back?

But she had spoken without giving any thought to the
animal beneath her. It never occurred to her that the
gelding might have a mind of his own. She had been
nervous on the ridge, it was true, but she had learned to
trust him. And, because he had brought her safely down
into the valley again, she had assumed she was in control.

However, her behaviour had unsettled Caesar. The animal had sensed her anger, and her frustration, without
realising it was not directed towards himself. Her tight
hold on the bridle, her anxious knees digging into his
sides, excited him. He was not usually a nervous beast,
but Laura's persistent use of the restraint disturbed him,
and he whinnied loudly as she tugged his head around.

What happened next seemed to occur as if in slow
motion. Jake had evidently sensed that the gelding was
becoming agitated, and he lunged for the reins himself,
as Caesar backed off. But although he managed to grab
the bridle, the horse was too excitable to control. He
reared wildly on his hind legs, almost throwing Jake off
his feet, and Laura slid off his back, with only a muffled
gasp of protest.

Jake let go of the animal then, and Caesar, finding
himself free at last, galloped away. But Laura didn't notice. She was too busy fretting over the fool she had

made of herself again, and hoping she didn't look as stupid as she felt.

But she barely had time to register the fact that the sleeve of one of her new blouses was covered in mud, before Jake flung himself on to his knees beside her. Uncaring that his daughter was still sitting on her pony, staring at them with wide, anxious eyes, he ran his hands intimately over Laura's body, checking her legs and arms, and skimming the slim curve of her waist.

'Come si sente?' he demanded hoarsely, and then, realising she was gazing at him uncomprehendingly, he translated, 'How do you feel? Are you all right?' He cupped her rueful face between his fingers. 'If Caesar has hurt you, I'll get rid of him!'

Laura's tongue appeared to circle her lips, which wasn't the most sensible thing to do in the circumstances. She could tell from the sudden darkening of his eyes that Jake was remembering how her tongue had felt in his mouth, and she guessed that if Luci had not been there he would have repeated the experience.

'I—I'm fine,' she assured him, a little unsteadily none the less, though he was not to know his nearness was as much to blame as Caesar's rearing. But it was difficult to think of anyone but him, when he was looking at her with passionately concerned eyes, shattering her defences, with the unmistakable tremor in his hands. 'Honestly,' she added, realising she was in very real danger of showing him her response, 'I just got a shock, that's all.'

'A shock!'

Jake's lips twisted, but before she could say anything else, Luci appeared at his elbow. 'The *signora*—she has hurt her head, Papa?' she asked, her English remarkably good for someone of her age, and with reluctance Jake released Laura, and got to his feet.

'Signora Fox is a little shaken, *bambina*,' he replied, offering Laura his hand to get up, and, although she would have preferred to get up independently, she accepted his assistance. She wasn't entirely sure her legs would hold her, and she was more than a little relieved to find she was able to stand without support.

'*Dov'e Caesar?*' Luci soon lapsed back into her own language, and Jake dragged his gaze away from Laura's pale face to reply that the horse was probably back at the stables by now.

'He'll be all right, won't he?' Laura ventured, running a trembling hand over her hair, and Jake's eyes darkened.

'Of course he will,' he declared succinctly. 'So long as you are.'

'Oh—oh, I am.' Laura nodded vigorously, and then winced at the sudden throbbing in her head. 'Well—almost,' she conceded, giving Luci a rueful smile. 'I'm sorry if I've spoiled your outing.'

Luci shrugged, not quite knowing how to deal with this situation. It was obviously not what she had expected, and her expression mirrored her indecision.

However, her father's terse rejoinder brought her head up. 'You haven't spoiled anything!' he declared, giving his daughter an impatient look. 'Luci, get on your pony. We're going back.'

There was nothing Laura could say. She knew she couldn't walk back to the *castello*, and she hoped Luci wouldn't blame her too much for ruining their outing.

Still, it wasn't until Jake captured the reins of his horse, and brought him back to where Laura was standing, that she realised what he was intending to do. Until then, she had assumed that he and Luci would ride back to the house, and probably return with some sort of vehicle to fetch her. Now, a shiver of panic swept over her at the thought of getting on to the stallion's back.

'You—you don't expect me to—ride him, do you?' she gasped, and Jake's expression softened.

'You and me both,' he reassured her gently.

Laura swallowed. 'Couldn't—couldn't I just—ride Luci's pony?' she murmured, and Jake expelled his breath on a heavy sigh.

'No,' he said, looping the horse's reins over his shoulder, and cupping his hands. 'Come on. Put your foot in here, and I'll help you. That way you won't get tangled up in the stirrup, and I can get up behind you.'

It wasn't a very elegant accomplishment, but when Jake swung into the saddle behind her Laura forgot her qualms in the sheer pleasure of feeling his muscled thighs enclosing hers. And when his arms came about her waist to take the reins, she felt the reassuring strength of his body all around her. It was pointless to deny it. No one else made her so aware of being a woman.

And, even though she had initially been alarmed at the idea of riding on the huge bay stallion, Laura was almost sorry when they trotted into the stable-yard some twenty minutes later. For the past fifteen minutes, she had abandoned any attempt to resist the desire to enjoy the experience, and it wasn't until Jake had dismounted and was reaching up to help her down, that she saw his strained expression. It was only then that she comprehended how her yielding body must have affected him, and the reasons why he had become progressively less relaxed during the ride were blatantly obvious.

'I can manage,' she said, a little breathily, but Jake ignored her. He waited until she had swung her legs across the pommel, and then lifted her out of the saddle. He lowered her to the ground slowly, allowing her to slide down the whole length of his body, and Laura couldn't help but be as aroused as he was by the time she found herself on her feet.

'*Ti voglio,*' he said, brushing her parted lips with his, and then walked away as Luci emerged from the stables.

Jake's parents were most concerned to hear that Laura had had a fall, and, although she tried to assure them it had been nothing, Sophia insisted that she rest for the remainder of the day.

'It is the shock that we do not always realise we have sustained,' she said, as they sat at lunch, in a delightful conservatory, overlooking the gardens at the back of the house. 'Is that not so, Nico? Laura must take care of herself.'

'I think Giacomo can be left to ensure that Laura does not overdo things, Sophia,' Count Lombardi replied smoothly, and Laura felt a renewed sense of duplicity for the ambiguity of her position.

'Your—your son—has been very kind,' she began, ignoring the intensity of Jake's eyes upon her. 'But—but really—I think my daughter——'

'Ah, yes,' Jake's mother broke into her stammered attempt at confession, with polite dismissal. 'We know your daughter, Laura. You must be very proud of her. She is a most successful model, is she not?'

'I—well, yes.'

Laura was taken aback, but, although she looked at Jake for inspiration, his expression was now unreadable.

'Yes, we met her in Rome,' went on Sophia Lombardi affably. She looked at her son. 'Giacomo introduced us.'

Laura swallowed. She suddenly realised how little she knew about her daughter's association with this family.

How little she knew about these people at all. For all she knew, they might condone their son's behaviour. And if even half what the gutter Press wrote was to be believed, sexual relationships, of one kind or another, were common enough among people of his background.

The maid came to clear their plates, and Laura decided not to say any more. If the Lombardis knew that she was Julie's mother, then maybe her daughter was expected to arrive that afternoon. She hadn't forgotten Jake's avoidance of an answer earlier, even if subsequent events had tended to overshadow its importance. She could only wait and see. She had discovered she didn't have the stomach to pursue it.

She escaped to her room after lunch, grateful that she had an excuse for doing so. But every sound she heard, every footfall outside her door, had her heart beating wildly, and she eventually gave up trying to rest, and went out on to the balcony instead.

It was very peaceful out there. The only sounds were those of the birds and insects, with the occasional drone of an aircraft to remind her this was the twentieth century. Everything else had an agelessness about it, not least the *castello* itself, and she found it incredible to believe she was actually here, a guest in such surroundings. It seemed a long way from Burnfoot, she reflected wistfully, and not just in miles.

She sighed. Or course, she would be going home tomorrow. Whatever happened—Julie notwithstanding—she had no intention of prolonging her stay. Which reminded her of the argument she had had with Jake earlier. She couldn't help wondering if she would have had the courage to leave today, if she hadn't fallen off the horse, and made such an idiot of herself. It was encouraging to believe she would, but now she was not so sure that she would have gone through with it. After all, if she had managed to ride back to the *castello*, she would still have had to find a way to get to Pisa. And what excuse could she have given Jake's parents? It wasn't their fault that she found their son so disturbing.

Her lips tightened. It was easy to be brave in the heat of the moment. But accomplishing her boast was something else again. Apart from anything else, she didn't even have a return ticket to London. A major drawback to your hosts' having their own private plane, she thought ruefully.

It was seven o'clock before Laura left the balcony to prepare for dinner. The afternoon had given way to evening, and the sun was leaving caverns of darkness in its wake. The valley was settling down for the night, and tiny pinpricks of light were appearing between the trees. Smoke drifted from the few farmhouses that nestled in the valley, and a solitary bell was tolling from the church in the village.

But apart from this evidence of human habitation, there had been no sign of any activity at the *castello*. Although Laura had spent the afternoon waiting for the sound of a car to prove that Julie had arrived, she was disappointed. Her daughter was not coming, she acknowledged flatly. Had she ever believed she was?

But she stopped thinking at that point. She knew that if she ever conceded she had had serious doubts about Jake's intentions before she'd left London there would be no living with herself. And if she ever allowed herself the luxury of admitting that she had come here, knowing that her daughter was unlikely to return from Los Angeles, and fly straight on to Italy, she was lost. For her own sanity, she had to go on believing. Anything else was madness…

CHAPTER TWELVE

LAURA packed her case before she went to bed. It was a small gesture, but she felt better after she had done it. It proved, to herself at least, that she meant what she said, and that was important to her.

Not that anyone was likely to offer any objections, she admitted painfully. She had thanked the Lombardis for their hospitality before coming upstairs, and if they had had any doubts about the arrangements they had been too polite to say so. Besides, she argued, climbing between real silk sheets, that she noticed had been changed after only one night's usage, she had only come for the weekend, and it was Monday tomorrow.

As for Jake, she preferred not to think about him. In spite of the fact that he had been waiting for her when she'd gone downstairs, and had wanted her reassurance that she had suffered no after-effects of her fall, she had left him in no doubt as to her feelings. Although it had been difficult to speak to him in his parents' company, her accusing eyes, and the determined way she had shaken off his hand, when he'd attempted to escort her into dinner, had been pointed enough; and Jake was no innocent. He knew exactly what was wrong with her, and during the meal that followed his manner had grown increasingly withdrawn. Only when he'd met her gaze across the table, had she glimpsed a little of what he was feeling, but she had refused to be distracted by his brooding contemplation. It was all his fault, she told herself tensely. He had tricked her into coming here, and now he had to face the consequences.

All the same, she couldn't entirely exclude herself from all responsibility. As she lay there, watching the curtains moving in the draught from the balcony doors, which she had left slightly ajar, she had to admit that she hadn't offered much resistance, when Jake had told her that Julie wasn't coming with them. She could have insisted on spending the night in London, and waiting until her daughter was able to accompany her, but she hadn't. And if she was perfectly honest, she would have to say that she had given in, as much because of her own guilty attraction to Jake as in response to his persuasion.

She sniffed, and rolled on to her side, as a fat tear overspilled her eye, and dropped on to the pillow. It was such a beautiful night, the moonlight shining through the crack in the curtains, giving the room a pearly luminescence. It was a night for love, she thought unhappily. And wasn't it a pity that the only man she might have loved was too young, too rich—and involved with her own daughter...?

She thought at first she was dreaming. When she felt the depression of the mattress, and a warm body curled, sensually, about her own, she responded with instinctive willingness. She had been thinking about Jake, and it wasn't the first time she had had dreams of this sort. Indeed, she seldom slept without dreaming about Jake these days, and, although in daylight it might seem pathetic, at night she was incapable of denying her fantasies.

But this was different. As she turned in his arms, and felt the heat of his naked body, she was puzzled. The strength of his embrace was so real, so physical, that she could actually feel the taut muscles that covered his belly, could even smell the musky scent of his skin. Always before, the dream had given way to substance; when she'd reached for him, he had melted; when she'd tried to hold on to him, he'd been gone. That was why she had always awakened, hot and frustrated, torn by emotions she had had no hope of fulfilling.

But not now. Now, she could wind her arms around him. She could press herself against him, and feel the instantaneous response of his body in return. Oh, God, she thought wildly, was she going mad? Was his arousal of her body the previous day responsible for this change in her perception?

But when his lips found hers, any previous perceptions fled. This was no dream, she realised, even while her mouth opened helplessly beneath the hungry possession of his. This was real. This was actually happening. Jake was in her bed, as naked as the day he was born, and she was coiled about him, as if she never wanted to let him go.

Reason was slow in coming, but, when it did, she fought to get free. Even though, seconds before, she had let him thrust his wet tongue into her mouth, she beat at him now with her fists, until he was forced to lift his head.

'Let go of me!' she choked, trying to wriggle away from him. 'You have no right to do this!'

'No?' Jake resisted her attempts to escape him without too much effort. 'I rather thought you were glad to see me.'

'Me?' Laura panted. 'You're crazy!'

'Well, a few moments ago——'

'A few moments ago, I was asleep,' she retorted,

aware that her struggles had driven her nightshirt up above her thighs. 'Jake, let go of me. Please.'

Jake shifted, but he didn't release her. He simply drew her closer, opening his legs and trapping her between them. It enabled him to free one hand to smooth the tumbled hair back from her temple, to brush her quivering lips with his thumb, and scrape his nail against her teeth.

'Keep still,' he said, and in the moonlight she could see the sensual twist of his lips, as he took every conceivable liberty with her body. Ignoring her frustrated efforts to fight him, he allowed his hand to trail down over her breasts, and her uncontrollable response made him smile.

'This—this is—unforgivable,' she gulped, using her anger to sustain her. But she knew that the longer he held her, the longer he played with her treacherous emotions, the less likely it was that she would win this unequal contest. One hand in the small of her back was urging her against his tumescent maleness, and the heat of him against her groin was driving all coherent thoughts out of her head.

'You want me,' he said, inching the nightshirt over her midriff.

'No——'

'Yes.' He sighed with satisfaction as the offending garment flipped over her breasts, and their fullness was exposed to his hungry gaze. He took the swollen globes into his hands, and squeezed them sensuously. 'Now, tell me about it,' he breathed, stroking their proud crests with his thumb. *'Ah, cara, sono belli, vero?'*

'I don't know—I don't know what you're saying,' protested Laura fretfully, but the possessive touch of his hands on her body was rapidly making everything else of little importance. He had removed the nightshirt completely now, and the fine dark hair that filmed his chest was disturbingly pleasurable against her skin. It arrowed down below his navel to the cluster of rough curls that cradled his sex. And as he moved, she involuntarily arched against him.

'I was only telling you you're beautiful,' he whispered huskily, taking one of her fluttering hands, and pressing it over his pulsating shaft. He groaned. *'Molta bella,'* he got out thickly. 'I want to be a part of you.'

'Oh, Jake,' she breathed unsteadily, but it was no longer an objection. The silky heat of his arousal against her hand had banished any lingering thought of resisting him. When his hand slid between her legs, she didn't try to stop him. She wanted him to touch her there. Her flesh was crying out for the quivering release he had given her the day before. But when his lips slanted over hers, and his tongue plunged aggressively into her mouth, she knew she wanted more. She could smell him; she could taste him; the musky male scent of his body was driving her insane. She could feel her readiness on his hands—readiness for him.

She wasn't aware of making any sound, but when Jake removed his hand she must have done, because he soothed her with a kiss. 'Be patient, *amorissima'* he said, though his own voice was far from controlled. He parted her legs with one hairy thigh, and moved until the throbbing pulse of his manhood was nudging her tight core. 'Let me love you,' he added hoarsely, and unable to restrain himself any longer, he thrust urgently inside her.

Laura gasped. She couldn't help herself. It was so long since she had known a man's body, so long since Keith had taken her virginity. It was as if she had never known a man before, and Jake was so big that he couldn't help bruising her.

'Laura! *Cara!*' he exclaimed, covering her hot face with kisses. '*Mi dispiace*, I am sorry! Did I hurt you?'

But Laura was finding that any pain she had felt was disappearing beneath the overwhelming pleasure of feeling his taut strength stretching the yielding source of her femininity. 'Oh, no,' she breathed, hardly aware of saying anything, as his body moved and swelled inside her. 'Oh, no, you're not hurting me,' she added, as her long legs curled about his hips. 'Oh, God, that feels so good! Jake—please! Don't stop now.'

It was as if she had been sleeping, as if every dormant nerve was awakening to the amazing awareness of her own sexuality. She had never felt like this before, never imagined she could feel such a tumult of emotion. She wound herself about him, meeting his invasion with an eagerness she simply couldn't deny. She no longer thought about who he was, or where they were, or anything outside this room, and this bed, and the satisfying thrust of Jake's hard body...

Of course, she had to think eventually. No matter how dramatic her personal fulfilment might have been, sooner or later, reality had to raise its ugly head. And it was ugly, she thought dully, as the wild heights of enchantment Jake had lifted her to, dropped back into a well of despair.

Oh, it was easy to be wise after the event, easy to berate herself for allowing it to happen, for letting Jake do what she had sworn he never would. But, the truth was, she was far too vulnerable where he was concerned, and he had known that, and used it to his own advantage.

And, as the ripples of delight faded away, and were

replaced by increasing waves of remorse, a chilling self-abasement sowed the seeds of disenchantment. What had she done? she asked herself bitterly. What kind of a woman was she? What kind of a mother, to make love with her daughter's lover!

A groan of nausea rose inside her, and, half afraid she might lose control of her stomach, as well as everything else, she struggled to get free of him. But Jake was a solid weight on top of her. Lying between her splayed legs, with his face buried in the moist hollow between her breasts, he was apparently quite content to prolong his pleasure in the moment. However, when she began to shift beneath him, she distinctly felt his immediate arousal.

'God—*no*!' she choked, as her own body quickened in response. Not again. But she realised she had to get away from him, and quickly, before he used her own weakness against her.

'Basta! Cosa fai?' he protested sleepily, as she made a superhuman effort to wriggle off the bed, and she wondered, somewhat painfully, if he was confusing her with someone else. Did he sleep with so many women that he couldn't keep track of their nationality? Dear God, this was a nightmare! If only she could wake up.

But when Jake lifted his head and saw her, there was only satisfaction in the dark sensual gaze he bestowed upon her. *'Bella Laura,'* he said, confounding all her fears about identity. *'Mi amore, ti voglio——'*

Laura's heart pounded. She would not have been human if she had not felt some response to the husky resonance of his words. When his mouth brushed her temples, his tongue feathering over her eyelids, they fluttered closed. And she could feel herself beginning to drift, the sensuous touch of his lips and hands a mindless provocation. Where was the harm? her senses cried. Why shouldn't she just give in?

Not again!

Forcing her eyes open, Laura turned her head away from Jake's questing tongue. 'No,' she said harshly. 'No, don't touch me! How—how can you do this? You're going to marry—Julie!'

'Che?' Jake's reaction was vehement, and he came up on his elbows, to glare down at her accusingly. 'What are you saying?' he demanded, and when she would have used the freedom he had given her to put the width of the bed between them he straddled her with his knees. Then, imprisoning her between his strong thighs, he said savagely, 'No!' And, although the word sounded more Italian than English, its meaning was unmistakable. 'No, I am not going to marry Julie,' he repeated emphatically. 'I do not know where in hell you got that from, but believe me, it is not going to happen!'

The postcard was lying face-up on the mat, when Laura opened the cottage door. It was a colourful postcard, the picture showing a view of the Hollywood hills, with the famous HOLLYWOOD sign, depicting the movie capital of the world, in the foreground.

It was from Julie, of course, thought Laura tensely, bending unwillingly to pick up the card. And she ought to be flattered that, even on such an exciting mission, her daughter hadn't forgotten her.

But, it was the last thing she needed at this moment. A reminder of where her daughter was, and what she was doing, and why she hadn't spent the weekend at Castellombardi.

Now Laura lifted her case into the tiny hallway, and inched herself round it, so that she could close the door.

Then, she collapsed somewhat tearfully back against it, allowing the pent-up emotions of the past twenty-four hours to have their way. It was so good to be back in her own home again, and without the postcard in her hand she could almost have convinced herself she was content.

But the postcard had changed things. No matter how unwelcome it might be, it had served to bring reality back into focus. She couldn't escape what she had done. She couldn't erase the events of the past forty-eight hours. What had happened, had happened, and she was going to have to live with it.

She closed her eyes, as a wave of weariness swept over her. She was tired, so tired. And it wasn't because Jake had exhausted her—not directly, anyway. She sighed, remembering the terrible row they had had over Julie. Whatever feelings Jake might have had for her, the bitterness of the words they had exchanged must have changed that, too. He hadn't appeared at breakfast. He hadn't driven her to the airport in Pisa. Indeed, she hadn't seen him since he'd stormed out of the bedroom the night before.

God! She pushed herself away from the door, and walked heavily into the cold living-room. While she was away, she had turned the heating off, and although it should have been warm enough she felt chilled right through. But she had the feeling that the coldness she felt came from within, not without, and no crackling fire or clunking radiators would make a scrap of difference.

She looked at the postcard again. She supposed she ought to see what Julie had to say, but she was loath to look at her daughter's handwriting. Not yet, she thought tightly, setting the postcard down on the mantelshelf. She needed a hot drink, before she could face that.

She took some time, watering her plants, and washing the coffee-cup she had used early on Saturday morning. Even that reminded her of the excitement she had felt when the chauffeur-driven limousine had called for her, and it took the utmost effort not to give in to tears again. She felt so lost, so empty; and she thought how naïve she had been to think that what she had felt when Keith had left her had meant anything at all. Then, she had been more concerned about what her friends would say, and learning she was pregnant had aroused feelings of panic, not unrequited love.

But this was different, *so* different. Now, the idea that she might never see Jake again filled her with despair, and she didn't know how she was going to survive it. There were times when she actually wondered whether it wouldn't have been better to know that Jake was going to marry Julie. At least, then, she would have stood a chance of seeing him again. And, although that might sound like the ravings of a madwoman, desperation came in many guises.

If only they could have met one another, without Julie's being involved, she thought now, filling the kettle, and plugging it in. Only, of course, there was no way someone like her would ever have encountered a man like him. It simply didn't happen. She was a north-country schoolteacher, whose only claim to fame was that the children seemed to like her. Well, other people's children, she ac- knowledged ruefully. She hadn't had such success with her own.

Nevertheless, the chances of a middle-aged teacher meeting a man like Giacomo Lombardi were virtually non-existent. She simply didn't move in the same kind of social circles, and without Julie's intervention their paths would never have crossed.

But they had, and, according to Jake, he had been attracted to her from the very beginning. Laura shook her head, scrubbing an errant tear from her cheek. Well, that was easy for him to say, she thought bitterly. How could he say anything else, when he'd just spent the last half-hour seducing the woman he was expressing his feelings to? And a man like him could be attracted to any number of women. It didn't mean anything. Not really. It was gratifying; flattering even; but it was just empty talk.

And she hadn't taken him seriously, she told herself firmly. She had known all along that any relationship between them couldn't last. Aside from everything else, there was Julie to consider, and Laura would do nothing to hurt her daughter.

Which was the reason she and Jake had had that almighty row, she remembered, with a shiver of dismay. So far as he was concerned, she was just using her daughter as a reason for denying what was between them. She didn't really care about Julie, Jake had told her contemptuously. She was just afraid of life, and Julie was a convenient scapegoat.

Of course, Laura had denied it. She had told him what Julie had told her, and, even if he hadn't believed her, it had opened up an unbreachable gulf between them. Besides, she wasn't sure she wanted the kind of relationship he had been talking about anyway. She was a conventional woman, with conventional needs. She simply wasn't the type to exist in that surreal world between what she knew and what she didn't.

Oh, he had told her he loved her. While he was making love to her, he had told her so in his own language; and, although Laura was no linguist, some words were unmistakable. But it meant nothing. In the throes of sex-

ual release, people said lots of things they didn't mean.
She had done it herself. Although what she actually had
said, when he had driven her to clutch at his hips and
cry out in ecstasy, she would rather not remember. Suf-
fice it to say, she had betrayed everything she had ever
believed in. She had given herself to Jake, wantonly and
shamefully, and he had been angry because she had
fallen back on the precepts of a childhood she had lived
with for almost forty years.

The kettle boiled, and she made herself a cup of instant coffee. Then, after giving the garden an uninter-
ested glance, she carried her cup into the living-room. It
was strange, she thought, settling herself in an armchair
beside the fireplace. In just three days, everything looked
totally different to her. The cottage; the garden; even this
room—which used to be so familiar to her—had lost its
appeal. She felt like a stranger in her own home. Well,
she was a stranger, she reflected painfully. A stranger to
herself at least.

But it was no use, she rebuked herself impatiently.
This was where she lived, where she belonged. Meeting
Jake—even *sleeping* with Jake—had only been a minor
deviation. It wasn't as if he wanted to marry her, or
anything old-fashioned like that. The way he had reacted, when she had suggested that Julie wanted to marry
him, had convinced her of that. An affair, yes. That was
something else. But how could she have an affair with
him, knowing that when it was over she would be left
to pick up the pieces of her life *alone*?

The postcard mocked her from its position on the
mantelpiece, and, pushing herself up from the chair, she
took it down. Hollywood, she thought ruefully. What
must the postman have thought?

Turning it over, she checked that it was addressed to

her. Yes, there was her name, and there was Julie's signature. There was no mistake. The card was for her. So
why not read it? She was going to have to eventually.

She frowned.

Hi Mum. Here I am in Beverly Hills, and loving every
minute of it. The weather's great, the hotel's fantastic,
and I've met so many gorgeous men that I've lost
count. David—that's David Conti, the producer—he's
been terrific. He's introduced me to ever so many important people—and he's single! He thinks I should
stay out here, and I'm really considering it. Sorry
about the Italian trip, and all that, but I don't suppose
you were too disappointed. You didn't want to go
anyway, and I'm sure Jake let you down lightly. Will
write when I have time...

Julie's signature was squeezed at the bottom, and
Laura bent her head towards the card to make sure it
was her daughter's name that was signed there. Of
course it was. Who else was likely to write to her from
Hollywood? Besides, it all fitted—except the bit about
the trip. She swallowed. Good lord, didn't Julie know
she had gone to Italy without her? Had Jake been expected to cancel the arrangements?

Julie hadn't put a date on the card, but as another
thought occurred to her Laura tried to decipher the post-
mark. After all, the card had travelled all the way from
California. For it to be lying on her mat, it had to have
been posted several days ago. But how many days?

After coping with the fact that the United States re-
versed the date and the month of the year, Laura eventually worked out that the card had been posted in Los
Angeles more than ten days ago. Which prob-

ably meant Julie had left for the States before Jake had telephoned her.

She breathed a little faster. So he had been expected to tell her the trip was off. So far as Julie was concerned, it hadn't happened. But, could she seriously be considering staying in California? What about her career? What about—Jake?

CHAPTER THIRTEEN

THAT question haunted Laura in the days to come, days that dragged interminably, until it was time to go back to school. There was no one she could discuss it with, no one she could confide in. Even Jess was unavailable, having taken advantage of the mid-term break to have a short holiday with her husband.

Not that Laura was convinced she would have confided in Jess anyway. After all, she had only told her friend she was accompanying Julie on a visit to her proposed in-laws. She had said virtually nothing about the fact that Jake was going with them. Oh, it had probably been taken for granted, she realised that, but what would Jess think if she told her she'd gone with him alone?

Well, she could imagine what Jess would think, Laura conceded. What anyone would think, given the circumstances. That she was desperate for a man, she acknowledged glumly. That even though she had known her daughter was away, she had jumped at the chance to take her place.

She refused to consider why Jake had chosen to deceive her. It seemed fairly obvious to her. After his abortive trip to the cottage, he had obviously given up the idea of seeing her again, but this opportunity had been too good to miss. And she had made it so easy for him—believing his ready lies, and saying nothing to embarrass his parents...

Back at school, it was easier to pretend that nothing had changed. There, no one but Mark knew she had spent a weekend away. And he didn't know all the details. She had simply said she was going to stay with Julie.

Nevertheless, he did ask her about her trip when he caught her in the staff-room one morning. 'I hope you didn't spend the whole weekend running after Julie,' he said, risking another rebuff, but for once Laura couldn't meet his eyes.

'No. No, I didn't,' she said, gathering her books together, and preparing to depart. 'It—er—it was very pleasant actually. A nice—break.'

'Well, good.' To her dismay, Mark accompanied her out of the door. 'It's about time she started looking after you for a change. Does this mean you'll be seeing more of one another from now on? I must say Mother thinks you should.'

Laura couldn't prevent a spurt of irritation that Mark should have been discussing her and Julie with his mother, but it didn't last. If that was all that he had to talk about, why get annoyed about it? They probably had her best interests at heart. Or Mark did, anyway. She wasn't so sure about Mrs Leith.

'As—as a matter of fact, Julie may be going to work in California,' she admitted, not knowing exactly why she should want to tell him that, and Mark frowned.

'You mean—on a modelling assignment?'

'Well—no.' Laura wondered if she simply wanted to say it out loud, to prove it to herself. 'I think she'd like to become an actress. You know: films and all that.'

Mark stared at her. 'You mean, she's going out to California on the off chance that she might——?'

'No.' Laura sighed, wishing now that she hadn't confided in him. 'Not on the off chance. She's been invited to have a screen test. Apparently David Conti——'

'David Conti?' Mark arched his sandy eyebrows. 'She knows David Conti?'

Laura could feel the beginning of a headache starting in her temples. 'Yes,' she said wearily. 'I believe she was introduced to him in London. But now, I'll——'

'David Conti!' Mark said the name again and shook his head. 'My God! I wonder how she met him.'

Laura knew she should just leave it there. She wasn't in the mood for long discussions, but unwillingly Mark had piqued her interest. 'Why?' she asked, giving in to the curiosity he had kindled. 'Who is David Conti? I don't think I've heard of him.'

'Of course you have.' Mark frowned now, evidently trying to think of a way to spark her memory. 'That film we saw at the Gallery, about six months ago. You remember? God, I can't recall what it was called, but it had won an award at Cannes. A black comedy, about eastern European rapprochement. Very topical, as it's turned out. Damn, what was it called?'

'*Social Graces?*' suggested Laura doubtfully, and Mark pounced on her words.

'Yes. That was it. *Social Graces.* Well, Conti produced that film—and many others, of course. He's an Italian, I believe, though he spends most of his time in the United States.'

Laura's mouth went dry. 'An Italian?'

'Yes.' Mark nodded. 'Why? Did you meet him?'

'Heavens, no.' But Laura could feel the betraying colour deepening in her cheeks. 'I—was just surprised, that's all. Julie didn't mention that he was an Italian.'

'Is it important?' Mark was curious now, but Laura decided she had said enough.

'Only to Julie,' she managed lightly, pretending to straighten the pile of exercise books in her hands. 'Now,

I really must go. My third-years will be climbing the walls!'

'Will I see you this week?' Mark called, as she started down the corridor, and Laura turned back rather reluctantly.

'Maybe—maybe next week,' she said, forcing an apologetic smile. 'With being away, I seem to have such a lot to catch up on at home. And you know how tiring housework can be.'

Nevertheless, she half wished she had agreed to go out with Mark when she got up on Saturday morning. The weekend stretched ahead of her, stark and uninspiring, and tackling household chores seemed the least attractive part of it.

Not that they took long. Despite what she had said to Mark, since her return from Italy she had had plenty of time to clean the house. Until she started back at school, it had been one way to fill all the hours in the day. He couldn't know that the last two weeks had seemed the longest two weeks in her life. It was hard to believe it was only fourteen days since she had left the cottage to go to the airport, in the limousine that had been hired for her. So much seemed to have happened in that time, and falling in love with Jake was no small part of it.

She was working in the garden, when she heard footsteps coming along the path that ran along the side of the cottage. She wasn't expecting anybody. She had even refrained from ringing Jess, because she hadn't wanted to get involved in awkward explanations. She assumed she would have to tell her friend one day. But, hopefully, not yet.

Now, however, she got up from her weeding, and looked rather apprehensively towards the sound of the footsteps. Her heart leapt briefly at the memory of another Saturday, when Jake had arrived so unexpectedly, but somehow she knew her visitor wasn't him. The foot-steps sounded too feminine, she thought uneasily. And although it might be Mrs Forrest, she wasn't really convinced.

Even so, she still felt a sense of shock, when Julie appeared around the corner of the house. The suspicion that it might be her daughter had already occurred to her but, nevertheless, seeing her doubts realised still caused a flutter of panic.

Not that Julie seemed at all unfriendly, as she came to the edge of the small sunlit patio, and subjected her mother to a resigned stare. On the contrary, she looked rather pleased with herself, and her attitude towards Laura was as patronising as ever.

'Whatever do you look like?' she exclaimed, making the older woman instantly aware of her mud-smeared dungarees, and sweat-streaked face. 'Don't you ever feel like wearing something—attractive?'

Laura stiffened. 'Sometimes,' she said, her own guilt not quite sufficient to quell her indignation. 'I'm gardening, Julie. You don't get dressed up to do gardening. You should try it yourself and see.'

'No, thanks.' Julie changed the green suede bag she was carrying from one shoulder to the other, and grimaced. She flicked an insect from the skirt of her striped crêpe suit, and visibly preened at the satisfying length of shapely leg below its short hem. 'I've got much better things to do.'

'Really?'

Laura found she couldn't keep the cynicism out of her voice, and Julie's expression hardened. 'Yes, really,' she said, tapping an annoyed foot. 'So—are you going to come indoors and offer me a cup of tea, or what? This is just a flying visit, I'm afraid. I've got to be back in London tomorrow morning. But I thought I ought to see you, before I go.'

'Go?' Laura blinked. 'Go where?'

'Back to Los Angeles, of course!' exclaimed Julie, glancing impatiently up at the sun, and then backing into the shade of the cottage doorway. 'Didn't you get my card?'

'Your card?' Laura stared blankly at her daughter, and then gathered herself sufficiently to follow her into the kitchen. 'Well—yes. Yes, I got your card.' She moistened her dry lips. 'But I didn't—you didn't——'

'I did tell you about David, didn't I?' Julie broke in, somewhat irritably. 'David Conti? The producer?' she added, emphasising the words, as she would to a rather backward child. 'I know I told you about having a screen test, when I phoned you about going to Italy. Oh—sorry about that, by the way.' She pulled a wry face. 'Still, I don't think I was cut out to be a *contessa*!'

Laura reached for the kettle, but it was an automatic action. She was hardly aware of what she was doing, and only when it started to hiss did she realise she hadn't filled it with water before plugging it in.

But had Julie really said she wasn't going to marry Jake? she wondered distractedly, almost scalding her hand as she took off the lid to fill the kettle. It certainly sounded that way, but she had been wrong before.

'Are you listening to me?'

Julie's complaining tone reminded Laura that she had indeed been allowing her mind to wander, and swallowing her confusion, she managed to shake her head. 'I'm sorry,' she said, steadying the rattle of the cups, as she took them out of the cupboard. 'I was just—so surprised, when you said you'd—changed your mind.'

'Changed my mind?' Julie frowned now, and Laura expelled the breath she had been holding rather quickly.

'Well—yes,' she said, feeling the heat invading her throat. 'I mean—you did say you wanted to marry Jake, didn't you?'

Julie sniffed. 'Oh, him!' She lifted her slim shoulders. 'I haven't seen him since before I left for the States.'

'No, but——'

'Oh, *Mum*!' Julie looked angry now. 'I'd rather not talk about Jake Lombardi, if you don't mind. Let's just say he and I have very little in common. I was wrong. I admit it. Let that be an end to it.'

Laura drew her lower lip between her teeth. 'But—I don't understand. I thought—I mean, you said he was the one!'

'Oh, God!' Julie groaned. 'Haven't you ever made a mistake?' Then her eyes glinted. 'Of course you have. How could we forget?'

'Julie——'

'All right, all right. That was below the belt. I'm sorry. But talking about Jake Lombardi brings out the worst in me. I thought he was in love with me, if you must know. But he wasn't. End of story.'

'He *wasn't*?' Laura knew she was risking a row with her daughter, but she had to pursue it. 'But—he did invite you to go to Italy with him.'

'Did he?' Julie didn't sound convinced. 'I suspect that invitation emanated from his parents. In any event, I don't think he had any intention of following it through.'

'You don't?' Laura could hear the kettle starting to boil behind her, but she paid it no heed.

'No.' Julie flung herself into a chair at the table, and propped her photogenic features on her knuckles. 'You see, it turns out that David is Jake's second cousin, or some distant relation like that. My guess is that Jake used that connection to get me off his back.'

'I see.'

Laura at last heard the kettle boiling, and turned to make the tea. It was quite a relief to do so, although her mind was still buzzing with what she had heard. Had Jake really arranged for Julie to have a screen test? Was the invitation to Italy intended for her all along?

'He was too old for me anyway,' Julie said, behind her, and Laura turned. 'He was,' Julie added broodingly, tracing the grain of the pinewood table with a crimson fingernail. 'I mean, you must have noticed what he was like, when he was here. Telling me what I should or shouldn't do. Trailing me round all those ancient monuments!'

Laura filled the teapot, and set it on its stand. 'You—you did say he was—old-fashioned,' she ventured. 'When—when you rang to say he wanted to—to meet me——'

'Oh, that was all my idea,' retorted Julie carelessly, helping herself to the milk. 'I mean—he was the most attractive man I'd ever met. And the richest, if it comes to that. And I'd heard that Italians place a lot of importance on the family. So—knowing what a homely little person you are, I thought for once I'd take advantage of the fact. But—it didn't work.'

Laura was staggered. 'You mean—it wasn't Jake's idea to meet me? You weren't on the point of getting engaged, or anything?'

'I never said we were.' Viewing her mother's shocked face, Julie shifted a little resentfully. 'I might have implied...' Her voice trailed away. 'Anyway, I don't see that it matters. It's not you who's been dumped, is it?'

Laura couldn't take it in. 'Are you saying that when you brought Jake here, you weren't already lovers?'

'Lovers?' Julie scoffed. 'What dear old-fashioned words you use, Mum! We weren't sleeping together, if that's what you want to know. Though I don't see why you're asking. It's nothing to do with you, is it?'

Laura sat down rather abruptly. It was all too much to take. Suddenly, the things Jake had said made sense, and she felt a searing pain for her own stupidity. Yet how could she have known he was telling the truth? She was Julie's mother. It was only natural that she should have believed her daughter. But that didn't alter the fact that she had probably hurt him deeply. That, whatever his intentions, it was her he had wanted.

'Are you all right?'

Julie was gazing at her a little curiously now, and Laura realised her feelings must be showing. But what could she expect, when her whole world had been turned upside-down? she thought bleakly. Oh, God! If only she'd known!

'You look awfully pale,' Julie continued, though the concern was tinged with impatience now. 'I expect it's with working outside, in that hot sun. You'd better start looking after yourself, you know. You're not as young as you used to be.'

Laura expelled a trembling breath. 'I'm all right.'

'Oh, well...' Julie was easily convinced. 'As long as you know what you're doing. So—aren't you going to ask me why I'm going back to California? You seem more concerned with Jake than how successful my screen test was.'

Laura's fists clenched on the table. The temptation to tell her daughter why that should be so was almost irresistible. But old habits died hard, and Laura still had no wish to hurt her. Besides, it was too late now to regret the past. That interlude at Castellombardi would remain her secret. Not a guilty one any more, just a poignant memory...

Almost a week later, Laura found Mrs Forrest waiting for her when she got home from school.

It had been another long week, enlivened only by the fact that it was one week nearer the summer holidays. And, from Laura's point of view, the holidays themselves would give her far too much time to brood about her mistakes. But she was hoping to get away for a couple of weeks at least, and she was clinging to the belief that time would heal all wounds.

However, finding Mrs Forrest sitting in her living-room, when she opened the cottage door, dispelled any personal considerations. Something was wrong, she thought. She knew it. Mrs Forrest's anxious expression, as she got to her feet, convinced her of that.

'Is it Julie?' she asked, dry-mouthed, only capable of one conclusion. Something must have happened to her daughter. She had no one else.

'No——' Mrs Forrest put down the handbag she had been clutching on her knee, and took an involuntary step towards her. 'There was a phone call, Mrs Fox. From—er—from Italy. The caller asked if I would deliver the message personally.'

Laura's knees sagged, and she reached for the back of a chair to support herself. 'From—Italy?' she got out unevenly. 'But—I—who——?'

'It was a lady, Mrs Fox,' said the cleaning woman eagerly. 'I think she said her name was Lombardy, is that right? Anyway, she said you'd know who it was. She wants you to call her back. Straight away.'

Laura caught her breath. 'Are you sure?'

'Oh, yes.' Mrs Forrest nodded. 'She said immediately.
That was the word she used—immediately.'

'No. I mean—about the name? Are you sure it was
Lombardi?' Laura stared at her.

'Oh, yes.' Mrs Forrest was adamant. 'That was the
name all right. You said it just like she did.' She bent
and picked up the pad beside the phone. 'Look, here's
her number. I jotted it down ever so carefully. She said
you can dial it direct. Marvellous, isn't it? Being able to
call somebody all those miles away.'

Laura nodded now, her mind busy with wondering
why Jake's mother should be calling her. For it had to
be Sophia Lombardi. She was the only female Lombardi
she knew—apart from Luci, of course.

Pressing her lips together, she tried to adopt what she
hoped was a casual expression. 'Well—thank you, Mrs
Forrest,' she murmured, glancing uneasily towards the
phone. 'I—er—I'll call her right away.'

'Oh...' Mrs Forrest looked a little disappointed now.
Clearly she had hoped Laura would be so anxious to
make the call that she might forget she was there. 'Then
I'd better go, hadn't I?'

Laura managed a smile. 'I do appreciate your staying.
To deliver the message, I mean.'

'You wouldn't like me to stay on?' suggested Mrs
Forrest hopefully. 'If it's bad news...'

'I'm sure it won't be,' said Laura, more confidently
than she felt. 'But thank you anyway.'

With the door closed behind the cleaning woman,
Laura was able to breathe a little more easily. But not
for long. Whatever reason the Contessa had for ringing
her, she would not have done so unless it was something

important. But what? Laura's brain simply refused to work.

A maid answered the phone to Laura's ring, and, although the woman's English was poor, a mention of the Contessa's name soon brought Sophia Lombardi to the phone.

'Laura?' she exclaimed, and hearing the relief in her voice, Laura's knees gave out on her. 'I'm so glad you felt able to return my call.'

'Um—not at all.' Laura sank down on to the arm of the chair. 'I—er—what can I do for you?'

'You did not mind me ringing?' the Contessa persisted anxiously. 'I realise it is something of an imposition, but I did not know what else to do.'

'No?' Laura shook her head bewilderedly. 'Really—it's not a problem.'

'You're very kind.' The Contessa let out her breath on a wispy sigh. 'But, even so, I am not sure I have done the right thing in calling you.'

Laura tried to contain her impatience. 'Why?' she asked, as a thousand different reasons presented themselves. 'I—please—is something wrong?'

'You could say that.' The Italian woman sounded rueful now. 'I—it's Jake, you see. He's—had an accident——'

'An accident!'

'—and I'm very much afraid he doesn't want to get better.'

CHAPTER FOURTEEN

LAURA came out of the airport at Pisa to find the Count's chauffeur waiting for her. She recognised the man immediately, not least because of his distinctive livery, though his good-humoured features and luxuriant moustache were surprisingly familiar. Probably because it was he who had brought her back to the airport after the shattering weekend at Castellombardi, Laura reflected tensely. There was nothing about that weekend she could forget.

'*Signora,*' he greeted her politely, installing her in the back of the limousine, as before, and depositing her single suitcase in the car's huge boot. '*Come sta?*'

'Oh…' Laura knew what that meant. 'Er—*bene,*' she murmured awkwardly. And then, with a tight smile, '*Grazie.*'

Nevertheless, she hoped the man wouldn't imagine she had taken a crash course in Italian. The few words she did understand had mostly been picked up from Jake, and in her present state of nerves it was difficult enough to remember her own language, let alone his.

However, after ensuring that his passenger was comfortable, the chauffeur seemed more concerned with negotiating the traffic around the airport than in conducting a conversation, and Laura was able to relax. Or at least try to, she amended, torturing the strap of the handbag in her lap. But, for the first time since speaking to Jake's mother, she felt she was actually making some progress towards her destination, and she forced herself to accept that for the moment there was nothing more she could do.

But it had been a terrible twenty-four hours since the Contessa's call. For the first time in her life, Laura had regretted the fact that she lived in the north-east of England. It had been impossible for her to get a flight to London the night before, and although she had caught the first available plane this morning she had still had problems about getting on a flight to Pisa. It was Saturday, and approaching the height of the tourist season, and all morning flights were full. In consequence, she had had to wait until the middle of the afternoon before she'd been able to continue her journey, and the flight to Pisa had seemed the longest flight of her life.

But she was here now, she told herself steadyingly, feeling the coolness of the leather squabs against her back. Until they arrived at Castellombardi, there was nothing she could do, so she might as well try and rest, and enjoy the journey.

Which was something she hadn't been able to do since she'd made that call to the Contessa, she admitted drily. But how was she supposed to react, after learning that Jake had suffered some kind of mental breakdown? she wondered. It was hard enough to cope with the reality of what Sophia Lombardi had told her. To believe that she herself might play some part in his trauma was sufficient to convince her she might never rest again.

She turned her face against the cool upholstery, and tried to stem the ready tears that burned behind her eyes. It was unbelievable. Things like this didn't happen to people like her. For nearly forty years she had lived a fairly conventional existence. Even having Julie was not such a remarkable event, and the problems they had had were common enough, even in families where there were two parents. She had been quite content to believe that that was all there was. Until Jake Lombardi had come into her life…

She stifled a sigh. What had his mother said exactly? That Jake had had a fall from his horse? Yes, that was it. He had been missing for almost eight hours, and when the search party had found him he had been unconscious.

God! Laura shivered, even though the air outside the car hovered somewhere in the high seventies. According to Sophia Lombardi, he had been found near the foot of the ravine, and, remembering the morning she had sat on Caesar's back looking down into the valley, Laura could only marvel that he hadn't broken his neck.

In fact, Sophia had said, no bones had been broken. He had had concussion, and multiple bruising, but somehow he had survived any serious injury. Of a physical kind, anyway, Laura conceded, remembering what else his mother had said. The accident had apparently happened the day after Laura had flown back to England, and since then Jake's mental condition had deteriorated rapidly. His family had thought at first that it was simply the after-effects of his concussion, but, as time went by, they began to realise that something more serious was wrong.

'That was when my husband began to suspect that Giacomo's accident might not have been an accident,' Sophia had explained unevenly. 'He is—he has always been—an expert horseman, and although at the time our relief at finding him alive, and apparently unharmed, blinded us to other considerations, it soon became apparent that all was not well.'

'Even so——'

'Even so, nothing.' Laura's shocked protest had been swiftly swept aside. 'You have not seen him, *signora.*

Believe me, he is not the man you knew—or the son I believed I did. I—we—are seriously worried about him.'

Laura had persisted even then. 'But—what do you think I can do?' she demurred. 'I mean, I——'

'I do not know if there is anything you can do,' Sophia had responded honestly. 'But—and it is a faint hope on our part—Giacomo did mention your name, while he was unconscious. When—when my husband found him, he said something, which we are now convinced was "Laura". Although I must also tell you that, since he has regained consciousness, your name has never been mentioned.'

A faint hope indeed, thought Laura now, pressing her face against the soft leather. But one which she, no less than his parents, could not ignore. According to the Contessa, Jake's withdrawal had begun the day she'd flown back to London, but whether that belief was based on truth, or a simple desire to manipulate the facts, Laura couldn't be sure. All she could be sure of was that Jake had told his parents he was bringing someone to meet them, whom he cared about. But in what context, and how deeply, only Jake knew.

She pulled a tissue out of her bag, and blew her nose. She would soon find out, she thought bleakly. Again, according to the Contessa, Jake had become virtually a recluse. He seldom left his apartments. When he did, it was always at night. He seldom spoke. Even Luci couldn't penetrate the wall of indifference he had built around himself.

Needless to say, he had lost weight, Sophia had continued. As no one seemed capable of persuading him to eat, the food prepared for him was returned to the kitchen untouched. He was simply not interested in anything, and, although it was obvious the Contessa was not happy about contacting Laura, she had felt she had no other option.

No doubt his parents blamed her for what had happened, Laura conceded tightly. They needed someone to blame, and she was vulnerable. Not that she resented it. It must be hell, when someone you loved wouldn't let you help them. It was hell even contemplating how she would feel if they were wrong...

It was almost dark when they reached Valle di Lupo. But the scent of the pine-strewn hillside was unmistakable, and as they drove down the steep track into the valley Laura tried to calm her suddenly fluttering nerves. What if Jake refused to see her? she fretted uneasily. What if he resented his mother's intervention? What if he simply insisted she turn around and go back home again?'

She closed her eyes against that possibility. What would she do if he did send her away? How would she cope, not knowing if he was alive or dead? Dear God, ever since she had spoken to Julie, and learned of the deception her daughter had practised, she had dreamed of seeing Jake again. How unbearable it would be if, having been given this chance, she was not allowed to tell him.

The huge limousine crunched over the gravelled fore-court in front of the house, and her nails curled into her palms. She was here. The time for uncertainty was over. Already the heavy doors of the *castello* were opening, and the Count's servants were coming out to meet them. She had to get out of the car and behave as if her arrival here was the most natural thing in the world, and not the single most important event in her whole life.

She was ushered into the huge baronial hall, just as she had been before, only then Jake had been with her, she remembered tensely. Now, she was on her own, and, in spite of her eagerness to get here, a timid sense of reluctance reared its cowardly head. Where was Jake's mother? Where was the Count? Suddenly the house seemed too big, too alien, for her limited ambitions. How could she presume on what had been, at best, a fleeting attraction? The Contessa must be wrong. If Jake was ill, it was nothing to do with her.

'*Signora!*'

A man, whom Laura vaguely recognised from her previous visit, was crossing the vast hall to greet her. She seemed to recall he was the Count's major-domo, or some equally archaic factotum, and her lips twisted as he came to a halt in front of her. Apparently she didn't warrant a personal welcome from Jake's parents, she thought bitterly. Whatever the Contessa had said on the phone, she was evidently not considered of sufficient importance to be granted a private reception.

But that wasn't this man's fault, and Laura responded to his greeting with a polite, '*Buona sera.*' It was all very formal and respectful, and, although she was grateful he didn't pursue a lengthy diatribe that she would not have been able to understand, she allowed him to escort her to the rooms she had occupied before with definite misgivings. What was she supposed to do? Behave as if everything was as it should be, and after a suitable interval go down to dinner, just as she had on that other memorable occasion? Without an alternative, what choice did she have?

By the time she had taken a quick shower, and refreshed her make-up, her nerves were as taut as violin strings. No one had come to inform her of the evening's arrangements, and, while she was fairly sure she was expected to join the family for dinner, she would have appreciated the confirmation. As it was, she had no idea how formal an occasion it was likely to be, and, remembering how elegant Jake's mother always appeared, she wished she had taken the trouble to pack an evening dress. But, when she'd been filling the one small suitcase she had brought with her, evening dresses had not been high on her agenda, and now her choice was limited to the cotton suit she had travelled in, and a simple linen tunic, packed more for its coolness than its style.

She eventually chose the coffee-coloured tunic. In spite of the sense of chill that emanated from some place deep inside her, her head felt hot, her hands clammy. She probably looked as if she was suffering from a fever, she thought unhappily, pressing the backs of her hands against her cheeks. If only she could be as cool and composed as the Contessa. Although, she had to admit, the Contessa had not been particularly composed the previous afternoon.

At eight o'clock, wanting any alternative, Laura left her room, and made her way downstairs. The house was quiet, unnaturally so, she reflected, remembering the buzz of conversation that had greeted her first appearance for dinner in the *castello*. But then there had been a dozen guests or more thronging the exquisitely appointed elegance of the library. Now, as she paused in the open doorway, she found she was the only occupant, the tray of drinks on a central table mocking her solitary attendance.

She frowned. This was ridiculous, she thought tensely, trying to summon anger as a counterpoint to panic. Where was everybody? Why had she been brought here, if she was to be abandoned to her fate? Dear God! A quiver of something approaching fear brushed the bare skin of her arms. It was almost as if she was a prisoner here. If she didn't hang on to her sanity, she would start believing Jake had planned the whole thing...

She glanced behind her, but there was no one there. No one to prevent her from leaving the *castello* now, if she chose to do so. Except that she was at least a hundred kilometres from the airport, she reminded herself bleakly. With no obvious means of transport at her disposal.

Feeling in need of something to bolster her crumbling confidence, Laura entered the library on tentative feet. There was Scotch on the tray, as well as gin, and Campari, and a dozen different liqueurs and mixers. Steeling herself for discovery, she lifted the whisky decanter, and poured herself a generous measure. Then, after ensuring that her audacity was unobserved, she swallowed a mouthful of the spirit, undiluted.

She was choking as the raw alcohol tore at her throat, when she sensed she was no longer alone. She turned, and through streaming eyes, she saw the shadowy figure standing in the doorway. Typical, she thought tearfully, dashing away the tears that caused her lack of clear perception. Whoever it was was seeing her at her worst, which was probably what they had intended.

'*Dio mio*, I should have guessed!'

Jake's hoarse exclamation was overlaid with tiers of self-derision, and while Laura tried, rather ineffectually, to regain her shattered composure, he turned sideways, and propped his shoulders against the door-frame.

'I—beg your pardon,' she got out at last, coughing to clear her throat of the constriction, which had little to do with the Scotch she had swallowed. 'Um—didn't you know I was coming?'

Jake rolled his head sideways and looked at her, his eyes dark with unconcealed irritation. 'Did you really think I did?' he queried, and, unable to sustain that cool, faintly mocking gaze, Laura's eyes flickered down over the lean contours of his body. Not that this exercise afforded her much satisfaction, she acknowledged ruefully. In spite of the earliness of the hour, Jake was apparently dressed for bed, his uncompromisingly black silk dressing-gown relieved only by the comparative paleness of his bare calves beneath.

'I—where is your mother?' she asked, instead of answering him, forcing herself to look into his face again. He certainly didn't look well, she thought, almost inconsequentially. But even now, here, faced with the undeniable evidence of what the Contessa had said, Laura still couldn't believe she was in any way responsible for his condition. Even though her heart palpitated at the thought that he might be suffering some inner mental torment, she couldn't bring herself to speak the words that might unlock his anguish. His mother could be wrong...

'Don't you know?' Jake responded now, his voice entirely without expression, and, realising she had to take the initiative here, Laura shook her head.

'Why should I?'

Jake studied her still-flushed face for a few seconds, and then straightened away from the frame. 'But it was she who invited you here, was it not?' he enquired flatly. 'I should have suspected something was going on, when she told me she was leaving——'

'Leaving?'

Laura was aghast, and Jake's mouth assumed a cynical slant. 'Yes, leaving,' he repeated, with the first trace of satisfaction in his tones. 'She and my father are spending the weekend in Rome—with Luci.'

Laura caught her lower lip between her teeth. 'I see.'

'Do you?' Jake's dark brows arched over eyes that had never looked more bleak. 'Well, I do not.' He raked a hand through his already tumbled hair, and, in spite of her anxiety about him, Laura found the fact that it trembled slightly gave her more hope, not less. 'Ever since—well, ever since I had a slight accident, a fall from my horse, nothing more—my mother has scarcely let me out of her sight. Then, suddenly, this morning, she announces she is desperate for entertainment. She says she has things to buy, people to see, a desire to visit the opera. All of which necessitate a visit to the city.' He made a gesture of impatience. 'I should have realised it was out of character. After all that had gone before, I should have known she would not leave, unless——'

He broke off then, and in spite of her own misgivings Laura guessed he was already regretting saying what he had. In a few words, he had endorsed most of what the Contessa had told her, and, although it was a long way from the interpretation his mother had put upon it, nevertheless, it gave Laura the opportunity she needed.

'Yes,' she ventured carefully. 'Your mother—did tell me you'd had a fall——'

'Really?'

The sarcasm in his voice was unmistakable, but Laura refused to be deterred. 'Yes,' she said again, smoothing her damp palms down the seams of the cotton tunic. 'She—also said you were unconscious when they found you.'

'All right.' Jake's fists balled in the pockets of his dressing-gown. 'So, I knocked myself out, when I fell. *Basta cosi!*'

Laura pressed her lips together for a moment. 'How—how far did you fall? The Contessa said you were found near the foot of—of the ravine.'

Jake's mouth hardened. 'Does it matter? As you can see, I am quite recovered.'

Laura trembled. 'I—don't think so.'

'What? You don't think it matters? My sentiments exactly.'

Laura tensed, but his derisive words did not deter her. 'No,' she said steadily, 'that's not what I meant, and you know it. I—I don't think you have recovered. And—and nor does your mother.'

'Ah.' Jake's lips twisted, and, leaving the door, he walked heavily across to where the tray of drinks was waiting. For a moment, Laura half thought he was coming towards her, and her pulse faltered in its mad tattoo. But then, as his real destination was revealed, her heart picked itself up again, battering away at her chest, as if it were some imprisoned creature, desperate to escape. 'Now, we come to the crux of the matter, do we not?' he remarked, pouring himself a generous measure of the spirit that had caused Laura so much discomfort earlier. 'My mother's opinion is of the essence, *no*? The only opinion worthy of any value.'

'What do you mean?'

Laura was troubled, not least by the way he was swallowing the whisky. Should someone in his condition be drinking alcohol? she wondered. But then, she chided herself, she didn't really know what condition that was.

'I mean,' he responded, after pouring himself another measure, 'were it not for my mother, you would not be here.' He studied the contents of the glass with bitter intensity. 'Still, that is not entirely your fault. I know how persuasive my Mama can be. Were it not for her silver tongue, I would never have attended the charity function in Rome, where I met your most estimable daughter. Ergo, we would never have met.' He raised his glass in mock salute. 'Like me, I expect you are wishing now we never had.'

'*No!*'

Laura's response was vehement. She could never wish that. Even though there had been times when she had wished for the ignorance of not knowing the torment Jake had brought her, deep inside her she knew it was a torment she would willingly face again, if it was a choice between her and Jake's happiness.

'No?' he echoed now, and, although the word was innocent enough, its enunciation wasn't. 'No, don't tell me. You've suddenly realised I'm the single most important thing in your life, and you were just waiting for my mother's call to fly here and tell me so!'

Laura hesitated, and then, realising he deserved nothing less than the truth, she nodded. 'Yes.'

'*Dio!*' The expletive that followed his curse was every bit as contemptuous as she had expected. 'I thought better of you, Laura. *Bene*, you have come here—at my mother's request, you have virtually admitted as much—and now, because you find my parents are not here, you think you can stand there and tell me you came because I needed you!' He swore again. 'What is going on? Are they *paying* you to say these things to me?'

Laura was appalled at the depths of his cynicism. Dear God, had she done this to him, as his mother had implied? Was she to blame for the bitter, world-weary lines that scored his face? He had lost weight. She had noticed that at once. But now she noticed how his bones bulged from the shoulders of his dressing-gown; how thin and angular were the hands that gripped his glass. The Contessa had not been exaggerating, she saw. Whatever the reason for Jake's malaise, something was tearing him to pieces from the inside out, and she knew she couldn't leave here without discovering what it was.

'No one's paying me,' she said now, bringing her hands together, and slotting her fingers. 'I admit it—I did come because your mother asked me to. But—but that doesn't mean I didn't want to come anyway. I—I did. I just didn't know how.'

'Liar!'

'I'm not lying.' Moistening her lips with a nervous tongue, Laura moved a step nearer to him. 'I—I did want to see you again——'

'To *see* me.'

'Yes, I did. But—how could I?'

'Is that supposed to be a serious question?'

'Yes.' She swallowed. 'You forget—I don't know where you live either in Rome or—or that place near Viareggio you spoke about. I don't even have your telephone number.'

'Julie would have told you.'

Jake was dispassionate, but Laura was glad he had mentioned her daughter's name. It gave her the opportunity to tell him what had happened. She doubted he knew. His mother had said he had refused to take any calls.

'I—didn't want to ask Julie,' she said, and, although it was the truth, its connotations were ambiguous, to say the least, and Jake knew it.

'No,' he conceded, agreeing with her when she least wanted him to. He swallowed the remainder of the whisky in his glass, and, to her dismay, poured himself another. 'We must not upset Julie, must we? Never let it be said that her happiness should take anything but prime position in your life. To hell with everyone else's happiness—even your own. So long as we ensure that dear little Julie gets everything she wants.'

'It's not like that!' Laura caught her breath despairingly. 'Please——' as he gave her a scornful look '—it's not! I—didn't understand before. Now, I do.'

'Do you?' Jake gave her a weary look. 'Or has Julie told you she is giving up her modelling career, in favour of an acting one, and you no longer feel the need to worry about her?'

Laura stared at him. 'Yes. No.' She blinked. 'How did you know about—about——?'

'Her acting career?' Jake's lips twisted. 'Didn't she tell you I introduced her to David Conti?'

Laura tried to absorb what he was saying. 'You mean—it was because of you, that—that——?'

'That he offered her a screen test?' Jake put down his glass, and wedged his hips against the edge of the table. Folding his arms across the parting lapels of his dressing-gown, he regarded her pityingly. 'You didn't honestly believe that a man like Conti would fly her out to Los Angeles, just to have a screen test, without some incentive!' He shook his head. 'She could have been tested equally well in London. And besides, the odds against someone like Julie, with no acting experience, and fairly average looks, attracting the attention of a well-known film producer, must be astronomical!'

Laura stiffened. 'Julie is a beautiful girl!' she exclaimed defensively, but Jake's mouth only took on an even deeper curl of derision.

'David knows hundreds of beautiful women,' he assured her flatly. 'Los Angeles—*California*—is full of them!'

'But—she says—he—*likes* her.'

'He does.' Jake shrugged. 'For some reason, best

known to himself, he is attracted to her. But do not go imagining that gold rings and orange blossom are on the horizon. They are not.'.

'As I did with you, you mean?' Laura countered quickly, and Jake's mouth hardened.

'There was never any question of my association with your daughter ending in marriage,' he told her harshly. 'If she told you there was, she lied.'

'Yes.' Laura's head dipped up and down. 'Yes, I know that now.'

'Because she told you so?' Jake regarded her coldly. 'So—you believe her, but not me.'

'I wanted to believe you——'

'But you did not,' retorted Jake, his lean face contorted with emotion. 'What kind of man did you think I was? Did you really believe I could sleep with Julie one week, and her mother the next?'

Laura shifted unhappily. 'I—I didn't know what to think.'

'Oh, no!' Jake wouldn't have that. 'I will not accept that even you were that naïve!'

Laura bent her head. 'And if I was?'

'It's not relevant.'

'It is relevant.' She lifted her gaze to his, her eyes seeking some minute trace of weakening in his contemptuous face. 'You—you have to understand, my— my sexual experience began and ended when I was sixteen. Oh, I know it sounds incredible, but it's true. Keith—that was Julie's father's name—he—he taught me everything I knew. And that was precious little, as— as you must have realised for yourself. You see, sex— sex with him was something—furtive; a forbidden experience, that I imagined would be—romantic. Only, of course, it wasn't. It—it only happened one time. As soon as he discovered I was a—that I had never been with a man before, he ended the relationship. By the time I realised I was pregnant, he had left town. I never saw him again.'

Jake's face was expressionless, and when he didn't say anything Laura hurried on, before her courage abandoned her completely.

'He was married, you see,' she added, biting her lips. 'I didn't know that, of course. And I don't think he ever intended his association with me to go as far as it did. It—it was my fault, for assuming—for assuming—well, for thinking he meant the things—the things he said.'

There was silence after she had finished. Jake still said nothing, and, had it not been for the fact that he had watched her intently throughout her fumbled explanations, Laura thought she would not have been unjustified in wondering whether he had actually heard a word she said. Or perhaps he had heard, but he still didn't believe her, she conceded wretchedly. And why should he, after all? It was a pathetic admission to make.

'So—so you see,' she appended at last, when the unnatural stillness was beginning to shred her already screaming nerves, 'you—you have to make allowances for my—my ignorance. I—I'm not like—not like the women you're used to—to dealing with.' A faintly hysterical laugh escaped her. 'I think—I think even you have—have to admit that.'

Jake moved then, and Laura jumped, but he only lifted his hand to massage the muscles at the back of his neck. She stood there numbly, while his fingers kneaded the taut flesh, and the lapels of his robe pulled apart and came together again in unison.

The action was magnetic. Laura tried to look away, but her eyes were drawn to that tantalising opening. All of a sudden, she was remembering the feel of his satin-smooth skin against her cheek. She was recalling how it had felt, when he had rubbed himself against her, and when she caught a glimpse of the disc of dark flesh that surrounded his nipple, she wanted to go to him, and take it into her mouth...

Her head spun, and, realising that if she stayed here any longer she was likely to do exactly as she was fantasising, Laura forced herself to look elsewhere. Her hands provided a satisfactory alternative, the knuckles white, as she dug her nails into her palms. She had to get out of here, she thought. She had to make a dignified exit. But how did one make any kind of exit in circumstances like these?

'Do you want to go to bed with me?'

The dispassionately spoken invitation stilled the madly churning turmoil of her thoughts, and Laura's eyes jerked to his in horrified comprehension.

'I—what did you say?'

'I said—do you want to go to bed with me?' Jake repeated, with a callous lack of delicacy, and Laura's control shattered into a thousand jagged pieces.

'You—you—how dare you?' she got out at last, all thoughts of humouring him swept away on the tide of humiliation that poured over her. 'What—what do you think I am?'

'That is what you came for, is it not?' he taunted, not a whit daunted by her feeble surge of indignation. '*Perche?* Did you find you liked it, after all? Or did your current partner not come up to your expectations?'

'I—I don't have a—a current partner,' Laura protested in a choked voice, and then, realising what she was doing, she said no more. She had no need to justify herself to him, she thought painfully. He had no right to say

these things to her. Just because his mother had asked
her to come here, and she had done so, did not give him
licence to treat her like some kind of high-priced whore.
It was sickening. It was obscene. And she had no intention of pandering to his perversions.

The door was still open, and she headed towards it.
The Contessa was wrong, she thought, blinking back
tears. Jake didn't care about her. He only wanted to destroy her. And she had given him the weapons to do it
quite successfully...

CHAPTER FIFTEEN

LAURA was pushing her belongings back into her suitcase, without much regard for their well-being, when someone knocked at her sitting-room door.

She was tempted to ignore it. It was probably one of the servants, she thought, come to see if she wanted anything to eat, but even the possibility that it might be Jake did not arouse any feelings of anticipation inside her. If it was him, he had probably come to finish what he had started downstairs, she thought bitterly, and she knew she wasn't strong enough to take any more of his accusations. Besides, he was right. If she was totally honest with herself, she would admit that she had come here to go to bed with him. But what he didn't know, and what he had completely failed to understand, was why.

The knock came again, and, although she was reluctant to waste any more time, courtesy demanded that she answer it. Crossing the floor, she paused to school her features into a mask of politeness, and then pulled open the door.

It was Jake, and even though none of her feelings showed in her face Laura realised she had known it all along. She was so deeply attuned to his mind that she had sensed that, however painful it might be, their involvement with one another was not over yet. But what she had not been prepared for was the fact that he had taken the time to put on a shirt and a pair of black trousers, and although his feet were still bare he looked more civilised.

'I'm sorry,' he said simply, and, because it was the very last thing she had expected him to say, Laura was briefly speechless.

Then, because something was obviously expected of her, she managed to shake her head. 'Are you?' she asked, in a tight, brittle, little voice. 'For what?'

'For this,' said Jake softly, putting out his hand, and wiping an errant tear from her cheek. 'For everything. Will you forgive me?'

Laura stared at him, her eyes burning with tears as yet unshed. 'I'm—I'm packing,' she blurted, glancing behind her at the clothes tumbling from the suitcase, clearly visible on the bed in the adjoining room.

'Then unpack,' Jake advised her huskily, stepping forward, so that she was obliged to move aside. 'I'll help you.'

Laura didn't know what to do. She glanced from him to the open door, and back again, and then, pressing her palms on top of one another over her midriff, she said unsteadily, 'I—I won't go to bed with you. Whatever you say, I—I won't be—used.'

'Who's using whom?' murmured Jake drily, and there was a wealth of self-derision in his tone. Then, as if losing patience with this stilted little conversation, he reached for her, his hands at the nape of her neck leaving no room for deviation. With grim determination, his mouth found hers, and the hungry urgency of his kiss drove all sane thoughts from her head.

He kissed her as if he was desperate to assuage all the pain and torment he had inflicted by his cold indifference. The heat and anguish of the words he muttered as he devoured her lips ignited a warming flame inside her, and the invading possession of his tongue incited an answering hunger.

Abandoning all hope of retaining any self-restraint with him, Laura wrapped her arms around his narrow waist, and pressed herself against him. This was what she wanted, she acknowledged raggedly. This was where she wanted to be. If he was only using her, then so be it. If he was taking advantage of the feelings only he could arouse inside her, then that was the way it had to be. She couldn't hold out any longer. Dear God, she loved him!

The intensity of the emotions they had unleashed made any kind of withdrawal impossible. With their mouths still melded together, Jake swung her up in his arms, and carried her to the bed, carelessly overturning her suitcase on to the floor, before collapsing on the mattress with her.

Then, holding her on his knee, he covered her face with kisses, murmuring to her in his own language, as he nibbled at her ear, deposited light caresses on her eyes, bit the quivering fullness of her lower lip. His hands cradled her cheeks, explored the sensitive hollows behind her ears, invading the scooped-out neckline of her tunic.

And while he brought every nerve and sinew of her body to shuddering awareness, he encouraged her to do the same. And she needed no second invitation. Already, her fingers were deep in the thick, silky hair that he had neglected, just like the rest of him. Her nails had grazed his scalp, before exploring the shape of his head, the size of his ears, the vulnerable curve of his neck.

The zip of her tunic was quickly dealt with, and she obediently withdrew her arms when Jake pressed it down to her waist. Her bra proved even less of a hazard, and then he was burying his face in the hollow between her breasts, and she could feel the heat of his tongue tasting her flesh.

For her part, she contented herself with unbuttoning his shirt, and as she eased its folds from his shoulders she caught her breath at the taut skin she had exposed. There was not an ounce of flesh on his shoulders, and if nothing else, it convinced her that she must have played some part in his breakdown.

Jake's mouth sought hers again, and his exploration of her body reached her knees, suddenly clamped tight together in his lap. With painstaking insistence, he massaged the taut bones that blocked his further invasion, and then, as the limbs weakened beneath his patient ministrations, he slid his hand along her thigh, to the throbbing junction of her legs.

Laura's senses rioted. Every part of her was awakening and expanding to the seductive pressure of his touch, and, between her legs, she was flooded with the proof of her need for him. With a helpless little moan, she wound her arms around his neck and pressed her tongue into his mouth, and his immediate response was both urgent and satisfyingly thorough.

Rolling her on to the bed beside him, he quickly disposed of the rolled-up tunic, and then startled her by bending to press his face against the dark triangle clearly visible through her lacy bikini briefs.

'Mi bella Laurissima,' he whispered, his voice ragged with emotion, and she was no longer in any doubt as to his need for her.

She helped him undress, smiling when she found he wasn't wearing any underwear. 'Well,' he said huskily, as his trousers joined his shirt on the floor, 'I hoped I wouldn't need them.'

'You don't,' she assured him unsteadily, winding her
legs around him. 'Oh, God, Jake, I want you!'

'I want you, too,' he told her, equally emotionally,
'and I really don't think I can wait any longer...'

Hours later, Laura discovered that the huge porcelain tub
was quite big enough for two people. Sitting between
Jake's legs, there was plenty of room to enjoy the frothy
depths of the water, and Jake assured her that he had no
objections to assisting her with her ablutions. On the
contrary, he seemed to take a definite pleasure in soaping
her rosy skin, and if his hand sometimes took the place
of the sponge Laura didn't care. The eroticism of his
caresses made a dizzying delight of this simplest of
tasks, and when she began to emulate his actions he
scooped her out of the water, wrapped her in a towel,
and carried her back to bed.

'Couldn't we——?' she began regretfully, looking
back over his shoulder at the bath, and Jake's lean mouth
curved into a sensual smile.

'I didn't want to shock you,' he remarked, lowering
her on to the bed, and beginning to towel her limbs dry,
but Laura merely pulled him down on top of her.

'You can do anything you like to me,' she breathed,
circling his lips with her tongue, and Jake needed no
second bidding. With the ease of growing familiarity,
his body slid slickly into hers, and the urgent lovemaking that followed left no room for any coherent conversation.

But later, after Jake had fetched a bottle of champagne
from the cellar, and they were sharing a toast, he said
huskily, 'Anything?'

Laura frowned then, not understanding what he meant,

and Jake prompted softly, 'You said I could do anything I liked to you.'

'Oh!' Jake was enchanted to see that she was blushing, her cheeks pink in the lamplight. 'Well—yes. Of course I meant it.'

'All right.' He nodded. 'Then that must include marrying you.'

Laura caught her breath. 'Marrying me?'

Jake's expression tensed, just slightly. 'Doesn't it?'

'Doesn't it—what?'

'Include marrying you?' said Jake, a little tersely. He looked down at the sparkling liquid in his glass. 'It's what I want. It's what I've wanted ever since I met you on the stairs at the cottage. And—I'd begun to believe you might want it, too. Was I wrong?'

'Oh, no!' Laura couldn't let him think that, and the tension in his face eased considerably. 'You know I love you. I never want to leave you. But——'

'But—what?'

'Oh——' Laura lifted her slim shoulders, unaware that when she did so the peaks of her breasts bobbed enticingly. 'What are your parents going to say? I am years older than you are.'

'You don't look it,' declared Jake thickly, leaning forward to brush his lips against those dusky peaks. 'And besides, I should think my father and mother can be left in no doubt as to what I want. You don't suppose they took themselves off to Rome, without anticipating what was likely to happen in their absence?'

'Even so...'

'Look!' Jake took her chin in his hand and turned her face to his. 'I love you. I want you. What else matters?'

'But Luci——'

'I'm tempted to say I don't give a damn what anyone

thinks, including my daughter,' declared Jake wryly. 'Anyway, Luci likes you. She never knew her own mother, so she doesn't know what having a mother is like.'

'All the same...'

Jake sighed. 'What else is there?'

'I just think your parents would have wanted you to marry someone else.'

'Really?' Jake shook his head. 'I think my parents will be incredibly relieved to know that they can stop worrying about us.'

'About you, you mean,' ventured Laura, regarding him anxiously. 'Did you—did you really miss me that much?'

'Stop fishing,' ordered Jake drily, but his eyes were eloquent with feeling. 'Of course, I missed you. *Dio*—when you walked out of here——'

He broke off abruptly, and Laura rubbed her cheek against his fingers, realising there was plenty of time to convince him he didn't have to miss her any more.

The moment was taut with emotion, and in an effort to restore their earlier inconsequence Laura said, 'Nevertheless, I'm sure your mother would prefer you to marry someone more—chic. More—sophisticated.'

'Which brings us back to rich again, doesn't it?' remarked Jake humorously, taking the point. He bore her back against the pillows, and pressed his face into her neck. '*Cara*, I married someone chic and sophisticated when I married Isabella. And it wasn't like this.'

Laura's eyebrows arched. 'Wasn't it?'

'No.' Jake bit her ear reprovingly. 'I told you before. I've never loved anyone as I love you.'

Laura shifted with sensuous grace. 'But what will your friends——?'

'My friends will envy me,' declared Jake huskily, and, losing patience with her questions, he found her mouth in a long drugging kiss.

But then, just as Laura was sinking into a deliciously erotic state of lethargy, he jerked back, cursing roundly. 'Damn,' he said, and when she gazed up at him uncomprehendingly, he pulled a wry face. 'I've spilled the champagne!'

Laura started to giggle, but she sobered somewhat when Jake pushed himself up to sit on the side of the bed. 'OK,' he said. 'I think the time has come to go back to my own bed.'

'No——'

Laura came up now, her eyes wide with apprehension, but Jake only regarded her with cool indifference. 'Yes,' he said, and then, as her expression grew anxious, he got up, and pulled her up into his arms. 'You didn't think I was going to leave you behind, did you?' he asked teasingly, his grin pure devilment. 'Oh, *mi amore*, what I have, I keep.'

Some time later, after they had transferred to the masculine austerity of Jake's suite of rooms, Laura brought up the one subject they had not discussed so far: Julie.

'I don't know what she's going to say,' she murmured sleepily, although the problem of her daughter seemed very far away at this moment. 'When she came to see me, before she left for California, I didn't even tell her I'd been here.'

'I shouldn't worry about it.' Jake was philosophical. 'You can invite her to the wedding.'

'Do you think she'll be very unhappy about it?'

'Unhappy?' Jake uttered a short laugh. 'Oh, *mi cara*, when has Julie ever cared about *your* happiness? Did it

ever occur to her that you might need a life outside that
existence you've been living for the last twenty years?'

'No, but——'

'No more buts,' said Jake flatly. 'From now on, we're
just going to look to the future, not the past.' He smiled.
'Now—do you know what? I am hungry. How does a
midnight feast sound to you?'

David Conti's house at Malibu was right on the beach,
with a huge sun-deck opening off the spacious family
room. According to Julie, the house was usually full at
weekends, with friends of David's and their families,
mingling happily with David's own children from his
three previous marriages.

Julie, herself, seemed happy, Laura thought, watching
her daughter from her position on the sun-deck. In the
year since she had come to California, Julie had lost a
lot of the brittleness she had had when she'd worked in
London, and although she and David were not married
yet Laura thought it was a distinct possibility, whatever
Jake said.

Her daughter had taken the news of her and Jake's
marriage with some belligerence at first, and their first
meeting after the engagement was announced had not
been entirely friendly. But Julie was like that, Jake told
her. She would always seek to dominate her mother. She
had done it for so long. But now, Laura had Jake to back
her up, and what might have been awkward had quickly
been defused. Besides, even Julie had been unable to
ignore their obvious happiness together, and perhaps she
had realised she was in danger of losing more than she
gained.

In any event, the idea of being related to the
Lombardis, if only by marriage, seemed to have per-

suaded Julie of its many advantages. It made her association with David Conti that much more serious. She was now *family*, after all. And she did have a pleasant life in Los Angeles.

This was Jake's and Laura's first trip to the United States since their marriage. Although it was almost ten months since that event had taken place, three months ago Laura had had a baby son, and during her pregnancy she hadn't wanted to travel so far. Besides, Jake had insisted she do nothing to upset either her, or the baby, and Laura had been quite content to enjoy his undivided attention.

It had also given her the chance to get to know her stepdaughter. Luci had been surprisingly eager to welcome her into the family, and it was not until the little girl had confided why that Laura had begun to understand her feelings.

Because her own mother had died before she was old enough to understand, Luci had spent most of her time with her grandparents, and although she loved them dearly, she loved her father best. But Jake had spent very little time with his daughter. He worked with his father, and because he'd had no wife to restrict his movements Count Lombardi had relied on Jake to accomplish most of their overseas business. In consequence, although Jake cared about his daughter, he had never been a proper father to her.

Now, it was different, Luci confided. Now they were a proper family, and whenever Jake travelled abroad he took his family with him. Especially Luci, Laura insisted, on those occasions when Jake would have preferred to have his wife to himself. She wanted the little girl to know she was just as important to them as the

new baby. There would be no misunderstandings this
time, she said.

Of course, they had a nanny for the children, and now,
looking towards the ocean, Laura could see Miss
Frobisher, tagging along behind Jake, Luci and David.
Jake was carrying Carlo, their baby son, and the dapper
little English nanny was trying valiantly to keep up with
their easy strides.

As if sensing her eyes upon him, Jake looked back
then, and waved, and Laura's heart turned over. It still
seemed incredible that it should be she whom Jake
loved, but he had proved it to her, over and over, in a
million different ways.

His parents had been amazingly supportive, too. But
then, no one could deny how good Laura was for Jake.
He had never looked fitter, so relaxed and handsome,
and when they were together their happiness was infec-
tious.

Now, Laura waved back, aware, as she did so, how
much she had changed, too, in the last year. Once, the
idea of sitting on a sun-deck in a bikini, sunning herself
in front of a crowd of strangers, would have sounded
totally daunting. But Jake's love had made her confident.
Because he thought she was beautiful, she felt beautiful,
too.

'You have a super tan,' remarked Julie suddenly, coming to take the cushioned chair beside her. 'I suppose
you spend a lot of time outdoors.'

Laura nodded. 'I suppose we do. We—er—we've
been staying at Marina di Salvo since Carlo was born,
and the sea air——' She shrugged. 'You know what it's
like.'

'Hmm.' Julie swung her long legs on to the lounger,

and adjusted her dark glasses. 'Marina di Salvo? Where's that?'

'Near Viareggio. Jake—that is, *we* have an apartment there.'

'Nice.' Julie closed her eyes. 'I guess it all worked out for you, didn't it?'

Laura sighed, wishing Jake were there to support her. But then, she rallied. She wasn't a silly spinster any more. She was Jake's wife, and whatever Julie said, she couldn't really hurt her.

So, 'Yes,' she said, in answer to her daughter's question. 'It did.'

'I'm glad.'

Nothing Julie said could have surprised her more, but Laura was sensible enough to be cautious. 'You are?' she ventured swiftly.

'Hmm.' Julie nodded. 'I guess I'd forgotten how young you really are. I'd gotten so used to seeing you as "my mother", in quotes. The schoolmistress! It's easy to be selfish, if you never look beneath the label.'

Laura expelled her breath slowly. 'I see.'

'I hope you do.' Julie opened her eyes again, and turned to look at her mother somewhat ruefully. 'I've been a bitch. I know it. And when you said you and Jake—well, I could have scratched your eyes out then.' She grimaced. 'But recently—well, I guess you could say I'm getting softer in my old age. It's obvious Jake is crazy about you, and I'd be a fool to deny myself the only family I've got.'

Laura's lips parted. 'Oh, Julie!' she exclaimed, and she had hardly time to squeeze her daughter's hand before her stepdaughter came dancing across the deck.

And Luci wasn't alone. Jake, and Carlo, were right

behind her, her husband's sable eyes dark and expressive, as they took in the scene they had interrupted.

'Are you all right, *cara*?' he asked, squatting down beside her, and giving Julie a wary look, and Laura smiled.

'Perfectly,' she said, taking their baby son, and tipping him over her shoulder. 'Julie was just complimenting me on my tan.'

'Really?' Jake didn't sound convinced, and Julie shook her head.

'Yes, really,' she declared, swinging her legs to the deck and getting to her feet. 'But don't say I don't know when I'm not wanted,' she added. 'Here—*Daddy*—you can have my chair. And stop looking at her like that. This is a respectable household.'

Jake grinned then, but he didn't argue, and after she had gone he lowered himself into the chair beside his wife. 'No problems?' he asked, linking his fingers with hers, and Laura felt almost too overwhelmed with happiness to speak.

'No problems,' she agreed huskily, and Jake gave a suitably contented sigh.

Chelsea figured life was just about perfect. Her business was thriving, and she'd raised a wonderful daughter who was off at college. But then that same daughter came home for the summer and turned Chelsea's safe little world upside down with her campaign to find Mr. Right for Mom. Because she did.

A MAN FOR MOM

Linda Randall Wisdom

Chapter One

"Okay, start talking."

Her glare the picture of righteous motherly wrath, Chelsea Brennan regarded her errant daughter, Colleen, who stood on the front doorstep at 1:22 a.m. on Friday the thirteenth.

The girl's initial bravado was rapidly disappearing. Even in skimpy silk pajamas that barely covered her feminine curves, her mother looked intimidating as hell.

To the man who stood behind Colleen, however, the lady looked just plain sexy.

Colleen winced, ineffectually crossing her arms to conceal the black sequined dress that barely covered her to midthigh. "I have a feeling you won't like it."

Chelsea's gaze flickered from her daughter to her companion. Oh, Lord. The man was definitely too old for a seventeen-year-old girl. Besides, Colleen had supposedly gone to the movies with her friend, Elaine.

Colleen sighed, envisioning being grounded until she was thirty.

"I suggest you begin by explaining what you're doing with this...gentleman," Chelsea prompted her.

"It's not what you think," the man started to explain.

Chelsea's hazel eyes snapped to the left. "Exactly

who are you, and what are you doing with my daughter?'' An unsettling thought occurred to her. ''Are you a police officer?'' Her eyes flicked suspiciously over his attire. Did undercover policemen wear jeans that tight and sexy leather jackets and have rugged good looks that spelled *male* in capital letters?

''No, I'm not a cop. The name's Mark Harrison.'' In turn he looked her over with a thoroughness most inappropriate for the mother of the teenage girl he was so tastelessly escorting.

She spoke crisply to deflect his brazen gaze. ''All right, Mr. Harrison, if it's not what I think, as you so quaintly put it, what exactly *is* it you're doing with my daughter?'' And to think she'd complained about Colleen's last date because the boy had worn an earring!

''I brought Colleen home to keep her out of trouble,'' he explained, looking all too self-assured for Chelsea's peace of mind.

''Oh?'' she said frostily, disbelief dripping from the single frozen syllable.

He rocked back and forth on his heels, his hands jammed in his pockets, his eyes blazing meaningfully into hers. ''So you can't believe I was just being an all-around nice guy?''

''Not at all.''

''Mom, I'm freezing,'' Colleen complained as she pushed past her mother and entered the house.

Chelsea opened her mouth to protest as the cradle-robber who called himself Mark Harrison boldly followed Colleen inside and closed the door. Too late. He was already in her living room. Well, she supposed she ought to hear his side of the story, too. She tightened the sash of her robe and marched after the twosome.

Mark prowled around her living room, touching a vase

here, running a finger over a framed photograph there. Looking altogether too much at home, he sprawled loosely on the couch.

Chelsea pulled in a deep breath. "All right, will somebody please explain what the hell is going on here."

Colleen winced. "Mom tends to get emotional about certain things," she explained to Mark as she sat in an easy chair, oblivious to the way her already short skirt rode up her slender thighs. Her mother noticed and was silently relieved that Mark didn't seem to pay the least attention to the exposed young flesh. Instead, he gazed up gravely in her direction.

"Well, you knew Elaine and I had plans for tonight," Colleen began.

"Yes, you told me you were going to the movies. Naturally, every teenage girl wears an eight-hundred-dollar dress to the mall multiplex."

Mark's deep brown eyes widened. "Eight hundred dollars for that little scrap of material?" He pointed at the strapless creation Colleen wore. "You're kidding, aren't you? I mean, no one pays eight hundred dollars for something like that, do they? I mean, she's only a kid. I wouldn't let my kid go out looking like that. Eight hundred bucks?" he repeated in outraged awe.

"A kid?" Colleen yelped, sitting forward.

Mark ignored her outburst and glared at Chelsea as if she were somehow to blame for his shock.

Chelsea spun on him. "All right, Mark Harrison, we've ascertained that you're not a cop, but you still haven't explained what you are. I'd like to know who I'm going to have arrested—call it an idiosyncrasy of mine," she said sweetly.

"I told you, I'm Mark Harrison. I'm also your daughter's savior. I protected her endangered virtue from a drunk hassling her at the club,'' he explained. ''For all the thanks I get,'' he added, grumbling.

Chelsea gasped. ''Club? What club? What on earth happened?''

Colleen rolled her eyes in disgust. ''Mom, it was no big deal. Mark just makes it sound like one. The other guy didn't touch me. Well, okay, he touched me, but not the way he wanted to. Well, what I mean is, he was drunk, and I doubt he could have done all that much in his condition, no matter what he thought.''

Chelsea groaned, unsure whether to laugh hysterically or cry. Closing her eyes, she collapsed on the couch. ''This is a nightmare. All I have to do is wake up and everything will be fine, right?''

Mark found his gaze riveted on the distraught mother of the adventurous minor. And why not? Talk about the kind of woman any man wouldn't mind having around late at night. Her honey brown hair was tousled, as if she'd just climbed out of bed. Considering what she was wearing, that was more than likely. Bed—the perfect place for a woman like her. Her cinnamon silk robe had slipped open just enough to reveal a slippery camisole and matching boxer shorts. While some men wouldn't consider glasses sexy, the tortoiseshell specs perched atop her honey-colored waves somehow added to her angry, offbeat allure.

Wait. If she'd been in bed reading, waiting up for her daughter, had she been alone? If so, where was Colleen's father—who would be, dammit, Chelsea's husband—and why wasn't he here ready to turn Mark into mincemeat?

''Mrs. Brennan...'' he began.

''Ms. Brennan,'' Colleen corrected smartly, then added, ''Chelsea.'' Chelsea glared at her.

So, the lady was single, Mark reflected. The evening was looking up. The evening. He abruptly remembered why he was here. "Let me make a long story short, Ms. Brennan."

"Please do." Her sarcasm was palpable.

"Colleen was down at Rick's Café with a friend." He held up his hand when Chelsea snapped forward, looking ready to kill anyone in her path—him first. "Some guy'd had a bit too much to drink, and when Colleen refused to dance with him, he made a fuss. She was smart enough to leave, but he was stupid enough to follow her out to the parking lot. I saw what was going on and guessed there might be a bit of trouble. I went outside just in time to prevent the guy from losing his chance to father children as Colleen and Elaine defended themselves. Since he was still a lot larger than they were, I stepped in to even the odds."

He paused, glancing briefly at Colleen. "I followed Elaine's car to her house to make sure the guy wouldn't try to tail them, then brought Colleen on home. She said she didn't think you'd be in yet, so I wanted to make sure she'd be all right."

Chelsea arched a disbelieving eyebrow. "Sure. And pigs fly."

He ignored the sarcastic remark. "Look, I didn't have to do this, but she seemed like a nice kid, and I didn't want to see her get hurt."

Chelsea stood. "That's true, you didn't have to do anything. After all, chivalry died ages ago, and men like you don't drive young girls home unless you feel certain said girl's parents aren't around and you'll have the opportunity to receive a proper thank-you."

"Mom!" Colleen was shocked. "Are you kidding? He's *old!*"

"I don't have even one foot in the grave yet," he said wryly. "And as for you, Ms. Brennan, you're too cynical for your own good."

She stood her ground. He might be the best-looking man she'd seen in a long while, but he had a healthy dose of arrogance to go with the attractive package. And she didn't like his telling her what was wrong with her. "Maybe I have good reason to be."

He got to his feet. "Maybe you do. So don't trouble yourself with a thank-you. Besides, even with the heavy makeup and—" he winced "—eight-hundred-dollar dress, Colleen is underage and could have gotten the club owner into a lot of trouble, even though she did drink just club soda. Why she was at Rick's is no business of mine—I'd say that was more her mother's department. But Rick is a friend of mine, and Colleen seemed like an okay kid, and I just saw no reason for the situation to get any worse."

Chelsea's eyes remained icy cold. "How commendable."

Mark didn't flinch. He merely gazed suggestively at Chelsea's long, sexy legs peeking out from the folds of the rob. "Look, Ms. Brennan, how you raise your daughter is no concern of mine. I only came in to explain."

Stung, Chelsea straightened and dismissed him with a chilly "Thank you for bringing Colleen home, Mr. Harrison.

He headed for the door. "Remember what I said, Colleen. You stay out of places like that until you're of age," he said over his shoulder.

"What, and deprive heroes like you of the chance to rescue the sweet young things?" Chelsea couldn't resist sniping as she followed him out.

He turned and faced her squarely. "I seldom explain myself to anyone, Ms. Brennan, but since you insist on being so wrongheaded about my supposed decadence, allow me to enlighten you. I don't hit on jailbait, and I don't hang out in singles' bars. But since Rick is a friend of mine and is rarely able to leave during operating hours, it's usually the only way I get to see him. If I were you, I'd be damn grateful that creep hadn't gotten his hands on Colleen. Otherwise, it *would* have been the police, not me, coming here to see you."

Chelsea watched the front door close behind Mark Harrison. She didn't move until she heard his car back down the driveway and roar off, unwilling to admit that his words had struck a painful chord deep inside her. Worry that something would happen to her precious daughter dogged her steps even more now that Colleen had suddenly reached the threshold of womanhood.

She took several deep breaths before turning back to her daughter. "Would you like to give me the whole story now?" she said with dangerous calm.

Colleen winced. "It's not what you think."

"Oh, really? What am I thinking?"

"You're thinking that Elaine and I went there to pick up guys."

"If you didn't go there to pick up guys, why did you go?"

Colleen shifted uneasily in her chair. "Would you believe to research a psychology report on the mating habits of today's singles?"

"Not a chance. School doesn't start until next week. How did you get the dress?"

"Elaine and I stopped by the shop. I'll pay for the lingerie," she hastened to add. "And I'll have the dress dry-cleaned. After all, Mom, you never sell the samples.

That's why I took this one. I figured you'd prefer my taking a sample than something off the rack.''

Chelsea raked her hair with her fingers, dislodging her reading glasses, which tumbled, unheeded, to the carpet. ''From the day you were born you never gave me a minute's trouble,'' she sighed. ''You slept all night, suffered from colic only twice, and you didn't even go through the terrible twos that so many other mothers moaned about. Even puberty, with all those hormonal changes, was a breeze. Are you trying to make up for lost time now?'' Her voice rose with her agitation.

Colleen stood up, sensing she was going to need every advantage she could get. ''We just wanted to see what Rick's was like. We weren't out for trouble.''

Chelsea was unmoved. ''Try again.''

''Okay, Elaine and I made a mistake in going there. But we were curious. You know, to see if singles' places are like they show in the movies. That's all!'' Colleen insisted.

Chelsea searched her daughter's features. She had always been grateful that Colleen never lied to her. She sincerely hoped the girl wasn't beginning now. ''All right, go on up to bed,'' she said finally. ''I'm not forgetting about this, though. From now until I say differently, you work at the shop every day until school starts to pay for what you took. When school starts next week, you can come in after school and on weekends.... And that doesn't mean your schoolwork slides, either. This year is too important for you to screw up.''

Colleen's eyes widened at the extent of her punishment. ''I have to pay for the dress, too?''

''The special dry cleaning alone won't be cheap, and, knowing your excellent taste—'' her sharp eyes took in the shimmering black silk stockings, and she imagined the remaining lingerie under the minuscule dress "—you can forget any after-school activities unless they have something to do with your education."

"Mom!" Colleen squeaked.

"My dear, you are well and truly grounded until further notice. If what Mr. Harrison said was true, you were very foolish and *very* lucky tonight." She stopped. "Now, do us both a favor and go upstairs before I lose my temper completely."

Colleen knew well enough to beat a hasty retreat. She scooted past Chelsea and hurried upstairs.

Chelsea bent down and picked up her glasses. What a day. First the bank had refused to extend her business loan. Then her business dinner had gone sour because the jerk of a manufacturer's rep refused to understand that she had absolutely no interest in going to bed with him. The shipment of silk camisoles due yesterday hadn't arrived and couldn't be traced. With the way her luck was going, they'd probably landed in Alaska.

"And now this," she muttered. She turned off the lights and headed wearily for the stairs.

"OH, NO, YOU MEAN your mom was already home? Did she talk to Mr. Harrison?" Elaine asked. Colleen had called her the moment she reached her room.

"He told her where we were," she groaned, flopping onto the bed, wrinkling the infamous dress. "As of now, I'm grounded for the rest of my life, and I have to work in the shop until I pay my debt to Mom and society. I guess I'm lucky she hasn't decided to lock me in my room for the next ten years." She adjusted the receiver against her shoulder and grimaced at the glittering sequins that were going to cost her so dearly. "Had your parents come home from their party yet?"

"No, it was cool," Elaine explained. "But, Colly, we're not going to be able to do this again. Next time, we might not be so lucky. If Mr. Harrison hadn't come outside when he did, I hate to think what might have happened to us. That guy was a real creep."

Colleen shuddered as she thought of the man, reeking of beer, who'd called her horrible names and told her he was going to show her just how grateful she should be he was paying attention to her. "Yeah, but I still haven't found anyone for Mom."

"What about Mr. Harrison? He's kinda cute."

"Yeah, he's cute for an old guy," she admitted grudgingly. "But he's so do-the-right-thing," she complained. "He's probably one of those boring types who doesn't know how to have a good time. He kept talking about how to raise a daughter, and he called me a kid!" she insisted, bristling anew at the major insult.

"If he didn't know how to have a good time, he wouldn't have been in Rick's," Elaine argued. "It's one of the hottest clubs around."

"Yeah, but he said he was only there because Rick is a friend of his. Not because he was looking to have some fun. Oh, I know he's cute, but someone that straight can't be cool, right? I'll just have to keep looking."

"I'm not sure that was such a hot idea to begin with, Colly. I mean, your mom might want to look for a man on her own. And there's no guarantee that she'll fall in love with someone we find. Oh, why do I bother going along with your crazy ideas?" she wailed. "We always get in trouble. And tonight was too scary for me."

"I just have to do some more thinking," Colleen said logically. "Look, El, we're entering our senior year, and then I'll be going off to college. I don't want Mom sitting around here all alone with just the shop for company then. She needs a man. She needs a sex life! After all, hard as it is to believe, according to all the magazine articles, she's in her sexual prime. She can't afford to let that important time of life pass her by.''

''You'd better not let her hear you say that, or you'll *never* get to leave the house,'' Elaine warned.

''She won't. Uh-oh.'' Colleen looked up as the object of their conversation entered the room.

Chelsea plucked the receiver out of Colleen's hand. ''Hello, Elaine. You two were very lucky tonight,'' she said. ''So I'm sure you'll understand why I'll be talking to your mother first thing in the morning. If you're smart, you'll talk to her first.''

''She'll kill me!'' Elaine wailed.

''Don't worry, we'll make sure you two have adjoining graves, so you can continue to get into trouble in the afterlife. And now it's time to go. Good night, Elaine.'' Chelsea replaced the receiver and reached down behind the nightstand to pull the cord out of the jack. She carefully wound the cord around the phone and began walking out of the room with the phone in her hands.

''But, Mom!'' Colleen protested with all the unearthly anguish of a telephoneless teen.

''I suggest you take off that dress before you ruin it completely,'' Chelsea said sweetly.

Colleen's pained wails followed her down the hall and into her own bedroom. As she pulled off her robe, she glanced down and suddenly remembered the brazen way Mark Harrison had looked at her. If her robe had gaped open, he might have seen her cinnamon-silk nightwear gleam against her lightly tanned skin. The thought unaccountably warmed her cheeks.

He was too old for Colleen, she reminded herself, recalling the man who was probably a good six inches taller than her own five foot six. And too young for her, she added firmly. He looked to be in his early thirties; she, on the other hand, was reaching forty sooner than she cared to admit. "And he was way too sure of himself," she muttered, scowling at the unwanted memory of his skintight jeans and buttery leather jacket.

Chelsea crawled into bed and pulled the covers over her head. "If I'm lucky, I'll wake up in the morning and learn this was all a bad dream."

"GOOD MORNING, Mother dear! Coffee, juice, toast with raspberry preserves, soft-scrambled eggs and two slices of bacon," Colleen sang out as Chelsea entered the kitchen. Colleen immediately handed her a mug of coffee.

"Nice try, sweetie, but you're still grounded." That didn't stop her from accepting her much needed morning jolt of caffeine.

Colleen looked more like her seventeen-year-old self this morning, dressed in navy cotton slacks and burgundy print blouse that Chelsea recognized only too well, since it usually hung in her closet.

"You said it looked better on me than on you," Colleen said before her mother could protest. "And I knew you'd want me to look nice in the shop."

Chelsea sat down to her breakfast. "I hate kids who are always right."

"You're the one who taught me good taste."

"Little did I know how it would backfire." Chelsea eyed her daughter. "Colly, we have to talk about last night." She searched her mind for the right words. "I know you broke up with Kevin not all that long ago, and you're probably feeling a little lost. After all, the two of you had gone together for six months, and at your age, that's practically a lifetime. But what you and Elaine did wasn't the way to go about finding someone new. You have no idea what kind of danger you could have been in if Mr. Harrison hadn't stepped in when he did.''

"I know that."

"And do you realize how much trouble you could have gotten the bar's owner into?" she persisted. "He would have lost his liquor license and probably even closed down."

"But we didn't order anything alcoholic," Colleen argued. "And we didn't let anyone buy us a drink."

Chelsea closed her eyes. "That's not it, sweetie. You were underage in a place that doesn't allow minors. I almost wish you were even younger, so I could take you over my knee for a spanking."

Colleen smiled. "You never put me over your knee even when I *was* younger."

Chelsea knew when she was fighting a losing battle. "That's probably why you turned out the way you did. I should have spanked you when you were a smart-mouthed little kid and I was young enough to keep up with you."

Colleen threw her arms around her mother's neck and dropped a kiss on her cheek. "As far as you're concerned, I'm still a smart-mouthed little kid, and as far as I'm concerned, you'll never be old."

"No?" She smiled wryly. "If you keep on pulling stunts like last night's, I'll be wrinkled and gray in a matter of hours."

Colleen looked at the clock. "I'd better head upstairs and finish getting ready. I know you like to get to the shop early, since Saturdays are usually so busy for you."

She paused in the kitchen doorway. "You know,

Mom, I read somewhere that sex keeps you feeling young. Maybe you should try it. I'm sure it would improve your disposition.'' With a twinkle in her eye, she danced off.

A horrified Chelsea stared at the empty doorway. Then she pulled a lock of hair down in front of her eyes, checking for gray.

"CHELSEA BRENNAN," Mark said out loud as he sipped his sixth cup of coffee since getting up that morning. "Honey brown hair, sparkling hazel eyes and those legs, those legs," he groaned, recalling the shapely bare legs topped by silky boxer shorts that looked better on her than men's underwear had ever looked on a man. He dropped his head until it thumped on the drafting table's paper-littered surface. How could he concentrate on the business at hand with thoughts of Chelsea Brennan crowding his brain?

He surveyed the blueprints that he'd been going over since dawn. Usually, this kind of chore only took him a couple of hours. Except usually he wasn't thinking about a leggy brunette with fire in her eyes.

He'd done his share of dating since moving to the Los Angeles area six months ago, but no woman had caught his attention the way Chelsea had. He leaned back in his chair, idly stroking his bare chest and daydreaming about the sexy, irate mom.

Chapter Two

"Hey, boss!" one of Mark's foremen called. "You'd better come out and take a look at this. Something's wrong with these measurements. I thought Friday the thirteenth was bad enough, but this Monday is proving to be a real bitch."

Mark swore under his breath as he snatched up his hard hat and strode out of his office trailer. "This isn't a project, it's a curse."

"Aw, you're just saying that," Steve teased as he walked alongside Mark. "Come on, admit you love the challenge."

"I admit nothing," he shot back. "It's days like this I wonder why I took on this job."

"We both know the answer to that. You want to prove to the old man you're ready to boss a big project all on your own. That's why you fought so hard to head up this one even though he wanted you on that minimall in Ventura."

"Shows how crazy I am. By now the minimall would have been done down to its last little detail. But here—anything that could go wrong around here has. The lead welder flunked a drug test, one of the carpenters was picked up for drunk driving last night, and my so-called assistant is going around looking as if his life is over because his girlfriend told him she didn't want to see him anymore.''

''If I didn't know better, I'd say you were suffering from one hell of a hangover and looking around for a cat to kick,'' Steve kidded him.

Mark combed his fingers through dark auburn hair that resisted any attempts at neatness. ''No hangover, although I wish I had that excuse. I just didn't get much sleep over the weekend.'' He wasn't about to admit the reason for his insomnia was a honey-haired honey who had looked at him as if he were the scum of the earth.

''You need to find yourself a good woman and settle down.'' The foreman spoke with the familiarity of a man who'd worked for Mark's family for the past twenty years.

''Yeah, well, that's easier said than done,'' Mark replied. ''Have you any idea how many women worry more about how they look than about what's going on inside their brains or in the world around them?''

Steve chuckled. ''Yeah, and have you any idea how many men prefer it that way? Why else do you suppose the gals go on that way?''

Mark conceded the point with a grumble and stalked toward the blueprints Steve had spread out on several concrete blocks. ''Okay, let's see what the problem is here before I *do* find a cat to kick.''

''DID YOU FIND OUT Elaine's fate?'' Chelsea asked her daughter.

Colleen wrinkled her nose. ''Before or after her mom threatened to put one of those electronic prisoner bands around her ankle? Her dad went off the deep end, too. He has a very long list of chores she has to do for the next six months. He also wishes they were Catholic, so he could put her in a convent. He's settled on no dates for the next ten years." She looked pained as she unpacked a delivery of colorful camisoles in whisper-thin silk and read off the style numbers and sizes while Chelsea checked them against the invoice. "At least they didn't bring up slavery like someone else I know." Colleen sighed, chewing on the end of a pen. "And all because Mr. Harrison butted in."

"It's a good thing he did," Chelsea pointed out, setting down her clipboard. "You finish up here, then find out what Gwen needs done. I've got a few errands to run."

"Terrific. From one tyrant to another," Colleen muttered.

"Thanks a lot, kiddo." Gwen, a tall, shapely brunette with model's features and a dramatic sense of fashion, groused. "Your mother said I was to crack the whip over you while she was gone."

"Where exactly was she going?" Colleen asked.

"To the bank. She should be back in an hour or so." Gwen glanced toward the door. "So, you want to tell me why you and your little friend decided to hang out at a classy meat market like Rick's last Friday night?"

Colleen wrinkled her nose, debating whether to answer truthfully or not.

Gwen looked sympathetic, and Colleen opted for honesty. "I was looking for a guy for Mom," she explained.

Gwen started to laugh, then abruptly sobered. "Oh, Colleen. And you went to Rick's to find that man? How were you going to handle it? Bring him home and instruct him and your mother to fall into instant love?"

"I don't know!" Colleen wailed, throwing her arms up and plopping down on a crate. "All I know is that

Mom needs a social life, and if she isn't going to do anything about it, I will. It isn't fair that I'm always going out and she stays home doing the books or having boring business dinners.''

"Colleen, your idea is charming, but it would never work,'' Gwen said gently. "Besides, your mom seems happy enough with her life the way it is now.''

"She only says that,'' the girl argued. "She hasn't gone on a date for ages.''

"So you intend to find Mr. Right for her,'' Gwen guessed.

"I hope to. It's not such a bad idea. There just weren't all that many likely guys at Rick's, so I'll have to keep looking. But not in bars,'' she added hastily.

"What about the guy who brought you home?''

Colleen rolled her eyes. "Nope. Not a fun type. He was too busy ticking Mom off by insinuating she wasn't a good mother. But I'll find someone. I know I will.''

Gwen thought back to Chelsea's description of Colleen's rescuer as one of those impossibly sexy guys who thinks he's God's gift to women. "You're in enough trouble now, don't you think? Why not let nature take its course?''

Colleen looked shocked at the very idea. "If I wait for nature, Mom will die a dried up, celibate old spinster!''

"Girl,'' Gwen said, "we really need to talk about your ideas of twentieth-century womanhood.''

"WILL YOU LOOK at that sweet thing?''

"I sure wouldn't mind having a closer acquaintance with those legs!''

"Now, there's a woman with a capital *W.*''

"Sure wish my wife looked like that.''

"If my wife looked like that, I wouldn't leave the bedroom for the next five years!"

"All right, knock it off, you animals," Mark ordered with a laugh as he approached the men from the rear. "There's a lot of women in the world who don't appreciate construction-worker cracks."

"Let me tell you, boss, if I wasn't a happily married man, I'd be out there getting the lady's phone number," one of the men told him as he adjusted his sweat-stained T-shirt over a generous beer belly.

Mark looked over the man's shoulder and did a double take. Those legs! Nice. Very nice.

"Yeah," he breathed.

The workmen grinned and nudged each other as they noticed their boss's absorption. Mark moved past them and headed for the sidewalk in a ground-eating stride.

"Ms. Brennan," he called out, waving an arm behind his back in a vain effort to stop the men's ribald comments.

Chelsea halted and looked over her shoulder. Her eyes widened as his identity registered.

"Ah, yes, the man who enjoys rescuing little girls," she said coolly. "Harris, isn't it?"

He grinned, knowing from her tone that she hadn't really forgotten his name. "Harrison. Mark," he said politely.

Her cool hazel eyes flicked over his worn jeans, faded blue T-shirt powdered almost white with concrete dust, his heavy work boots, and back up to the battered Angels cap on his head. She couldn't miss the late-afternoon shadow of a beard on his face, nor the sweat rings under his arms and the damp line down the front of his shirt, Mark realized unhappily.

Chelsea didn't miss a detail of the man's raw maleness, an unfamiliar—and unnerving—element in her experience. The man was made for carnal adventures, and this mom wasn't in the market for adventuring. She'd have to stay cool. "I gather you work with that group of overage adolescents back there?" She nodded in the direction of the men still watching with obvious interest.

He looked back. Why wasn't he surprised to see his crew raising their arms and making all sorts of asinine remarks? He frowned at them, which only made matters worse.

"Yeah, I guess you could say that." She'd been so busy checking *him* out, Mark noted with satisfaction, that she'd overlooked the sign that declared to one and all that Harrison Construction, Inc., was in charge of the project.

She tipped her head back to take in the tall steel-and-concrete supports. "The ideal setup for the man who likes to stay on top of things," she mused.

"Yeah, I do like to be on top," Mark drawled, his gaze sweeping over her with lazy regard, so she couldn't possibly miss his meaning.

Chelsea gave an icy smile, but her stomach was busy doing somersaults from the heated expression in his eyes. The man was pure sex on the hoof! And the worst part was, he knew it. How she'd love to knock him off balance. "Yes, I imagine some *boys* never outgrow their passion for Erector sets." Her eyes gleamed in triumph as the fires flaring in his indicated that she'd scored a direct hit.

"What exactly do you do here, Mr. Harrison?" she said quickly, a little unsettled by her momentary boldness.

He watched her play of expressions for a moment,

then answered easily, "Oh, a little of this and a little of that."

He let his gaze drift over her slim, tailored skirt and dynamite legs, then glanced at the row of tiny buttons dotting her creamy blouse. Fantasies about loosening each and every last one of those buttons to discover just what was underneath danced through his mind. He silently cursed the tight fit of his jeans and forced himself to look into Chelsea Brennan's cool eyes, the better to imagine he was standing in the middle of an Arctic blizzard.

"This mall is going to be something when it's finished. Three stories' worth of shops and entertainment centers," he said conversationally.

"I know. I've seen the plans." She tucked her clutch bag more securely under her arm. "I hope you take great care on the upper stories."

He grinned. "Afraid I'll fall off and hurt myself?"

She shook her head. "No, my shop will be up there, and I don't want my customers to fall through the floor because someone forgot to hammer in a nail or whatever it is you do." She flashed a bright smile and began walking away. "Goodbye, Mr. Harrison. Have a nice day."

Loath to let the firecracker go, Mark stepped forward. "You have space here? That's great! Hey, how about our having a cup of coffee? We could talk about the construction of your shop."

She continued walking. "No thanks."

He scowled and pulled the bill of his baseball cap down over his eyes.

"You shouldn't ignore your little friends in the sandbox for too long," she called over her shoulder.

"Hey, Boss, you seem to be losing your touch," one of the men hooted. "Didn't the lady like your looks?"

Fuming, Mark watched Chelsea until she was out of sight. "It ain't over 'til it's over," he muttered.

CHELSEA BLAMED her swift walk as the reason for her shortness of breath. Better to blame it on that than on the man she had just encountered again. Even in sweaty work clothes, Mark Harrison looked like every red-blooded American woman's dream.

"Doesn't that man own anything other than jeans so tight they must cut off his circulation?" she muttered, resisting the urge to fan herself as visions of his broad chest, lean hips and cocky stance invaded her mind.

"Stop it, Chelsea! He was wrong for your daughter, and he's all wrong for you," she reminded herself. "Besides, he's so young, I doubt he even knows what gray hair is."

Yes, but wouldn't you like to peel off that shirt and see if you could find some? her brain jeered.

The mental picture sent heat rushing to her face.

"Early menopause," she declared to herself, making a sharp turn to enter a nearby drugstore to cool down in its air-conditioned interior. Yes, that's what it was. Just a few hot flashes, nothing more. She hit the glass door with the flat of her palm. "Yeah, right."

"HOT WHAT?"

The minute Chelsea was out of sight, Mark headed for the trailer to phone the leasing agent for information on Chelsea Brennan.

"Hot Stuff," Ariel Cummings repeated. "She specializes in high-fashion lingerie. All unique and very expensive. Husbands are known to tremble when their wives look in the shop windows, because they know the ladies won't stop at looking, and their credit cards and checkbooks are in grave danger. Funny, though. They never seem to regret the expense once they get home.''

Pricey lingerie, huh? Talk about the fantasies that conjured up. ''What else can you tell me about her?''

''What's to tell?'' Ariel said candidly. ''Chelsea is that rare woman who seems to keep her life sane by keeping men from messing it up. She has her business and her daughter, and she concentrates on those.''

''Is she divorced? Widowed?''

Ariel hesitated. ''She doesn't talk about her daughter's father, and some of us are polite enough not to ask,'' she said pointedly. ''But I can tell you she isn't easy prey.''

Mark's eyebrows shot up. He hadn't imagined Chelsea to be an unwed mother. But then again, if he hadn't met Colleen, he would have found it hard to imagine her as a mother, period. ''Maybe you'd put in a good word for me?'' he asked.

''Chelsea's a very serious lady, Mark, not someone out looking for a good time.''

The remark stung. ''Did you ever stop to think *I* might want more than fun and games?''

''You forget, my sweet, I've known you and your family for a long time. You like playing the field too much.''

''Maybe I have it out of my system,'' he argued, shifting from one foot to the other.

''Chelsea has enough to do keeping Colleen in line,'' Ariel persisted. ''She doesn't need you complicating her life. Why not pick on someone more your style to charm into bed?''

In a fit of pique, Mark muttered, ''People can

change,'' and he slammed the phone down. Then he tapped his pencil thoughtfully on the drafting table, wondering who he could buy some underwear for.

Chapter Three

"You're awfully jumpy today. Still worried about the bank loan? Or are you fretting about your renegade teenager?" Gwen asked her friend and partner as the two women set up new window displays after the shop closed that evening.

Elaine's mother had called with an invitation for Colleen to have dinner with them, and, with the assurance of strict parental supervision, Chelsea had sent her off. Now she studied the emerald green, silk peignoir in front of her and reached out to adjust the hem before replacing it over one of the tiny chairs that dotted the shop. "I knew that man was trouble the moment I saw him," she muttered, carefully tucking the price tag inside the bodice. "First he hits on a hapless seventeen-year-old, then..." She paused and grumbled, "Some men have no scruples."

"Could the man you're talking about be Colleen's rescuer?" Gwen asked archly. "I know Colleen wasn't too keen on him—no doubt it's hard to admire a guy who turns you in to your mom—but he sounded pretty yummy. Could he be a serious prospect?"

"Serious? He's probably the kind of bozo who believes serious reading material is the Sunday funnies."

"Come on, Chels," Gwen chided. "You've only talked to the guy once. And from what Colleen said, it was only to yell at him for daring to save your daughter from a drunk. Not exactly the best way to make friends and influence people—especially men."

"Twice," she snapped.

"Twice? So tell me, when did you see him the second time?" She studied her friend's flushed features. "Aha! It was today, wasn't it? When you went to the bank?" she guessed. "Of course! No wonder you came back so flustered. Did he make a pass at you?" she asked with her usual candor. "Get under your skin until you wanted him under your sheets?"

"Gwen!" Her shout echoed in the empty shop.

Unperturbed by her friend's distress, Gwen scrunched down to look in the mirror hanging over an antique chest, where lingerie spilled out of the drawers in charming disarray, inviting browsers to pick up and touch, ultimately, to buy. She licked the tip of one finger and used it to smooth her eyebrows. Dressed in a bright red jersey dress that clung to her angular body, she radiated a fire that belied her cool porcelain features. Gwen's wintry beauty was a perfect foil for Chelsea's warm glow.

"Chelsea!" she mocked. "Sweetie, you're thirty-nine, not ninety-three. In fact, my aunt is seventy-eight, and she still enjoys an active sex life. You could take a few lessons from her. Actually, we all could," she added dryly.

"I've had enough of men, thank you very much." Chelsea turned back to her careful draping of a silk-and-lace bra and tap pants against a cream-colored silk pillow. A garter belt in the same shade of emerald appeared to have been tossed on the floor of the display window next to a pair of sheer stockings similarly artfully arranged in "careless" disarray. It gave the impression of peeking into a woman's boudoir, with a trail of clothing leading the way to a bed offstage, where, naturally, a man awaited. "What would you think of putting that stool in here and setting the satin mules next to it?"

"Sounds sexy," Gwen agreed, heading for the other side of the shop to pick up the delicate satin cushioned stool. "You know, considering the way you decorate the windows, people would think you actually enjoy sensuality, rather than living the life of a nun. Come to think of it, a nun's social life is probably more active than yours."

"I am happy with my life the way it is," Chelsea stated between gritted teeth.

"So tell me again—what does Mark Harrison look like?" Gwen asked innocently.

The sudden question caught Chelsea off guard, and, without thinking, she answered it.

"Tall—about six feet—dark hair, brown eyes, muscular build, probably from his work in construction. Looks great in tight jeans. Has the kind of buns you wouldn't mind taking a bite out of and—" Then it hit her. "Gwen!" She looked as if she wanted nothing more than to strangle her best friend.

Gwen merely smirked. "I rest my case. You've got the hots for the guy. And, believe me, he sounds worth it. There's so few good men around."

"If you think he's that great, you can just head over to the mall construction site and pick him up yourself. I surely won't be seeing him again."

Chelsea clenched her teeth as she arranged the high heels and nervously made unnecessary adjustments to the resulting display. Didn't she have enough problems without fantasizing about some macho, arrogant construction worker? Gwen's comments about the sensuality of her work notwithstanding, Chelsea had never much liked men who were overly cocky about their sexuality or anything else. So what was so special about Mark Harrison? And why did he bother her so much? As Gwen had said, he'd only tried to help.

She tried to push him out of her mind, reminding herself that she had enough to occupy her attention, what with her loan and getting the new shop off the ground. No luck. Was it really Mark's lack of scruples that bothered her? Or was it something else? Some...hidden chord he struck inside her.

"This just isn't working," she grumbled, hiking up her skirt and kneeling in the window to fiddle with the display.

"Now I'm really curious to see this man," Gwen mused, tapping her forefinger against her chin.

"He's all yours," Chelsea said through clenched teeth, shifting her position in the small space.

BOLD TEAL SCRIPT on a pale gray sign overhead declared the shop to be Hot Stuff, lingerie and evening wear for the sensual woman. The window displays on either side of the door were enough to knock a man's socks off— among other things, Mark reflected.

A cream velvet backdrop prompted visions of a woman's bare skin, while a frosty blue nightie made up of nothing more than a few scraps of lace and sheer fabric had him thinking of ice pressed against heated flesh. He stared at the small ornate table topped with an antique frosted-glass perfume bottle, conjuring images of an old-fashioned canopy bed with a deep, feathery mattress.

"Wow," he breathed, unable to take his eyes from

the sensual setting. Curious now to see the second window display, he reluctantly moved on, disappointed to spot the Closed sign tucked in the glass door as he passed. His disappointment quickly fled when he noticed a familiar figure kneeling inside the next window. Her position revealed a great deal of nice-looking thigh.

Finding it difficult to keep a grin from blossoming, he stood smack in the middle of the sidewalk, certain that, sooner or later, she'd have to notice him.

"Gwen, I need more tape," Chelsea called out.

"My, my, my, I do believe I see one of those few good men," Gwen fairly purred, looking over Chelsea's head as she passed her the tape.

Chelsea glanced over her shoulder and almost dropped the satin mule she was holding. "Oh, no!" she moaned.

Mark grinned broadly and gave a cocky thumbs-up signal. "Very nice," he mouthed.

"You mean he's the one?" Gwen sounded delighted as she waggled her fingers at Mark.

"Unfortunately."

"Unfortunately, my foot. He's gorgeous!" Gwen headed for the door and opened it. "Hi there," she greeted him. "I understand you're the man who rescued the fair Colleen from a fate worse than death."

"Guilty as charged." He tucked his hands into his jeans pockets and rocked back and forth on his heels, looking about as "Aw, shucks, ma'am" as a timber wolf. "Interesting shop."

"Why not come in and get a better look?"

"We're closed!" Chelsea protested.

Gwen flashed her a sly look. "Come on, Chels, let's get a male point of view here. You know very well some of our best customers are men." She held out her hand as Mark walked inside. "I'm Gwen Blake, Chelsea's partner in crime around here."

"Mark Harrison." He eyed her long red-lacquered nails dubiously. "Do you have those things registered with the police as lethal weapons?" He grinned engagingly. "And they say females are the weaker sex. Well, you couldn't prove it by me. You two—and your window displays—are downright dangerous."

Gwen preened, and Chelsea glared. "My, aren't we cute," Chelsea mumbled.

He grinned. "Oh, we try."

Gwen looked from one to the other. "Well, people, as much as I hate to miss what might happen next, I think it's time for me to leave. Bye." She sailed out the door before Chelsea could open her mouth to protest.

Chelsea wanted to say something nasty, but she just couldn't make herself. Not when there was a weird, tumbling sensation going on in her midsection. "What do you want?"

Mark rocked back on his heels before leaning forward to whisper in her ear. "Never ask a leading question, sweetheart, unless you're prepared to hear the answer."

Chelsea turned red. She looked away from him as she climbed out of the window, pretending the fact that her skirt had ridden up practically to her waist wasn't all that embarrassing.

She turned around, fully prepared to politely tell Mark it had been a long day and she needed to get home. Instead, she found him strolling through the shop, stopping here and there to study something. He put out his hand to cautiously finger a silk robe, then hastily withdrew it.

"It's all right to touch it," Chelsea said quietly. "That's why we display the merchandise the way we do. People use their senses in choosing clothing. If it feels good, they're more tempted to buy.''

He looked over his shoulder and smiled. ''Maybe so, but hands like mine aren't meant for touching something this delicate. I'd snag the fabric. Calluses come with my line of work.''

The image of hands roughened from manual labor stroking her bare skin in a caress both rough and sensitive made her nerve endings quiver.

She cleared her throat. ''Not all the men who come in here have perfect manicures. If I'm not worried, why should you be?''

He tentatively fingered a black silk-and-lace chemise, then bent to peer at the tiny price tag. ''A hundred and fifty dollars?'' His voice rose.

''It's French lace,'' she explained, doubting that many construction workers would buy French lace for their wives or girlfriends. Was Mark shopping for a special woman? Something deep inside her told her he was unmarried. For all his faults, he seemed too open to deceive a wife by flirting with other women.

''At that price, might as well fly to France directly for it.'' Mark straightened up. ''Give me cotton jockey briefs anytime.''

Chelsea's eyes dove to his faded denim jeans, and suddenly the room seemed close and sweltering. She fingered the top button of her blouse, furtively easing the collar from her throat.

''If you don't mind, the shop is closed, and I need to get home,'' she choked. She hadn't craved a cigarette for the two years since she'd quit. Right now, though, she'd kill for a smoke.

Mark leaned against an armoire. ''Why?''

''Why?'' she echoed, unsettled and confused.

"Why do you need to get home right away?"

"Because it's been a long day, and I'm tired."

"So you're not rushing home to your daughter?"

"No, she's having dinner at Elaine's," she replied without thinking.

Mark nodded. "You know, I'm not such a bad guy. I don't drink too much, I'm kind to animals, I like kids, my family will vouch for my sterling character, and I don't scratch or belch in public. My car and truck are paid for, and I can afford more than a hamburger at the local steak joint as long as you don't order the large fries."

"Are you asking me for a date?" Chelsea questioned incredulously. She was grateful for the dim lighting, which hid her blush, but the intimate atmosphere it lent made her nervous. What was it about this man that made her simultaneously so skittish and yet so bold?

He cocked his head to one side and considered her question. "Yeah, I guess you could say I am."

"I don't think that would be a good idea."

Mark rubbed a hand over his jaw. The soft rasp of beard bristles seemed loud in the charged silence. Then he straightened up and walked over to her with the loose-hipped stride that made her think of a jungle animal stalking its prey. "Okay, then, we won't call it a date. Just two people interested in the mall construction having dinner together."

This man just wouldn't take no for an answer. And, for the life of her, Chelsea could barely remember why she was trying so hard to make him.

"How old are you?" she asked suddenly.

"I'll be thirty in a couple of months. Why?"

Even younger than she'd thought. "I'm thirty-nine."

"So?"

"So I don't date younger men."

He halted in front of her. "Why not?"

The question never having arisen before, she had no logical answer. "I just don't."

He stood so close to her she could feel the heat of his skin, inhale the musky aroma of manly sweat, see the sparks in his dark eyes.

"It has nothing to do with my being younger, does it?" His soft voice set the downy hairs on her arms on end. "It has to do with your being scared."

"Scared!" she scoffed with false bravado.

"You're scared to go out with me. Scared to enjoy yourself. Scared to let yourself in for a situation you can't completely control." He backed away from her. "Hell, I only asked you to dinner, not for a night of debauched sex. But I guess even a dinner out would be too much for you." He headed for the door. "Sorry if I ruined your day, Ms. Brennan."

"Wait!" Her cry sounded torn from her throat.

He stopped at the door but didn't turn around. He was leaving it all up to her.

"You're right," Chelsea said haltingly, crossing her arms in front of her chest. "There's nothing wrong with our going out to dinner. After all, you did rescue my daughter, and I owe you for that."

"You owe me zip."

A second nicotine fit clawed its way up her throat. Would that she'd bought a pack of cigarettes that afternoon in the drugstore. "I'd like to freshen up first, but I could meet you in an hour or so."

"Fine. I'll swing by my place and clean up, and I'll pick you up in an hour." He opened the door.

She didn't want him at her house again. "I can meet you and save you the effort."

Mark shook his head. "Nope. A gentleman always picks up his date." The grin he flashed her was anything but gentlemanly, and Chelsea felt the slim remainder of her peace of mind flutter in the breeze as he opened the door and walked out, whistling as he went.

CHELSEA CONTINUED reminding herself that this was simply a courtesy dinner, nothing more. It would give her an opportunity to verify his honorable intentions about rescuing her daughter, and then they could go their separate ways.

"And I can remind Gwen that, yes, I have dated a living, breathing male who had nothing to do with our business," she said out loud with satisfaction as she freshened her makeup. She had changed into taupe evening trousers and a chiffon blouse in swirling shades of rust, gold, soft orange and tan. Now she worried that the blouse might be a little provocative, with its sheer sleeves and back, even though the mocha silk camisole she wore underneath hid everything important. She hadn't worn this blouse yet, and as she dabbed on perfume she nervously wondered why she had chosen tonight to do so. Suddenly she heard the back door open and slam shut.

"Hey, Mom, where are you? You can run, but you can't hide from me." Colleen's laughing voice drifted upward. "I saw your car in the garage."

"Darn, and here I tried so hard," Chelsea called back. Suddenly she wished she had been gone before Colleen got home. That way, she could have left a note that she'd gone out with a friend. Now, Colleen would learn the truth.

Colleen appeared in the doorway. "Whoa! That outfit

can't be for lounging around the house," she said slyly. "What gives?"

"I'm going out for dinner." Chelsea tried to sound casual. "Why aren't you still at the Curtises'?"

Colleen plopped onto the bed and leaned back against the brass headboard. She picked up one of the burnt orange-and-bronze-striped pillows and hugged it against her chest. "We finished dinner an hour ago, and I didn't want to jeopardize my time off for good behavior by staying out too late," she grumbled good-naturedly. "So, who are you going out with?"

Chelsea swallowed a sigh. As Colleen had said, she could run, but she couldn't hide. "Mark Harrison." Her back was to her daughter as she pulled out a taupe leather clutch bag and transferred items into it.

"Him?" Colleen sounded pained. She scooted down and stretched out on her back, studying her mom through narrowed eyes. "Why would you go out with Mr. Straight-and-Narrow?"

"Because he asked me." She tried for a nonchalant air but failed miserably. She began searching through her jewelry chest for her hammered bronze earrings.

"If you're looking for those bronze discs, I've got them." Colleen jumped up from the bed and ran out of the room to retrieve them.

"I should have had a boy who wouldn't borrow my clothes and jewelry," Chelsea groused.

"Yeah, but that would have stuck you with Little League, Boy Scouts and dirt tracked into the house on football cleats all day long." Colleen returned and dropped the earrings into her mother's palm. "And he probably would have demanded a python for his birthday instead of asking for a car—that I still haven't seen."

"And won't for a very long time. As for everything else, you're right, sweetheart. Instead, I was team mother for powder-puff softball, assistant leader while you were in Girl Scouts, driver for your out-of-town soccer games, and I swept dirt out of the kitchen several times a day from your running shoes. How on earth did I end up so lucky?"

"You never had to escort me to the mens' room," Colleen pointed out.

Chelsea looked into the mirror as she fastened her earrings. "I'm sure I could have handled it."

"Do you think Mark Harrison is cute?"

Chelsea stilled at her daughter's abrupt change of topic. "I haven't really thought about it," she lied judiciously.

"Well, I think you can do better," Colleen announced, grateful her mother didn't know of her plans to find her the right kind of man. "You know, find someone...livelier."

Chelsea raised her eyebrows at the thought of someone livelier than Mark Harrison. "Why don't you go do something useful, daughter dear?"

"Such as lock myself in my room?"

"Sounds good to me."

Colleen levered herself up off the bed. "I was just offering my opinion," she declared with a martyred air.

"A son wouldn't have done this to me," Chelsea muttered, carefully applying her lipstick. She froze when she heard the peal of the doorbell. She quickly finished and hurried downstairs.

The moment her hand covered the cool metal doorknob, she took a deep breath and pasted a bright smile on her face. Then she threw open the door.

"Hi," she greeted Mark, stepping back to let him enter.

"You look lovely," Mark said huskily.

Chelsea put her hand over her stomach to stop the butterflies from their war dance. When the man cleaned up, he cleaned up beautifully.

"Th-thank you." She found herself drowning in his big brown eyes.

Mark raised a hand as if to touch her, but he was stayed by two short bursts of the doorbell.

Chelsea couldn't stop looking at him. "I—I guess it must be a friend of Colleen's," she whispered, forcing her lethargic limbs to move as she gestured Mark toward the living room and turned to open the door again.

The moment Chelsea caught sight of her unexpected visitor, she knew he couldn't be one of Colleen's friends. She *prayed* he wasn't one of Colleen's friends. Otherwise, her daughter wouldn't be allowed to leave the house until she was thirty.

The man was in his midforties, deeply tanned, with several gold chains adorning his half-bared chest. In addition, he was probably quite bald when he wasn't wearing one of the worst toupees Chelsea had ever seen.

"Hey, baby, I'm here to see Chelsea," he greeted her with a shark's grin. "I understand she's looking for a real man."

Chapter Four

"So, who was your admirer?" Mark asked casually. "For a lady who talks about not dating much, you seem pretty popular," he added as the cocktail waitress set a plate of hot hors d'oeuvres in the middle of the small table.

Chelsea grimaced. Herman's nightmarish arrival would remain stuck in her mind for a long time to come—and a certain seventeen-year-old girl would have reason to remember as well. She took a stick of fried zucchini. "I guess you noticed that Colleen suddenly couldn't leave her room." She wrinkled her nose. "Herman told me he read my ad in a lonely hearts column—about how I was looking for a good man in hopes of having a 'meaningful' relationship. I don't think he believed me when I told him I hadn't placed that ad."

She suddenly giggled. "The poor man. When that gust of wind came up and tipped his toupee over one ear…" Chelsea succumbed to full laughter. "I honestly tried not to laugh, but— By the way, what did you say to him that made him even angrier?" Mark had made his presence known and escorted the man to his car.

"I suggested he either try a stronger glue for his toupee or go without it. That a lot of women find bald men very sexy." He winced. "He told me to shave my head and see if I feel the same way afterward."

Chelsea sighed and sipped her drink. "I do know one thing. Colleen and I are going to have a very long talk when I get home. I just can't believe she did that. And why."

Mark eased his chair closer to hers. "Since I don't intend to get you home very early, I'm sure she'll be able to come up with a wonderful tale."

Chelsea felt a shiver of delight travel up her spine at his words, and she struggled to suppress it. "She'll stick to the truth if she knows what's good for her. And, like my daughter, I also have a curfew."

"Self-imposed, I'm sure. And rules are meant to be broken." And he gave her a smile that Chelsea was sure could break any rule—and any heart.

"I'm too old for you," she whispered weakly.

"You and I both know age has nothing to do with it." Mark was idly circling the rim of his glass with a bronzed forefinger while his eyes probed hers. "We're both consenting adults, who are getting to know each other...." His voice trailed off meaningfully.

Chelsea couldn't keep her eyes off the sensual way Mark touched his glass. It didn't take much imagination to envision him touching her with that same reverence— a light, provocative stroking that would send helpless shivers along a woman's skin.

She forced herself back to the present. "I..." She coughed to clear her throat. "I run a demanding business, and I'm raising a daughter who's entering a challenging time in her life. As I told you before, my free time is very limited, and most of that I choose to spend with Colleen."

"And you call that an excuse for not dating? Forgive

me, but Colleen doesn't seem like a clinging, helpless child, and your line of business suggests to me that you're not exactly a dried up old hag yourself.''

Chelsea silently congratulated herself on not throwing the plate of appetizers at him. Instead, she bit almost violently into a wedge of toasted Brie, at a frustrating loss for words and composure.

Mark threw back his head and laughed at her reaction. ''You're one prickly lady,'' he teased. ''Come on, loosen up. Tell me about yourself—and not just about your daughter and your business. Why don't you start with the men in your past?'' He smiled when he noticed the wary look on her face. ''I have to admit that I'm curious about Colleen's father.''

''Colleen's father didn't want to be a father. He took off when he learned I was pregnant,'' she said quietly, fingering her glass. ''After that, I didn't want to get serious with anyone. I had a baby to raise and school to finish.''

Not because of Colleen, but because she didn't want to get hurt again, Mark thought to himself.

She looked up suddenly, as if startled by her own frankness, and pasted on a bright smile. ''Now it's your turn. Tell me about your scandalous past.''

''Not much to tell,'' he said promptly, hurting inside for her but grateful no other man had yet claimed her.

''I can't believe that.''

''Believe it. Oh, there were the usual...flings, and one long-term relationship. She decided her career was more important than me, so we parted company. And, right now, this mall takes up a lot of my time.''

''You never said exactly what you do there,'' she pressed.

He grinned. ''Promise you won't get mad?''

Chelsea narrowed her eyes. "Why would I get mad?"

He shrugged. "The company in charge of the mall is Harrison Construction."

She stared at him. "Such as Mark Harrison?"

"Such as Don Harrison, my dad, and my brothers and myself. I'm the youngest."

She wanted to be angry about his earlier charade, but she realized that she, after all, was the one who'd automatically assumed he was just one of the work crew. "As I said before, don't screw up the second floor," she advised.

"Sorry I'm not a run-of-the-mill tradesman?"

Chelsea smiled. "Well, I have a rickety front step that's been driving me crazy."

The maître d' approached them with the news their table was ready. As they walked into the dining room, Chelsea glanced around appreciatively. The restaurant was fairly new; one she hadn't been in before. The semisecluded seating, dim lighting, ornate table settings and hushed atmosphere bespoke quality and elegance.

"This seems like the kind of place that has ten waiters for every table," she murmured over the top of her menu after they had been seated and handed the leather-bound folders listing the day's offerings in elegant calligraphy.

"Yup," Mark confirmed. "If I showed up here during the day, they'd, oh, so politely usher me out the back door before the patrons got a load of a real working person. I bet they even checked my credit rating while we were waiting for our table."

Chelsea swallowed a giggle, and he grinned, leaned across the table, and lowered his voice conspiratorially. "To be honest, some of these places give me the creeps. I figure they're trying to decide where I bought my tie and whether my suit was off the rack or tailor-made."

"Then why did we come here?"

"Because I wanted to impress you," he said easily. "I wanted to show you that under all the dirt and calluses, I can be a classy guy." He leaned closer. "I wanted you to enjoy tonight so much that you won't give me such a hard time the next time I ask you out."

And I want to see all of that silky thing you're wearing under that blouse that drove me crazy as I followed you through this room, he thought.

Chelsea studied her nails. "Mark, I—I'm serious about my limited free time," she said softly. "I'm happy with the life I have, and, well, there's very little room left in it for anything else."

Mark cocked his head to one side. "Basically, this is a 'Thanks for asking me out, just don't bother doing it again' speech, right? I gotta give you credit, Chelsea, you didn't even wait until the end of the evening to tell me. You waded right in before we even ordered our meal. I must have made a great first impression for you to just spit this out." He made a show of studying his hands. "Let's see, I remembered to clean my nails before I picked you up."

"Stop it!" she snapped. "You're taking this the wrong way."

He rubbed his jaw. "Yep, I did shave."

Chelsea's fingers curled around her wineglass. How upset would people get if she threw it at him?

Mark shrugged. "So, what's my unforgivable crime?"

"Have you decided what you wish to order?" The waiter had suddenly appeared.

"Perhaps the lady would appreciate some steak tartare to sink her teeth into," Mark murmured.

Chelsea winced at the deserved jab and fitfully collected herself sufficiently to order—a civilized, cooked entrée. Why did this man get her so angry? He wasn't anything like any man she'd ever dated in the past, and on a minute-to-minute basis he seemed to challenge her very sanity.

"Do you act like this with every woman you take out?" she asked once their waiter had glided away as silently as he had come.

"No, I usually sit on my motorcycle in the driveway and gun the engine until she comes out, and then we head for one of the truck stops on the edge of town. There's a pretty good selection of bars out there, too. Sometimes I even shave and put on a clean T-shirt, just to give a girl a thrill."

"Damn, you mean I missed out on something that thrilling?" she bantered.

"Sorry, babe, maybe next time." Mark gave that lethal grin of his.

The idea of a next time with him suddenly appealed to her very much. Proof positive that she *was* losing her mind.

"Are you going to keep your other shop once the mall opens?" he asked conversationally, now that the ice was broken again.

"I thought about it at first, but I decided two shops so close by would only compete with each other. But the new shop will be about twice the size of my old one, so I'll be able to expand my stock and institute a few things I can't now."

"Such as?"

"More dressing rooms, more evening wear and accessories. Definitely a larger stockroom and an open area for fashion shows in the future."

"Lingerie fashion shows, huh?" he said, arching his eyebrows.

She shook her head in mock despair. "You men do like to ogle lovely models wearing skimpy garments, don't you. Well, men do shop at Hot Stuff along with women, so I guess we have to put up with you. I'm planning to have special showings around the holidays, Valentine's Day and Mother's Day that ought to help men with their choices. Last Christmas we served coffee and pastries and did everything possible to put men at ease, and it turned out to be such a success, we plan to repeat it."

Mark thought of the many sensual textures and colors spilling out of drawers and draped around the cozy shop. While he personally hadn't felt uncomfortable there, he realized that some guys might feel like intruders in such an exclusively female world unless specially invited. Personally, he wondered if Chelsea's bedroom displayed such colors and textures.

"Why lingerie?" he asked, although he believed he knew the answer. Underneath the all-business mom lurked one sensual woman.

She shrugged uneasily. "Why not? It's become a large business over the years. The growth of Victoria's Secret is proof positive. Women like pretty things, and lovely lingerie makes them feel more feminine. One of my best clients is a stockbroker for a very conservative firm, and she has to wear dark colors and severely cut suits to please her superiors. Little do they know underneath those ultrastraight suits she wears some incredible lingerie. But she knows, and she likes the feeling."

"So do you wear your own merchandise and savor the secret feelings?" he asked huskily.

She thought she would drown in his gaze. To save

herself she answered archly, "Well, what kind of merchant would I be if I didn't appreciate my own wares?"

"Are you tonight?"

"Am I what tonight?"

"Wearing your own sexy wares. If so, I'd be happy to provide a male endorsement later."

"Dream on," she huffed.

Mark looked at her with admiration warming his eyes. "Oh, I will. You're pretty quick on the comeback when you want to be, aren't you."

"A seventeen-year-old daughter keeps me on my toes," she said pointedly.

"Ah, we're back to safer subjects. All right, you win—for now. So, how long have you had your shop?"

That was a subject she'd happily talk about. "Almost seven years. I scrimped and saved to open it, and there were times I wasn't sure I'd manage," she admitted. "But I was determined I wasn't going to fail. With a child to support, I couldn't afford to."

"It sounds like you haven't," he told her with warm sincerity.

He paused as the waiter whisked away their salad plates and replaced them with their meals, then continued with, "So, the lady doesn't need anything or anybody. She's completely self-sufficient."

"Obviously, you're still young enough to believe in the tooth fairy."

He shook his head, amused by her sniping. "Cut the jive, Chelsea. You're not some wise old woman of the world, and I'm not some kid still wet behind the ears," he said softly but dangerously. "And I sure as hell didn't ask you out because I need a mother figure."

She gazed at him, then pointed at his plate. "Eat your green beans," she said in her best motherly scold.

He grinned. "Be grateful they didn't serve peas. I might have embarrassed you by hiding them under my knife until I had a chance to sweep them under the table."

"I was that way about carrots," Chelsea admitted. "My older sister told me if I ate them my hair would turn orange. Since I was six and she was ten, I believed her. My parents would coax and threaten, but it didn't do any good. I refused to eat them. I spent a lot of evenings at the dinner table until my bedtime."

They exchanged other horror stories, and, without knowing just how it had happened, Chelsea found herself having a wonderful time.

"How about a nightcap somewhere?" Mark asked as they waited for the parking lot valet to bring his car to the door.

Chelsea reluctantly shook her head. "It's a workday for me tomorrow, and I have a chamber of commerce breakfast to attend in the morning."

With a mysterious smile, Mark graciously ushered her into the waiting car and drove her straight home. Chelsea had expected an argument about the night still being young, and the fact that Mark didn't say anything prompted her to wonder if perhaps she wasn't all that great a date. Of course, she had tried to discourage him. So why did she feel so let down? She actually had to battle the urge to pout.

"Here we are, safe and sound," he announced, stopping the car in her driveway.

Chelsea pasted on a smile. "Thank you for dinner. It was—" But she was talking to thin air. Mark had hopped out of the car and walked around to open her door.

"I was taught always to walk a lady to her door," he

informed her, taking her hand and helping her out. "Now, the evening didn't go all that badly, did it? In fact, I think it went pretty well. So there's no reason not to try again."

All her fears came rushing back, and Chelsea dug in her heels the moment they reached the front door. "Mark, I—" She had opened her mouth to argue, but not another word escaped. Not when Mark's mouth covered hers in a sizzling good-night kiss.

He didn't just kiss; he stroked and caressed and nibbled his way along every millimeter of her mouth. His tongue dipped inside and invited hers to play hide-and-seek. And his hands—they were lethal to a woman's sanity! His fingers traveled down her spine, then back up again.

"Now," he breathed once he'd kissed her senseless, "that wasn't so bad, was it? In fact, I'd give it an *A.*" He tapped the tip of her nose. "Good night, Chelsea. Sleep well." He walked back to his car whistling a jaunty tune.

Still in shock, Chelsea finally forced her legs to move one at a time and ordered her hand to unlock and open the door.

"Hi, how was your evening?" Colleen clattered down the stairs.

Praying that her daughter's sharp eyes would miss her dazed, glassy-eyed look, she murmured, "It...it was all right," as she walked woodenly toward the rear of the house.

Colleen's amused gaze followed her mother. "Does this mean you're not mad about Herman?"

"Mad? I'm furious. And...and we'll discuss it first thing in the morning."

Chapter Five

"Why, Ms. Brennan. Fancy meeting you here." The voice was male, smooth and much too utterly charming for seven o'clock in the morning.

Chelsea looked up from her cup of coffee. Mark not only sounded utterly charming at this ungodly hour, he looked damn good, while, after a largely sleepless night, she looked like something dragged out of a swamp. It was bad enough that the last place she wanted to be was this city business leaders' breakfast and monthly meeting. It was worse to confront the man responsible for her insomnia and to see him look so damn gorgeous! It would be relatively easy to hate him, she mused.

"Go away," she said succinctly.

His broad smile didn't waver as he straddled a chair alongside her and rested his crossed arms along the back. "Not a morning person, I take it. Now me, I love mornings. There's nothing more breathtaking than watching the sun come up. Unless it's watching the sunrise with a beautiful woman. Although then I usually miss the sunrise."

Her jaw ached from clenching it so tightly. "Shut up."

He was undeterred. "I like to go running first thing in the morning. There's usually no one out."

"Because they're all smart enough to be in bed where they belong."

"Yep, there's nothing like running on a misty morning with the fog rolling around you." He sighed. "Pure solitude, as if there's no one else in the world but you. Unless of course, you've got a beautiful woman with you. Then you really could care less what the weather is like."

"Vampires retreat to their coffins at dawn, and normal people wait until the sun is well and truly up before venturing out of bed." She sipped her coffee, closing her eyes with relief as the caffeine seeped into her system.

Mark arched an eyebrow. "Have trouble sleeping last night?"

She wasn't about to answer that. "I slept like a baby," she lied with aplomb, hoping that the extra layer of concealer under her eyes hid the dark circles she'd faced that morning after a restless night of reliving a kiss she shouldn't have responded to to begin with.

He nodded knowingly, letting her know he knew she was lying but was magnanimous enough not to mention it. "I'm going for some of that breakfast buffet. How about you?"

The last thing her flip-flopping stomach wanted was food. "Just coffee is fine for me."

He shrugged as he straightened up. "Save my seat."

"Not if I can help it," she muttered, watching him walk away. "No man should look that good this early in the morning."

"Just think what he probably looks like before he's gotten out of bed." Mercy Hampton, owner of a card and gift store in town, took a seat next to her. She flipped a stray lock of dark blond hair behind her shoulder. "I can see him now—unshaven, heavy-eyed, bare chest— and bare everything else. Yummy." She broke off a piece of her blueberry muffin and popped it into her mouth.

"You've got to quit reading those romance novels, Mercy," Chelsea reprimanded. "They're giving you ideas."

"Those kinds of ideas I can live with." She plucked a tiny container of cream out of the basket in the middle of the table and poured it into her coffee. "You weren't here the first time he showed up at a meeting. All the women practically had heart failure. Yours truly included. I haven't missed a meeting since. Unfortunately, he doesn't show up all the time."

Chelsea looked around. Unless she was mistaken, there *were* more women present than usual. And a good percentage of them were looking Mark's way. They also looked extremely hungry, and she sensed it wasn't for the breakfast buffet.

"So, how did you meet the gorgeous Mr. Harrison?" Mercy asked, drawing Chelsea's attention away from the horde of usually dieting women who'd suddenly developed an interest in trying a bit of everything at the buffet tables.

She shrugged. "His company is building the new mall."

"Well, I know *that*. I'll have a shop in there, too, remember? Come on, Chels," she prodded. "The man acted as if he knew you real *well*, if you get my drift."

Chelsea turned in her chair and eyed her friend. "We met through Colleen. We had dinner last night, and that was it."

Mercy looked crestfallen. "Damn, nothing exciting ever happens around here," she groused.

"Get a life, Mercy."

"I have one, and it's about as boring as watching grass grow. My two cats have a better social life than I do, and both of them are neutered!"

"I can relate to that," Chelsea murmured.

"What?" Mercy looked up.

Chelsea shook her head. "Nothing. Just talking to myself."

"Better watch that. They say it's a sign of old age," she teased.

Chelsea's answering smile was a bit strained. Age wasn't something she liked to consider, with the big four-oh looming closer and closer on the horizon. "I won't worry until I start answering myself. That's when it gets dangerous."

"Dangerous? Talking about me?" Mark set a loaded plate on the table, sat down and reached for a napkin. He shared an engaging grin with both women, but his eyes seemed heated when directed Chelsea's way.

"Actually, we were discussing age," she said pointedly. She glanced at his plate, which appeared to have large helpings of pretty much everything. "I guess you were hungry," she commented dryly. "Did you leave anything for the others?"

"A few crumbs. Besides, a woman I know keeps implying I'm still a growing boy." He bestowed that heartstopping smile on her again, picked up a biscuit and buttered it liberally. While Chelsea didn't usually eat breakfast, the hot buttered biscuit in his strong, masculine hands suddenly looked like a tiny piece of heaven. So much so that her mouth practically watered at the sight.

To her surprise, he held it out to her.

"You look hungry," he said softly. "You'd make me feel better if you ate something."

Hungry indeed. With trembling fingers she accepted the biscuit and took a tiny bite before placing it on the small plate next to her coffee cup.

Mercy, who was busy looking from one to the other, spoke up.

"So, you met through Colleen," she said to Mark.

Mark nodded as he munched on a slice of bacon. "Yeah, Colleen had car trouble one night," he lied shamelessly, to Chelsea's eternal gratitude, "and I gave her a lift home." Eternity evaporated, however, with his next words. "Chelsea and I met and hit it off instantly. A match made in heaven," he declared with satisfaction. "She asked me out that very night."

Chelsea's eyes grew saucer round. "I did not! You coerced *me* into going out with *you!*"

"Is she always like this?" Mark appealed to Mercy, who was trying very hard not to giggle.

"No, usually she's worse," she confided, leaning forward as if imparting a deep, dark secret. "I'm surprised that she even agreed to go out with you, since her idea of a hot night is having her legs waxed."

Chelsea buried her face in her hands. "I knew I should have slept in," she moaned.

"So, you think I might have a chance with her?" Mark slanted a wicked glance Chelsea's way as he directed his question at Mercy.

"If you play your cards right."

"I can't believe this," Chelsea went on. As if anyone were bothering to listen to her. She glanced around the table to see what other civic leaders might be eavesdropping on this humiliating conversation. An older gentleman who owned several dry cleaning shops winked at her, and she moaned again.

"So, how long have you known Chelsea?" Mark inquired.

"About three years. My card shop was next to hers until rent hikes forced me to find a cheaper space. But now I've gotten a great deal with the new mall's leasing company, and I can't wait to move in." Her dark blue eyes sparkled with anticipation.

Chelsea eyed her friend, trying to see her as a man would. Mercy was pretty in an old-fashioned way, with her long ash-blond hair pulled away from her china doll features. The delicate lace blouse and calf-length blue print skirt completed the look of a gracious bygone era. Mark seemed indifferent to the entire effect.

"With luck, it won't be too long now," he told Mercy. "We've pretty much made up for the delays caused by last spring's rains."

Several of the others at the table began questioning Mark about the mall's construction, and they were soon engrossed in a general conversation about the placement of ramps, escalators, elevators and walkways. Chelsea got up from her chair and walked to the buffet table to refill her coffee cup. As she returned, she sneaked a glance at Mark. He was dressed in charcoal gray twill slacks and a Wedgwood blue V-neck sweater with a white dress shirt underneath.

"No wonder the women are practically falling all over themselves," she muttered. "He's brawny, broad-shouldered and downright beautiful."

A woman stopped her on her way back to her table. "Chelsea, do you have those new bustiers in yet?"

"Not yet, Lorraine. They should be in by the end of next week," she replied, halting at the woman's chair.

"But I did get in a new shipment of camisoles you'll love. Some nice strong colors that just glow against your skin. Some are plain with spaghetti straps, and others have lace insets in the neckline."

"My charge card loves you," Lorraine groaned. "I'll be in tomorrow to see them."

Assured of a sale, Chelsea resumed her walk back to her table. As she slid into her seat she looked at Mark, who turned his head in her direction.

"Still hungry?" he whispered.

She frowned. "The biscuit did me just fine, thank you."

He arched an eyebrow and leaned closer. "I can do much better than a biscuit, you know. And you can thank me when we're alone," he murmured.

Chelsea would have loved to bat down his blatancy, but not when they had an avid audience in the background. She was grateful it was time for the speaker. Anything to keep her mind on business!

Except it didn't work. Not with Mark seated so close to her. It wasn't as if he did anything to achieve her notice, but then, he didn't have to. He simply sat there listening to the speaker with the same rapt attention he gave to everything else, and she was enraptured simply looking at him!

She couldn't understand herself! This was not her usual style. Before, she had always found it easy to compartmentalize men as necessary evils for the propagation of the species and other sundry tasks. But now...

How did he do it? she wondered on a grumbling note. After all, they'd shared one of the hottest kisses in history last night, and here he was acting as if she were just another business person at a chamber of commerce breakfast meeting.

Realizing her wildly contradictory impulses toward the man, she began to fear that, if she wasn't careful, she'd begin to act like a love-crazy female. And that was one thing she'd vowed never to do. Once again firm in her convictions to take no chances and suffer no feminine foolishness, she decided to leave early before she had time to reconsider.

"I've got to get to the shop," she whispered to Mercy as the speaker began to wind down. She was grateful their table was situated near the rear of the room so she would cause no commotion while she made her escape.

"Lunch tomorrow?" Mercy whispered back.

"Sounds good. Call me later." She scooped up her purse and crept out as quietly as possible. She wasn't sure whether to feel irritated or relieved that Mark hadn't even turned his head while she retreated. And then she was irritated with herself for even considering the question! Darn Mark Harrison and all the kinks he was throwing into her thinking!

Once inside her shop, Chelsea looked at the stack of paperwork waiting for her on her minuscule desk and determinedly turned her back on it. Checking her present stock for reordering would be infinitely more fun.

Now, where had that thought come from? And since when did fun come before responsibility? Unsettled by her untoward temperament, Chelsea had just finished changing a display of robes when a pounding on the service door startled her. She glanced at her watch.

"Oh, Gwen. Did you forget your key *again?*" She laughed, pushing open the door.

"Shouldn't you ask who's there before you open the door?" Mark demanded, walking inside.

"I should have this time."

Ignoring her retort, he loomed over her, glaring

darkly. "You never know who might be out there. Some
maniac or robber or murderer."

"Now, wouldn't that be peachy reading in the morning paper?" She felt the fluttery feeling in her stomach
again. "What are you doing here?"

He eyed a rack filled with colorful silk chemises and
teddies and fingered one. "I didn't get my kiss."

"Your kiss?" Her voice rose an octave. "You got
your kiss last night, bub. I should know. I was there."

Mark turned around and slowly advanced. "That was
a thanks-for-going-out-with-me kiss." He waved his
hand back and forth. "I missed my thanks-for-a-
breakfast-biscuit kiss."

Chelsea's feet felt frozen to the floor, and she was
certain her heart had stopped beating. How did this man
do this?

Mark was now close enough to touch her, and he did,
slipping his arms around her waist and drawing her to
him. "Now, *that* is what I'm here for," he breathed,
lowering his face.

Any form of protest was wiped from Chelsea's mind,
along with other remotely coherent thoughts, as his
mouth captured hers in a kiss that promptly stole all the
breath from her body.

His tongue didn't request entrance; it took it. His
mouth didn't just explore; it devoured. And his hands!
What his hands were doing to her had to be illegal somewhere in this world! They stroked up and down her back,
fingertips pressing against her spine just above her buttocks, meandering slowly upward until they traced patterns against her nape. His body heat enveloped her in
a blanket that was more sensual than comforting, and
the low rumble of his voice as he talked about her skin,
her eyes and her hair was enough to weaken her knees.

"How many of these bits of lace and silk do you have in your own closet, Chelsea?" Mark breathed, pressing butterfly kisses against her eyelids. "What did you decide to wear under that sexy dress of yours today?" His fingertips sought the snap holding her wrap dress closed.

It took a great deal of effort, but Chelsea called on every ounce of willpower to pull away from him.

"Don't count on finding out." She hated that her voice came out as soft and silken as the mocha teddy she had chosen to wear under her green jersey dress.

His thumb was all too close to that one snap closure, and if it became undone, the belt would be almost useless. His hips rocked gently against hers, leaving her in no doubt of his arousal. Her breath caught in her throat at how easy it would be to...

He cocked his head to one side in thought. "Satin and lace, I bet," he murmured.

Chelsea was positive her face was bright red. Did the man have X-ray eyes?

She pulled a deep breath into her lungs.

He grinned, knowing he had unnerved her.

She put her palms up and pushed him away. "Out, Harrison. Out. Now." Her eyes bored into his. Her courage may have been faltering, but she did a remarkable job of faking it.

Mark knew enough to back off. "Yeah, I'm late for work already." He glanced at his watch. "And it's all your fault. Bye, sweetheart. See you later."

And, with that, he ambled out the door, leaving Chelsea simultaneously furious, frustrated and slack-jawed in amazement.

Finally collecting her badly tattered wits, she ran to make sure the door was securely locked.

"DAMN THAT MAN!" she cursed, slamming down her accounts ledger an hour later, still unable to concentrate for thoughts of sizzling kisses and sexy hands.

"Honey, no man is *that* bad," Gwen drawled, standing in the doorway to the small office. Today, her form-fitting dress was a bright sapphire blue with a hot pink leather belt cinching her narrow waist. Her high heels matched her belt and the ribbon threaded through her French braid. She batted her mascaraed eyelashes. "Don't tell me you're talking about that adorable hunk who was by here last night? Chelsea, that man is *all* man. Testosterone extraordinaire. Don't let him get away."

Chelsea grimaced in a mixture of agreement and despair. "He's not my type," she said weakly.

Gwen burst out laughing. "Honey, he's everybody's type." Her smile dimmed a little. "Chelsea, you've been alone too long. Obviously, you went out with him last night, and, obviously, he showed you a good time. Why not go with the flow and enjoy yourself?"

Chelsea sighed. "There's more than just my pleasure involved. I have Colleen to think of."

"She's a big girl. Believe me, she isn't going to begrudge you some fun. I say go for it."

"That's just it!" she moaned, nervously rolling her pen between her fingers. "How can I 'go with the flow' with a man who'll soon be gone with the wind?"

"You're worrying too much about the wrong things," Gwen said. "That guy is most definitely interested in you, and there's no reason to believe that it's short-term only in his mind."

Chelsea wanted to crawl under her desk and hide until this insanity over Mark was done with, but she knew it was going to take more than just hiding out, so she resisted the urge.

"I hate people who think they're so smart," she muttered.

Gwen grinned. "Correction, you hate people who are right." She wheeled around and walked back into the main part of the shop.

Chelsea couldn't help yelling after her, "I also hate people who feel they have to have the last word!"

Chapter Six

"Mom, are you going to ask Mark to the beat-the-blues barbecue?"

Colleen casually tossed the bombshell at her unsuspecting mother as Chelsea and Gwen arranged new stock.

"I'm sure he has better things to do than come to a barbecue." Chelsea plopped a box into Colleen's arms. "Here, make yourself useful for a change. I've got some paperwork to finish up."

"It would be a good way for him to meet more people, since he's fairly new in town," Colleen persisted.

"What is this sudden interest? An inquisition?" Chelsea demanded.

"I know I'd look forward to your barbecue even more if that adorable guy was coming," Gwen piped up none too helpfully.

Chelsea shot both a warning look. "I've already drawn up the guest list, and I'm sure Mark Harrison is quite capable of meeting people on his own. Look at how easily he met *you,* my darling daughter."

"Come on, Chels, what's one more? That's usually your favorite phrase." At her partner's glare, Gwen quickly pretended to adjust a deep burgundy nightgown displayed on a padded hanger.

Chelsea clenched her teeth. "Fine," she spat out, "I'll ask him, but I'm sure he already has plans."

She marched into her office and shut the door so quietly it was more unnerving than if she'd slammed it.

"Well, we were subtle about that, weren't we?" Gwen said dryly.

"Mom doesn't know from subtlety," Colleen argued. "Remember that guy in the shop last Christmas? He did just about everything but stand on his head, and she still had no idea he was putting the moves on her." Colleen rolled her eyes in disgust. "I mean, even I could tell he was hot for her."

"That was Troy," Gwen reminded her. "A name we don't mention in her presence if we still want to live, remember?"

Colleen groaned. "Oh, yeah. He wanted Mom to let him wear her shoes."

"I don't think that would be Mark's idea of fun," Gwen observed.

"Nah. He's way too stuffy." Colleen's voice was muffled as she crawled around on the floor looking for a pin she'd dropped.

Gwen's eyebrows rose. "Stuffy? Mark? Sweetheart, trust me, the last thing that man is, is stuffy."

How DID she do it?

Mark stood transfixed in front of a window display that sent his blood pressure sky-high. He couldn't have forced his feet to move if he'd tried. There was a much shorter route to his bank, but he couldn't resist checking out Hot Stuff's intriguing windows. Just a look at the ever-changing displays was enough to fuel any man's fantasies about the woman who decorated them, and this one was the ultimate in his book.

A stack of three pale peach towels sat on a white wrought iron chair, with a sheer mocha-colored nightgown draped over them as if the owner had dropped it there before stepping into the hot, steamy bath silently implied by a floral bath powder tin, a loofah sponge and a sexy romance novel ditched by its drowsy reader. An ornate canister filled with bath crystals lay on its side with the crystals spilled across the floor, possibly leading to the fictitious bathtub.

Mark swore he could smell their sensuous fragrance, hear the quiet splash of a woman's body moving through the bubbles. As if that wasn't bad enough, his tortured gaze fell on another decorative bottle filled with body lotion. He muttered a curse under his breath at the notion that a window could arouse him so easily.

"Good morning, Mr. Harrison. Looking for something in particular?" The throaty voice only splashed more fuel on his heated dreams.

He turned his head. "Ms. Brennan, you've got quite a knack with windows."

Chelsea turned to study the display. With her arms crossed in front of her and head cocked to one side, someone might have thought she was seeing the window for the first time. "How do you know my partner didn't design this window?"

"This one has your signature on it." He indicated the second window, which had gone to the other side of the color and mood spectrum, with splashy cherry-red silks and multicolored glitter. "Gwen likes her displays to shout—to reach out and grab you with color and vibrancy. While yours—" His voice lowered to a husky murmur that sent shock waves along Chelsea's nerve endings. "Yours whisper of soft sensual pleasures, an aura of intimacy. For instance, the woman soaking in the tub, thinking of her lover, waiting for her in the bedroom."

A flush of color moved up Chelsea's throat to her cheeks. "I don't recall indicating the bather had company."

He gave a wicked grin. "The book was tossed to one side. Obviously, she didn't want to read about it, she wanted the real thing." His dark eyes delved into hers.

Damn him! She silently resolved to change the window that very day. She almost wondered if he knew she'd unwillingly been thinking of him as she arranged the current display.

"You have quite an imagination." Her voice didn't come out as light and airy as she'd hoped. Her hands, which were now clasped together in front of her, were damp with perspiration. Her whole being felt tense, expectant, as if she were on the brink of some dangerous but enthralling adventure. As if loving this one man was all she would ever desire. As if he could be the fulfillment of all her dreams, and she of his.

What an improbable, impossible dream, she thought, suddenly blinking back tears.

Mark noted a fleeting sadness in Chelsea's eyes. "Go for a drink with me tonight," he coaxed gently, surprising even himself. He wanted time alone with her, and not here in the middle of the sidewalk, where the world could intrude on them at any time.

"I'm not sure I'm up for drinks and clever conversation."

He grinned. "I'd say we're well past the clever conversation part, wouldn't you?"

Images of his kisses flooded her brain and again sent

color staining her face. "You enjoy being brash, don't you?"

Mark stepped closer until the warm scent of man and a faint hint of after-shave filled her nostrils. "Maybe I just like to see you blush and look all flustered while I remember how you felt in my arms the last time I kissed you."

He stepped back before he gave in to the temptation to touch her. "I'll pick you up at your house around seven."

"I might have plans," she said.

This time he did touch her, but just the tip of her nose. "You might, but you don't." He studied the café au lait silk blouse topping deep mocha pants. "I just bet that nightgown looks great on you." With a jaunty wave he walked off.

Chelsea could only stand there wondering how the temperature had risen so quickly. She also wondered where she could be at seven o'clock that night, coward that she was.

"WANT TO GO OUT on an ice-cream binge tonight?"

Colleen looked at her mother as if she'd suddenly lost her mind. "The last time I suggested such a thing, you told me it took you a month of heavy-duty aerobics and a million hours on the stair climber to work off the calories."

"So I double up again for awhile." She waved her hand airily. "But doesn't that sound good?"

Colleen narrowed her eyes. "You sound too eager to consume a million calories in one evening. What gives?"

She looked properly affronted. "I have to have a reason to want to spend time with my favorite daughter?"

"Your *only* daughter," Colleen pointed out.

Chelsea rolled her eyes. "A mere technicality."

Colleen clearly didn't believe one word. Then the light bulb of understanding clicked on. "I remember one time I didn't want to be home because Kevin wanted to come over to continue our last fight after I'd walked away from him. Tonight, *you* don't want to be home because someone you're afraid of seeing is coming by. Someone...male." She suddenly shrieked with laughter. "Mark is coming by tonight, isn't he? He is!" she squealed when she noted the telling flush on her mother's cheeks.

She hastily rearranged her expression to a more sober one. "Mother, you should be ashamed of yourself. You really should follow the advice you force on your poor daughter. Running away doesn't get you anywhere. You must face your problems squarely." She giggled. "So, what time is Mark coming over, and where is he taking you?"

Chelsea knew when she was defeated. Why did she have to have such a smart kid? "Seven, and he said something about drinks."

"Is he coming to the barbecue?"

"I forgot to ask."

"Gwen would say you didn't want to ask him."

"Colleen, let's drop the subject."

Colleen shrugged. "So, what are you going to wear tonight?"

"Heavy armor," Chelsea muttered, scowling.

"Yes, I hear chain mail is very popular this year."

"Smart-mouthed kid."

"Everyone says I take after you." She schooled her expression to one of supreme innocence. "It is cool outside tonight, so if I were you, I'd wear something warm." Her face lit up. "And I know just the outfit. Wait right here!" Colleen tore off to the other end of the house.

"Nothing short and tight," Chelsea called after her, following at a slower pace. Her daughter's ideas regarding dress codes for dates were a bit more eclectic than her own.

By the time Chelsea got upstairs, Colleen seemed to have dragged out half the contents of her closet.

"Now, where is it? I know it's here because I picked it up from the cleaners a couple of days ago," Colleen muttered, pawing through a dresser drawer. "Great! I found it!" She held up a bright orange tunic with purple lightning bolts dashed across the front. Next she pulled out a pair of purple leggings.

Chelsea backed away as if fearing her daughter would forcibly dress her in the wild outfit. "No. No way."

"Are you kidding? This would look fantastic on you. Although Mark's so stuffy, he might not appreciate it." Colleen got busy rummaging through the small antique chest on her dresser that held her jewelry. "I've got some purple earrings, if I can find them, and your purple flats work great with this. I know, because I always wear them with it."

"Colleen, women my age don't wear outfits like this," she protested, finding herself just a little bit tempted. Most of her clothing was a shade on the conservative side. But an outfit like this would really give Mark something to think about. "I have plenty of suitable outfits to wear."

"Suitable!" Colleen screwed up her face as if the thought of a "suitable" outfit was as appealing as a dose of cod liver oil. "This is not a time to look suitable, Mom. This is a time to look hot. There's no reason you can't wear this. I don't know why you're so worried. You don't look your age, and you have a good figure," she pointed out. "You should be proud of yourself for not letting yourself go. Some of my friends' moms look terrible."

"Thanks, I think." Chelsea eyed the bright outfit dubiously. Still, a crazy new part of her mind whispered, what was so wrong with breaking out of her usual conservative mode?

She took the clothing out of her daughter's hands before she regained her sanity. "Oh, hell," she muttered, walking out of Colleen's bedroom.

"I'll bring in the earrings once I find them," Colleen called after her.

"No thanks, I've got some that will work."

Chelsea laid the items on the bed and walked into the bathroom to turn on the shower. After this afternoon, there was no way she was stepping into the tub for a relaxing bubble bath!

"I found the earrings!" Colleen stood in the doorway holding up a pair of dangling bright purple earrings elaborate—and long—enough to rest on the wearer's shoulders.

Chelsea sighed. "Don't you have any homework to do?"

"I'll get on it after you leave," she promised. "Actually, there's only some reading for my lit class and a paper to finish for psych."

"And?"

"That's it, I swear."

Chelsea shook her head in disbelief. "I always had tons of homework during my senior year."

"Yeah, well, sometimes I think they're afraid if they

give us too much homework we'll drop out or something.''

A slight frown marred her young features. ''Mom, why are you so against going out with Mark?'' She looked down, biting her bottom lip. ''It's not because of me, is it? I mean, you're not embarrassed to see him because he had to bring me home that night, are you?''

''No, Colleen, that's not it at all,'' Chelsea rushed to assure her. ''It's just that...''

Just what? Just that there's something so magnetic about him that he scares the hell out of me? That he makes my safe little world seem suddenly dangerous? That he makes my blood sing and my heart dream dreams it has no right dreaming?

She heaved a deep sigh.

''He turns you on, doesn't he?''

Chelsea looked heavenward for assistance, but none seemed forthcoming. ''I don't want to discuss it.''

Colleen grinned. ''You didn't want to discuss the birds and the bees with me, either. Remember? But you survived, and so did I.''

''I *had* to discuss that with you,'' she muttered, pulling open the shower door and adjusting the water temperature. ''You were convinced babies came by way of the Easter Bunny.''

''That's what Elaine's brother told us. At the age of six, I thought it sounded logical. So, come on, admit it. Mark turns you on, doesn't he? Who knows? He might even turn me on if he was about ten years younger.''

''Terrific.'' She walked purposefully to the door and closed it in her daughter's face.

''It doesn't have anything to do with Mark being younger, does it?'' Colleen yelled through the door.

"It's the in thing now, Mom. Younger men and older women. Look at Cher. It doesn't bother her."

Chelsea was glad to have a heavy stream of hot water drown out Colleen's probing questions.

By the time she finished her shower and applied her makeup, she felt ready to enter her bedroom, and if need be, face her inquisitive daughter again. A lilting voice in the distance told her Colleen was on the phone, which gave her a much needed reprieve. She glanced at the clock, only to see that time was growing short.

Chelsea slipped the thigh-length sweater over her head and quickly pulled on the bright purple tights. While it wasn't her usual attire, she had to admit the soft mohair covered her body in a sensual caress. A caress a little like...

"Stop it!" she frantically ordered herself when she realized where her thoughts were leading her. As she found her earrings, a quick glimpse in the mirror told her that any more blusher was unnecessary. Her cheeks were more than bright enough. Still, in a fit of daring, she pulled one side of her hair back and secured it with a purple clip. Her amethyst earrings weren't as bold as Colleen's, but she felt they added just the right touch.

"You look great, Mom." Colleen sauntered in and dropped onto the bed. "You should carry stuff like that in the shop."

"And have you in debt to me for the rest of your life because you wouldn't be able to resist anything?" she retorted, transferring her keys and wallet to a purple suede clutch bag that matched her flats.

Colleen wrinkled her nose. "You're never going to let me live down that sequined number, are you."

"I think you can use a reminder or two of the consequences of mischief-making." Chelsea dabbed on perfume and walked out of the room with Colleen on her heels.

"Well, you see, there's this dance coming up soon," Colleen said, "and we both know how expensive party dresses are, so I figured I'd save you money by wearing the black one again."

Chelsea turned on her heel and bestowed a loving smile on her daughter. "No."

"Mom!" she whined in perfect teenager-ese.

At that the doorbell chimed, and Chelsea hurried to open the door.

"Mark, tell her it's for a good cause!" Colleen appealed to the man standing on the doorstep.

"It's for a good cause," he echoed.

Chelsea shot him a look that clearly said to keep out of this. She looked back at Colleen, pressed her fingers to her lips and blew the girl a kiss. "Good night, sweetheart. Study hard, and, for the last time, no."

She closed the door on Colleen's wails of protest.

Chapter Seven

"I guess you didn't want me offering my opinion back there." Mark held the car door open for Chelsea as she slid into the passenger seat.

"You are so right."

He braced his hands on the window frame and leaned toward her. "Am I forgiven if I tell you how great you look this evening?" he murmured.

That reckless feeling was once more racing through her veins. She'd thought she could keep it under wraps, that wayward side of her personality. "You can try, but I don't believe in making things easy."

He leaned in even closer. "Not even for me?"

Any closer and they'd be in each other's skins! "Especially not for you. No doubt you've always had it easy with the opposite sex, and I'm not about to be added to your list."

He straightened up. "Sweetheart, one thing you'll never have to worry about is joining any list. You're strictly in a class by yourself." He walked around to the driver's side and got in.

The minute Mark settled in his seat, Chelsea felt all the air leave the car's limited confines. All she was aware of was the man seated next to her wearing that

unbeatable combination of denim and leather that so
suited his rugged looks. She stared out the window in
hopes of regaining her equilibrium.

"How do you usually manage Colleen's cut ups—
when I'm not around to interfere, that is?" he asked,
half turning in the seat as he backed down the driveway.

"If I want to keep my sanity, I have to stay ten steps
ahead of her at all times," she replied. "Conveniently,
she often finds it hard to believe that I just might have
been a teenager myself once upon a time and conceivably know a lot of the tricks of the trade."

Mark found it difficult to keep his attention on the
road. He was seeing a new Chelsea tonight, and this one
intrigued him just as much as the remote but sexy one
he'd first been drawn to. Not only was her clothing different, even her perfume was lighter, more carefree than
the warm, extremely feminine fragrance she usually
wore. He quickly revised his first idea of where to take
her.

"So *do* you keep your sanity?" he asked, turning left
instead of right.

Chelsea's low chuckle warmed his blood, especially
since he was already more than a little overheated by
the sight of her long, shapely legs sheathed in some soft
purple fabric.

"What do you think?" Her throaty laughter started
him thinking about chucking the idea of a drink and
heading directly for his place.

"I think you manage. You couldn't run a business
without it. And Colleen seems pretty well adjusted."

"I'm thankful she is," Chelsea answered. "Basically,
I offer her the respect of treating her as an adult as long
as she acts like one. Oh, we have our battles at times,
but usually she's pretty responsible."

She looked around as the car rolled to a stop. "And Colleen thinks you're stuffy." She gestured to the neon sign. "Isn't this the place where my darling daughter got into trouble?"

"I thought you might like to visit the scene of the crime," Mark said as he assisted her out of the car. He looked around the crowded parking lot and then back at her. "Stuffy, huh? Is that what *you* think of me, Ms. Brennan?"

She looked up. *Not on your life,* she thought. "I could think of other ways to describe you," she said cheekily.

Chelsea winced at the strident sound of rock music assaulting her ears as they entered the crowded club. Only Mark's hand resting firmly against the base of her spine kept her moving forward through the masses as he directed her to an unoccupied table.

"Hi, Mark." A waitress wearing black leggings and a hot pink tunic appeared. Her smile was warm as she set a bowl of pretzels on the table. "Haven't seen you around here for awhile. What can I get you?"

"Jack Daniel's and water for me." He looked inquiringly at Chelsea.

She opened her mouth to order her usual wine when some imp inside claimed her voice and said, "I'll have a screwdriver."

The waitress nodded and moved off.

In the same unfamiliar spirit of risk taking, Chelsea heard herself say impulsively, "I know this is late notice, but I'm having a barbecue this Saturday, and—"

"What time?" he asked promptly.

She laughed. He hadn't even given her a chance to finish her invitation! "It usually begins around two and goes on until whenever."

He leaned over and whispered in her ear, "I'll be there."

"Mark, hey, great to see you! Renee said you were here." A man of medium height slid into a chair across from them. While he spoke to Mark, his eyes devoured Chelsea with hungry male appreciation. "Well, well, well. Now I understand why I haven't seen you much lately. Sweetheart, let me give you a piece of advice— I'm a much better bet than ol' Mark here."

Mark grimaced. "Chelsea, this cretin is my buddy Rick. If you ignore him, he'll usually slink away like a good boy."

Chelsea shot Mark a sly glance as she responded to Rick. "Oh, really?"

Rick gave a killer grin that didn't do half as much for Chelsea's hormones as Mark's smile did. "Really. So why don't you ditch the guy before you break his heart and come away with me? We'll fly off into the sunset to somewhere exciting, just you and me."

"And leave my poor little girl alone?"

"Little girl? As in daughter?"

She nodded. "A seventeen-year-old daughter."

Rick blinked. "Seventeen?"

She nodded again.

"Like in high school?"

"A senior," Chelsea confirmed.

"So you're a mom, huh?" Rick said, looking dumbfounded.

"A very serious mom. PTA and all that mommy stuff."

Rick heaved a sigh as he heaved himself upward. "Mark, we need to talk. Moms can be dangerous creatures. If you're around them too long, you start thinking like a parent." His hand rested on his friend's shoulder before he moved away. "Drinks are on the house. Something tells me you're going to need them."

"Does he come on to all your women friends that way?" Chelsea asked oh, so innocently once they were alone.

Mark dipped his head and nuzzled the soft skin behind her ear. "Only the gorgeous ones."

She quivered under his touch. "You should think about having your eyes checked."

Mark grasped her chin gently and raised her face to his, only to see the waitress approaching with their drinks. Once Renee discreetly hurried away, Mark attempted to pick up where he'd left off, this time to be interrupted by a cry of, "Chelsea, is that *you?*"

Gwen materialized by the table with a man in tow.

Mark released Chelsea's chin and muttered a curse of frustration.

"Yes, Gwen, it's me." Chelsea looked amused by Mark's irritation.

Gwen greeted Mark with open delight and happily eyed Chelsea's glass. "Something tells me there's more than orange juice in that glass. Hmm. Hard liquor, and quite an outfit. Things must be looking up around here," she said gaily.

Chelsea looked past Gwen's dazzling, electric blue formfitting sequinned dress to her date. "Who's your friend?" she prodded politely.

"Oh, this is Beau." Gwen quickly made introductions before leaning over to murmur in Chelsea's ear, "He thinks I'm fantastic, so it's a beginning." Waggling her fingers, she waved her goodbyes and moved off, Beau hot on her high heels.

"Does this guy know what he's in for?" A bemused Mark watched them leave.

Chelsea shrugged in amusement, picked up her glass and sipped her drink. She sat back, savoring the tart orange flavor mingling with the sharp, cold bite of the vodka.

The alcohol wasted no time in racing through her veins and leaving her with a rich warm feeling. She closed her eyes to better appreciate it. "I only hope he sees more than her looks. Although, men tend to choose their dates more by bra size than by brains." She opened her eyes, surprised at her own bluntness but rather enjoying the liberated sensation. She eyed Mark narrowly. "Is that how *you* choose?" she asked.

Mark found himself falling under the spell of her tawny eyes. "Once upon a time, maybe, when I was young and stupid. I soon learned that a woman who could carry on an intelligent conversation was infinitely preferable when the service in a restaurant was a little slow."

Chelsea continued sipping her drink. She'd eaten little that day, and the alcohol pleasantly drizzled through her system without interference.

"Ready for another?" the waitress asked brightly, reaching for Chelsea's now empty glass.

Chelsea beamed at the younger woman. Right now, she felt warm and fuzzy inside, with more than a dash of daring thrown in. She didn't want to lose that feeling. "Yes, please."

Mark placed a hand over his own glass, which was still half full. "I'm fine. Uh, Chelsea, don't you think you should slow down a bit?"

She looked at him as if he'd lost his mind. "Are you kidding? I very rarely get out," she confided. She narrowed her eyes in reflection. "Unless you count that male strip show a group of us went to for a friend's fortieth birthday.'' She plucked up her drink the moment the waitress set it down. "Thank you. Anyway,'' she continued, lifting the glass to her lips, "Rachel was feeling sorry for herself over the big four-oh, but by the time the evening ended, she didn't feel the least bit sad."

Mark shoved the bowl of pretzels under her nose. "Have one."

"No thanks. Too much salt isn't dood for you." She choked back a laugh. "I mean, good for you. I guess I'm more tired than I thought. It's been a long day." She giggled happily.

"Two drinks and she's snockered," he muttered, rising to his feet. "I'll be back in a minute. You stay here, okay?"

Chelsea looked up with wide eyes. "Where else would I go?"

"That's what worries me." He hurried to the back of the club, silently praying she'd still be there when he returned.

The minute Mark found his way back to the table he discovered Chelsea sipping another drink, obviously supplied by the adoring male sitting in Mark's chair.

"I really need the vitamin C," she solemnly informed him. The vacant smile and bright eyes told him she needed much more than vitamins. "This is Brad. He's in stocks."

Mark glared at the other man until he muttered something about seeing a friend of his and hastily vacated the chair. "Something tells me you need a pot of coffee a hell of a lot more," he muttered, grasping Chelsea's arm and pulling her to her feet.

She reached down. "I didn't finish my drink!"

"You're not leaving, are you?" Gwen appeared behind them and touched Mark's shoulder. "We were going to see if you two would like to hit some of the other clubs with us.''

"I think Chelsea has had enough night spots," Mark said through clenched teeth.

"Gwen, tell him he's being a spoilsport," Chelsea injected, unaware her words were slightly slurred.

Gwen stared at her partner. "Did you get her drunk?" She looked incredulous.

"No, some creep tried that while I was in the rest room." Mark refused to let go of Chelsea, who was still trying to reach for her drink. She missed the glass by several inches.

"Chelsea doesn't drink hard liquor, only wine," Gwen explained.

"Then this was a hell of a time to start." Mark headed for the door, dragging Chelsea behind him.

"'Night, Gwen," Chelsea called over her shoulder as her heels skidded on the floor. "Mark, I can't walk that fast!"

"You can if you turn around and walk properly." He gripped her fingers even tighter as he pushed open the door and pulled her outside.

"I never knew you had this bossy side."

Mark continued on to his car and not so gallantly deposited Chelsea in the front seat. Within moments the car was leaving rubber on the asphalt as he raced out of the parking lot.

"Hey, you're not going the right way for my house," she told him.

"The last thing I'm going to do is have Colleen see you this way," he replied. "We'll go to my place, where I can make you some coffee and, hopefully, sober you up." He shook his head in wonderment. "What possessed you to drink so much if you're not used to hard liquor?''

"I don't know. I guess because the first drink left me feeling reckless, and I didn't want the feeling to go away." Her head dropped back against the seat with a thump. "I wasn't always such a poopy partner, you know."

He resisted the urge to grin. "Oh, really?"

Her head bobbed up and down. "Yeah, I used to be a real party girl. Dance all night. Go to school the next morning. Never did drink much, though." She leaned over until her mouth brushed his ear as she breathily confided, "I don't have a head for it."

Mark coughed to cover his chuckle. "Yeah, somehow I already guessed that."

Chelsea shook her head back and forth vehemently. "No, really," she went on as if he had given her a negative reply. "I don't turn weepy or anything, I just get dizzy." Mark would have questioned her further, but he had to concentrate on parking in his apartment building's underground lot. He inserted the magnetized card in the slot, waiting for the gate to open. He parked in his assigned space and helped her out of the car.

"This is spooky." Chelsea leaned into Mark's side as they walked to the elevator. "We should have gone to my house."

"Not until I get some coffee into you." He pushed the button for the fourth floor.

She leaned back against the elevator wall, watching him through narrowed eyes. "Tell the truth now."

"Truth about what?"

"You brought me up here to show me your etchings, didn't you?"

"I don't have any etchings."

Chelsea looked shocked. "You don't have any etchings! Well, what kind of libid—libidid—libidinous bachelor are you?" She stumbled over the words. "Oh, hell, I mean, how are you supposed to seduce me if you don't have any etchings to show me?"

At the precise moment Chelsea asked her question, the elevator door opened to reveal an elderly couple, who looked shocked as Mark hustled Chelsea past them.

"This used to be a quiet building," the woman huffed, glaring at Mark as she and her husband stepped into the vacated elevator car.

"Is she one of your neighbors?" Chelsea asked, following Mark down the hallway. "What a prune! Trust me, Mark, dealing with people like her will only ruin your day. I'd move if I were you. Find a place that won't mind your having etchings."

Mark unlocked his door and pushed it open, quickly ushering Chelsea inside before any more of his neighbors had the misfortune to run into her. "Yeah, well, you're doing a good job of getting me tossed out of here." He reached around the doorjamb and flipped a light switch.

Chelsea walked in with a slightly unsteady gait and looked around. "You don't spend very much time here, do you?"

Mark headed for the kitchen and rummaged through the cabinets for coffee. "There seem to be more nights than I'd like when I'm sleeping in the trailer at the construction site. The interior work is coming along on time, but lately I've had a lot of paperwork to catch up on. Since it isn't my favorite chore, I tend to put it off until I have no choice but to settle down and get reports out to the head office."

Chelsea perched herself on a barstool at the breakfast

counter, where she could watch Mark measure out coffee and water. She rested an elbow on the counter and propped her chin in her cupped palm.

"Do you have any Irish cream to go in that?"

He shook his head. "I think you'd be better off drinking the coffee full strength."

She sighed dramatically. "Then I'll just return to my old stodgy self, and I, for one, know I'm not always a lot of fun. Not since back when I was a crazy teenager anyway," she rambled. "Back then, I was convinced that life was meant to be one day of fun after another." She grew pensive. "Then the day came when I had to grow up. That was when I decided that the fun-loving Chelsea would have to go, and the hardworking Chelsea would take her place."

Mark began pouring coffee. "Maybe you could have blended the two together," he quietly suggested, already guessing that the day she forced herself to grow up was the day she discovered herself pregnant with Colleen and learned her boyfriend wasn't as willing to give up a free and easy life-style.

She shook her head. "No, you can't be a mom and run around with your friends all the time. Usually they feel uncomfortable around you anyway. Know why?" She didn't bother waiting for a reply. "Because they're afraid you're contagious, and the last thing they want is to be pregnant. Can't blame them," she said matter-of-factly. "Your head's in the toilet every morning, and sometimes in the evenings, too. Your ankles swell, your clothes don't fit you anymore, and toward the end you waddle like a duck. It's not a pretty sight." She sighed.

Mark visualized Chelsea pregnant. He doubted he'd find one thing wrong with her. "I've heard some men are turned on more when their wives are pregnant," he murmured. Hell, the idea sure turned him on! At the same time, his saner side warned him that Chelsea wasn't going to be any too pleased with either of them when she sobered up and realized just how much she had revealed about herself while under the influence.

"Yeah, well, they're not the ones who look like an overinflated basketball." Chelsea eyed the coffee cup set in front of her. "If I drink coffee, I might not be able to sleep tonight."

"Drink," he said gruffly, pushing it right under her nose.

She wrinkled said nose as she picked up the cup. "You're very bossy. No wonder you're in construction. Such a macho profession." She narrowed her eyes to focus on her wobbling cup.

He blinked at the abrupt turn of subject. "Yeah, that's been said. Now, drink up." He carefully tipped her cup upward.

Chelsea twisted her features as the bitter brew attacked her taste buds. She tried to push the cup away, but Mark wouldn't allow her to. "This is terrible!"

"I doubled the strength. I figured you'd need all the help you could get."

This time Chelsea successfully pushed the cup away. "I would think you'd enjoy having me up here at your mercy," she accused, pursing her lips. "After all, isn't that what you've been working toward from the beginning?" The last words were delivered in a throaty rush.

Mark seriously thought about loosening his tie. There was only one problem. He wasn't wearing one. He looked down into her slightly glazed eyes and began to worry that even a whole pot of coffee wouldn't sober Chelsea up.

"Chelsea, as much as I'd like to pursue this further,

I'm afraid you'd regret it in the morning," he said finally, pushing the coffee cup back under her nose.

She sighed and picked it up, draining the contents in several gulps. "Honestly, Mark, you need to loosen up. Take chances. Of course, Doug used to say that a lot." She frowned. "The only decent thing that guy ever did was give me Colleen."

Mark straightened up at this piece of news. "So we have Doug to thank for Colleen," he commented.

She nodded, then grabbed hold of the counter to keep her balance as her body started to list to one side. She grimaced as she watched him pour more coffee into her cup. "Yeah, but personally, I just ignore any part he had in her conception. There was a point when I was so angry at him for rejecting Colleen that I wanted to curse him with eternal impotence."

He winced. "That's pretty heavy-duty."

"Well, he was a heavy-duty jerk. You know the kind. Keeps declaring 'I love you' until you've given him what he wants. Then refuses to accept the consequences. Oh, I admit he didn't do it all by himself, but it wouldn't have hurt him to admit he had a daughter. I never expected financial help from him. You know, this coffee is starting to taste all right." Her sudden change in subject again took him by surprise. "You know what's really good is to put a pinch of cinnamon in the grounds. Now, tell me when I can inspect my store space."

Mark took a deep breath. She kept changing the subject so often, he wasn't sure where she'd end up next.

"I'd say about a week or so. The interiors are almost finished, and painting will start soon."

"I chose soft rose and ivory for the color scheme," she informed him, emptying the second cup as rapidly as she had the first. "It should accent the clothes without

overpowering them. That's so important in retailing.
And they're relaxing colors.''

''What's Gwen's part in the shop?''

''She handles the evening wear and accessories and
takes care of advertising and marketing. We balance
each other perfectly. She gears me up, and I keep her
feet on the ground when she looks too high too soon.''
She raised her arms over her head and stretched her fingers toward the ceiling. ''And sometimes we trade
places.'' She grinned. ''Do you realize how good you
look in jeans?''

Mark felt like shaking his head to clear it. Did she
keep track of how many times she'd switched subjects
so far? This new Chelsea was turning out to be better
than any television show.

''Why don't you tell me how I look?'' he invited,
leaning over to caress the back of her neck.

She lowered her eyelids a fraction, then swept her
gaze up and down him in a leisurely study. ''Better than
any bare-chested, muscle-bound model I've ever seen,''
she said. ''You could probably pose for one of those
beefcake calendars. You know, with no shirt and your
jeans half—''

''Maybe I should have taken you home to your daughter after all,'' he mumbled.

She waved her hand. ''No, she'd just fuss over me,
and I hate being fussed over. I hope she meets a man
like you when the time is right.'' She leaned forward as
if confiding a secret. ''You should see the boys she
dates. Not a pimple in the lot. And so polite it hurts.''
She suddenly giggled. ''They call me ma'am. Please understand, I'm not complaining about their manners. I just
wish they'd use another form of address. Ma'am? Makes
me feel ancient.''

Her lips curved in a sexy smile. "You wouldn't call me ma'am, would you, Mark?" Her voice lowered to a husky drawl. "No, I don't think you would." Her words came out breathy as she leaned forward until her lips were close to his. "But what would you call me when you got around to doing something like this?"

And without warning she grabbed hold of his shirt collar and hauled him toward her. And he wasn't about to protest when her mouth covered his in the kind of kiss no man in his right mind would say no to.

Chapter Eight

Chelsea's fingers combed through Mark's hair, rubbing his scalp in a caressing motion that sent electric messages all through his body while her mouth worked its own magic on his. She bit down gently on his lower lip and tugged.

"I won't break if you touch me, Mark," she murmured, dipping her tongue between his lips.

"Maybe you won't break, but I'd definitely go insane if I touched you the way I want to," he insisted on a ragged note. He concentrated ferociously on keeping his hands on her waist while they itched to move upward under the soft wool and find warm bare skin. "Honey, you had too much to drink tonight, and you don't know what you're doing."

"Silly, of course I know what I'm doing. Kiss me," she softly ordered, twining her arms around his neck and pulling his face back to hers. "Make my head spin."

"Sweetheart, I think both our heads are spinning right about now." He laughed hoarsely, unable to stop himself from pulling her off the barstool and fully against him.

"But it feels so good." She drew the words out as she shimmied her hips against him. "You feel so good."

Mark felt as if he were hanging by his fingers on a

precarious ledge. He hated to believe it was only the alcohol talking, but this Chelsea wasn't one he was used to. He silently ordered himself to behave, even as he fell further under her seductive spell. Soft lips whispering encouragement were nicer than his cautious brain shouting warnings inside his head. And warm, satiny skin felt better than soft wool. His fingers had somehow reached the edge of her bra.

"What color is it?" he whispered in her ear, biting down gently on the lobe.

"Purple passion." She giggled. "Silly name, but it does help sell the products." She breathed unevenly against his throat. "Want to see?"

Mark closed his eyes, groaning. And before he could stop her, she had tossed all caution to the wind and whisked her sweater up and off. He gazed hungrily at the demibra that pushed her full breasts upward enough to nearly spill out over the rich purple fabric. He uttered a pithy prayer for strength.

"The clip is in the front," she pointed out.

He took several deep breaths. "Yes, I can see that." This was all so crazy! he told himself. He felt his control slipping out of his hands and didn't know how to regain it. Or if he even wanted to.

"Chelsea," he said finally, "while I'd like nothing more than to steer you into my bedroom, I'm not sure this would be a good time."

She looked up with wide eyes glazed with both alcohol and desire. "But I thought... I mean, you are..." Her eyes dropped to the area below his waist. "Wow," she breathed.

"Exactly. And while I'm going to hate myself in the morning for even saying this, I think the alcohol you had tonight has gotten the better of you." He groaned,

closing his eyes against the delectable sight before him.
"I want you, Chelsea. Damn, how much I want you. But
I want both of us sober when we go to bed together. I
want you aware in every fiber of your being that you
want me as badly as I want you."

Her eyes clouded. "You don't want me?"

He gnashed his teeth. "Chelsea, listen to me. I want
you. Badly. But I don't want *you* hating *me* in the morning for—forgive the cliché—taking advantage of your
condition."

A semblance of sobriety finally penetrated Chelsea's
carefree daze. Mark's rejection had accomplished what
his coffee hadn't. Her fingers trembled as she bent down
and retrieved her sweater.

"You can take me home now," she muttered, not
looking at him.

"Chelsea, we need to talk about what just happened,"
he urged.

She grabbed her purse and headed for the front door.
She stood there watching him until he got the message
and snatched his keys up from the counter.

The ride back to her house was silent as Chelsea
looked out the window, pretending great interest in nothing. The euphoria from the alcohol had dissipated, leaving her feeling drained and humiliated. Mark had barely
stopped the car in her driveway before she had the door
open and was running up the walk.

"Chelsea!" he called after her as he scrambled out of
the car. But the slamming of her front door was his only
answer.

"Son of a bitch!" He smacked the top of the car with
the flat of his hand.

"Mom? Mom!"

Chelsea wanted to ignore the pounding on her bathroom door. Wanted to black out her daughter's insistent demand for a reply.

"What?" she sputtered as water from the shower filled her mouth.

"You're back early," Colleen called through the closed door. "Are you okay?"

Chelsea turned around and braced her hands against the tile, allowing the hot water to pound her back. "I'm fine," she shouted. "Just tired. Did you finish your homework?" Her facial muscles constricted with the effort of trying to sound normal.

"Yeah. I'm going to watch that movie on cable. Wanna come down and watch with me? I'll make popcorn."

"No, I'm going to bed now. It's been a long day, and I want to get to the shop early tomorrow."

"Okay. 'Night."

Chelsea finally twisted the shower knob off with a violent flick of the wrist. She skimmed her wet hair away from her face and stepped out of the tub, reaching for a towel.

She quickly dried off, gritting her teeth when the nubby terry passed over still sensitive breasts.

"Fool. You should be grateful the man had principles," she reminded herself, flipping on her hairdryer and brushing her hair with vicious strokes.

With that particular self-flagellation completed, she crawled into bed and pulled the covers over her head. But she couldn't block out the truth. After years of keeping a tight rein on herself, of being a stable, responsible parent and citizen, she had stupidly let every unfulfilled hunger, every unrealized dream, rush to the surface.

And, as a result, she had almost run headlong into disaster again. Hadn't she learned the last time?

"No more screwdrivers," she vowed, closing her eyes. "And no more Mark."

"SHUT IT OFF, Mom!"

The pounding on the door sounded like a legion of bass drummers, and if that wasn't bad enough, she'd swear there were millions of bees buzzing around her head.

"Go away," Chelsea moaned, rolling over and pulling the pillow over her head.

"Mom, shut off your alarm. It's loud enough to break glass!" Colleen shouted from the other side of the closed door.

Chelsea rolled back over and stared at the buzzing, taunting clock. She'd overslept by fifteen minutes! She groped for the button and slapped it down. The silence was glorious.

"I've got to get over to the school early for drama club orientation, so I'm leaving now. See you later."

"Right." Chelsea slowly rotated her neck, gingerly maneuvering her aching head. Unfortunately, the memory of the previous night flooded it all too swiftly. She moaned softly and buried her face in her hands. "Why didn't I just tear the man's clothes off, throw him to the floor and have my way with him?"

The mental picture of Mark in naked splendor was all too explicit. Calling herself horrible names, she climbed out of bed and dragged herself to the bathroom, where she intended to take another long, soothing shower.

But by the time she'd dressed and applied makeup, she still didn't feel refreshed. Instead, she felt more off center and erratic than ever. Images of Mark kept pop-

ping into her head as she choked down a cup of coffee
and a slice of dry toast.

"Chelsea, you will never do anything so stupid
again," she muttered, heading for her car. Then she
cursed when she realized she was about to back the car
out of the garage without activating the automatic door
opener. "Get a grip, Chelsea."

"WELL, WELL, WELL. Look who strolls in an hour late,"
Gwen sang out when Chelsea entered the shop through
the rear door. She looked her partner up and down. "Are
we in mourning?"

Chelsea looked down. "I just grabbed the first thing
I came to," she mumbled, actually meaning she'd
grabbed the first thing that wouldn't jar her sensitive
eyeballs. She wondered if she could get away with wearing her sunglasses in the shop without attracting too
much attention.

She was spared any more comments from Gwen when
the bell over the door softly rang, announcing the arrival
of a prospective customer.

"Fran, how good to see you!" Gwen trilled. "We
recently got in some beautiful sequinned tops that're perfect for you. Let me show you one of them."

"Thank goodness for Gwen." Chelsea sighed, closed
her eyes and sank into the desk chair. Oh, Lord. The
barbecue! she suddenly remembered. How could she
have forgotten? How was she ever going to face Mark?
She opened her eyes, disconcerted to find herself facing
a sheer black nightgown.

MARK WASN'T having it any easier as he walked through
the mall interior, dealing with carpenters and electri-
cians.

"Hey, boss, are you awake?" Steve teased. "You seem to go off into space every time we hit the second floor."

"It's just one of those days. I can't seem to keep my mind on anything." Sure, he went off into space every time he found himself within ten feet of Chelsea's store space. And his mind was on something, all right: a purple-passion clad beauty with a lot of tears locked up inside her.

"Must be a woman."

"What makes you say that?" he growled.

"Simple. You've got that look that says a woman's got you pretty much hog-tied and nowhere near hollering for help. If that isn't what you want, you'd better start backpedaling pretty quick," he advised. "My fourth wife caught me off guard and had me before a justice of the peace before I knew it. Let me warn you, boss. Women are husband-hunters, pure and simple."

"Women are nothing pure and simple. They're complicated," Mark replied, thinking of the varied sides of Chelsea he'd seen the night before. Damn. He still couldn't believe he'd acted the gentleman in the face of such temptation!

"Complicated?" Steve chuckled. "Uh-oh. You must have it bad, friend."

"Yeah." His mind made up, Mark headed for his trailer office to make a call.

"Good afternoon. Hot Stuff. How may I help you?" came Gwen's bright greeting.

"Hi, it's Mark. You can help by getting your partner to the phone without telling her it's me," he replied.

"I would if I could, but she left on a couple of errands about a half hour ago, and I don't expect her back for probably another hour," she told him. "I can have her call you when she gets back."

He tamped down his disappointment. "Yeah, do that."

"I guess I'll see you at Chelsea's barbecue this weekend," Gwen said easily.

"Let's hope so," he said, wondering if Chelsea would ever want to see him again. "Anyway, have Chelsea call me." He set the receiver down.

"I don't think Chelsea needs to call you."

Mark turned around to find Chelsea standing in the trailer doorway. She looked uneasy, as if unsure of her welcome.

"Hi," he said softly, afraid if he spoke too loud she might run off.

It didn't take much to see she was suffering from a hangover. Her black jacket and skirt told him she had probably chosen a look as subdued as she felt. She still looked great to him.

"Gwen said you were running errands. Does this mean I'm one of them?"

The tight motion of her head indicated no. "This was more…spur of the moment when I drove by." She stared down at the leather clutch bag she held. "I came to apologize."

He purposely kept his distance as he leaned against the edge of his desk. "Apologize for what?"

"For the way I behaved last night. For the things I said." She spoke so low he had to strain his ears to hear her. "I'm not used to having more than one drink, especially hard alcohol. I don't know what came over me, having so many drinks last night. I guess I wasn't thinking straight." She still refused to look at him. "Basically, I wasn't myself," she concluded miserably.

He smiled. "Maybe in some ways you were more your real self last night than you've been in a long time."

Now she did look up at him, and the pain in her eyes hurt him. "No, that wasn't me. I have to keep myself in check." Her contradictory confession left her lips before she could pull back the words.

"Because you're afraid I'll take advantage of you the way Colleen's father did?" he asked gently, straightening up and walking over to her. "Chelsea, are you that afraid of men? Or just that afraid of your true emotions?" He fingered the gold pin on her jacket collar, aching to kiss away the sadness etched on her beautiful downturned lips.

"Pretty," he murmured, leaning forward.

Faint color tinted her cheeks. "The pin, you mean. I look terrible, and you know it."

"Fishing for compliments?" He braced a hand on the doorframe behind her shoulder, effectively trapping her. He inclined his head and breathed in the spring-fresh scent of her perfume, then smiled at the faint catch in her breath. So he was getting to her even sober, was he?

She forced her gaze upward from his open collar to his face. "Let me go."

"No." Again he was pleased to hear that tiny little catch. "I want you to stop being afraid."

"I'm not afraid of anything or anyone," she murmured.

"You're afraid of me. Of what I do to you."

"Your ego is astounding, Mr. Harrison. But then, perhaps that's a function of your age."

A knot tightened deep in his stomach at her condescending, distancing tone. "Oh, you're good, Chelsea, very good. There's only one thing. You're not going to put me off with that age crap, because you already know it means zip to me, and you don't give a damn about it, either. Because you've already discovered we can be very good with each other.'' His mouth moved lightly over the top curve of her ear before opening and tenderly biting down. ''Maybe I shouldn't have been such a gentleman last night. Maybe I shouldn't have taken you home after all.''

''It only would have made things worse. Sex doesn't turn the world right on its axis. It only complicates things.'' Despite her words, her hips unconsciously nestled against his.

''Or allows two people to see each other in a new light. A true light. The light of real intimacy.'' Now he was nibbling his way toward the corner of her mouth as he pressed lightly on her back, drawing her even closer to him. ''Come on, Chelsea, admit you want to see me that way.''

She braced her hands on his chest and pushed him away.

''Work on the ego, Mark,'' she advised, safely distant again and reaching behind her for the doorknob.

He deliberately waited until she walked out of the trailer. ''I'm looking forward to the barbecue,'' he called.

She stiffened and spun around, a look of astonishment on her face. Then she turned back around and walked off.

Mark braced his shoulder against the doorjamb and watched until she was out of sight.

''Damn, that woman makes me crazy,'' he said with a sigh.

Chapter Nine

"So, you made it," Chelsea said by way of a greeting to Mark. She led him toward the rear of the house.

This casually dressed Chelsea was different yet again from the various versions of the woman he'd seen before, and Mark found himself unable to keep his eyes off her as he followed her through the house.

"Sorry I'm late. A conference call to my dad took longer than I expected," he explained, itching to carry her off to a distant bedroom and have his wicked way with her. He wondered how long her barbecue lasted and was determined to be the last to leave.

"You never said what the occasion was," he said, hoping to prompt conversation. "So what's the occasion?" He looked out the open French doors that led to a spacious patio, where he could see several guests lounging around the pool soaking up the early-fall sunshine. Others were splashing about, and a few sat at two long picnic tables set on the grass. "Gatherings this large are usually in honor of some holiday."

"I call it my beat-the-fall-blues barbecue," she replied, steering him outside. "Colleen was always depressed because school was starting up again and her summer fun was over, and I was depressed because she was depressed. So about four years ago we decided to have a joint party and each invite an equal number of friends. Before we knew it, we'd started sort of a tradition, and we seem to invite more people every year. The big difference this year is that Colleen was invited to spend the weekend in Santa Barbara with Elaine and her family and wasn't about to miss that," she said dryly. "There's wine, beer, soft drinks—everything for your pleasure."

"I already know what I want for my pleasure."

Mark's softly spoken words brought a wave of warmth over Chelsea's entire body.

"Too bad the pool is heated. I'd say you could use a good cold dunk," she murmured, stepping away.

"Hi, Mark, glad you came." Gwen greeted Mark with a kiss on the cheek before taking his hand and pulling him out onto the patio.

Mark snagged a can of beer from the bed of ice, popping the top. "This is quite an impressive spread," he commented.

"Mark, here's some people you ought to meet." He turned around to find Chelsea standing between a smiling gray-haired man and an equally smiling redhead wearing a minuscule bikini.

"Mark Harrison, this is Vicki Carson and her father, Lawrence." She made the introductions. "Lawrence owns Pacific Coast European Motors, and Vicki is the fleet manager there." She turned to Lawrence. "Mark is in charge of the new mall construction. I thought today's party would give him a chance to meet some of our local movers and shakers."

The men shook hands, while Vicki looked Mark up and down as if he happened to be the day's main course.

"Chelsea, where on earth did you find this one?" she

purred, placing a hand tipped with long vermilion nails on Mark's arm.

Mark hoped he wasn't just imagining that Chelsea's smile was a trifle strained at Vicki's blatant interest.

"Actually, I have Colleen to thank. She met Mark and introduced us," she said smoothly, turning away as someone called her name. Just before she walked off, she looked briefly over her shoulder at Mark.

Hurrah! Mark silently cheered. She didn't want to leave him! He smiled broadly, hoping to indicate that there was nothing to fear, even from this female barracuda.

Before long, several other women noticed the new arrival and floated over for introductions. Mark shifted uneasily, beginning to feel like a coveted object on an auction block. He just hoped people realized he wasn't for sale.

"Since no woman likes to be part of a crowd, I guess I'll do a little circulating," Gwen said casually.

He grabbed her arm. "Don't you dare," he growled in her ear. "I need all the protection I can get." He glared at her as her shoulders shook with laughter.

CHELSEA OPENED several cabinet doors, muttering. "I know it's here." She slammed one door shut and opened another. "Why do I let Colleen put things away? I can never find them when she does."

"That wasn't very nice," Mark reprimanded her, stepping into the kitchen.

Chelsea paused a split second before lifting herself up on her tiptoes to reach an upper shelf. Mark stepped behind her and easily grabbed the dish and set it on the counter in front of her, reluctant to pull his arms away from their loose embrace around her.

"I don't know if it's safe for you to run around in those shorts," he murmured in her ear.

Chelsea willed her hands to stop trembling as his tongue tickled her ear. She swore under her breath when the dip she was trying to transfer plopped from the spoon onto the counter. She reached blindly for a dishcloth.

"Here." Her hands were gently pushed out of the way while Mark easily snagged the cloth and wiped up the mess, still sticking to her like glue. "There, good as new."

Chelsea breathed in sharply when his hips made intimate contact with hers and she felt his arousal. "Don't," she whispered.

"It's kinda hard not to be this way when I'm around you." He wrapped his arms around her middle so there was no chance for her to escape. "I wish we were alone," he said softly.

"We are alone."

"Not the way I'd like us to be alone. And if I see that old man Carson mentally stripping your clothes off again, I'm going to punch him out." He didn't bother to mask his irritation.

Chelsea sniffed. "He's not old. He's prematurely gray."

"He's a dirty old man probably out there hitting on every bikini-clad beauty within range," he told her while he leisurely nibbled on her neck.

She allowed her head to fall backward against his chest. "You're doing it again."

"Doing what?"

"Th-that," she said weakly.

"Is it working?"

"Yes," she said with a sigh.

"Damn, and we've got all those people outside!" His

comic frustration invited her reluctant laughter. "Okay, I've got it. I'll just march out there and tell them we've discovered a nasty bacteria in the food and they all have to go home so we can have the house fumigated."

"You don't fumigate for bacteria," she pointed out.

"You can fumigate for anything your little heart desires, as long as it isn't me."

A kiss whispered a message against her temple. She closed her eyes, savoring his touch the way she usually savored a hot fudge sundae. "You make things sound so easy." She sighed.

"They are if you want them to be." His hands moved downward until his fingertips touched the sides of her breasts. "All right, so you won't let me kick them out. Then the least you can do is protect me from those female sharks. If it hadn't been for Gwen running interference, I would have lost my virtue by now out there. And that's something I'm saving for you." He dropped a kiss by the corner of her eye. "You gonna let them know I'm already taken?"

She chewed on her lower lip. "And if I don't?"

"I'll just stand here and continue seducing you until you say yes."

Her laughter was tinged with frustration. "Oh, Mark, what am I going to do with you?"

He turned her in the warm circle of his arms. "I should think you already know the answer to that question. Think about it, and we'll explore the subject in depth after everyone has gone. Okay?"

She drew in a deep breath and finally nodded. "But that doesn't mean you're going to get your way," she warned him.

"No, but I can hope, can't I?" he whispered dramatically. "Now, come on. I'll help you carry this stuff out. The sooner they eat, the sooner they'll be gone."

"This is not the barbecue I envisioned," she told him, picking up two platters and handing them to him.

"Don't worry, you can handle anything that comes along," he promised, unable to resist stealing a kiss that lingered as his mouth whispered across hers. By the time he stepped back, she was smiling. "See how well you handle me?"

"If I handled you well, I wouldn't be in this mess," she retorted, picking up a stack of paper plates and the dip dish and walking outside ahead of him.

As they headed for the long table set up for food, Mark admired Chelsea in her tan shorts jumpsuit coupled with a bright apricot T-shirt. Her hair, brushed into soft waves, was caught behind her ears with two combs. She looked as soft and fresh as a breath of spring. And he realized he was well on his way to falling in love with her.

"Now all I've got to do is convince her," he muttered.

Chelsea looked over her shoulder. "Convince who of what?" A suspicious look marred her delicate features.

"You. Of how good I am for you." His innocent smile would have done a Boy Scout proud.

Chelsea was immediately drawn into conversation with another new arrival, and several other guests introduced themselves to Mark. It didn't take him long to see that Chelsea's friends warmly welcomed newcomers into their midst, and while he would have liked nothing more than to be alone with her, he did begin to enjoy himself.

"I drive by the mall site about once a week," Jeremy, who owned two stereo stores, told him. "I can't believe it's going up so quickly."

"Yeah, I've got a great crew," he replied, covertly looking around for Chelsea, who seemed to disappear the moment he caught sight of her. "The way things are going, we'll be finishing right on schedule."

"I heard you're opening an office in the area. Will it be a branch office of your dad's firm, or are you striking out on your own?"

Mark stifled a sigh of frustration as he realized he wouldn't be able to hunt Chelsea down just yet. "My brothers and I will each have separate offices with our own subspecialties, under the general umbrella of Harrison Construction, Incorporated. My oldest brother builds homes, while another specializes in schools, churches and public spaces. I prefer commercial building myself."

Jeremy eyed Mark. "You're pretty young for such a large responsibility, aren't you?"

Mark flashed a brief smile that didn't come anywhere near his eyes. "Well, we all have to start somewhere, don't we?"

"Yeah, that's true."

Jeremy looked over his shoulder when someone called his name. "Hey, there's Suzanne. Talk to you later."

"How do you happen to know Jeremy?" Mark asked when he finally caught up with Chelsea for a few moments.

"I bought my stereo system from him," she explained. "He offered a pretty good deal."

"Yeah, I can imagine." Jealousy darkened his tone. "I bet he tried to throw himself in as a bonus."

"Maybe he tried, but I wasn't listening or interested."

Mark grinned. "You sure know how to brighten my day," he murmured in her ear.

"Come on, meet some other people," she invited.

Mark held her back. "I hate to tell you this when you've been such a great hostess, but I'm getting pretty tired of all these people. I want to be alone with you."

While her smiling features looked innocent, her eyes sparkled with devilry. "Could you maybe consider this a way of heightening the anticipation?"

"Lady, you're pushing your luck," he warned, but secretly he was delighted at the return of the high-spirited Chelsea.

"I know," she whispered, walking away.

Chelsea was aware just how much she was pushing her luck, and she marveled at the changes overtaking her. She always enjoyed fun, but blatant flirting was pretty new to her. Mark had somehow managed to break down some strong emotional barriers, and for once she didn't care.

"Chelsea, wherever do you find such gorgeous men?" A sloe-eyed brunette cornered her. "That Mark Harrison looks positively delicious. And while I'm not all that crazy about older men, that silver-haired Lawrence Carson does have an air about him."

Chelsea leaned forward as if imparting a state secret. "That's not all he has, Kira," she murmured. "I understand that Lawrence has a very healthy bank account, and the lady in his life recently left for the East Coast and a lucrative modeling career. The poor man could probably use some serious consoling."

Kira's eyes lit up, and her lips parted in a wide smile. "That poor dear," she cooed. "All alone, is he?"

Chelsea nodded. "And while Mark appears to be a great guy—" she paused significantly "—well, we all know construction types. A bit more...crude, shall we say? You know what I mean—beer and football and such." She shook her head pityingly. "I thought if I invited him here he could make some useful business contacts and perhaps even smooth out his rough edges...."

Kira wet her lips. "Hmm, while 'rough edges' are nice at times, I think I'll go over and have a cozy chat with Lawrence," she decided. "I always wanted to know more about foreign cars."

Chelsea patted her arm. "Yes, you do that." She watched the brunette stalk the older man with the grace of a man-eating tiger.

"Oh, you're good. You're very good," Gwen said with a chuckle, handing Chelsea a plastic cup filled with wine.

Chelsea sipped her wine, looking very pleased with herself. "I'm sure I don't know what you mean."

"Come on, Chelsea, by the time you finished, you had Kira steered away from Mark and practically drooling over Lawrence. Little does she know that Carson's most interesting topics of conversation are his golf game, his boat and how his imports outclass American-made cars."

Chelsea nodded her agreement. "And what does Kira talk about?"

"Her hairdresser, her manicurist, herself."

"Right." Chelsea nodded. "Ergo, Kira will have a rich, self-involved man attending to her every wish, and Lawrence will have a beautiful, self-involved woman on his arm. A match made in heaven." She glanced down at her watch. "I'd better put the rest of the food out and get the grill fired up."

"Honey, if you need to get a fire going, just track down Mark. Those sexy eyes of his will provide more than enough heat," Gwen teased.

Chelsea gave her a playful push. "Go line up a couple

of volunteers to man the barbecue while I fetch the rest of the food.''

With the ease of a veteran, Chelsea soon had bowls of salads, crocks of baked beans, baskets of potato chips and an assortment of condiments arranged on the serving table, while Mark and two other men grilled hamburgers.

''I'm impressed with all the work you've done.'' Mark finally sat down next to Chelsea, carefully balancing a loaded plate on one knee. ''And you've obviously got a lot of nice friends who think the world of you.''

''I'm lucky that way,'' she said modestly. ''And I'm glad I have a yard big enough to accommodate them.''

Suddenly she noticed his mile-high hamburger, which appeared to have everything on it but the kitchen sink. ''Are you sure you're going to be able to get your mouth around that? It looks big enough to feed three.''

He shot her a pointed look. ''I figured I'd give in to at least *one* of my appetites. Besides, a hamburger with everything on it is the best kind.'' He leaned over and whispered in her ear, ''Although, for your sake, I did forgo the onion.''

She smiled as she held up her own loaded burger and took a large, unladylike bite out of it. She chewed thoughtfully and swallowed. ''That's funny, I didn't.''

Chapter Ten

"I thought they'd never leave!" Mark intoned dramatically as he opened a large trash bag for Chelsea.

Chelsea's frown wasn't convincing. "You all but threw them out, what with the way you kept yawning and staring at your watch," she reproved. She leaned over the serving table, gathered all the trash into the middle of the paper tablecloth, and dumped the entire bundle into the bag Mark held.

"Well, they'd been here practically forever," he defended himself. "Besides, I didn't hear anyone complaining. Except maybe that one guy who showed up late."

Chelsea groaned at the memory of the unknown, unexpected visitor who had asked for her by name. She'd fled to the kitchen, leaving Mark to deal with the oversize, tattooed biker. "I can't believe Colleen struck again! And to invite him to the barbecue!"

"At least his arrival got everyone else thinking about leaving," Mark said.

"Your little here's-your-hat-what's-your-hurry spiel right after Vince mentioned he should probably get going since he had an early day tomorrow didn't hurt either.'' She swatted him with a paper plate. ''That was rude.''

Mark danced out of her reach. ''Hey, I did you a favor. You must be exhausted by now.''

''Some favor.'' She wadded napkins into a large ball and lobbed it into the bag.

Mark dropped the bag and clasped Chelsea's hands. ''Are you really mad at me?''

''No, but I should be,'' she murmured.

''What if I found a way to make it up to you?''

She tipped her head to one side. ''You'd better have an excellent idea.''

''Oh, I do.'' His words were heavy with meaning. ''And I'm sure you'd agree with me, too.''

''There's certainly nothing wrong with your ego, is there?''

''You mean a lot to me, Chelsea,'' he said in a low voice suddenly throbbing with intensity.

She had to tip her head back to look at him, and at once she was mesmerized by the dark lights in his eyes. Working outdoors had tanned his skin deeply and carved tiny creases by his eyes.

''I don't take things lightly, Mark. I can't afford to. For many years I've had no trouble keeping men at arm's length, but you've somehow managed to shoot down every one of my defenses. Perhaps I'm a fool to admit it.'' She frowned. ''And that's just it. I've been a fool before. And that kind of pain I never want to go through again.''

More than anything Mark wanted to hold her in his arms and assure her that everything would be fine. But he knew she had to trust him of her own accord.

A tiny smile curved her lips, now bare of the peach-bronze lipstick she'd worn earlier. ''Yet you turned my life upside down, and I feel I have no choice but to see this out to its bitter end."

"Quite a choice of words, Chelsea. You act as if it's over before we've even had a chance to truly begin. Do you know something I don't?"

"I know that every beginning has an ending, and not necessarily a happy one."

This time Mark did step forward, grasp her and pull her into his arms. "There's no ending for us, Chels," he murmured, bringing her closer to him. "Just all beginnings. Trust me."

Her reply was to raise her head slowly and allow him to capture her mouth with his, as if, as she'd said, she had no choice but to give in to him and to her inner self. Her lips parted under his probing tongue, and she tasted beer and man. In no time he pulled her so tightly against his body that a sheet of paper couldn't have slid between them.

She savored the warm, musky aroma of his skin as she suddenly, frenziedly, pulled her mouth away enough to nibble at his throat and revel in his growling reply.

Mark inhaled the faint scent of perfume in her hair as he buried his face in the soft waves that tickled his nostrils.

"I want you, Chelsea," he whispered, running his open mouth over the graceful curve of her neck while his hands kneaded her hips, pressing to fit them against him. "I need you."

"Yes." Her reply was a faint exhalation, her body taut with anticipation. "God help me, but I can only say yes."

Mark didn't give her any time to rethink her answer. He picked her up in his arms and carried her inside. He walked unerringly toward the stairs, climbing each step with a deliberate stride. Chelsea draped her arms around his neck and buried her face against the slightly rough surface.

When Mark switched on the bedside lamp, he was pleasantly surprised by what he found. Here was the tangible proof of the true Chelsea, the Chelsea he was so certain he knew.

A rich, fiery-colored comforter covered the king-size brass bed, topped with lush silken pillow shams. The shaded lamp itself cast a soft, sensual glow of warmth over the room.

He laid her down on the bed and stood there for a moment to gaze down at her. "You're so beautiful against that fiery material," he whispered.

"Fire can be dangerous," she warned him in a voice gone helplessly husky.

He stretched out next to her, fingering the straps to her outfit. "Couldn't you have worn something easier to get off?"

She arched an eyebrow. "I thought you liked challenges."

"There's challenges, and then there's challenges."

He edged one hand under her back while the other found the side zipper of her jumpsuit and eased it down. Its soft rasp and the sound of labored breathing quietly rent the silence.

Chelsea closed her eyes against the sensations racing through her body. Mark had hardly touched her, but it didn't seem to matter. The way he looked at her was almost as potent as lovemaking itself.

But suddenly that wasn't enough. She needed more. She reached up, touching his cheek with curious fingertips. She allowed him to lower her jumpsuit and peel her shirt off over her head, and she smiled when he pulled in a sharp breath at the sight of her lacy mint green camisole and the matching lace bikinis that barely covered her hips.

"Is this legal?" he murmured, tracing the narrow shoulder strap until his fingertip reached the top of her breast. He drew patterns against her satiny skin, feeling her shivers of delight under his touch. He moved downward along the camisole until he reached bare skin at her waist. His fingertip glided over the small indentation of her belly button, and when he reached the lace topping her panties, she moaned softly.

"One...of our...newest items," she gasped. "Like it?"

"Like? Hell, I like it so much, I may need CPR." He pressed his palm against the warm area between her thighs and rotated the heel slightly. Then he leaned down and covered her mouth with his in a kiss so possessive and explicit that it took her remaining breath away.

His tongue parted her lips, darting inside to rediscover the sweetness he knew was there, and it wasn't long before all clothing turned into an unbearable restriction. Chelsea began tearing his off, and, growling a curse, Mark kicked everything to the foot of the bed, uncaring as comforter and clothing slid to the floor in a heap. Right now, he cared only about seeing all of her.

"Mark," she moaned as his hand slid under her camisole to cup her full breast. His callused thumb rubbed the nipple, sending shock waves throughout her body. She twisted and turned until Mark released her from the delicate silken prison. Then she blindly reached out for him, needing to touch him.

"Just relax and let me love you," he whispered, pressing light kisses all over her face as his hands roamed her body with loving strokes. He gently nudged one knee between hers, parting her legs, feeling her damp heat seduce him. Then he lowered his head and fastened his mouth on her nipple. Chelsea gasped and bucked upward under the intimate touch, and Mark softly urged her onward, urged her to give in to her feelings. With his hands, his lips and his hot whispered words he sent her racing into the flames.

Under his loving touch, Chelsea gave herself up to the fires within her. She rubbed her fingertips against his nipples, watching the copper-colored circles harden into tiny nubs under her touch. Never before in her limited experience had she felt uninhibited enough to fully explore the male body the way Mark encouraged her to do. With his moans and his movements he showed her how much she pleased him, and she continued to caress him, stroking his hair-roughened skin, kissing his expressive mouth and learning what he liked best. All shyness melted away in his heat, and when she encircled his powerful erection with her fingers, he moaned what could have been a prayer or a curse, muttering something about dying and going to heaven.

But time for leisurely exploration was rapidly running out.

"Wait," Mark said hoarsely, scrambling to find his jeans and to reach into a pocket. He might dream of someday seeing Chelsea pregnant with his baby, but he wanted it to be a joint decision made at the right time Such as after she agreed to spend the rest of her life with him.

Conscious that it had probably been a long time for her, he took it slow and easy, even though he felt he would explode if he didn't have her right away. He entered her carefully, watching her face for any signs of discomfort. She whispered her desire and arched up to draw him deeper into her. He silently called upon all his willpower to wait for her to fully accept him before he began the age-old movements. Even then, he continued to be slow and deliberate, wanting her to share it all with him.

Chelsea watched him, her lips moist and parted, her eyes glazed with desire. This total trust, this infinite tenderness, was new to him. Special. And he knew that this one-of-a-kind woman was what he'd been looking for all his life. And he wasn't about to give her up, no matter how stubborn she might try to be later on.

He shifted his weight in a way that brought a moan to her lips and had her wrapping her legs around his hips. "Stay with me, Chelsea, all the way."

A sob escaped her as she closed her eyes. She didn't think she could stand the pleasure much longer, yet she needed it as much as she required air to breathe. She writhed uncontrollably, murmuring his name.

"Open your eyes," he ordered in a raw, primitive voice. "Look at me, Chelsea." He deliberately halted all movement, and his muscles screamed in agony as he waited for her to comply. Her eyes slowly opened, glazed with passion and a stunned, silent questioning.

"Just look at me," he breathed. "See what you do to me, what we do to each other, what we have together. See how well we fit, how perfect we are together. We wouldn't have that with anyone else."

By then, Chelsea couldn't have looked away if she'd wanted to. She was under Mark's sensual spell, powerless to resist. A faint sheen of perspiration coated her skin, and Mark's body, too, gleamed under the soft light.

Chelsea looped her arms around his shoulders, looking down to where they were joined and back up at

Mark's taut features. He was right. They were perfect together. And there was no more holding back.

He coaxed her into a maelstrom of color and light, and a kaleidoscope of fire seemed to whirl around every thrust of his body into hers. And she tumbled gladly to the very center of the inferno they had created.

MARK COULDN'T STOP touching Chelsea. Her damp skin felt like heaven to his callused fingertips. And the sleepy, satisfied smile on her lips was pure paradise. Her makeup was smudged, her hair a tangled mass of curls, but he doubted he had ever seen her looking so beautiful.

"That was incredible." His voice was hushed, awed.

She opened one eye. "Is that the best you can come up with?"

He burst out laughing while relief flooded his veins. No guilt, no regrets, just sheer satisfaction. "You are something else, Chelsea Brennan." He lowered his head and pressed a light kiss on lips already sweetly puffy from kissing. "You do things to me I never knew could happen," he said. "You make me feel things I never thought I would." His eyes, so brown and dark with desire, coasted into hers. "Which is the real Chelsea?" he mused. "The smooth, sophisticated owner of Hot Stuff lingerie? The harried mother of a teenage daughter who brings crises—and creeps—to her very doorstep? The free spirit at Rick's, who attracted every man in the place? Or the incredibly sexy woman I just made love to? Which one is the real you?"

She looped her arms around his neck to bring his face even closer to hers. "I have an idea you just jumbled all of them up and turned them into one whole person," she whispered, gently clamping down on his lower lip with her teeth and pulling it into her mouth.

She rubbed her fingertips against his muscular arms, slowly making her way downward past the crisp hairs on his chest to his narrow waist and flat stomach. Then she glided down even farther to the nest of dark, coarse hair, where she found him already erect and pulsing against her feathery strokes.

If Mark had thought he was tired, he learned differently as his body leapt under her teasing touch. Her fingers encircled him, and he shuddered with pleasure.

"We may set a world record for recovery time," he murmured, nuzzling her throat and inhaling the sweet scent of her.

Her soft laughter was music to his ears as he rolled over and buried himself deep in her damp velvet warmth. Her eyes gleamed gold fire as she arched to draw him in even farther.

"Maybe there's something to be said for younger men after all."

Chapter Eleven

"Mark. Mark, wake up. Please, you have to wake up now!"

Eyes still closed, he smiled as he turned over and reached out. His smile turned to a slight frown when he found something soft to the touch but not as enticing as bare silken skin. He opened one eye, hoping his fingers were lying to him. They weren't.

A frantic-looking Chelsea was clothed in an oversize fleece top and floral print leggings. Even his sleep-befuddled mind knew something was awry. This was not what he expected to wake up to. Shouldn't Chelsea be wearing something made of silk and lace, or, better yet, nothing at all?

"Mark, you have to get up," she ordered, pulling on his arm.

"Is there a fire or something?" he mumbled.

"No, but—"

"Well, then, why don't we start a blaze of our own?" He tried to grab her.

She evaded him. "Mark, you have to get up now," she ordered, pulling off the sheet covering him.

"I am up." He grinned wickedly, reaching for her again.

"That's not what I mean, and you know it!" She stopped and took a deep breath. "Colleen just called. They had car trouble, and they're on their way home. She can't find you here."

Her words were more effective than a cold shower. He dropped back against the pillow. "Are you so ashamed of what we had last night that you don't want your daughter to know?" he asked quietly.

"I need to set an example for her. I don't want her to think her mother is easy!" she cried.

"I see," Mark said. He pushed the sheet aside and climbed out of bed. He wasn't surprised to find his clothing picked up, neatly folded and stacked on the dresser. "Well, I guess I don't have to ask if you'll respect me in the morning," he said sardonically, picking up his clothes and walking into the bathroom.

Chelsea dropped onto the bed, staring down at her trembling hands. How could she feel so wonderful one minute and so thoroughly miserable the next?

"Why couldn't I have played this cool, as if I did this all the time?" she murmured. Then her lips twisted. "Probably because I don't do this all the time."

"Did I ever imply I thought you did?" Warm hands covered hers. Mark hunkered down in front of her, rubbing her icy fingers back to life.

She raised her head. Tears glistened in her eyes. "This is all so new to me, Mark," she whispered. "I may have a daughter, but I've never spent an entire night with a man. I know it isn't very sophisticated to admit, but it's true."

Warmth flooded his heart at her admission. "And you're afraid you'll lose her respect if she knows you've made love with a man who isn't your husband?" he guessed.

"We've talked about the difference between making love and sex," she murmured, mesmerized by the slow motion of his hands on hers. "I know I can't rule her life, but I don't want her to make the same mistakes I did."

"Chelsea, Colleen is a smart kid. She wouldn't think you were terrible for letting me stay over. By now she has to know there's more between us than just lust," he told her. He silently urged her to smile. "Hey, how about fixing us a glass of orange juice?" He rocked the hands still encased in his. "There's no set rules for this kind of thing. We'll make up our own as we go along, and we'll make sure Colleen doesn't get any wrong ideas. Together we can handle whatever comes along, okay?"

Her lips twisted. "You've obviously done this before."

"Not as often as you seem to think. I happen to prefer quality over quantity. Now, stop worrying about such unimportant stuff. If and when Colleen finds out we're lovers, we'll handle it. And it won't hurt to see two adults in a caring, committed relationship. It sure beats a parade of men through her mother's bedroom, right?"

She stared at him. "Is that how you see us? Committed?"

"You don't think I've put up with all your mean-mouthed stubbornness just for a quick roll in the hay, do you?"

She couldn't help but smile at that. "Now you're teasing me."

He touched her cheek, sliding the backs of his fingers over the warm surface. "You are a unique woman, Chelsea. And I'm glad I didn't have to fight some other guy for you."

She laughed at the possibility.

Mark shook his head. "I would have fought any guy who tried to stand in my way. I think from the first moment I saw you, I must have known you were the woman for me." He grinned. "Even if you are stubborn as hell and determined to give me a hard time."

"I can't believe you were attracted to a woman yelling at you," she said, fingering his shirt hem.

He shrugged. "Not only attracted, I was knocked out. You were showing concern for your daughter's well-being and anger over her wrongdoing. You were frightened for her safety, and I was an unknown, potentially threatening entity. You were a mother defending her child—and you were downright beautiful." He smiled. "Chelsea, you've told me you have a full life. All I'm asking is to be allowed to be a part of it. I do have my uses, you know." He leaned over her, gently forcing her back onto the tumbled covers until her head lay pillowed on his forearm.

"Such as?" Her voice was husky and languid.

"Oh—" he nuzzled her throat "—I know a bit about plumbing."

Her breath caught. "I can change washers myself."

"Carpentry..." His teeth nipped the tender skin.

"I know how to use a hammer," she breathed.

"Mowing lawns, raking leaves..." he murmured.

There was a catch in her voice as his hand snaked its way up under her top. "I have a gardening service."

"Well..." He pulled up her top, and his mouth found her bare breast. "There is one other thing I have some talent for."

"Such as?"

And she sighed as he proceeded to show her.

"YOU ALSO HAVE a talent for making coffee." Chelsea lifted her cup and saluted Mark, who now sat well and properly dressed at the small round table in the breakfast nook.

"Told you I had my uses." He leaned back in his chair, happily sated. "But I can't make waffles like these. Breakfast is usually whatever I find at the doughnut shop in the morning."

She wrinkled her nose. "Jelly doughnuts for breakfast?"

He put a hand over his heart. "Hey, I'm just a poor bachelor, sweetheart. I'm not supposed to know how to cook. That way, you'll feel sorry for me and cook me wonderful, nutritious meals."

She groaned and stood to clear away the dishes, but he reached out and dragged her onto his lap.

"Mark!"

"Aw, come on," he teased, circling her waist with his arms and holding her captive. "Give us a kiss."

"You are insatiable!" She laughed. With her hands full, she was helpless to fend him off. But suddenly she needed him to touch her, and she knew her hunger was for much more than just his physical possession. She wanted to crawl inside his heart and fill it to bursting, the way hers was. The feelings inside her were so intense they almost frightened her, but Mark had proved that there was nothing to be frightened of. That they were right together. Hadn't he?

"How old were you when you first kissed a boy?" he murmured, surprising her with sudden lightness.

"Six. And I socked him in the nose for it," she admitted.

He grinned. "Bet you wouldn't have socked me."

"How could I? You weren't even born yet," Chelsea shot back.

Mark tensed at the remark, but she seemed to be only teasing. So, for the time being, he resolved to simply enjoy this lighthearted Chelsea who smiled merrily and seemed eager to return his caresses.

Her face was free of makeup, but her lips were rosy from his kisses, and her cheeks were flushed a bright pink. Even her eyes shone. And he dared to begin to hope for even more.

"Chelsea…" he huskily began. But he was halted by the shrill ringing of the phone.

"I should get it," she murmured.

"It's probably just somebody selling something you don't want or need."

She reluctantly left the warm haven of his arms. "It might be Colleen."

It was.

As Chelsea put down the plates and picked up the receiver, Mark leaned over and grasped her around the waist, pulling her back onto his lap.

"Yes, the barbecue went just fine," Chelsea said brightly. Too brightly.

"Personally, I enjoyed more what happened afterward," he whispered in her other ear.

She batted at him, but he merely laughed softly and tightened his hold.

"Actually, I'm just lazing around enjoying the peace and quiet without you running around the house looking for something that's always found in your room."

"Lazing around. I like that idea." Mark slipped his hand up under her top and found a bare breast. "C'mon, let's laze some more."

Chelsea's eyes widened as her nipple hardened under

his teasing fingers and a tingling sensation began making its way through her body. She swallowed hard.

"What?" She sounded dazed. "No, I just thought I heard someone at the front door," she said slowly.

"No, I think it's wonderful the problem with the car didn't turn out to be major after all. So you're going to stay in Santa Barbara?"

"Colleen, you're a kid after my own heart," Mark whispered, clearly pleased with the news. "Have fun, stay as long as you like. Don't hurry back on our account."

Chelsea pressed her fingertips against his lips to silence him. Grinning against her fingers, he proceeded to tease them with his tongue.

"Yes, I'll be fine. I'll think about it, but I'm doing just fine on my own, thank you," Chelsea said weakly. "Bye, hon."

Chelsea tried to pull away from his imprisoning arms. "Mark, let go. I need to hang up the phone."

His embrace tightened. "Tell me what she said."

"They're staying in Santa Barbara after all."

"And what are you supposed to think about?" he coaxed.

"Colleen said I should call up a friend and get out," she replied.

"Aren't you lucky? I can save you that phone call."

Chelsea pried his hands loose and stood up, hanging up the phone and standing back a safe distance. "I don't think you were the person she had in mind."

He cocked an eyebrow as he pulled his shirt over his head and playfully flexed his muscles. "I'd be a hell of a lot more fun than Gwen."

Chelsea could feel her face redden as she stared at his

bare chest, and her fingers itched to tangle themselves in the thick curls. "You don't play fair."

"What's unfair? I'm suggesting something we both like to play at," he said seductively.

She found herself weakening but rallied firmly. Tempted as she was to give in entirely to her newfound spirit of play, part of her urged a return to some form of equilibrium. "We can't spend all day in bed. Besides, I have some paperwork to catch up on."

Mark considered her words, as if gauging her sense of vulnerability. "Okay, we'll go roller-skating," he stated.

"Roller-skating?" Her voice squeaked with dismay. "I can't go roller-skating. I have work to do."

He stood up, pulling his shirt back on. "Sure, you can go roller-skating. Paperwork you can do later."

The dancing lights in his eyes caught her off guard, and though skating was hardly a way to guarantee equilibrium, she found herself unable to send Mark away.

"I'm no expert at roller-skating," she warned him.

Mark waved a dismissing hand. "There's nothing to it."

"It is when it's your butt you're landing on," Chelsea argued, positive she could already feel the hard floor connecting with her posterior. She should have known that Mark would be into a lot of physical activity. Most of hers consisted of crossing the parking lot.

"Don't worry, I'll make sure you stay up," he promised, grabbing her hands and pulling her out of the kitchen.

She looked toward the sink as she felt all resolve leaving her. "The dishes!"

Mark's suggestion regarding the dishes was physically

impossible but interesting. He grabbed her hand and almost dragged her out the door.

"But I want to call my insurance agent and make sure my life insurance is up-to-date!" she wailed even as she was led, she was certain, to her doom.

"MY LEGS WILL NOT cooperate," Chelsea argued once Mark had laced her into a pair of skates and pulled her to her feet. She dug her fingers into his forearm with a death grip.

"You're just fine," he soothed, leading her toward the rink.

Chelsea could already feel her knees buckling as one foot went one way and the other went in the opposite direction. She held on even tighter.

Mark didn't seem to mind in the least. Her glare bounced right off him.

"If I so much as break a nail because of this, I will hold you personally responsible."

"Come on, we'll take it slow and easy," he crooned, gliding out onto the rink.

"I'm going to fall," she complained as her ankles wobbled dangerously.

"No, you're not," he assured her, sliding one of his arms around her waist. "You're doing fine."

She heaved a silent sigh of relief to feel his arm around her. "Mark, I feel like a fool out here."

"Hey, you can do it," he urged. "And if you fall, no sweat. Look at that kid."

Chelsea watched a small child who was whirling around and plopping down and picking herself up on a regular basis. "Everyone knows kids bounce much better than adults do," she muttered.

"Cynic," he teased, brushing a kiss against her temple. "Come on, lady, let's get wild and crazy." He moved forward, ignoring her yelp of protest as he kept hold of only her hands and skated backward as he led her across the rink's perimeter.

Chelsea gasped when she began sliding to the right while Mark was still going to the left. He quickly guided her in the correct direction.

"You're worrying too much. Just relax, go with the flow."

"I hate people who tell me those things," she grumbled, keeping a firm hold on his fingers. "Don't you dare let go of me or I'll never forgive you!"

"Sweetheart, I don't ever intend to let go of you."

Chelsea looked up at the intensity in his voice. The dark glint in his eyes sent that now familiar flash of fire through her veins. "Mark..." Her voice trembled.

"I wish we were alone," he complained, swinging her to a halt against the rink wall and leaning into her. "Then we could try something like strip skating."

She ran her tongue across her lower lip. "How would we play that?"

"Every time one of us fell down, we'd take off a piece of clothing."

"I'd be naked in no time!" she exclaimed.

"I know," he said, eyes twinkling.

"Oh, you!" She slapped his arm, then looked at him suspiciously. "And what, pray tell, would you be doing during this display? I would think you'd want to participate yourself."

His lips curved upward in his rakish grin. "I'd be watching, of course—and waiting to catch you. Get the idea?" he asked huskily.

Chelsea smiled in challenge and ducked under his arm. And while her first steps were more than a little wobbly, she was able to skate off without falling down, and it took several minutes for Mark to feel ready to catch up. She laughed in triumph.

Finally he skated alongside her, sliding an arm around her waist and catching hold of one of her hands.

"You're clever, lady, very clever," he murmured through the loud rock music.

"I've had an excellent teacher," she retorted.

Mark threw back his head and laughed. "I think we'll have to come back here more often."

"I'd rather have root canal work done, thank you," she said primly.

He roared with laughter. "You're one stubborn lady, you know that?"

Her lips curved upward. "You mean, you've just now figured that out? My, my, and I thought you were faster than that."

"By now you should realize slow and deep is more my style."

Chelsea shook her head. "You have a one-track mind," she accused him.

"Where you're concerned, absolutely. Now, tell me how much fun you're having."

"I never said this was my idea of fun," she argued.

He inclined his head close to hers. "True, I liked my idea more. Want me to yell fire and get rid of everyone so we can try it?"

With his arm around her and his thigh moving rhythmically against her, Chelsea found herself actually tempted.

She felt her face burning. She had never thought of herself as such a free-spirited woman until Mark came into her life. And now he had her thinking and saying

sexy things, and, more, giving free rein to some mighty
powerful emotions. And she wasn't sure entirely she was
really ready for any of it.

Chapter Twelve

"Mom, if you stay in there any longer, you're going to melt and slide down the drain."

"Go away. You have your own bathroom. Just leave me to my pain."

Colleen pounded on the closed bathroom door. "You've been in there for an hour and a half, and you keep refilling the tub, so there's probably no hot water left. And all you've done is tell me to go away. Well, I'm not going!"

Chelsea shifted her legs in the steamy water and moaned softly at her aches and pains. "And he said we'd have fun," she muttered, sinking down until her chin rested on the water. "He didn't say anything about falling down and bruising every inch of my body."

"Wimp!"

She privately damned Colleen's excellent hearing. "Colleen, go call Elaine or something."

"Mark's on the phone for you."

"Tell him I'm not talking to him."

"Are you mad at him just because he took you roller-skating?" she said in disbelief.

Chelsea sighed. "No, why should I be mad simply

because I let him talk me into doing something I'm physically incapable of doing?''

''This from the woman who told me to try to share some of my boyfriend's interests, such as noisy, obnoxious stock car races?'' she hooted. ''Double standards, Mom? Actually, come to think of it, I'm surprised Mark suggested something that fun. Maybe he's not so uptight after all.''

''Uptight?'' It was Chelsea's turn to hoot. ''Just tell the stuffed shirt that I'm soaking the aches and pains from my almost forty-year-old body.''

Chelsea waited until her daughter finally obeyed her by leaving.

''What that man does to me!'' she muttered, then sputtered as water trickled into her mouth.

She'd hoped the long bath would not only soothe her battered bones but also cool her feelings for Mark for a little while. Instead, the slide of the hot water, made silken from bath oil, reminded her of the slide of his hands across her bare skin, the heat of his body covering hers.

She closed her eyes, reliving the hours she'd spent with Mark. Last night he had shown her a new side of herself—that of a passionate woman as hungry for him as he was for her. Despite Colleen's origins, she had never thought of herself as wanton. Had Mark proved her wrong? Lovemaking with him was addictive, and even now she could feel her body tingling in remembrance, her breasts swelling and nipples peaking for his touch.

She moaned softly as she shifted her aching body. ''I was better off celibate.''

''CONGRATULATIONS! I was so glad to see you and Mark acting like a real couple!'' Gwen pounced on her the minute she entered the shop.

"Wh-what do you mean?" Chelsea asked, wondering just how much Gwen—or any of her other guests—had seen.

"Chelsea, the entire time at the barbecue, the man looked at you as if you were better than any of the food we served."

Chelsea shook her head.

"Is that no, we're not admitting we're a couple?"

"It's no, I'm not telling you one thing."

"Then it must be absolutely delish." Gwen's dark eyes gleamed.

Chelsea looked around the crowded stockroom. "Did you talk to the mall office this morning?"

Gwen recognized her friend's not so subtle way of changing the subject. "First thing. The interior will be painted this week, and we can make our inspection of the premises next week. There's no reason we can't move stock in there by the first of the month."

"It'll be a zoo when the mall first opens," Chelsea guessed, perching on the edge of the desk and smoothing her mallard blue knit tunic over her slim skirt. She stared down at her taupe pumps as if something about them fascinated her, while the truth was, she felt uncomfortable under her friend's shrewd eye. Gwen had a nasty habit of seeing right through her.

"As long as they buy, we can't complain about the extra work," Gwen reminded her as she held up a hot pink sequined cocktail dress displayed on a black velveteen padded hanger. "Hmm, I knew I should have ordered an extra one of these for myself. I'll have to call today and see if I can have another one rushed out." She hung it back on the rack of evening clothing that would be moved to the new shop once the interior was finished.

"Where do you wear all the clothes you buy?" Chelsea asked in wonderment. Gwen's closet was huge, and it was stuffed to the gills with elegant evening clothing.

"I go out a lot in hopes of finding Mr. Right." She cocked an eyebrow. "Maybe I should get Colleen to do my searching for me. She sure did a great job for you."

"Oh, yeah, look at Mr. Black-Leather-and-Chains who showed up at the barbecue," she groaned.

"Not everyone can bat a thousand. Still, she did fine with Mark. And I saw the way he was looking at you at the barbecue," Gwen pointed out. "He might as well have placed a brand on your hip."

Chelsea thought of the tiny love bite on her left hip and concentrated on not blushing. She'd done too much of that lately, thanks to Mark. "You're imagining things," she muttered.

"Am I?" Gwen looked her over from head to toe. "Hon, you practically floated in here today. That is not the look of a woman who spent the rest of the weekend doing housework."

Chelsea slid off the desk and looked around for something, anything, to occupy her hands. "We did go roller-skating."

"Excuse me, could you repeat that statement? I don't think I heard correctly." Gwen playfully cupped an ear.

Chelsea braced her hands on her hips. "We went roller-skating, and I fell down a lot. Now are you happy?"

"Yes!" Gwen raised her fist to the sky. "It's about time somebody prodded you out of your responsible mom routine."

"Easy for you to say. You're not the one with a black-

and-blue butt," Chelsea muttered. "I could barely walk last night and had to spend the evening in a tub of hot water."

"Not alone, I hope."

"Most definitely alone, with Colleen pounding on the door every five seconds. When she was little, I thought it was kind of cute that she missed me so much. But I *was* looking forward to the day she'd outgrow that trick and I could enjoy my baths in peace. It looks as if I'm going to have to wait until she goes off to college."

"Oh come on, you're going to miss her next year, and you know it," Gwen insisted.

Chelsea sighed. "You're right. I will miss her. After all, we practically grew up together."

"So maybe someone will be moving in before Colleen leaves." Gwen eyed her slyly.

Chelsea looked down at her hands and began fiddling with her bangle bracelets. "You're getting ahead of yourself, Gwen. Way ahead of yourself."

"A man who walks by this shop practically every day in hopes of catching a glimpse of you isn't your typical fly-by-night guy just looking to get laid," Gwen said bluntly.

Chelsea looked up, startled by this piece of news. "What do you mean?"

"What I mean is, I've noticed Mark walking past the shop many times, and each time he's looking in as if he's window-shopping for the love of his life, which we both know happens to be you. The guy is nuts about you, Chelsea. I know *I* wouldn't mind finding someone that wonderful."

"It's still so new, so...fragile," she confessed. "We still have so much to learn about each other." *Such as how he likes to be kissed between his shoulder blades.*

Or how he responds to tickling. Or— She shook her head to banish the erotic thoughts racing through her mind. "Not to mention that Harrison Construction isn't based awfully close by. For all we know, Mark will be taking off as soon as he's finished with the mall."

Gwen smirked. "Chelsea, Mark is opening an office here in town. He talked about it Saturday. And he's putting a bid in to build the new office complex slated for that cul-de-sac off Margarita Road."

Chelsea was surprised at that piece of news and wondered why Mark hadn't mentioned it to her. Of course, she wryly reminded herself, they hadn't done much talking Saturday night, and yesterday she was too busy concentrating on not falling for the umpteenth time.

Gwen watched the play of expressions cross Chelsea's face. "Okay, no more teasing," she said quietly. "I know it's been a long time since you've been in the man-woman game, but Mark is so crazy about you, I don't think he can even think straight. Put him out of his misery and let him know you're just as crazy about him."

"Hey, I'll be the first to admit he's the best thing to come along in my life since Colleen, but I'm not the type to rush into things." Or at least she hadn't been, before Mark. Chelsea glanced at the clock on the desk and headed for the front of the shop to unlock the doors. "Next thing I know you'll be talking about Colleen getting married and having babies. And if you dare bring up such a horrible subject," she tossed over her shoulder, "I'll murder you." After turning the sign from Closed to Open, she flipped on the soft lighting in the two display windows. She looked around the shop's interior, making sure everything was in place, although the stock was always tidied up each evening after closing.

"We're going to have to make room for our holiday stuff soon."

"What would you think about doing something different from the usual reds and greens this holiday season?" Gwen asked, busily changing accessories on a gold lace dress that only the trimmest woman could comfortably wear. "Something more offbeat."

"Sounds good to me. Everyone else will be decorating with those colors, and it does get to be a bit much," Chelsea agreed. "Are you by any chance thinking of using that pink sequined dress as your centerpiece?"

"It could be fun. The sequins have a silver shimmer to them, so I could go with it under a moonlight spot."

"Those folding doors are supposed to be delivered by the end of the week. For the other window I thought we could make it look as if the passersby were peeking into someone's bedroom."

Gwen's eyes lit up. "That could be really sexy," she breathed.

Chelsea nodded. "Done right, it should bring in a lot of new customers curious about the place. We ought to stop by LeeAnne's this week to see how our ads are coming along." The same graphic artist who had designed their logo also produced all their advertising material. The young woman's innovative designs were just right for Hot Stuff, tastefully portraying just enough spice to tempt almost any woman to check out the boutique's fanciful wares.

Gwen grinned broadly before moving off to greet a customer. "I just know this will be the beginning of something very big," she predicted. "And to think that Mark is behind it all. I mean, he is the one building the mall. How apt that he should appear in your life!"

Chelsea sighed, sensing again that her life was slowly flying out of control. "Yes, how apt."

"SO, WHADDYA think, boss?"

Mark tilted his head back to look at the stained glass skylight that rained a colorful shower of light into the atrium at the center of the three-story mall. Then he gazed at the workmen hurrying around, arranging ornamental trees and bushes by the wooden benches set up for weary shoppers. Earth-toned tile flooring and the lush greenery gave the impression of a quiet getaway, a refreshing image for a busy mall.

"We did a fine job, Steve," he said finally, turning on his heel to gaze upward toward the space where Chelsea's shop would be.

Early that morning he'd seen painters applying a soft rose enamel to the wooden window frames under Chelsea's direction. He hadn't been able to see her in two days and had hoped to stop by the shop, but several executives from the corporation that owned the mall came by requesting an extensive tour. Mark wished he could have palmed the job off on someone else, since all he wanted to do was to be with Chelsea. But by the time he had finished his duty and could get away to return to Chelsea's shop site, only a few stray carpenters were there, working on the interior.

He tried calling her that evening when he finally had a free moment, but only to get her answering machine.

"Dammit, Chelsea, where are you?" he roared into the receiver.

He heard a few clicks, and then her precious voice rang in his ears. "Actually, I was running the water and didn't hear the phone right away. Why are you screaming into my answering machine?"

With a sigh of relief, he dropped into his chair. "I miss you."

"You saw me two days ago," she gently reminded him.

"That was two days ago. And I spotted you this morning up in the new shop, but I was nursemaiding a couple of mall executives, and by the time I finished, you were gone." He ran a hand over his face. Only a minute before he had felt so tired he doubted he could stand up straight, but just connecting with Chelsea had revived his spirits. "Have you forgiven me yet for taking you roller-skating?"

"I forgave you," she admitted. "I just wanted to make you suffer a little."

"I'm going to look for office space tomorrow. Want to come along? I'd love to have your opinion."

Her sigh gave him her answer before she spoke. "I can't, Mark. I have another meeting with the bank tomorrow about extending my loan for the new shop."

He nodded. "Okay, then, I'll call you when I finish."

"You're not going to yell at my poor, defenseless answering machine again, are you?" she teased.

"Just don't stay out of reach, okay?" he grumbled.

"As in reaching out and touching someone?" she purred wickedly. "As you can see, I'm only a phone call away."

Mark groaned. "That's just it, wench. I *can't* see you, and it's driving me mad," he said melodramatically.

"Well, if you think it will help any, you can picture me wearing that black nightgown you admired so much."

"You mean that lacy number that shows more than it hides?"

"That's the one I'm wearing," she confirmed, her voice pure mischievous seduction.

Mark groaned more deeply. "I have a good three hours of paperwork ahead of me tonight. Do you honestly expect me to handle that after what you just told me?"

She laughed softly. "You're a big, strong man. I'm sure you can handle just about anything. I'll be a good girl now and let you return to your work. Good night, Mark," she sang.

As the dial tone buzzed in his ear, Mark ran his fingers through his hair, knowing there would be no use attempting to work tonight.

"YOU GOING OUT to look for an office today?" Steve asked, stepping into the trailer the next morning.

Mark nodded. "While I'd prefer visiting the dentist, it has to be done. The realtor I spoke to has several sites in mind."

Steve grinned, familiar with Mark's dislike of being cooped up in an office when he could be out in the thick of things. "Management is hell, ain't it?"

Mark grinned back. "You got it." He looked down at his dust-smeared clothing and noticed a spot of grease on the knee of his jeans. "Guess I should change first. Can you make sure everything's ready for the final inspection?"

The foreman nodded. "Everything will be fine. You go on and find a fancy office, so you'll have an excuse to hire a good-looking secretary with a great pair of—"

"Out," Mark said, moving off.

THE REALTOR was the kind of woman he might have taken to not that long ago, Mark realized. Attractive, intelligent, and definitely flirtatious, sending him unmistakable signals that she was more than amenable to an instant no-strings-attached fling.

But he was surprised to find himself not the least bit interested. He selected the third office space he visited, concluded the deal and asked to have the documents sent to Harrisons' main office. The woman smiled her regrets that he wasn't free for dinner, and Mark left the realty office hungry not for food but for the sight of Chelsea. He climbed into his car and sped off, for the first time in his life totally uncaring that he'd left behind a sure thing in pursuit of something more elusive but infinitely more appealing.

He reached Chelsea's house and smiled to see lights on.

His smile dimmed when Colleen answered the door and told him her mom was out.

"She and Gwen are at a private fashion show. Some new lingerie designer who's hoping to get his line out in time for the holidays is pulling out all the stops for the local retailers," she explained. "I'm on my way to Elaine's, but you could come in and wait for her if you want."

Mark thought of his empty, Chelsea-less apartment. "Yeah, I'd like that," he replied.

Colleen ushered him in, gathered up a stack of books and headed for the door. "There's beer and soda in the refrigerator, so feel free. I doubt Mom's going to stay late because she hates those things." She stopped at the door. "Oh, Mark, I want to apologize for thinking you were stuffy. I think you're really good for Mom, and, what with me going off to college soon, she could really use a nice guy around." She grinned. "Just make sure your intentions are honorable, okay? Oh, and, now that

I think of it, tell Mom I'll be spending the night over there.'' With a wink and a thumbs-up sign, she left.

Mark felt the air leave his lungs. So much for their worries about how Colleen might take their relationship. He shook his head in wonderment for a moment. Then he slipped off his jacket and decided to prepare a proper homecoming for Chelsea to make up for the time they'd been apart.

Chapter Thirteen

"It's about time you got home. Do you know how late it is? Here I've been slaving over a hot pizza box, and you've been out carousing at some professional peep show. So, how was it? Were there half-naked men showing off the new look in madras boxer shorts and silk body shirts, strutting their stuff down the runway while the ladies screamed and salivated?"

Chelsea froze in the act of setting her purse on the entryway table and spun around at Mark's voice. All she could see over the back of the living room couch were his bare feet nonchalantly propped up on the coffee table. Her heart leapt to realize how good indeed it felt to have this man to come home to.

Her instant response was to mask her excited pleasure. "Feet off the table, if you please," she ordered mildly, acting as if she found him in her living room every night of the week. "And, actually, I have heartburn from weird hors d'oeuvres and cheap wine and a headache from loud music and dubious cigarette smoke. Does that tell you how much fun I had?" Still keeping a safe distance, she plopped down in a chair in the foyer and eased her shoes off her tired feet.

"Isn't there something else you'd like to say?" Mark piped up.

Chelsea stretched. "What kind of pizza?"

"Mushroom and sausage," he muttered.

"With extra cheese?"

"Yes," Mark grumbled. "I think I'll go reheat it," he offered brightly.

"Just give me a minute to swallow some aspirin and take—"

Chelsea's mouth dropped open as Mark passed her on his way to the kitchen. The man was wearing nothing but black bikini briefs and a sexy-as-sin smile!

"TALK ABOUT making someone crazy," Chelsea muttered, pawing through her closet. "I guess I should be grateful he was wearing underwear." She stopped and pressed a hand to her stomach. The buffalo stampeding through it had nothing to do with cheap wine and everything to do with the half-naked man downstairs.

She breathed in deeply, then suddenly smiled as a thought occurred to her. In an instant she found what she was looking for, then took the time to freshen her makeup and brush her hair.

"Perfect timing," Mark greeted her over his shoulder as he pulled a foil-wrapped package out of the oven. The enticing aroma of tomato and cheese teased Chelsea's nostrils.

She sat on one of the bar stools at the breakfast counter, casually crossing her legs.

"So you say Colleen is spending the night at Elaine's, huh?" she commented.

"Yup," he said. He turned around—and nearly dropped the reheated pizza.

Chelsea managed a look of concern. "Did you burn yourself, sweetheart?"

Mark remained wide-eyed and speechless.

Chelsea looked down. "What's the matter? Don't you like my at-home wear?"

"What at-home wear?"

"Mark, I am as decently covered as you are."

"Decent? You have no top on!" His voice cracked.

"I do so." She flicked the tawny peach lace tunic. "Oh, I guess I did forget the liner," she said innocently.

Mark couldn't keep his eyes off her as he slid the pizza onto the table.

"Mmm, I'm starved," she said, reveling in giving Mark a taste of his own medicine. She grabbed a slice and took a healthy bite.

Mark continued to peruse the lace covering her bare skin. Then he leaned over and stole a bit of cheese from the corner of her mouth. And before Chelsea knew what had hit her, she was in his lap, and his mouth was feasting on hers.

"Never knew pizza could taste so good," he murmured.

"Perhaps you never tasted it from the right place," she breathed.

"And now that I have, you can be damn sure I won't try any other place."

Chelsea stared into his eyes, reading the unspoken meaning in his words.

"I don't want any other woman," he confirmed softly. "I just want you."

"I'd say you already have me."

"But not exactly where I want you," he replied, bumping his hips against hers.

"You are incorrigible," she whispered back, unable to stop smiling.

"Yeah, and you love it."

I love you. The words popped into her mind so unexpectedly that she almost fell off his lap.

· And suddenly Mark stood and set her on the counter with her legs dangling over the edge. He grasped the hem of her lace tunic and lifted it off over her head. He covered her breasts with his warm palms, and Chelsea closed her eyes as lightning raced through her body.

She moaned, sliding her hands under the waistband of his briefs and pushing them down as far as she could reach. As Mark stepped back to finish the job, Chelsea gasped, "Mr. Harrison, you are a very dangerous man."

"THIS SHOULD BE the last of the new orders," Gwen told Chelsea as they leafed through their notes on the previous evening's show. "What would you think about ordering those satin and lace teddies in teal and mocha?"

Chelsea nodded as she jotted down the colors. "And the silk camisoles and briefs in raspberry, melon and copper. Maybe we can find silk flowers to coordinate with those colors. We have to make this a grand opening to remember."

"How about having Marianna hand out sachets to customers?" Gwen suggested.

Chelsea nodded at the reminder of the model they'd used in the past for their fashion showings. "That would really create a sensation. She could wear a tap pants and camisole set. She's so good with people that, no matter how sexy she is, she doesn't seem to threaten women or incite men. Why don't you give the agency a call and see if she's available?"

Chelsea looked at the ever-growing pile of notes relating to the upcoming event. "You know, it's funny. I thought opening the new shop would be a breeze after all we went through putting this one together. I guess I should have known better. Every time I cross something off my list, I add five more tasks to it. I have this fear that opening day will come and we'll still be running around finishing up things."

"It's too soon for preopening jitters," Gwen scolded, pointing at her friend with a vivid scarlet-tipped finger. "Now take a deep breath, let it out and remember that soon we're going to be rolling in profits!" She laughed, throwing her arms out as if to embrace the world.

Chelsea couldn't help but be caught up in Gwen's joy. "I swear there are times you are so positive you're almost sickening."

"Fancy that. And I'm not even the one in love."

That stopped Chelsea cold. "How did you know?" she blurted.

"I only had to look at you. You stare off into space, obviously daydreaming about Mark, then you suddenly get red in the face, which tells me that the daydream must have been pretty hot," she teased. "Besides, it couldn't have happened to a nicer person. So when's the wedding?"

"Whoa! Wait a minute!" Chelsea held up a halting hand. "Mark has never even said he loves me."

"Sweetie, this is the nineties. A woman is allowed to say the words first."

She glared at her friend. "I can't stand smug people."

"You mean you can't stand people who are right," Gwen said in her favorite refrain.

"That too." Chelsea fiddled with the pens and pencils scattered on her desk, carefully aligning them until they lay in a neat row. "Mark just...swept me off my feet, without allowing any arguments on my part." She grimaced under Gwen's knowing look. "All right, I argued, but he didn't listen." Gwen's raised eyebrows forced her to qualify still further. "All right, so he listened to my arguments. He just didn't agree with any of them."

"A man of logic."

Logic? Chelsea thought of Mark's impulsiveness—particularly in the kitchen last night. "A man, all right."

"Go with the flow," Gwen ordered. "You deserve someone like Mark, who will give you love and laughter. Why not just hold on tight and enjoy the ride?" She straightened and headed out of the office as the tinkling of the bell announced a customer. "And since you're acting so fidgety, you can be the one to supervise the furniture delivery at the new shop this afternoon," she said, adding on a teasing note, "Maybe you'll run into Mark while you're there."

Chelsea didn't argue. What was the point? As she'd said, lately no one seemed to heed to her arguments anymore.

"SO, ARE YOU pleased?" Steve asked Mark as the two men stood in the parking lot looking at the mall's exterior.

Mark's gaze moved over the three-story stone-and-glass structure, noting the gold-lettered banner announcing its opening date flapping in the afternoon breeze.

"There were days I wondered if we'd ever get to this point," he said quietly. "I spent a lot of nights worrying I'd bitten off more than I could chew—and fearing an earthquake would shake it all down." He broke into a broad grin. "But, damn, we did it, Steve!" He clapped the older man on the back. "The stores inside are taking

shape, the landscaping crew finished yesterday, and before too long that building is going to be filled with eager
shoppers ready to spend their money.''

''It's also going to boast that pretty lingerie lady
you've been seeing,'' Steve teased. ''Who'd have
thought you'd fall for the mother of a teenager?''

''Yeah, and what a mom,'' he mused, still grinning.
''Too bad I couldn't find office space closer to the
mall.''

''Just as well. We'd never get you out to a job site
again.'' Steve watched his boss with a keen eye. ''So
when do you take her home to meet the family?''

''When I feel she can handle the horde. Soon, I
hope.''

The older man shook his head. ''You're really serious
about her, aren't you?''

Mark nodded. ''About as serious as you can get. But
she's still a little jittery, so I've got to take it slow and
easy.''

''You, slow and easy?'' Steve said in patent disbelief.
''Ah, women never know what they want until you show
them.'' With that piece of sage advice, Steve started to
walk away. ''Some of us are unwinding after work.
Want to have a couple beers with us?'' he asked over
his shoulder.

Not too long ago Mark would have accepted without
hesitation. ''I'll let you know later,'' he said instead.

Steve grinned. ''Maybe you should bring the little
lady along to give us roughnecks some class.''

''And have you try to beat my time? No thanks!''
Mark retorted. ''Okay, get to work and earn those big
bucks I pay you.''

''Don't I wish!''

Mark was still grinning when he walked through the

main entrance. While he'd participated in building other structures, this was different. This was all his own. His baby. He looked around, feeling about as proud as any new papa.

Not surprisingly, his feet took him in the direction of the new Hot Stuff boutique. They slowed as he spied a familiar figure directing two burly men hauling an armoire around the shop.

"No, up against that far wall," Chelsea instructed, pointing.

"Lady, this thing weighs a ton. Are you absolutely sure this time that that's where you want it?" one of the men asked with an exasperated huff.

"I told you that was where it belonged in the first place, but you so politely informed me it wouldn't fit. Then the spot you were certain it would fit in didn't work," she pointed out. "If you'd listened to me in the beginning, you wouldn't have had to move it again, would you?"

"Just do it, Ray," the other man said wearily, resting against the piece of heavy furniture.

Chelsea was so involved in her battle that she didn't notice Mark approaching until he stole up behind her and his lips nuzzled her nape. The moment their warmth registered, all her nerve endings flew into overdrive.

"Wow, lady, you're a toughie, aren't you?" he said huskily, wrapping his arms around her waist. "Hey, guys."

She covered his hands with her own. "With you nibbling on my ear, it's difficult to keep up the image of a bad guy, bud." But she allowed herself to relax against him. "What's up?"

"Besides me?" He chuckled in her ear.

"Behave yourself, Harrison."

He laughed. "I've been outside admiring my handiwork. Now I'm up here admiring yours."

He sensed her smile. "My handiwork?"

"Among other things." He inhaled the soft floral fragrance of her perfume mingling with her own personal scent. He wiggled his hips against her bottom. "Why don't you get rid of the gorillas so we can fool around in the stockroom," he growled in her ear.

"I thought I told you to behave yourself."

"Kinda difficult with a sexy woman in my arms."

"Mark, I'm trying to get this furniture set up, and these men love to remind me they're being paid hourly," she told him weakly, forcing herself to move out of his arms.

"You want the lady's undivided attention, buddy, you'll let us get this damn cabinet where it belongs," one of the men told Mark.

Mark stood back and watched Chelsea direct the placement of the armoire and two large chests of drawers, which he knew she would fill with colorful silks and satins to tempt the buyers. As he watched her, he couldn't help wondering what she wore under her blush-colored sweatshirt and the slim black jeans that faithfully followed her every curve. Knowing her, he sincerely doubted he would find ordinary cotton. No, he'd discover something frothy, with silk and lace.

His temptress-in-hiding, he mused. An apt image for Chelsea, whose life had led her to keep so much of her spirited self under wraps. Fortunately, despite her best intentions, which had misguidedly convinced her to overcompensate for years for perhaps the one moment of freedom she'd ever known, her true nature had not been completely squelched. Her feisty, well-adjusted daughter was testimony to the positive powers of her personality. And her shop itself was testimony to the sensual woman within her who might want to run but who couldn't hide forever. Not from him, anyway.

Funny, he mused further, how this complex, captivating woman had so easily captured his heart. Funny, too, how commitment, anathema to a bachelor, didn't seem so scary anymore.

Yeah, he decided. He wanted to be the one to walk Colleen down the aisle when she got married, and tease her about how much he was going to enjoy watching some other guy have to deal with her. And he wanted to see Chelsea have his child, see her body ripen and grow heavy with their baby. The baby might have colic all the time and keep them up most nights, but neither of them would complain because they'd be too busy marveling over the perfection their love had created. Hell, he'd even learn to change dirty diapers. Well, he quickly amended, maybe.

And, above all, he knew he wanted to grow old with Chelsea. To hear her bitch about the new wrinkles she would convince herself she found every morning, while he'd look in the mirror and insist he was losing his hair.

He straightened up as the present intruded on his fanciful thoughts. Yep, it was getting time to stake a permanent claim on the lady, whether she was ready or not. And the process shouldn't be painful in the least, since the way to this lady's heart was, clearly, through her lingerie!

Chapter Fourteen

"I cannot believe a simple delivery of furniture took more than two hours!" Chelsea fumed after the deliverymen left the store, muttering about women who didn't seem to know their own minds and cursing the need for so much furniture in a fancy underwear store. She paced into the storeroom, waving her arms around in frustration.

"Hey, babe, calm down," Mark said. "Here, let me massage some of the kinks out of your shoulders." And, tugging her toward him and turning her around, he proceeded to do just that.

"Ah, that feels marvelous," she said, letting her head roll loosely on her shoulders.

"It's even better without a shirt," he suggested innocently.

"You are so bad," she said huskily, but he could hear the smile in her voice.

He grinned. "Guilty and proud of it. There's something about you in a pair of jeans and a sweatshirt the color of your blush when I do this—" his hands slipped around to briefly cup her breasts "—that starts me thinking." At her sharp intake of breath, he leaned forward and whispered a few graphic suggestions in her ear. "What do you say?"

Her breathing accelerated, and he just *knew* she was blushing. "I think you'd probably be laid up in traction for at least six months if we indulged in all of your ideas," she murmured.

"I just bet you're wearing something really sexy under this." Mark let his busy fingers slip under the sweat-shirt's neckline. "And who says you wouldn't be in the the next bed?"

"Because it's a well-known fact that women can stand up to physical stress better than men." Chelsea was like-wise busy, reaching backward until her hands cupped his denim-covered rear. She chuckled throatily when he froze under her caresses. Finally she turned around in his arms and ran one finger under the waistband of his jeans. And when she reached the metal button, she didn't stop there.

"Honey, with what I have in mind, the last thing you'd have to worry about is standing up." He dipped his head and nuzzled her ear. "You always smell so good," he whispered. Then, with a jolt he gasped, "Do you realize where your hand is?"

"I certainly do. Why, does it bother you?"

"Yes!"

She started to extract her hand. "I'll stop it then."

"No!" He looked around frantically. "Damn! This floor is cement! How about making a quick run to my apartment?"

Her hand began its magic ministrations again. "Are you sure you want to walk out now?"

He hissed a curse as her fingers danced up and down his heated length, and his reasoning slowly came back to life. The structure was buzzing with workmen, and there was a good chance of someone wandering in here looking for him.

"Chelsea, as much as I hate to say this, we should probably think about continuing this later," he told her in a raw voice, gently pulling her hand out of his jeans.

Trying to steady his breathing, he pulled her up against him, feeling their heartbeats gradually returning to normal. "How about dinner tonight?" he said finally.

"Why don't I cook?" she suggested.

"You won't catch me saying no. What time?"

"Six-thirty?"

Mark nodded and stole a quick kiss before straightening up and heading for the door.

"Mark?"

He turned to find Chelsea sending him a saucy grin and raising the hem of her sweatshirt to flash him a glimpse of the most X-rated bra he'd ever seen. He groaned and grabbed the doorjamb for support, certain he had to get the hell out of there before he completely disgraced himself.

He exited to the musical sound of her laughter, wondering just who was reaching whose heart through a lady's lingerie.

"I CAN'T BELIEVE you're actually cooking something that didn't come in a microwave tray," Colleen announced theatrically as she chopped vegetables and tore greens for a salad.

"I do not nuke food every day of the week," Chelsea protested, setting the roast she'd marinated earlier in the oven.

"Oh, really? When was the last time you cooked a dinner from scratch?"

"Why it was..." she paused. "No, it was...well, I've cooked. I know I have."

"You just want to impress Mark with your cooking skills," Colleen teased. "Although, I don't know why you'd have to bother, since he already seems more than impressed with your other assets."

Chelsea knew she was blushing and was powerless to stop. "The idea of discussing sexual matters with my daughter is very daunting," she muttered, setting out ingredients for a mousse.

Colleen's eyes widened with mock innocence. "Why, Mother, whatever made you think your innocent little girl was thinking such a thing?"

"Colleen, you haven't been innocent since the day I explained the facts of life to you and you corrected me on a few points. Now, is that salad ready?"

Undaunted, Colleen grinned. "So, I guess I should get lost tonight, huh?"

"I have good news for you. You're no longer grounded. Now, what was that about a fall dance?" Chelsea reminded her daughter.

"Okay, I'll be gone." Colleen sighed dramatically, arranging the salad until she deemed it perfect. She picked up the bowl and carried it to the refrigerator. "Need help with anything else?"

Chelsea shook her head. "I'm going upstairs to clean up. It's amazing how dirty you can get setting up a shop. The clean-up crew seems to think that sweeping the plaster dust from one end of the room to the other constitutes a job well done, and evidently the paint smell won't go away until someone gets the bugs out of the ventilation system." She wrinkled her nose. "I'm going to take in some potpourri tomorrow and scatter it in the chests and dressing rooms in hopes that it will help banish some of the odor before the store owners' cocktail party next week. I'd hate to have anyone smell paint on the clothing.''

Colleen trailed her up the stairs, but not, evidently, to glean wisdom on shopkeeping.

''If Mark proposes to you, will you accept?'' she asked out of the blue.

Chelsea's foot nearly missed a step, and if she hadn't grabbed the banister, she would have fallen flat on her face.

''Proposes? Whatever gave you the idea he'd propose?'' Her voice came out in a croak.

''Oh, come on, Mom, you wouldn't cook for just any man,'' she observed wryly. ''And Mark doesn't seem like the kind of guy to want just an affair. I've seen the way he moons over you, and if that isn't love, I don't know what is.''

Chelsea slowly continued up the stairs. ''I'll tell you what. If we come to any important decisions, we'll make sure you're the very first to know.''

''Sounds good to me,'' Colleen said airily.

THE MOMENT Mark entered the house, he sensed something slightly out of sync. Colleen gave him a cheery smile and wave as she left the house. Chelsea seemed a bit uneasy as she chattered about nothing in particular and nervously busied herself fixing him a drink and making sure he was comfortable. He tried to decipher the restlessness as he feasted his eyes on Chelsea in copper-colored silk pants with a cropped short-sleeved top. A bronze beaded necklace swung between her breasts in a very enticing sway, and she'd brushed her hair into a mass of loose curls that made him want to run his fingers through it. He also wanted to kiss that burnt-orange lipstick from her lips, among other things.

"I hope you're hungry," Chelsea commented as she handed him his drink.

He deliberately allowed his fingers to brush against hers as he accepted the glass. "Oh, I'm hungry all right," he murmured.

"Dinner first," she said firmly, allowing him a few minutes to sip his drink before leading him into the dining room.

Mark looked down at the table, stunned at the bountiful feast. A platter filled with light pink slices of roast beef jostled a heaping bowl of fluffy mashed potatoes, a tureen of fresh mixed vegetables and a beautiful green salad.

"Is there a holiday I forgot about?" he asked. "I can't remember the last time I saw so much food on a table."

Chelsea laughed and gestured for him to sit.

"It sure looks better than what I usually eat," Mark told her, taking the chair she indicated.

"Take-out food?" she guessed.

"That and microwave marvels," he confirmed sadly. "My mom would be horrified at my eating habits. Although she kept telling the family she hated to spend hours in the kitchen, only to watch the food disappear in less than ten minutes. We once argued that we didn't eat that fast, but she shot us down when she timed us on Thanksgiving. Nine minutes, forty-six seconds." He helped himself to seconds of mashed potatoes and roast beef.

Chelsea smiled secretly at his speed. "I sympathize with your mother. I wouldn't be too happy, either."

Mark finally relaxed in his chair. "So, I hope it's not

too late to ask you to go to the mall's cocktail party with me.''

She looked at him over the rim of her wineglass. "Are you asking me if you're too late in asking me? Or are you asking me to the party?"

"Both," he admitted.

"You just want me to hear everyone praise you for building such a beautiful complex," she teased.

"That too," he cheerfully admitted. "But then I'll take *you* out to dinner, and we'll make a night of it."

Chelsea watched Mark under the cover of lowered eyelashes. He'd obviously shaved again before coming over and in the process had nicked his chin. For a reason she couldn't explain, she found the tiny cut endearing.

"Would you like coffee with your dessert?" she asked, her voice coming out with a tenderness that surprised her.

"Maybe later," he said. "I don't think I could eat another bite right now." He stood up and began picking up plates, carefully stacking them on top of each other.

Again she felt a wave of tenderness wash over her. "Hey, I didn't invite you over to wash dishes," she protested, trying to take the plates from him.

He held them out of her reach. "I know. I just want to show you how handy I can be around the house. Lead me to your dishwasher."

Chelsea smiled. "I never put my good china in the dishwasher," she informed him.

He looked downright pitiful. "Good china?"

She nodded.

"You mean it all has to be washed by hand?" he said bleakly.

Still smiling, she nodded again. "The glassware, too. I don't put the good crystal in the dishwasher, either."

"Well, I hope the detergent you use is kind to hands."
He walked into the kitchen as if facing his doom.

"I have a better idea," Chelsea called as she gathered
up the meat platter and vegetable bowl. "We could rinse
them off and leave them in the sink for Colleen to
wash."

Mark cocked his head. "She'd hate us!"

An evil grin curved her lips. "Yes, she would."

"She'll think we did it on purpose."

"We are. It'll be character building."

He turned around and leaned against the counter.
"Well, then I wouldn't want to deprive your daughter
of such a positive growth experience."

He straightened and moved toward her. He wrapped
his hands around the back of her neck, pressing his
thumbs against the taut muscles there. "Come on, you
must be tired. Let's go get comfortable." He led her into
the family room and dropped onto the couch, pulling her
down onto his lap. "Comfy?"

"Too comfy," she blurted out. "I'm afraid I could
get used to this."

He tilted his head back and looked at her long and
hard. "You mean you could see this happening for the
next fifty or sixty years?"

Her mouth dropped open. "I wasn't exactly considering that long a term."

Mark winced. "You make it sound like a prison sentence. I was thinking in a more positive light."

Chelsea's eyes widened, and her mouth dropped open
in shock. "I—I'm not the kind of woman you need,"
she finally sputtered.

"And how do you know what kind of woman I
need?" He scowled at her.

"I know you don't need a woman who's probably

going to be broke putting her teenage daughter through college," she explained. "Believe me, single mothers *know* they aren't all that popular with men. I'm not apologizing for what I am or for what I've done in the past, but I am being a realist."

"I don't recall ever dispensing any judgments." Mark pulled her around to face him, all the while keeping her firmly in his embrace. "Did you think I was going to throw your past up in your face?" he said slowly. "Hell, you were just a kid who wanted something most horny nineteen-year-old boys promise but don't come through with. But you grew up fast—and strong—when you realized you'd ended up with something very precious. Colleen. And you've done a great job raising her without any help. That's what counts, Chelsea. And that's what's made you the wonderful woman you are today."

"You're not even thirty yet. How can you be so wise?" She rubbed her cheek against his shirtfront.

"It isn't age, or even experience, that gives you wisdom, it's what you do with what you have," he countered. "And no more age cracks if you please."

"But, Mark," she argued, "I'll be *forty* in less than a month. And while men might age gracefully, most women don't."

"Yeah, my mom has sometimes said pretty much the same thing. But my dad, who's twelve years younger, just can't seem to get worked up about it."

Her head snapped up. "You're making this up."

He shook his head. "No, I'm not. In fact, they created quite a scandal when they got married, since they'd met when she was a teacher at his high school." He grinned. "Ironically, her subject was biology."

Her mouth dropped open. "You're kidding!"

"Cross my heart. Dad used to say that Mom's private

tutoring in biology was a hell of a lot more interesting than what she taught at school.'' Mark grinned.

Chelsea arched an eyebrow. "Are you saying that while he was a student...?"

"No, although Dad said he fell in love with her the minute he saw her in the classroom. It was close to the end of the school year before he got up the nerve to tell her about his feelings. She let him down easy, explaining that a lot of students developed crushes on their teachers, and that as he got on with his life he'd be happy he'd waited for someone his own age.

"He joined the air force after graduation, but when he returned home four years later, he tracked her down, and this time he wasn't about to give her a chance to say no. They were married six months later," he concluded.

"It's nice to know some true-life love stories have a happy ending," Chelsea said faintly.

"Absolutely." Mark lifted her hands to his lips. "Now, what time is Colleen due home?"

"Not for awhile, why?" She looped her arms around his neck while his hand roamed up and down her back in a sweeping caress. What a perfect way to spend an evening.

"I didn't think you'd appreciate it if she walked in and caught us necking on the couch." It wasn't easy, but he kept his massage nonsensual.

"You're right. It wouldn't be a good idea." Her gaze roved to the small clock on the VCR. "Considering her curfew, however, she shouldn't be home for another two hours."

He pulled her into his arms and nuzzled her throat. "Then I guess we'd better make the most of the next two hours, because I intend to prove to you once and for all just how well matched we are.''

"I thought I'd already discovered that," she remarked, wiggling her hips in a way that brought a groan to Mark's lips.

"I decided you could use some extra convincing," he growled, "and I vow to give my all to the cause." Chelsea laughed throatily as he dipped his head and ran his slightly open mouth down her neck. "And since there's only one hour and fifty-nine minutes left before Colleen's due home, I suggest we not waste any more time."

Chapter Fifteen

"I'm afraid I'm going to be crazed with work for the next few days," Mark said.

Chelsea clutched the telephone receiver so tightly that her knuckles turned white. "I—I see." She stumbled over the simple words, afraid she did indeed see. All too clearly.

"It's nothing personal," he hastened to assure her. "I just have some Harrison Construction stuff to catch up on."

Her mouth opened, but no sound came out.

"I still intend to take you to the cocktail party, so don't worry about that."

A cocktail party was the last thing she was worried about. A lifetime of loneliness was more like it. Why couldn't she get the words—any words—out?

"I'll see you then, okay?" Mark said.

She blinked, feeling the moisture on her lashes. "Okay."

She had never felt so alone as she did the moment she set the phone down.

CHELSEA FRETTED. She worried. She agonized. She wondered if she could work up the nerve to track Mark down and tell him she loved him and that she refused to let him get away. She wondered if he'd gotten tired of waiting for her or just plain tired of her. When she remembered his intensity on their last evening together, she found it hard to believe the latter. Still, failing to come up with a strategy to end her torment, she did the next best thing. She moped.

She missed Mark's laughter. She missed his loving even more. And, as she grumbled and growled at Gwen and Colleen, she missed the woman she'd become in the arms of this man who'd had the moxie—and the manliness—to greet her in a pair of scandalously skimpy black briefs.

Even throwing herself into finalizing the new shop's setup didn't stop her from dipping into her memories and deciding she needed a plan of action.

"Well, Chelsea, it's time to fish or cut bait," she told herself as she arranged a ruby red camisole with a matching pair of tap pants.

Gwen slapped her forehead with her palm. "Oh, no, she's spouting those old sayings again!" she moaned, looking heavenward. "But could this one mean she's finally come to her senses?" she added shrewdly.

"I thought you were here to help, not heckle." Chelsea fixed her with a warning look.

Gwen ignored the warning. "Have you told Mark how you feel yet?" She peered at her partner. "You haven't, have you?"

"I—I almost did. But that's when he backed off, and I'm afraid now I may be too late."

"Then, sweetie, I suggest you get your affairs in order in a hurry. Believe me, you don't want to lose this man."

Chelsea resisted the urge to scream.

Gwen looked at her watch. "What time is the cocktail party tonight?"

"Seven," she said gloomily.

"Is Mark still taking you?"

"The last time he talked to me he said he was." She hated sounding so testy.

"Want some advice?" Gwen murmured.

"No!" she said quickly.

"You're going to get it anyway. Wear something incredibly sexy tonight. Something that's going to make Mark feel he's died and gone to heaven. And, honey, if that doesn't make him propose, then take the bull by the horns and do it yourself."

Chelsea turned away, the glimmering of an idea sparking in her brain. She didn't bother telling her friend that she had the perfect outfit hanging in her closet at home and that she'd just never had the nerve to wear it yet. One look at the dress was guaranteed to send Mark into cardiac arrest.

MARK WASN'T SURE what to expect when he picked Chelsea up that evening for the mall's preopening get-together, but the flushed, agitated woman who opened the door wasn't it.

"Hello, Mark." She flashed him a harried smile as she stepped back to admit him. "I'm almost ready. I'm sorry, I don't know what happened, but I somehow ended up running late. I guess I took too long in the tub. Don't worry. I'll be ready in no time."

"You look incredible," he breathed, staring at the sexy vision standing before him.

Chelsea inclined her head. "Thank you. I'll only be a moment." She hurried upstairs.

Mark watched her ascend, noticing the gold-dusted

sheer stockings, the bronze high heels, the sleeveless V-neck dress that skimmed her body to end inches above her knees. A pair of dangling earrings danced against her neck, and a wide bangle bracelet circled one wrist. Her hair was brushed into light airy curls held back from her face with a headband that matched the golden dress.

"I can't let her out of this house looking like that," he muttered, pressing his fingers to his chest to still his rapidly beating heart. "Every wolf will be on the prowl the minute she shows up."

"Did you say something?" Chelsea called from upstairs.

"Nothing important," he called back, coughing to clear his throat.

When she returned, her lips were glossed, and a rich, heady perfume wafted around her.

"Don't you think you should wear a jacket or coat?" he asked as she headed for the door.

She looked over her shoulder. "It didn't seem all that chilly out. I don't think I'll need a wrap."

"The restaurant might be air-conditioned for the event." His eyes were fixed on the scanty front of her dress. Was she even wearing a bra? He didn't think so.

Chelsea seemed to ponder his statement. "Well, all right. I do have a wrap that will go with this." She opened the closet door. Mark's sigh of relief evaporated as he watched her drape a sheer gold shawl around her shoulders.

"That's it?"

"Mark, I'll be fine." She patted his arm. "Now, shouldn't we go so we won't be late? I've held us up long enough."

Was she crazy? Chelsea asked herself as Mark helped her into his car. She hadn't missed the stunned look on his face when she opened the door, nor the way he kept glancing at the front of her dress.

And why wouldn't he be floored by her appearance? she thought wryly, settling herself in the passenger seat, smoothing her dress down as close to her knees as it would go, which wasn't all that close. She was nearly naked.

Suddenly her brazen plan seemed just plain crazy, and she felt her earlier courage start to recede.

Mark seated himself behind the wheel, resting his hands on it as he stared out the windshield as if he were preparing himself for an immense task. Chelsea waited with bated breath.

"To say you look beautiful wouldn't be enough," he said quietly, still staring ahead. "I—I'm proud to be the man accompanying you."

She leaned over and placed her hand on his arm. The muscles tensed under her touch. "And I'm proud to be the woman accompanying you," she murmured.

Mark took a deep breath, and the warm oriental scent Chelsea wore filled his lungs. With the way she looked, he wasn't sure he'd survive the night with his sanity intact.

"Let's get this over with," he muttered, quickly switching on the engine.

THE GET-ACQUAINTED cocktail party for the shop owners was held in a fancy restaurant situated at one end of the mall. As they crossed the courtyard, Mark noticed Chelsea's preoccupation and her covert glances upward in the direction of her shop.

"Is something wrong?" he asked her.

She shook her head. "No, just something I thought of." She flashed him a brilliant smile. "But I guess it doesn't matter. I doubt anyone will notice." She picked up her pace as she draped the chain to her small purse over her shoulder.

Warning bells clanged in his head as he watched her shawl slip, exposing her barely covered chest. "Notice what?" he croaked.

She continued smiling and patted his arm. "Look, it's not worth mentioning. Don't worry. Everything will be fine."

He clenched his teeth together so hard his jaw ached. "Chelsea..." he began.

She threw her hands up. "All right. If you must know—" she leaned closer "—I told you I was running late, and I knew you'd be at the house soon, so I just forget something. It's nothing terribly important."

Mark didn't like the sound of this. "What did you forget?"

Her face turned a light pink. "Mark, not here," she murmured, looking around. "Someone might hear us."

"What did you forget?" he said through gritted teeth.

Chelsea sidled closer until her breasts burned an imprint on his arm. She laid her hand on his shoulder as she raised herself up on her tiptoes and whispered in his ear, "I forgot my underwear."

"You—" He bit off the rest of his question. Without thinking, he slid his hand down her back and felt...nothing. "Do you mean to say you don't have anything on under your dress?" he rasped.

She shook her head.

He resisted the urge to loosen his shirt collar. "Not even..."

Again she shook her head.

All the breath left Mark's chest in a mighty whoosh. He opened his mouth to tell Chelsea they were going back to her house, *now*, when someone called out her name.

Before Chelsea turned to reply, she whispered to Mark, "Don't worry. No one can tell." And she waved to her friend and began walking toward the restaurant.

"*I* can tell," he muttered darkly, following her as close as he could while wishing he could drape his suit coat around her shoulders and button it up to her lovely throat, which, right now, he was ready to throttle!

Chelsea greeted people right and left, very much aware of Mark hovering over her. She wished she could tell him it was taking every ounce of courage she had for her to go through with her crazy idea. She'd even thought about slipping out of the party and running upstairs to her shop to pick up some undergarments. But she was determined to see this through.

"See? Everything is fine," she murmured to Mark, spinning around to greet someone. Her abrupt motion sent her shawl slipping down her shoulders.

Mark carefully pushed the flimsy fabric back up, then stared longingly at the bar. He had a feeling it was going to be a long evening.

"Here, you look like you need this." Gwen plopped a squat glass into his hand.

Mark tossed the drink down in one gulp.

"Thanks," he wheezed. "I did need that."

Gwen looked from the empty glass to Mark's face. "That was twenty-year-old Scotch you just abused." Her eyes slid around him to Chelsea, who was talking to the manager of one of the chain bookstores. "The last time I saw that dress, it was on a hanger in our stockroom. I never would have thought Chelsea would choose such a daring number. I'm glad she did, though. It looks wonderful on her. It makes a statement, wouldn't you say?'' she added slyly.

"I didn't think she had to make any statements," he muttered, thinking about getting another glass of Scotch.

"Well, then, honey, you still have a lot to learn about women." She patted his arm. "Better keep an eye on Chelsea, Mark. There's a lot of men here who wouldn't mind getting to know her better."

"Not if I can help it," he growled.

Gwen shrugged nonchalantly and went off to play social butterfly.

Mark was in agony every time he looked at Chelsea, visualizing what was—or, rather, what was *not*—underneath that skimpy excuse for a dress. He vowed to stick to her like glue, which wasn't easy in such a crowd. He was sidetracked by various store owners who were interested in further expansion, and, despite the opportunity to drum up business, he discovered he had no patience for shoptalk. Watching Chelsea was driving him mad. If a man touched her, Mark wanted to break the man's arm. If he smiled at her, Mark was positive the man had noticed her provocative lack of undergarments and was plotting her seduction. He wanted her dressed in flannel from neck to toes. He wanted them out of there.

He glanced at his watch. "Look, why don't you call my office and we'll set up an appointment," he told the owner of a small electronics firm as he handed him his business card. He then headed purposefully toward Chelsea, whose shawl was now looped over her elbows and swinging loosely against the small of her back. Without thinking, he slid his hand down her back and felt...nothing. If he hadn't prided himself on being an adult, he would have whimpered like a lost puppy.

No more Mr. Nice Guy, he decided. It was time to reclaim his woman.

"Excuse me, but I'm afraid we're going to miss our dinner reservation if we don't leave soon." He presented Chelsea a tight smile that looked decidedly frayed around the edges.

"Never come between a man and his dinner," one of the women chuckled. "Since Chelsea's shop is next to mine, I'm certain I'll be seeing her again."

"Just my luck to be next door to the candy store," Chelsea said with a laugh. "I'm sure Gwen and I will be taking turns coming in for some of the rich fudge you're known for." She leaned back slightly as Mark's arm slid around her waist. "The man has perfect timing. I'm starving."

Chelsea was lucky to get those words out, because, before she knew it, she was being ushered rapidly into the mall. "I thought we were going to dinner," she protested as Mark pushed her none too gently up the stairs to the second level.

He grasped her hand and dragged her down the walkway until they skidded to a stop in front of her shop. "I'm sure you have a key."

She looked at the two windows she and Gwen had decorated that morning, then back at Mark. "What are we doing here?"

"We're here to get you dressed. You need to add at least a few important items to your wardrobe before we go anywhere else." He held out his hand. "Key?"

Chelsea shook her head in mock puzzlement as she dug into her small bag and pulled out a key ring. "I don't know why you're so worried. Just as I told you, no one noticed."

He stood behind her. "*I* noticed."

"*You* already knew." She pushed the door open and walked inside. "I just hope the night watchman doesn't come by and think the shop's being broken into. I'd hate to have to explain the situation to the police."

"Forget the police," he told her, snapping on the lights as he entered and closed the door behind him.

Chelsea kicked off her shoes and circled the perimeter of the shop. "It came out beautifully, don't you think?" She gestured to an armoire with clothing spilling out its doors in colorful disarray, then bent to finger a basket of lacy sachets.

She straightened up and spun around. "It's not easy to create the right atmosphere, especially one where a man will feel comfortable shopping. You'd be surprised how many men buy lingerie for their ladies." She opened a drawer and casually pulled out a handful of scrappy bikini panties. "So, give me your male opinion. Which color would you prefer I wear?" Her voice lowered to a purr as she walked over to him with her hands outstretched, the silk spilling over her palms.

Mark resisted the urge to poke his finger inside his shirt collar and roll it around his neck. He looked at the scanty panties she held, then back up at her luminous eyes and glossy, kissable lips.

"You know more about these things than I do," he croaked.

Chelsea continued smiling. "But I want your opinion. What about this pair?" She held up what looked to Mark to be nothing more than a few strings of black lace. She frowned. "No, these aren't quite right. How about this pair?" Just as scanty, in a bold, candy-apple red.

"I—I don't think so," he muttered.

She walked over to a hanger displaying a shockingly

sexy bustier. "What would you think of something like this? It's cut low enough that it wouldn't show."

She stood back, eyeing Mark. "I think you should be the one to choose, since it seems so important to you that I be properly dressed."

Right now the need to breathe felt very important. Mark wondered if the air-conditioning had failed; he was feeling mighty warm. "I think we should forget this."

"Forget it? It was your idea that I be fully clothed before we go to the restaurant. I'm just asking your opinion on what I should wear." She moved forward a step. Mark moved back. "Mark, what's wrong?" she murmured, moving forward again. "You're not afraid of me, are you?" she purred.

Something finally clicked in his brain, and he reached out and gripped her upper arms, pulling her to him. "You're doing this on purpose!" he said. "You're deliberately trying to make me crazy."

She looked up with a smile on her lips. "Did it work? I'm afraid I haven't had too much practice in seducing a man. At least not sober."

"Don't worry, you've got it down pat," he muttered just before capturing her mouth in a soul-stirring kiss.

Chelsea hung on to his shoulders, afraid if she let go her knees would finally give out. But Mark took matters into his own hands—literally—by sweeping her up into his arms. He carried her through the rose-and-ivory drapes into the dressing room area, muttering several colorful curses.

Chelsea touched the throbbing pulse in his neck with the tip of her tongue, then buried her face against his throat to muffle her laughter. "Having trouble, Mr. Harrison?" She swept one hand downward until she found his zipper and the bulge straining behind it. "Yes, I'd say you are."

"Lady, any trouble I'm having you caused by parading around that party without any underwear," he growled, shouldering his way to an ornate chaise where he unceremoniously dumped her before following her down. He began kissing her hungrily, and she was soon busy kissing him back, pulling his tie loose and unbuttoning his shirt.

"Oh, Mark." She sighed, running her hands across his bare chest. "I do love you."

Chapter Sixteen

Mark hadn't thought it could get any better. He'd been wrong. This time when he held Chelsea in his arms and felt her mouth moving over his, he felt as if he'd died and gone to heaven. She'd finally uttered the magic words.

He wanted to take it slow. He wanted to take it fast, so they could start all over again. Instead, he inhaled the scent of Chelsea's skin, savored the soft sounds she made when he entered her, shivered with desire at the way she moved so sweetly beneath him.

He had to stop before he exploded. But he couldn't stop, because she felt so good, so welcoming. She drained and fulfilled him all at the same time.

He groaned and covered her mouth as their motions quickened and together they reached a shattering climax. Gasping to recover his breath, he rested his forehead against hers, then began dropping lazy, satisfied kisses on her face.

Her half-closed eyes opened. "Oh, Mark," she murmured, running her nails down his back, tracing random patterns on the taut skin as she rotated her hips.

"That was wonderful," she breathed.

"I'd call it magic," he said. He raised his head to look into her eyes. "Chels, I love you."

She gifted him with a smile that sent flashes of lightning through his system. "You'd better, Mark Harrison. Otherwise, I never would have allowed you to ravish me on a five-hundred-dollar silk-covered chaise lounge."

He laughed out loud and clasped her against him.

BOTH WERE GRATEFUL the night watchman was nowhere around when they finally crept out of the mall, with Chelsea still minus the items they'd gone into her shop for.

When they arrived back at her house, Mark followed her inside.

"Colleen is spending the night at Elaine's," Chelsea said, yawning luxuriously and dropping her purse and shawl on the entryway table before slipping off her shoes. "How about an omelet?"

"Sounds good, since we never did get the dinner I promised you."

Mark sat at the breakfast table watching Chelsea move around the kitchen.

"Chels, will you marry me?"

Chelsea spun around at the abrupt question and saw him looking as stunned as she felt.

He gave her a weak smile as he shrugged. "I didn't expect to just blurt it out that way. Actually, I wanted to do this in a more romantic setting. You know, candlelight, soft music, all that good stuff. But I couldn't put it off any longer."

"Really?" she whispered.

He slowly climbed off the barstool and walked toward her. He took the omelet pan out of her hand and set it on the stove.

"I hated waiting," he told her. "But I knew you had to think things over. Come to grips with everything. But I've been ready—and waiting." He smiled. "You know, I think I fell in love with you that first night, when you yelled at me for rescuing your daughter." His smile widened at the memory. "You in those skimpy pajamas, with those glasses on top of your head, carrying on like a she-tiger defending her young."

"Oh Mark, you are crazy," she moaned, remembering that night only too well. She hadn't considered it one of her better times.

He shook her gently. "So, are you going to put me out of my misery and marry me? I'm sure Colleen would give you her permission."

"Give her permission? She'd probably happily give me away," she said wryly. "Are you sure you know what you're getting into? Teenagers can make you go gray real fast."

"Then maybe we'll have to have a new baby to make us feel young again." He frowned. "Why are you looking at me like that?"

"The idea of having a child with you..." Her eyes glistened with happy tears. "Oh, Mark!" she said with a sigh, wrapping her arms around his waist and resting her cheek against his chest. Then she straightened up. "But you're just getting a new office started. I'm getting a new store started. What are we doing even thinking about marriage right now?"

He dropped a kiss on the top of her head. "No more excuses, Chelsea. No way am I letting you go now. So, do all your arguments and dire predictions mean you're saying yes?"

She slowly nodded, amazed at the idea that her life

was coming together in ways she never would have dared to dream.

Then she actually let out a giggle. "Just be prepared for Colleen to remind us this was all her doing. She'll never let us forget that if she hadn't broken the rules, we never would have met."

He picked her up and swung her around in a circle. "We'll handle Colleen. Hey, together we can handle anything—even a teenager," he assured her. "And, Chels," he murmured just as his mouth moved over hers.

"Hmm?" She smiled as his probing tongue slipped between her parted lips.

"Get that bustier thing you showed me tonight. I want the chance to take it off you—maybe on our wedding night."

"Mmm. Hot stuff," she breathed.

Young widow Diana Thatcher and her two girls needed help—male help—someone to fix the plumbing when it broke, and that sort of thing. Her advertisement for a live-in handyman produced a guy who didn't know a nut from a bolt, but when it came to fixing broken hearts, he had talent to his very fingertips...

THE FIX-IT MAN

Vicki Lewis Thompson

1

"MOTHER, I HATE TO INTERRUPT you in the middle of Harold's lesson, but—"

"Mom! The toilet's running again!" shrieked Allison from the top of the stairs.

"I'm telling her, bimbo!" shouted Laurie. "Now the whole neighborhood knows about it."

Oblivious to anything but the sheet of music in front of him, Harold blew diligently on his tuba. Oompah, oompah, oompah. Diana kept time with one hand and pushed her dark hair back from her face with the other. "Did you wiggle the handle?" she asked, keeping her silver-gray eyes focused on Harold's technique.

"It flops around. I think it's really broken this time."

"Mom! You'd better get up here!"

"She's coming, Allison! Will you be quiet?" Laurie turned and raced up the stairs to enforce her command.

Diana closed her eyes and took a deep breath then glanced apologetically at the small boy holding the giant instrument. With a downward wave of her hand she ended his puff-cheeked rendition. "Continue working on measure seven, Harold. I'll be back in just a moment."

"But Mrs. Thatcher, measure seven has only one note, held for four beats."

"Then work on measure eight, Harold," Diana advised,

one ear tuned to the sound of running water and the other to her daughters' vehement arguing.

"You didn't tell her loud enough," Allison insisted as Diana mounted the stairs. "How's she supposed to know it's an emergency if you say in this little voice, 'Mother, I hate to interrupt.' Sounds like you broke your little toenail, not like the whole house is about to be flooded from—"

"The windows are all open, Allison," Laurie responded through clenched teeth. "And you're up here shouting about toilets. Gross."

"What'll be gross is if this thing overflows, and we—"

"Make way, ladies," Diana said, pushing past them to the upstairs bathroom. Shoving the sleeves of her green gauze blouse to her elbows, she lifted the chipped porcelain tank top and bent over the mysterious inner workings, then jiggled the chrome handle on the side of the tank. Water continued to pour through the tank. "Go away girls," she said wearily. "I'm about to swear."

"Is it going to flood?" Allison asked, her blue eyes wide and her blond ponytail bouncing.

"I don't think so, but I'll have to call a plumber."

"Uh-oh." Laurie took her younger sister's arm and propelled her down the hall. "Come on, Allison. You know how she gets when we have another repair bill to pay."

The chiming of the doorbell floated up the stairs.

"One of you could answer the door while I figure out how to turn the water off to this thing!" Diana called after them.

"I will," Allison replied as her sister dragged her away.

"And Laurie can direct Harold for a while. After all, he's just a beginner."

"Fine." Diana crouched on the linoleum floor and searched for the shut-off valve. God, it was hot upstairs. If only one of the electric fans worked. "Damn you, Jim," she muttered. "I can handle lonely nights. I can deal with the girls. But I can't fix the damned john!"

Tears mingled with her mascara, and her eyes stung as she found the valve and turned it angrily. They weren't tears of grief. She'd wrung those out months ago, and now she was just plain mad at Jim for dying, at the house for being old, at money for being scarce and most of all at the toilet for breaking down. She treated herself to a colorful string of expletives.

"Mom, are you crying?" Allison stood uncertainly in the bathroom doorway.

"No, honey. This is just...sweat. I can't remember a July this hot, can you?" She fumbled for a tissue and dabbed at her swimming eyes.

"Nope." Allison looked unconvinced. "I hate to tell you this, on top of everything, but Mrs. Eckstrom was at the door."

Diana plopped down on the edge of the old tub. "Not Beethoven again?"

"Her rose bed is a shambles, she said, and if we can't keep Beethoven penned up, she's calling the pound."

"Oh, damn." Diana looked up guiltily. "Oops. Sorry, sweetheart."

"That's okay, Mom. Laurie's tying him to the clothesline. Want me to fix the fence? I could work Dad's saws. I know I could."

Diana smiled wanly. "And fix the toilet and the electric fans and the kitchen faucet? And paint the windowsills?"

"Well, maybe not all at once, but—"

"Allison, you're a talented girl, but I know what we need around here." She slapped her hands against the knees of her white slacks and stood up. "And I've just decided what to do about it."

"What?" Allison trotted after her. "What do we need, Mom?"

"A man, Allison. I'm placing an ad in the *Journal* right this minute."

"An ad for a man? Freaky!" Allison trotted down the stairs after her mother. "Laurie, Mom's putting an ad in the paper for a man."

"She is not, bimbo. All right, Harold, let's try the last four measures again."

"She is, too! Ask her."

"Mother?" Laurie stopped directing and watched Diana pick up the telephone. "You *are* calling a plumber, right?"

"As soon as I place this ad, Laurie. Oh, Harold, you may go now. I'll give you a longer lesson next week to make up for this one."

Laurie tossed her dark bangs away from her face. "What ad?"

"For a live-in handyman."

"You wouldn't." Laurie's gray eyes, a shade darker than her mother's, narrowed suspiciously.

"Yes, she would," answered Allison with a smug grin. "I told you she was doing it."

"Goodbye, Mrs. Thatcher. Goodbye, Allison. Goodbye, Laurie." Unnoticed, Harold packed up his tuba and lugged it out the door.

"Mother! Bring a complete stranger into this house?"

Laurie wailed. "You're going to let some man we don't know sleep and eat here?"

"I'll get complete references." Diana temporarily replaced the receiver and launched into the arguments that had been floating in her head for weeks. "Wouldn't you like to have the fence repaired so Beethoven doesn't get out almost every day?"

"I bet I could fix it," Allison argued stubbornly.

"Maybe after you take shop in seventh grade, but the job needs to be done now. And how about the toilet? I hate to think what kind of bill the plumber will send us, but any man with a lick of sense could fix that in no time. And we would have more money for other things."

"Like clothes?" Laurie's gray eyes shone with interest. "I saw a really neat outfit at White Oaks Mall."

"We'll see, Laurie, but yes, I think we might have more money for things you girls want. Maybe a new tape now and then, a new pair of drumsticks for you, Allison. And your flute could use a little repair work, Laurie."

Her oldest daughter sat silently for a moment, her dark head bent in thought. "I'm not sure it will look so good, having a strange man living here."

"I've thought of that. But people will only talk if we give them something to talk about. Besides, what if he turns out to be sixty-five years old?"

"Oh, Mom, you wouldn't consider somebody that ancient, would you?" Allison looked horrified then began to smile conspiratorially. "How about somebody...say... twenty-five?"

"I don't want some kid," Diana protested. "Anyway, age has nothing to do with it. If he's clean and neat and knows how to fix things, what difference does it make if he's got white hair?"

Allison rolled her eyes. "A lot. He'd probably complain every time I practiced my drums or played my tapes an eensy bit loud or wanted a slumber party." She perched on the arm of the couch. "Your music lessons aren't so quiet, either, Mom. What about the Bad News Brass every Friday afternoon? Those three boys could blow the feathers off a chicken."

"Yeah," Laurie chimed in. "And what if the fix-it man disturbs us? Susie's grandpa lives with them, and he gets up early on the weekends and starts *whistling*. I couldn't stand that. I need my sleep."

"I know what, Mom. Don't get anybody older than you are. That's plenty old."

"Watch your tongue, young lady." Diana tugged Allison's ponytail.

"Yeah, bimbo. That wasn't nice. Mom's not old."

Allison's blue eyes shifted uncomfortably. "I know, but lately it seems…"

"What?" Diana asked.

"Well, you *act* older than you used to, Mom."

"Is that so? Maybe because I *am* older than I used to be?"

"Not that old. Even Mrs. Eckstrom says it's a shame for someone as young as you not to have a—"

"Allison," Diana interrupted sternly. "We've had this discussion before, and I know where it's leading."

"Yeah, Allison. Quit trying to marry Mom off. She might pick someone we didn't like."

"No, she wouldn't."

"Besides, it'll be hard enough getting used to a fix-it man. I don't want to start thinking about a new father."

"Exactly." Diana hurried to put Laurie's fears to rest. "I

have no marriage plans. That's why hiring someone is the answer. If he doesn't work out, we can fire him. Simple as that. What do you say?"

Laurie took a large pink comb from her back pocket and ran it through her short hair. "I still say it won't look right. And what if his being here changes everything?"

"We won't let that happen, Laurie."

"Oh, who cares," Allison said. "I think it's a great idea. I'm tired of the fans not working and the toilet running and Beethoven getting out all the time."

"That's two against one fence sitter," Diana said. "I'm placing the ad. Who knows? Maybe I won't have any takers."

SECRETLY DIANA WONDERED if anyone would be enticed by her offer of low rent and free meals in exchange for handyman duties. Was Springfield, Illinois, big enough to contain any men like that?

The first caller admitted to being seventy-five years old and complained on the telephone about his arthritis. Scratch one prospect. The second sounded young—too young. Anybody who used Allison's favorite "freaky" in every sentence didn't qualify as Diana's handyman. But the third man intrigued her, and she advanced him to step two—a face-to-face interview.

She'd forgotten to ask his age, but he had sounded very mature. His primary reference was the California high school where he'd taught until this year, when he had taken a personal leave to finish his doctoral dissertation on Abraham Lincoln's Springfield years. Diana called the school, deeming the long-distance charge worth her peace of mind, and heard nothing but praise for the character of Zachary Wainwright.

A high school teacher. A Lincoln scholar. She imagined horn-rimmed glasses and tweeds, a shy manner and a sunken chest. Zachary Wainwright might be the perfect maintenance man and the perfect boarder. Perhaps he'd be so meek that he wouldn't have the nerve to object to a little noise now and then. She had to admit the Bad News Brass took some getting used to.

Diana set the stage carefully for the interview. She sent the girls across the street to spend the morning at the Nelson Center pool, so that their presence wouldn't make the poor man nervous—or suspicious about a possible noise problem.

She'd chosen her dress, a soft white shirtwaist with a touch of lace at the collar, deliberately. Despite the damp heat of the morning Diana looked cool and poised but, she hoped, a trifle vulnerable. Zachary Wainwright mustn't think he should argue for a lower rent. After all, she was a widow, a fact she had included in her ad with the purpose of appealing to the gallantry in the men who applied for the position.

Trying to ignore the steady tick of the grandfather clock in the living room, Diana ran a feather duster over the carved black walnut furniture. Her mother-in-law had insisted that the antiques stay with the house when she and Jim had bought it twelve years ago, and as a young bride Diana had been delighted. Now she found the dark wood and the hand-crocheted antimacassars a trifle depressing.

When the doorbell chimed, she hung the feather duster in the cleaning closet and smoothed her dress. She wondered at her quiver of trepidation, feeling almost as if she were going on her first date. Ridiculous! This man, if he seemed suitable, would be her employee, and she would be the employer. He should be the nervous one, not her. She was perspiring because the morning was already very warm, that was all.

As she walked toward the front door, she could see him dimly through the frosted glass, and he appeared bulkier than she imagined a Lincoln scholar should be. And a little taller. With a smile of welcome to put him at ease, she opened the door.

How long they stood facing each other, she didn't know, but her smile was completely gone by the time he spoke.

"Mrs. Thatcher? Or are you her daughter?" He raked his fingers through sandy hair that had been streaked blond by the California sun and dampened by the Illinois heat.

Diana knew at once that this man didn't spend all his hours huddled over books. Nor was his chest sunken, nor were his deep blue eyes—made bluer by a dark tan— rimmed in thick glasses. He held a pair of sunglasses in one hand, but she would bet money they didn't correct a vision problem.

She cleared her throat. "I'm Diana Thatcher."

"The widow?" he croaked. "I expected white hair and a cane."

"And I expected thick glasses and a tweed sport coat, Mr. Wainwright," she said with a tiny smile, realizing how illogical her imaginative picture had been.

"In this heat? You've got to be kidding."

Diana's gaze swept over the man who stood on her front porch looking like an ad for Hawaiian Punch. His light blue T-shirt was tucked into white cutoffs, and the ragged fringe dangled over tanned muscular thighs that tapered to well-formed calves and ankles. She wouldn't have been surprised at bare feet, but instead he wore a battered pair of blue running shoes without socks.

"How old are you, Mr. Wainwright?"

"Getting older every time you call me that. How about Zach, before I begin to gray at the temples?"

Diana shook her head. This man would never do. "All right, how old are you, Zach?"

"Thirty-one, Diana."

"That old?"

He nodded soberly. "That old. Could we possibly continue this fascinating discussion inside? Your living room has got to be cooler than this porch."

She stood back from the door. "Inside isn't much better, I'm afraid, but we could sit down. Would you like some lemonade?" Why was she asking him in? Why not tell him straight out? *No, thank you, Mr. Beach Bum. I can't have someone like you sleeping in the guest room.*

"Love it."

"I'll be right back." She disappeared into the kitchen, only to hear his voice right behind her.

"I'll help. Where do you keep the glasses?"

She jumped. "The cupboard left of the sink. But you don't have to..."

He grinned, and Diana stared in fascination at the beautiful smile spreading slowly across his bronzed face. "Wouldn't want you to think I'm lazy."

"Oh." The steady drip of the kitchen faucet was the only sound in the room.

"Then I might not get the job," he continued, laying his sunglasses on the counter and regarding her earnestly. "I want it very much."

Diana turned away from the mesmerizing blue of his

eyes and opened the refrigerator. "Well, actually, I don't think that you—"

"Your offer is perfect for me, Diana. Motel bills will eat me alive before I can complete my research."

"On Abraham Lincoln." She felt better discussing his scholarly background. And when not looking at him.

"Yes. The sociological impact of this town on his future behavior as a president was immense, as I'm sure you already know. I needed to see Springfield for myself, but it's an expensive proposition. Your plan is a godsend."

His words soothed Diana's jangled nerves. He *was* a scholar, in spite of his muscles and his tan. And muscles were important for a handyman, weren't they? She closed the refrigerator and turned, the frosty pitcher of lemonade clutched in both hands. "We can take this into the living room, if you like."

"The kitchen suits me better, if you don't mind." He placed two glasses with fruit painted on them in the middle of the table. "The living room's so dim and formal."

Diana rummaged in a drawer and pulled out two terry cloth coasters. "My mother-in-law's furniture," she explained, rushing to let him know the room didn't reflect her taste. And then she chided herself for caring about what he thought. "Actually, it's beautiful furniture, when the sun comes in that room," she added to soothe her conscience. "I keep the drapes drawn in the summer, to make it cooler in there. My students..." Her voice trailed off as she realized he was listening to her babbling with mild amusement.

"So you're a music teacher. I saw the piano when we came through. Well, that's okay. I'm sure a few little girls tinkling on the keys won't bother me." He took the coaster she handed him and slipped it under his glass.

Diana poured the lemonade. A few little girls tinkling on the keys? He didn't know the half of it, but his perception of her teaching wasn't the crucial factor. His tanned good looks were. She could hear the neighborhood gossips now. "Have you seen that California beachboy living at the Thatchers'? Diana says he's a maintenance man, as if we'd believe that." Diana took her seat slowly as she tried to figure out how to tell Zach Wainwright he wouldn't be around long enough to be disturbed by the tinkling of piano keys.

He raised his glass to his lips and gulped down half its contents before setting it back on the table with a sigh. "I was parched. You're right, it is hot in here, but it's also very quiet. I like that." He stretched his legs under the table and leaned back in the chair to survey the neat but outdated kitchen. The appliances were nearly twenty years old, he estimated. "What are those flowers in the window?"

"African violets."

"The leaves look like velour or something. Pretty."

"Thank you," she replied, racking her brain for a tactful way to maneuver him out of her house.

He swallowed the last of his lemonade and flashed his dazzling smile. "How about it, Diana? Can we strike a bargain?"

She grasped at the first excuse that occurred to her. "I don't think you could concentrate here, Zach. I didn't mention this in the ad, but I have two daughters, twelve and thirteen. They're not at home this morning, but they can be quite noisy at times. And my music students don't all play the piano. There are other instruments..."

Zach's smile widened indulgently, and Diana felt her pulse responding to his charm. "Don't forget, I've been teaching high school for several years. Two young girls don't frighten me, nor a few music students. I can tell what kind of person you are just by looking at that dress and those delicate purple flowers, Diana. You're not the type to live in bedlam."

Diana glanced down in confusion at her dress. She'd set the scene so carefully to snare a quiet mild-mannered bookworm, and what had she caught? A bronzed Adonis had swallowed the bait.

"That's just what it is around here, Zach," she said desperately. "Bedlam."

"Nonsense. You haven't seen bedlam until you've taught high school for a few years. So, what do you say?"

Diana traced the cluster of grapes painted on the side of her glass as she was thinking, her mind keeping frantic time with the dripping faucet. What was so hard about just saying no? She didn't have to give him reasons, did she? She didn't have to tell him that he was too handsome, too virile, too tanned. She didn't have to say he scared her to death with his open, breezy California manner.

"What is it, Diana? What bothers you about me?"

"You're—not exactly what I had in mind," she said shakily. The faucet kept up its steady beat.

"Which was?" he prompted.

"Someone a little...older."

He chuckled. "I've been told I'm very mature for my age."

In spite of herself Diana laughed. "Me, too. Just recently." She thought of Allison. Allison would tell her to hire Zachary Wainwright in a minute. Diana had tried to brush her youngest daughter's comments aside, but they nagged at her. *Was* she turning into an old lady? Having a man like this one around might be good for her—for all of them. Of course Laurie had been dead set against change, any change, since Jim had died.

"You can always kick me out if we don't get along."

Diana looked up and imagined the ocean reflected in his eyes. She'd never been to the seashore, never walked along a beach or played tag with the waves. She'd never known someone like Zachary Wainwright. Diana took a deep breath, as if she were about to dive from a cliff into deep mysterious waters. "When can you move in?"

2

ZACH BLINKED. He hadn't expected her to say yes, considering she'd been against him from that first moment on the porch. For some reason she was afraid of him. What a laugh. Afraid of a teddy bear.

"How about tomorrow morning?" he suggested, not wanting to miss his chance. Diana. Wasn't that the Roman name for the Greek moon goddess? She looked like a moon goddess, with her milk-white skin and silvery eyes. A shame someone like her had ended up alone.

"Might as well. Would you like to see your room?"

He chuckled, amused with himself. Shouldn't his accommodations have been his top priority? Instead he'd been imagining how nice it would be to gaze into those fascinating eyes every morning over coffee. "Sure. Will I be upstairs or down?"

"Upstairs. The master bedroom is down here."

"Oh." And he was acutely aware that there was no master anymore, that she slept solo in a big bed. Or did she have lovers? He studied her discreetly, noting the shirtwaist buttoned to her creamy throat, the nervous motions of her hands toying with the glass. Lovers were doubtful. His heart warmed with sympathy, but he didn't kid himself that was all he felt when he looked at Diana Thatcher.

"Come on, I'll show you the room."

Once again he was following her, and that's exactly

what he'd do from here on out—follow her lead. He
hadn't figured the Widow Thatcher would look like Diana, but he wasn't at all sorry that she wasn't old and
plump. The scent of violets trailed after her, or was he
imagining it because of the flowers in the kitchen window?

"Here we are. This first room on the right."

He reached for the porcelain doorknob, which had
some sort of flower painted on it. He turned the knob, almost afraid it would break off in his large brown hand. As
he opened the door, the hinges creaked. Somewhere he'd
read how to take care of that. Shouldn't be too hard. He
stepped inside the room and took quick inventory, not
that he cared what it looked like. He had already made his
decision downstairs—maybe on the front porch.

The floor was polished hardwood and probably
creaked worse than the door. He'd have to watch his pacing. The dressing table and double bed looked like antiques of the same vintage as the living room furniture
that she didn't much care for. But for his needs, the decor
would provide the perfect atmosphere for digging into
the past. He even liked the musty smell of the wood floors
and faded wallpaper.

"There's no desk," she explained, "but the dressing table might work. I could get you a better chair."

"And I can even watch myself study," he said with a
smiling glance at the wood-framed mirror attached to the
dressing table.

"Perhaps this isn't suitable, after all," she said quickly.
"I'm sure you have other options, so maybe we should
forget—"

"I have no other options, Diana." He looked at her
steadily across the room. "This will be just great." And incredibly hot, he acknowledged silently as sweat trickled

down the middle of his back. Not even a hint of a breeze stirred the sheer curtains at the open casement window. The white paint on the sill was blistered and peeling. Painting wasn't too complicated, though. He could do that.

"This room has one of the nicest views," Diana said, walking over to the window.

"And how appropriate." He joined her by the window to gaze out at the huge oak trees and lush greenery across the street. "Lincoln Park."

"That's true." She smiled up at him, and his breath caught in his throat. He focused quickly on the park again. God, she was lovely! "I have the same view," she continued, "but the height of this room gives a better perspective."

So her bedroom was directly below his. An inkling of the problems that fact might present to his concentration began to penetrate his heated brain. "I bet it does." He glanced sideways, wondering if she felt the heat. She looked so cool and calm in her white dress that he longed to fit his palm to the nape of her neck under the clouds of dark hair to see if any dampness lingered there.

She was so pale, even in the middle of summer. Had he ever made love to a woman who didn't have a suntan? He caught himself. Diana Thatcher might never be more to him than a landlady. For all he knew, she was still grieving for her dead husband, for God's sake, and he wasn't about to trample on any memories.

"The bathroom's down the hall," she explained, moving away from the window, and he gave himself a mental shake. "You'll have to share it with the girls."

"No problem. My mother taught me to put the seat down."

Diana's cheeks grew rosy.

"Sorry. Chalk that remark up to my California tongue. I forget that people in Springfield are more..."

"Civilized?" she replied archly.

He couldn't resist. "I was going to say inhibited."

She met his laughing gaze with more poise than he'd expected. Classy lady. "Are you saying you're uninhibited?"

"I suppose that's a relative term, Diana. Compared to my brother-in-law, who goes skinny-dipping in the Pacific Ocean, I'm inhibited. But compared to a man who wears pajamas to bed, I'm not."

Diana's pulse began to race as she realized where her boldness was leading them. She should be more careful. "I see," she said unsteadily, backing out of the room. *Change the subject, Diana.* "Then we can expect you in the morning?"

"Do you want me to sign anything, pay my rent in advance?"

"Uh, yes, I suppose I should collect a deposit. That would make everything official, wouldn't it?" she said over her shoulder as she started back down the stairs and he followed. "Have another glass of lemonade, and I'll get my receipt book."

When they reached the first floor, she ducked into her bedroom where the bookkeeping supplies were kept, and he returned to the kitchen to pour himself the suggested lemonade. Diana found him standing by the kitchen window, examining her violets. How gently he touched the velvet leaves...

Her skin began to tingle in a way she'd almost forgotten it could, and she fought the insane urge to invite his gentle hands to soothe that tingle away, to—her imagination screeched to a stop. What in heaven's name was she thinking of? Her cheeks burned with shame.

"How about the first month's rent in advance?" she asked, her voice sounding loud in her ears. "Is that fair?"

He lifted his fingers from the soft leaves and turned toward her, his lemonade glass in one hand. "Better than I'd find in California. My apartment complex there requires first and last month's and rights to my firstborn." He set his glass on the counter and reached in his back pocket for his checkbook. "But then I've seen some of the beer busts my neighbors throw, so I guess the landlord's attitude is justified."

Diana looked at him in alarm. "Zach, you aren't—how do the girls say it? You aren't a party animal, are you?" He threw back his head and laughed, and Diana found herself smiling in response to his amusement. "Is that a silly question?"

Zach wiped his eyes and laid the check on the counter. "Of course not," he said, clearing his throat. "You wouldn't want a—" he pressed his lips together, but his eyes twinkled "—a party animal would never do in this refined white clapboard house with flowers on the bedroom doorknobs." The corners of his mouth twitched. "I drink an occasional beer, a glass of wine when it's handy, but I don't get drunk. I haven't been here long enough to meet any eligible young women, and besides, I'm in Springfield to work. I think you'll find my social behavior acceptable."

"That's good." She colored. "I mean—I'm sure you wouldn't—I didn't intend to imply—"

"Hey, don't apologize. You're in a vulnerable spot here, a widow alone with two young girls. I can understand that the respect of your neighbors is important to you."

Diana sighed with relief. "Yes, it is, more for the girls' sake than mine, but I care, too. To tell you the truth, bringing you into the house will start tongues wagging as it is."

"Even if they understand my role here?"

"Yes. You see, I thought you'd look...different."

"The tweeds and thick glasses? I won't promise about the tweed jacket in this heat, but if it would help, I could scrounge around for some awful-looking horn rims."

Diana smiled. "I'm afraid that wouldn't do it. There's still the matter of your gorgeous tan, and your body—" She broke off in horror. Glancing quickly away from him, she prayed the kitchen linoleum would swallow her up.

His voice was soft when he spoke at last. "You're wonderful when you blush."

She bowed her head, hiding her face with her hair.

"Diana, is my presence going to cause problems with you?"

Somehow she found the courage to meet his sympathetic gaze. "Probably."

"Shall we cancel the agreement?"

"I...no."

"Why not?"

She couldn't tell him the real reason, that she'd tasted the heady sensation of being near him and couldn't imagine sending him out of her life—not just yet. "I must hire someone to help me around here, and I don't believe Springfield is overflowing with suitable men whom I'd have in my house. Your high school raved about your sterling character, Zach. What chance have I of finding someone else who comes so highly recommended?"

He grinned. "They raved, huh? They're long on talk and short on cash, I guess. And wonderful though they think I am, they're going to lose me if I can land a university position."

"Which is why you're in Springfield."

"Right. Stanford might be impressed by the thoroughness of my doctoral research. I certainly hope so."

Diana quickly wrote his receipt and picked up the check from the counter. "Well, then, it's settled. Tomorrow you move in."

"You're sure?" He retrieved his sunglasses.

She nodded her head decisively. "Yes. The neighbors may talk, but they'll soon realize this is exactly what we say it is, a business arrangement." She folded her arms and tried her level best to look imposingly official.

"Okay." He surveyed her prim demeanor with a sparkle of humor in his blue eyes. "I'll be over around ten, if that's convenient."

"Of course." Diana handed Zach the receipt then walked with him through the silent house to the front door.

"Until tomorrow," Zach said with a soft smile.

"I'll be here." She held the door open, and his gaze met hers for a brief moment. Then he crossed the porch and bounded down the steps with an exuberance that reminded Diana of Allison. As she watched him stride down the walk to an older-model orange Corvair with California license plates, she noticed again how wide his shoulders were under the blue T-shirt and how the low-slung cutoffs hugged his lean hips. "A business arrangement," she said softly, as if committing the phrase to memory. "Simply a business arrangement."

He pulled away from the tree-lined curb with a wave of his hand, and she raised hers in response. Tomorrow morning he would be back. To stay. She wandered into the kitchen and ran her fingers around the rim of his lemonade glass then pulled off the coaster and rinsed the glass in the sink. The faucet continued its steady plunk, plunk, plunk after she'd twisted the handle as hard as her strength would allow. Well, she did need a man around, she thought defiantly. And why shouldn't he be great to look at?

"WHEN'S HE GETTING HERE, MOM?" Allison flipped the dish towel impatiently at Laurie, who was painstakingly scraping the last bit of egg from the breakfast plates. "Hurry up, slowpoke. I don't want to be doing dishes when he shows up."

"Ow!" Laurie feigned great injury from the towel. "Make her stop that, Mom. When is he coming, anyway?"

Diana opened the oven door and peeked at the browning cinnamon rolls. "Pretty soon."

"Are you baking those rolls for him?" Allison accused slyly. "You haven't made any for a long time."

"Of course I'm not baking them for him," Diana insisted, ripping a paper towel from the roll and dabbing at her damp forehead. *Or am I?* she wondered with a start. Had she made cinnamon rolls since Jim had died?

"I don't care why you're doing it. I'm just glad you are," pronounced Laurie. "Only thing is, the kitchen's getting awfully hot."

"Then why don't both of you go out in the backyard and play with Beethoven? He needs a break from that clothesline, and you might find a breeze under the maple tree." For reasons she didn't examine, Diana wanted the scene peaceful when Zach arrived. He'd find out soon enough what life in the Thatcher house was like, but she hoped this first day would run smoothly.

"Okay," Laurie agreed. "Right after I comb my hair."

Allison made a face. "'Right after I comb my hair,'" she mimicked. "You'll be bald some day from all that combing, and I'll laugh my head off."

Laurie shrugged haughtily. "I guess you won't care about how you look until you mature."

"Oh, brother," Allison groaned. "I'm going outside. Call me when he comes, Mom." Her ponytail bouncing, she skipped out the door and let the screen bang shut after her. A few moments later Laurie followed, taking care to close the screen door softly behind her.

"Thanks, Laurie," Diana said automatically. Bless Laurie for her consideration, she thought. But then life would be dull without Allison around. Diana cherished what each of her daughters brought to her life, even when pandemonium ruled.

She opened the oven and removed the tray of fragrant cinnamon rolls then mopped her brow again as she glanced at the kitchen clock. Soon. She tucked the tail of her pink shirt more securely into her tan slacks then fidgeted with her collar. Was she trying to parade her culinary skills for this California beachboy? Shaking her dark head, she reached for the powdered sugar just as the doorbell chimed. The bag of sugar fell from her nerveless fingers, and a puff of white coated her face and chest.

"Dammit," she swore softly, grabbing the dishcloth and patting it over her face and the front of her blouse. The doorbell rang again, and she tossed the cloth in the sink and walked quickly to the front door.

This time his cutoffs were denim, and his shirt was green, but otherwise he looked the same—muscular, tanned and smiling. "Something smells heavenly, but I can't imagine you cooking on— Who threw you in the flour?"

"It's powdered sugar," she said, self-consciously brushing her cheeks. "For cinnamon rolls."

"You turned on the *oven* on a day like this? Dear lady, the heat has frazzled your brain."

"The girls love them," she said lamely, ushering him into the sweltering atmosphere.

"So do I, but not in the middle of summer without central air. How big are these girls? Did they tie you to the stove and threaten you with bodily harm unless you baked them cinnamon rolls?"

"No, of course not. I just thought... Never mind!" She whirled abruptly and stalked back into the kitchen.

Zach stood in the middle of the living room, sweating and thinking, and then he followed her into the kitchen. "Did you bake these in honor of my arrival?"

"Not on your life!" She ripped a paper towel from the roll and dampened it under the faucet.

"It's a wonderful gesture. Do you have an electric fan?"

"Three." Diana wiped the last of the sugar from her face. "And they're all broken. Why don't you just move your stuff in and leave me alone in this steambath of a kitchen?"

He watched her frantic motions as she brushed the sugar from her blouse. The process made her breasts quiver, and he looked away, fighting a warmth that had nothing to do with summer and a hot oven. "Why don't we sit on the porch with some lemonade until the house cools down?"

"Not now. I have too many things—"

With a screech, Allison flung open the screen door and raced into the kitchen. A howling, dripping-wet Laurie dashed after her.

"You'll pay for this!" bellowed Laurie. "You ruined my hair, you bimbo!"

"But you said you were hot!" protested a giggling Allison, grabbing Diana and using her as a shield. "Protect me, Mom. She's gonna kill me."

"You bet I am." Laurie struggled to get past her mother's outstretched arm. "With great pleasure."

"Girls! Stop it this instant," Diana commanded, her face

aflame with anger and embarrassment. So much for smooth beginnings. "We have a guest."

"Oh, no." Laurie stopped struggling and looked past her mother. "Oh, no!" she wailed again, throwing her arms over her head and running from the room.

"He's here?" Allison spun around, and her blue eyes widened. "Freaky! I—I mean, glad to meet you. I'm sorry we made so much racket, Mr., uh, Mr.—"

"Zach."

"Mr. Zach."

"Just Zach. My last name's Wainwright."

"Oh." Allison digested the information and nodded approvingly. "Mom's right. You don't look anything like a history teacher."

Diana gasped. "Allison!"

Zach chuckled. "I'll take that as a compliment."

"It is," Allison said, looking him over from head to toe. "Are you a surfer?"

"Sort of."

"Figures. That's a great tan. D'ya like rock?"

"Allison, that's quite enough questions for now," Diana said reprovingly. From upstairs came the whine of the blow dryer. "I assume you doused your sister with the garden hose."

Allison studied the pattern on the linoleum. "Yeah. Sorry about that. But she kept combing her dumb old hair and complaining about the heat instead of playing with Beethoven, so I—"

"Cooled her off."

"Uh-huh."

Diana could have sworn that she heard a muffled snort from Zach. "Sounds like a great idea to me, Allison," he said. "Maybe after I finish unloading everything from the car, you can turn that hose on me."

Diana trained an icy gaze in his direction. "Not until she's apologized for her behavior to you and to her sister."

Zach composed his face into a grave mask. "Oh. Right. Better do that, Allison."

Diana knew from the twinkle in Allison's eyes that Zach had just won a champion for life. From now on Zach would be able to do no wrong as far as Allison was concerned.

"I'm sorry, Zach," Allison said with an attempt at contrition.

"Apology accepted."

"And your sister," Diana prompted.

Allison trudged to the foot of the stairs and waited for the sound of the hair dryer to stop. "Sorry, Laurie," she called then waited. "Sorry, Laurie," she said again. "Sorry—" She swallowed her words as the recipient of her apology descended the stairs, fluffing the dark hair that barely grazed her collar.

"It's only what I'd expect from a child," Laurie said airily as she breezed past her sister and sailed into the kitchen. "I'm Laurie," she said with an engaging smile at Zach.

Zach gave a slight bow. "Pleased to meet you, Laurie. I'm Zach Wainwright."

"I know." Laurie stood there, not saying anything, smiling contentedly at the man standing in their kitchen.

Diana stared at her daughter. Was this the same girl who worried about how it might look to have a strange man living in the house? All three Thatcher females were literally fawning over Zach Wainwright! Allison drooled over his tan, Laurie restyled her hair, and she—she was worst of all. Right on cue, like one of Pavlov's dogs, she'd settled into her homemaking role and baked cinnamon rolls.

After a year of not having a man to cook for, she'd begun to enjoy the freedom from baking the sweets Jim used to insist on, but let Zach Wainwright show up, and she put herself right back in harness. Well, she could take herself out again.

"If you'll excuse me, Zach," she said, "I have some shopping to do. Go ahead and unpack, and if I'm not back by lunchtime, the girls can show you where we keep the bread and bologna." With an aloof smile she took her purse from its hook by the back door and left without a backward glance. In reality she had no shopping whatsoever to do, but she, for one, was not going to hang around this morning and dance attendance on the captivating Zach Wainwright!

Having made her speech, Diana felt honor bound to stay away and window-shop in the White Oaks Mall until early afternoon. She took her time over a hamburger and soft drink, and by the time she returned, the house was quiet. Two notes rested on the kitchen table. One was from the girls, who had apparently made peace with each other and gone to the pool. The other was from Zach, and she studied the unfamiliar scrawl with interest.

Diana—
Cinnamon rolls are great. The girls helped me move in, and I'll be studying in my room for the rest of the afternoon if you need to discuss anything. Do you have an extra front-door key?

Zach

So he'd enjoyed the home-baked goodies, after all. Too bad, because she wasn't doing that number again! She just bet the girls had helped him. He may not have moved a single one of his gorgeous muscles this morning.

After the cool comfort of the shopping mall the house seemed especially hot, and Diana wondered how Zach was faring in his room. Heat rose, and by afternoon the upstairs bedrooms were pretty bad. There she was, doing it again, worrying about him like a mother hen. Still, she couldn't subvert all her humanitarian instincts. If he had a fan that worked...

And then it dawned on her that he might be able to fix her broken fans. After all, wasn't that the idea, for him to repair what needed repairing? She'd take him the newest one first and see what he could do with it before dumping the others on him. Time for Mr. Zachary Wainwright to make himself useful.

She dug in the hall closet for the best of her three oscillating fans then climbed the stairs to his room. The door stood open, and she tapped on the doorjamb.

"Come in."

He was propped against the headboard of his bed with open books spread around him and a legal pad on one bent knee. All he wore were his denim cutoffs, and Diana caught her breath at the picture he made—golden skin against the white hobnail bedspread and white lace-edged pillows supporting his broad back. *Jim didn't have that much chest hair*, she found herself thinking then was ashamed of herself for making the comparison.

Zach finished the sentence he was writing and glanced up. "Hi." He smiled in welcome, and she clutched the fan to her chest. "Shopping all done? Don't tell me you bought me a fan."

Her warm glow of admiration evaporated. Did he imagine she would cater to his every need, as the girls apparently had? Her laugh was brittle. "Not quite. This is one of our three broken ones, and I'd like you to take a look at it."

He grinned. "I'm looking." Good grief. Fix an electric fan?

She held on to her temper. "I meant you might fix it."

"I know. I have a maddening tendency to tease people. Sorry." Zach put his notepad aside and swung his tanned legs over the edge of the bed. *Buy time, Zach. You can't admit to her that you thought a handyman might have to oil a few hinges, caulk around the bathtub, easy stuff like that. She expects you to fix an electric fan, for God's sake!* "Why don't you leave it, and I'll see what I can do," he said, standing barefoot in front of her.

Diana held the fan like a shield. "Um—okay." She thrust it toward him. "Here."

He breathed deeply of her violet-scented perfume. It wasn't his imagination that she wore it. Where? Behind her earlobes, on each wrist, in the valley between her breasts? He struggled to rein in his imagination. Perhaps being alone in a bedroom with her fueled his indecent thoughts. Maybe the heat was getting to him. He wanted to strip off her clothes and his and stand under a waterfall together. But the shower would do.

"I may not get to the fan this afternoon," he said, grateful that his hands were occupied. He had to get her out of here, and fast. "I'm in the middle of some compelling research material, and I'd like to finish my notes before suppertime." Compelling research material? He knew exactly what was compelling him at this moment, and it wasn't his scholarly notes.

"Oh!" Her eyes darkened with guilt. "I'm sorry if I disturbed you." She scurried back to the doorway, creating a breeze with her perfumed body as she moved.

"No problem, but I do want to complete this one section." What had he done, moved in with a tempting goddess and set things up so he couldn't touch her? Damn!

"Dinner will be at five-thirty," she said.

"Why not wait until later, when it cools down?"

She looked at him strangely. "We don't eat fashionably late, I'm afraid. You may be used to that in California. You probably even have happy hour, but we have our evening meal at five-thirty."

Zach sighed. "I wasn't worried about fashion, just about heat. I'll be down at five-thirty, Diana."

"Wear a shirt."

"Of course."

With one last glance at his bare chest, she fled down the stairs.

He stood still for a moment, savoring the fragrance she left behind. "Oh, Diana," he muttered, shaking his head, "if you knew how you affect me, you'd tell me to ride my surfboard out of here before sundown."

3

Zach spent the night on sheets damp with sweat, and several times he got up and leaned against the sill of the open window to catch any errant breeze from the park across the street. The curtains hung limp and lifeless in the pale light from a tiny sliver of moon. Was it this hot in Diana's room downstairs? And did she sleep, as he did, with nothing on? The thought did little to help cool him off.

"Tomorrow the fan gets fixed," he muttered, flopping back on the twisted sheets.

In the morning he smuggled the fan out and ran through a drizzling rain to the Corvair parked at the curb. Even the rain was almost warm, and he dreaded the muggy heat that would envelop Springfield when the sky cleared. A working fan would make this afternoon's research session almost bearable.

With the lower cost on room and board, Zach figured he could afford to have the fan repaired. Who would have imagined that Diana expected an electrician, as well as a handyman? But this was the first thing she had asked him to do, and he hated to disappoint her on the very first request.

The repair shop was busy, so that the clerk advised him to leave the fan for several hours. He decided to put in some time at one of his favorite haunts, the historical library in the basement of the old capitol building. By the time he emerged from the building, the rain had stopped. The damp sidewalks of the pedestrian mall around the capitol were crowded with produce vendors, and he bought a fire-engine-red tomato and bit appreciatively into the tangy pulp. He hadn't realized what tomatoes were supposed to taste like until this summer in Illinois. Licking the juice from his fingers, he glanced at his watch and decided the fan should be ready.

As he paid the repair bill and drove home, he tried not to think about the cost or the necessarily sneaky way he'd accomplished the task. He was halfway up the stairs to his room when Diana's voice floated up to him, and he thought he'd have to confess everything.

"Zach? Is that you?"

"Yeah. Be down in a minute!" he called, taking the stairs two at a time to get the fan into his room. Once safely inside the steamy room, he found a plug and turned the fan on high. Ah, heaven! He stripped off his shirt and stood in the full blast of air with his eyes closed.

His pleasure lasted several seconds before his conscience began to prick him—no one else in the house had a working fan. With a sigh he pulled his shirt back over his head, unplugged the fan and carried it downstairs, where he found Diana making tuna sandwiches in the kitchen.

"Here you are. All fixed. Thought you could use it in here, or maybe in your bedroom."

"It works?" Diana looked at Zach with new respect. "You must have done it last night, because I know you were gone all morning."

So she'd noticed. He liked that. "Yes. I, um, had some work to do at the library."

"You ought to save that for the heat of the day, considering the library's air-conditioned."

"Guess you're right." He thought how terrific she looked, standing by the sink in crisp white slacks and a green gauze blouse. Nice, but too formal for this kind of humid heat. "Don't you have any shorts? I'd think you'd be a lot cooler in—"

"No, I don't have any shorts." She continued spreading mayonnaise on the bread.

"Why not? Wait—cancel that question. Too personal. I'm sure you have your reasons." He busied himself finding the best position for the fan. Diana might have a giant birthmark or something. How could he know what her reasons were?

Her silver eyes were the coolest things in the room as she turned to him. "Shorts are for young girls. And surfers."

"Good grief, Diana, you sound like you're a million years old." He felt a wave of relief that she wasn't hiding some horrible disfigurement.

"Older than you."

"By how much? One year? Two?"

"Three."

"Oh, Granny, how do you manage to totter up and down stairs at your advanced age? Diana, thirty-four is not too old to wear shorts."

"I'm also a widow."

"What's that got to do with it?" He flipped the switch on the fan and watched with satisfaction as she turned her face toward the cool breeze.

"I have to be careful not to appear to be flaunting myself for any man in sight."

"Flaunting yourself? You? Whistler's Mother is more blatant about her sexuality than you are. I've never known a woman so reserved, so...so *covered up*."

"That's because you're used to California, where they

parade around the beaches in next to nothing. This is Springfield, Illinois, and I don't wear shorts!"

Zach raised both hands. "Okay, okay. But you'd be a hell of a lot cooler if you did."

"That's my problem." Diana washed and dried her hands before walking to the pantry, where she stood on tiptoe and lifted two more oscillating fans from the top shelf. "When you have time, maybe you could take care of these, too. One could be for your room, of course."

Zach took the fans without comment. At this rate his financial edge would dwindle fast.

"Would you like a sandwich?"

He raised one tawny eyebrow. "If it's not too much trouble." Apparently she'd mellowed since her stalking-out speech yesterday at lunch. Were repair jobs the way to her heart?

"No trouble. I'll set the plates out if you'll call the girls. I think they're both upstairs."

The four of them had a noisy congenial lunch at the kitchen table. The meal was much more to Zach's liking than the previous night's heavy supper in the dining room. The roast, mashed potatoes and gravy Diana had prepared last night would have been delicious on a cold winter evening, but not when the temperature was pushing ninety. A few subtle questions directed toward the girls convinced him that eating a substantial evening meal in the dining room was hallowed family tradition, but he thought this was silly. A picnic on the back porch made more sense in this heat.

Diana bit into her sandwich and watched Zach laughing and talking with the girls. He was so relaxed, so wonderfully casual, and she was frankly envious. Shorts would feel better, now that she thought of it. Or now that Zach thought of it, to be more precise. Maybe a pair of

Laurie's... But no. She had lessons this afternoon, the first batch since Zach had moved in. Better not send the kids home with tales of a strange man *and* their teacher's new mode of dress.

After lunch Zach disappeared into his room to work, and the girls took Beethoven for a walk while Diana taught her first two lessons of the day, one for piano and one for flute. She moved the fan to a corner of the living room, but it had little effect unless she stood directly in front of it. At two-thirty the Bad News Brass arrived, and as the sound of three trumpets, not always in perfect harmony, resounded through the living room, Diana heard Zach's door close. *Too bad*, she thought, as the heat and noise took their toll on her good humor. *I warned him.*

Five minutes later the girls paraded through the room, their fingers in their ears, and Diana heard Beethoven start to bark. Probably Mrs. Eckstrom's damn cat was deliberately taunting him, now that he was tied up and couldn't chase her. As Diana directed the three boys, she brought her palms slowly downward, indicating lowered volume, but the Bad News Brass hadn't learned how to do that yet. Neither had Beethoven, Diana realized as the cocker spaniel became more vociferous in his disapproval. The telephone rang, and Laurie pounded downstairs to grab it, but not before it had pealed several times.

"You'll have to speak up, Jenny!" Laurie shouted into the receiver. "We've got quite a racket going on here."

Laurie and Jenny continued their high-pitched conversation, and when Diana thought her ears could hold no more, Allison began practicing her drums.

"Diana."

Zach was right behind her by the time she heard him, and she jumped three inches from her chair. Several seconds later she managed to get the attention of all three trumpet players, and they ceased their bugling.

"Yes, Zach?" *Let him complain. He wasted the entire quiet morning,* she decided belligerently.

"This is impossible."

She turned to him, an innocent expression on her face. "You knew I taught music."

"Yes, but I thought it was mostly piano."

"I never said that," she insisted.

"Okay, but the dog—"

"You knew we had a dog."

"Yes, but he looks so small. How can he make so much noise?"

"He has excellent lungs, and he's bored because he's tied to the clothesline."

"Okay, but does Allison have to play her drums right now, Diana? Isn't she supposed to be on vacation or something? Who practices an instrument in the summer?"

"All my students, including Allison." Diana was determined to brave this one out, especially considering the three pairs of round eyes staring at her and Zach. "I don't see a problem." She smiled sweetly, hoping the drop of perspiration sliding down her temple wasn't erasing her cool and calm image.

He waved his arms helplessly in the air. "You're all going at once! Right when I'm trying to work upstairs."

"Then don't work." She could almost see his frustration level rise like the mercury in a thermometer.

"But I have to!"

"Zach, you threw away this morning, choosing to mess around doing Lord knows what. I have to earn a living, you know. Allison needs to practice, and Beethoven—" She broke off as inspiration hit. What a perfect way to demonstrate to her three students, who would undoubtedly run home with tales of this encounter, what Zach's exact position was in the Thatcher household.

"I suppose Beethoven has to practice barking," Zach grumbled, wiping his damp brow with the arm of his T-shirt.

"He's barking because he's tied up," Diana repeated, "and I imagine Mrs. Eckstrom's cat is prancing around just out of reach. You obviously can't work on your dissertation right now, so why not take the time and fix the fence? Then Beethoven can run around, and he'll stop barking, which will solve at least one noise problem."

Zach scratched his head. "Fix the fence?" His blue eyes grew worried. "Uh, with what?"

"Why, the tools in the basement, of course. You'll find everything you need." She leaped up and dashed to the kitchen for her purse. "This should cover the cost of any boards you have to buy, and there are several cans of nails sitting around." She handed Zach thirty dollars, which he took with obvious reluctance. "After all, a deal's a deal, right?" Her silver eyes challenged his blue ones.

Zach's face tightened with sudden determination. "Right." He tucked the money into his pocket and strode out the front door.

With a bright laugh of success, Diana turned to her students. "Okay, boys, let's take it from the top."

"Mrs. Thatcher, who is that guy?" piped one young voice.

"He's our handyman," Diana replied with a tiny smile.

For the rest of the afternoon she taught music and listened to the rewarding sound of sawing and hammering in the backyard. Now she was getting somewhere! Her fans would be fixed and the fence mended. Next she might have him tackle the kitchen faucet. Well, maybe she'd give him a few days off first.

After Zach had been working for about an hour, Allison came downstairs. "I'm going out to help Zach," she announced. "He looks like he could use it."

"Oh, I'm sure he can," Diana replied solemnly, knowing full well Allison would manufacture any excuse to be around Zach, and a building project only sweetened the pie. It was amazing that Laurie wasn't pitching in, except that she hated to get sweaty and mess up her hair. Even Zach couldn't overcome that.

Once during the afternoon Allison raced through the living room, mumbling that she needed a bandage for Zach's thumb, but other than that the afternoon proceeded smoothly. When the last student left, Diana straightened up the living room and strolled out the kitchen door to inspect the repaired fence. Her expectant smile faded at the scene before her.

Not surprisingly, both Allison and Zach were sopping wet, and the garden hose lay nearby, ready for the next time they decided to cool off. But what arrested Diana's attention was the fence.

Zach stood to one side, petting an unchained and happier Beethoven, while Allison hammered in the last few nails. Most were crooked and had to be bent sideways, so that the boards looked as if they had been put up with very large staples. A few bent nails wouldn't have mattered so much, but why hadn't Zach matched the lumber to the wood of the existing fence? And why were the boards different sizes, and crooked, and what was that big Z of two-by-fours holding it all together? The fence looked as if it had been repaired by...by a twelve-year-old. Apparently Zach had allowed Allison to do almost all the work.

"Whatcha think, Mom?" Allison's blue eyes sparkled with joy at her accomplishment. "Freaky, huh? Beethoven will *never* get past this fence again. Zach and I've built this baby to *last*." She pounded on the fence with the hammer for emphasis.

"I can see that," Diana said weakly. "Looks like you did a lot of work, Allison."

"Zach did, too," her daughter maintained. "Don't we make a great team, Mom?"

Diana glanced at Zach, who seemed pleased as punch with the job he and Allison had completed.

"Al's great at this sort of thing," Zach said, throwing an affectionate arm around the young girl's shoulders. His thumb had at least three bandages taped around it. "We had lots of fun, too."

Diana's eyes narrowed. Al? She shuddered at the masculine nickname for her daughter.

"Yeah," Allison echoed enthusiastically. "Zach doesn't mind getting wet like *some* people. Say, are you ready for one last spray from the hose, Zach? Sort of a celebration for finishing?"

Zach laughed, and his teeth showed very white against his tan. He'd taken off his shirt, and his muscles rippled in the late afternoon sun. "Why not? Care to join us, Diana? Sure feels good on a day like this."

"Uh, no thanks." Diana backed warily toward the door.

"Come on, Mom. You never have any fun anymore."

Zach threw a challenging look Diana's way. "Is that true?"

She shrugged under the scrutiny of his blue eyes. "I don't know. I have fun."

"She used to laugh a lot more," confided Allison.

Diana glared at her daughter, but Allison pretended not to notice. "You two did a great job on the fence," Diana said hurriedly. "I'd better start dinner, or we won't eat on time." She turned toward the door.

"So what?" Zach called, and Allison giggled at the audacious suggestion that they eat late.

"I like an ordered existence," Diana said primly and spun on her heel. Obviously Allison and Zach were out to sabotage her efforts to maintain some sort of routine, but they wouldn't succeed that easily, she vowed. However, once inside the kitchen, Diana gazed longingly past her neat row of violets to the scene outside the window, where Zach, Allison and Beethoven frolicked in the spray from the hose.

An ordered existence. Jim had always preached it, giving her the freedom to be the more carefree one of the two of them. But Jim was gone, and she had the responsibility for providing order in all their lives. Her girls needed that stabilizing influence, the security of tradition, she told herself. Wearily she wiped beads of perspiration from her forehead with the back of her hand and tried to forget that she'd rather be standing under the splashing water in the backyard instead of molding hamburger into a very dull meatloaf.

Allison spent the dinner hour describing the repair job in detail, and Diana marveled that Zach had allowed her to make so many decisions about the fence. But Allison looked so pleased with herself that Diana didn't have the heart to find fault with the job, atrocious though it was.

She couldn't remember Allison glowing this way since Jim had died, and that meant a lot more than a beautiful fence. Her handyman was helping in ways she hadn't envisioned, she mused, glancing across the table at Zach. His freshly washed hair was combed back from his bronzed face, and his white knit polo shirt emphasized his deep tan. *He's very good-looking*, she admitted candidly.

Zach raised his eyes and caught her assessing gaze. When she blushed, he smiled and pushed back his chair. "How about letting the girls clean up while we sit on the back porch where it's a little cooler?" he suggested, picking up his dishes.

"That sounds nice." *He's smooth, too*, she thought, clattering her dishes a little too loudly as she stacked them into a pile. *Has me making all the right responses.*

"It's Laurie's turn to dry," Allison said. "I've been dryer two times in a row, and it's more work because the dryer has to put away."

"Yeah, but last time you left half the dishes on the counter, and I put them away, bimbo," Laurie retorted. "So that gives me the right to wash again."

Diana frowned. "Don't bicker, girls."

"Tell you what," Zach said with a winning smile. "Allison washes, Laurie dries, and I'll put away later."

Allison laughed. "You? You don't know where anything goes."

"Then it's time I learned, if I'm going to be living here. Your mother will show me. In fact, I'll throw in an extra bonus. I'll finish clearing the table right now." He disappeared into the dining room.

Laurie pulled a dish towel from the rack. "Sounds fine with me. Let's go, Allison."

"Call me Al."

"Al? Why? That's a boy's name."

Diana paused with one hand on the screen door to hear her younger daughter's answer.

"Not if it stands for Allison," she replied, tossing her blond ponytail. "And I like it."

Laurie rolled her eyes. "What a bimbo. Okay, make with the soapsuds, Al."

Diana shook her head and pushed open the door.

"Just leave the dishes on the counter," Zach directed. "Your mother and I will be out here if you need anything."

Diana settled into the cushioned porch swing, and Zach sank down easily beside her. After trotting up the white wooden steps, Beethoven stretched contentedly at their feet. The murmur of the girls' voices in the kitchen and the creak of the swing as Zach and Diana moved lazily back and forth were the only sounds in the evening stillness, and the air smelled of wet peat moss and Mrs. Eckstrom's roses.

Then Allison must have moved near the door, because her words were easily understood. "It sounded nice when Zach said that part about 'your mother and I will be out here if you need anything.' Dad used to say things like that. It's almost like Zach and Mom are married."

Diana's gaze flew to Zach's face in alarm. He was grinning.

"Kids," he said, his blue eyes twinkling.

"Especially Allison," Diana murmured, looking away. "She speaks without thinking."

"I haven't been a teacher for nothing, Diana. I'm used to hearing all sorts of painfully candid statements."

She still couldn't look at him. "I would never want you to think I was looking for—that I advertised because I—" She stopped in confusion.

"Don't worry. I don't." His eyes grew warm. "But surely someday you'll consider remarrying, won't you? You're far too lovely to—" He stopped abruptly at the frightened look in her eyes. "Oops. California tongue again. Sorry."

She smiled uncertainly. "You shouldn't have to apologize for giving me a compliment."

"I wasn't. And I'll say it again. You're lovely, Diana."

She smiled once more and dropped her gaze.

"But I have no right to pry into your plans for marrying. I don't even know how long—that is, when—"

"A little over a year ago."

"I bet you've had a tough year." The hand that rested on the back of the swing brushed sympathetically against her shoulder.

Diana felt his touch, which lasted only a fraction of a second, through her whole body. When was the last time a virile caring man had touched her? The few men she knew didn't even believe in shaking hands with women. "Yes, it's been a tough year," she agreed, wishing his hand would drift back to rest against the thin gauze covering her arm. A harmless casual touch. Surely they could afford that tiny luxury.

"What was he like?"

"Strong, disciplined. Hard-working. Probably too hard-working, but we didn't realize he had a heart problem."

"Sudden, huh?" Zach said, his voice gentle.

Diana nodded. "I've had well-meaning people tell me it was better that way, but I had no chance to prepare, emotionally or financially."

"How did it happen?"

Disarmed by Zach's compassion, Diana found herself telling him the entire sad story—Jim's struggle to sell tractors in a depressed market, his worry over finances and then the sudden chest pains that preceded a fruitless race to the hospital. She described the emptiness, the numbness when grief was too vast for tears, and the moment when she had had to tell Laurie and Allison their father was dead. She had no idea how long she talked and he listened, giving only a nod or murmur of understanding. She only knew that at last someone cared to hear what she'd bottled up for more than a year.

The anger, the resentment, the fear and anguish poured out, and Zach absorbed it willingly, encouraging her to continue until there were no more words. When at last she was finished, they sat silently, creaking back and forth in the old porch swing for long minutes.

At last Zach spoke in an unsteady voice. "Diana, I'm really sorry. You were both so young, and the girls—" His hand cupped her shoulder, and this time he didn't move away.

Diana sat very still and enjoyed the electric current running between them where his hand lay against her thinly covered skin. She imagined she understood both signals pulsing through that touch. He did feel sorry for her, but that wasn't the message that both soothed and excited at the same time. He also wanted her. For so many months she had conditioned herself to the role of widow and mother, but now, sitting here with Zach, she felt the stirrings of a forgotten role—woman.

Slowly she turned her head, and her silver gaze sought his face. Yes. What she felt in his touch was smoldering in his blue eyes. She watched his lips move.

"I wish there was something..."

She didn't respond. The answer was there for him to see, and she didn't look away. Silently each accepted the truth written clearly on the other's face. Then she gave a brief shake of her head, and he understood, better than if she'd shouted her refusal. His blue eyes darkened with regret.

"Yoo-hoo, Diana!"

They both started as the moment was destroyed.

"Yes, Mrs. Eckstrom?" Diana rose from the swing, and Zach followed her down the steps and over the fence, where the tall gaunt woman was standing on tiptoe and straining to examine Zach and Allison's repair job.

"See you got the fence fixed," Mrs. Eckstrom commented, moving her reading glasses down on her nose and staring pointedly at Zach as she flapped a pleated fan rapidly back and forth beside her face.

"Yes. Allison and Zach did it this afternoon, so Beethoven shouldn't be a problem in your rose garden anymore."

"That's good." Mrs. Eckstrom continued to peer at Zach over her glasses.

"And I'd like you to meet my handyman, Zachary Wainwright," Diana said quickly then hurried on. "He's in Springfield working on his doctorate in history. He needed an inexpensive place to stay, and I needed someone for small repair jobs, so we—"

"I see." Mrs. Eckstrom's lips pressed together into a thin disapproving line. "Where're you from, young man?"

"California."

"Uh-huh. Thought so." Mrs. Eckstrom nodded wise- ly and continued her fanning. "How do you like our Illinois summers?"

"Warm."

"So you fixed this fence, did you?"

"AI—I mean, Allison and I did, yes."

Diana broke in. "Allison insisted on doing most of it, Mrs. Eckstrom."

"So I see. I hope you're better at history than fixing fences, young man."

"Thank you, Mrs. Eckstrom," Zach said gravely, as if he'd been complimented.

Diana almost choked on her repressed laughter as Mrs. Eckstrom peered at Zach in confusion.

"Land's sakes," the gray-haired woman muttered then cleared her throat noisily. "Well, it's getting too dark for an old lady to be out. Good night to both of you." With a curt nod she walked away, fanning furiously as she went.

"Good night, Mrs. Eckstrom," Diana called then grinned at Zach. "By tomorrow the whole neighborhood will know I have a California surfer living in my house."

"Who did a lousy job of fixing your fence."

"I don't care about that. Not really. Allison had a wonderful time helping."

"Actually, Diana, Al—"

"But do we have to call her Al?"

"You don't think that's cute?" Zach picked up a stick and threw it for Beethoven.

"Sounds tomboyish."

"I think it fits her." He leaned down and pried the stick from Beethoven's mouth.

"Hold still," Diana commanded and slapped at Zach's bare arm.

"Hey, if you don't want me to use the nickname, just say so," he chuckled, glancing up in surprise.

"Mosquito," she explained, brushing the crushed remains from her palms. "We'll have to go in or be eaten alive."

"You mean just when the temperature out here becomes bearable, the mosquitoes attack and drive us in? What a place!"

Diana chuckled. "Perhaps you should put the weather and the mosquitoes in your dissertation. Maybe what we thought was a mole on Lincoln's face was a giant mosquito bite."

Zach swiped at his neck, where another spindly insect

had settled. "I don't doubt it. Hey, what's that over there?" He pointed toward a large bush in the corner of the yard where several pinpricks of light flashed, and his voice grew excited. "Are they fireflies?"

"We call them lightning bugs, but yes, that's what they are."

"Why didn't I see them around the motel?"

Diana thought about it. "I guess because they don't show up too well when there's a moon, and it's darker tonight."

"Let's catch one."

"Catch one?" Diana laughed. "That's the girls' department. Haven't you ever seen them before?"

"No, and I want to catch one."

"In our hands?"

"Sure. Come on, Diana." He lóped toward the bush, and she watched him make frantic passes at the flickering insects.

"Slower," she cautioned, crossing to him. With partially cupped palms she carefully tracked one of the tiny winged creatures then gracefully closed both hands around it.

"Got him!" she crowed.

"You're a real pro," Zach proclaimed, and Diana laughed again in delight. "And I love to hear you laugh, Diana. Let me peek inside and see that firefly or lightning bug, or whatever you call him."

Diana held her cupped hands up and opened them a crack. Zach took both her hands in his and brought them up to eye level.

"Yep. There's that little sucker, winking away. Amazing." Then he took both her hands and opened them to allow the insect to escape. "Thank you."

"You're welcome." She took a shaky breath, trying not

to make too big a deal out of the fact that he still held both her hands.

When he spoke his voice was husky. "When you let yourself loosen up a little, you're a different person, Diana. That...fascinates me." His thumb stroked lazily across the back of her hand.

She tried to breathe normally. "I can't be that person very often, Zach. Somebody has to...to be the adult in charge."

"What a shame, lovely Diana. Did anyone ever tell you your eyes are the color of moonlight?"

"No," she whispered, leaning toward him in the gathering dusk.

"Or that your skin is as pure white as a moonbeam?"

"No."

His breathing grew harsh. "God, I want to kiss you."

She jerked backward, her heart pounding. "Oh, Zach, no. We can't. I mustn't. I'm a widow—with two daughters. I—"

Abruptly he released her hands. "Then run in the house quick, Widow Thatcher. Before neither of us wants you to go."

4

HORRIFIED AT HER REACTION to Zach, Diana lay awake most of the night, planning repair projects. She would allow no more of those idle moments on the back porch swing. The solution to keeping Zach—and herself, she was honest enough to admit—in line was the same solution that worked so well in guiding her daughters away from mischief. She'd keep him busy.

When Zach arrived at the breakfast table looking none too rested himself, Diana handed him coffee and a plate of bacon and eggs then smacked an extensive list down next to his fork. He picked up the paper, and she watched with satisfaction as his blue eyes widened.

With a low whistle he tossed the list to the center of the table. "Judging from this, the house qualifies for urban renewal funds. Is everything on there urgent?"

"Would you like to reconsider our arrangement?"

Yes. Our sleeping arrangement. Her sleeveless blouse gave him his first glimpse of her milk-white shoulders. God, she was beautifully made! "I didn't say I wouldn't do the work, Diana. Aren't you eating?"

"I've already had something."

"In that case I appreciate the extra trouble to fix my breakfast."

"It won't happen often, believe me."

He calculated the frost level in her cool gray eyes. "You're upset about last night, aren't you?"

"Zach, be quiet. The girls—"

"Are sound asleep, like normal adolescents during summer vacation." He dug into his breakfast.

"But you never know, and sound carries through this old house. I heard you...pacing last night."

"Did you? Why didn't you use the 'old broom handle on the ceiling' trick? I would have stopped." So she had heard him. Subconsciously he'd probably wanted her to. Maybe he'd even hoped she might come upstairs and ask him to be quiet.

"Next time I will," she said crisply. "I hope you don't make a habit of it."

"I pace when I'm frustrated."

"Or bored?" She stood facing him, both hands on her hips. "I realize Springfield doesn't offer the nightlife you're used to in California, but I'm sure you could find female companionship if you tried."

"Dammit, Diana!" The coffee sloshed in his cup as he slammed it down. "I am not some stud who has to have a woman every night."

"You could have fooled me." She recoiled from the flash of pain in his blue eyes. "I take that back. I'm sorry." She rubbed her bare arms nervously and looked away. "I'm reacting about as maturely as one of my daughters. The fact is, you scare me, Zach."

"Diana—" He rose and made a movement toward her.

"Stay put," she warned him, backing away. "Don't feel sorry for me. That's how we got in trouble before."

He sank back onto the chair. "Perhaps I *should* leave. You obviously don't trust me. I've made you uptight."

She smiled faintly. "Uptight. That's certainly a California word. But I guess it fits."

"So what do you want to do?"

Diana gazed at him silently for several seconds as the

dripping faucet added a primitive rhythm to her thoughts. What did she want to do? He would be shocked to the tips of his brown toes if he knew the fantasies that had paraded through her head last night. Indecent fantasies about his sun-bronzed body—how her pale fingers would explore and caress this blond Adonis who had invaded her house and her mind. How he, in turn, would bring her to mindless ecstasy. The steady beat of the water pounded in her ears.

"Diana, when you look at me like that I don't understand why we're playing these games."

She dropped her gaze immediately, whirled toward the sink and twisted the chrome handle. "Stupid faucet! We have to stop this dripping."

"Today?" He wondered frantically how he could smuggle a plumber in without her noticing.

"No, not today, but soon. Maybe after school starts. Right now, with the girls home all day, I use the sink too much to have it torn apart for several hours."

"Then you want me to stay?" Zach knew the answer. He just wanted her to say it. She not only wanted him to stay, she wanted him, period. How complete was her control? How strong were the Midwestern ethics she'd made a part of her life for better than thirty years? And if her control snapped, and they would find themselves in each other's arms, would he be able to make love to her, knowing the recriminations she'd heap on herself and on him afterward?

"The girls seem very pleased you're here, Zach."

"How about their mother?"

She sighed and fingered the velvet leaves of the African violets on the windowsill. "I wish—"

"Me, too."

She glanced at him curiously. "You don't know what I was going to say."

"Yes, I do. It's the same thing that I thought over and over last night. The same thing men and women all over the world say when they meet the right person at the wrong time."

She flushed then bowed her head so that her cloud of dark hair covered her cheeks. "I should send you packing, Zachary Wainwright."

"Don't do it just yet."

"No good can come of this."

Zach picked up the list and grinned wryly. "Oh, I don't know. Lots of civilization's accomplishments are the result of rechanneled sexual energy."

Diana couldn't look at him. Her face was aflame, and she knew it.

"I'll put in time on my dissertation this morning and tackle something on the list this afternoon. By tonight I should be too exhausted to, ah, pace."

"Fine. Pick whatever you like on the list."

"What I would like isn't on the list."

"Zach!" Her voice was strangled.

"Okay. I'll be good." He scanned the piece of paper and groaned inwardly. Plumbing needs were big in this house. She'd written down a few rewiring jobs, too. Maybe he should enroll in a technical school at night. "I think I'll start with painting." Any fool could do that. Even a bumbler like Zachary Wainwright.

Diana took a deep breath and turned to face him. "All right. As you may have noticed, the paint on the window sills and sashes is blistered and peeling. I'd rather you started out there and worked in."

"Take care of outward appearances first, huh?"

"In more ways than one. Your presence on a ladder in

the yard will give credence to your position as the handyman around here."

"I see. Reputation time. I'll also be farther away from you. Unless you're going to help?" he finished hopefully.

"Nope. That's why you're here. I have plenty of my own work to do."

"All work and no play—"

"Keeps temptation at bay."

"Very clever." He drained his coffee cup and stood up. "I take it that means you won't join me in another cup of coffee before we begin the day?" He approached the sink with his empty plate and cup.

"No, thanks," she said hurriedly, moving away from the sink to give him room. "I have errands, and I'd better start before the stores get crowded. I'll pick up the paint when I'm out. See you at lunch." She fled from the kitchen, his amused chuckle ringing in her ears.

AFTER LUNCH ALLISON WANDERED out to the back porch, where Zach was stirring a can of paint. "It always reminds me of melted vanilla ice cream," she commented.

Zach held up the wooden stick and let the paint run back into the can. "You're right."

"You've done all the scraping already?"

Zach looked up. "Scraping?"

"Yeah. Dad used to spend about half a day scraping the old paint off. You done already?"

"Uh, not exactly. Just checking the paint." When she stared uncomprehendingly at him, he felt obliged to add another explanation. "You know, for color."

"Oh."

"Before I scrape."

"Oh." Allison watched him stir a while longer. "Need any help?"

"If you don't mind, why don't you get the—ah—the scraper."

"The what?" Allison looked puzzled. "You mean the wire brush?"

"Right. The wire brush."

"You've never scraped off old paint before, have you, Zach?"

"To tell you the truth, Al, no."

She gave him a sunny smile. "I guess people don't have to scrape old paint in California." She skipped down the porch steps and disappeared into the garage. While she was gone, he wiped off the wooden stirring stick and pressed the lid back on the paint can. Al had just saved his reputation. His position here was precarious at best, and if Diana found out how much he didn't know…

Several times during the morning he had considered telling Diana that he wasn't particularly well-versed in home maintenance. But then the sultry look she had given him this morning would intrude on his good intentions. Somehow he'd work his way through the list of repair jobs. On the next library trip he'd look for some books on the subject, and maybe the hardware store would yield a comrade-in-arms.

"Here you go." Allison handed Zach the wire brush.

"Thanks, Al. The ladder's set up, so I might as well begin with the second floor."

Allison glanced apprehensively at the tall extension ladder propped against the side of the house. "It doesn't look right."

"What do you mean? A ladder's a ladder."

"The ladder looks okay, but I remember it being tilted more. It's so straight up and down."

Zach felt his patience waning. At least he knew how to position a ladder, didn't he? "I'm sure it's fine, Al." He put one sneakered foot on the bottom rung. The làdder rocked a little but not dangerously. He climbed until he was even with Allison's bedroom window.

"Don't look into my room!" called Allison from below him. "It's a mess."

"Don't worry. I won't tell your mother. I'm just the handyman, remember?"

"You are not. You're a friend, too."

"Why, thank you." He steadied himself against the house and began scrubbing away at the flaking paint.

"Did you ever meet any movie stars while you were living in California?"

"I never met any, Al, but I caught a glimpse of Burt Reynolds once."

"You did? Freaky! I wish I could go there sometime." She sighed. "I've never seen the ocean. Atlantic or Pacific."

"You'd love it. I can picture you playing in the surf, having a ball."

"Oh, I know I would. But Laurie wouldn't. She'd always be worried about her *hair*. Do you know that when we go to the pool she swims with her head out of the water, just like a dog, so she won't get her precious hair wet?" She giggled at her own joke. "Just like a dog. I'll have to tell her that."

"Now, Al. Don't buy trouble. Maybe someday you'll worry about your hair, too."

"Ha! Why should I? She only fiddles with her hair because she's boy-crazy. I think boys are stupid."

Zach smiled. "You do?"

"Oh, I didn't mean you. Zach. I meant *boys*. The ones in my grade are dumb to the max. Did you hear that? See, I know some Valley Girl talk. Do they talk that way in California?"

"No more than they do here, I bet," Zach said, laughing. "I think teenagers are pretty much the same all over."

"Well, I'm not a teenager yet. And from what I've seen of Laurie since she became one, you can have that teenager stuff. You should see her after she's put on makeup. She's over at Jenny's right now, trying out eye shadow with sparkly junk in it. Yuck!"

"I hate to say it, Al, but most girls go through that."

"Not me."

"If you say so, but I wouldn't—"

The sound of loud barking drowned out the rest of his sentence.

"Beethoven, leave that cat alone!" Allison yelled, chasing across the yard.

Zach stopped scraping and glanced down in amusement at the trio weaving a frantic pattern around the yard. Mrs. Eckstrom's cat must have miscalculated and figured Beethoven was still tied up. Its gray stripes became a blur of motion as it cut left and right, searching for an escape route. Beethoven bounded right behind, barking gleefully, and Allison brought up the rear.

The cat leaped to the second rung of the ladder before Zach had realized the animal's intention, and as the feline scrambled upward, Beethoven pounced on the bottom rung of the ladder. Zach felt it sway and grabbed for the windowsill, but he was too late. He glimpsed Allison's horrified expression as the ladder went over backward, and then he twisted his body and instinctively flung out his arms to break his fall.

Allison screamed his name just before the grassy yard rose to meet his outstretched hands. A sharp pain shot through his right wrist, and then he rolled away from the metal ladder that clanged down beside him. He lay there, dazed, as Allison raced toward him.

"I'm gonna kill that dog! Mom! Come quick!"

Slowly he sat up as Allison crouched down beside him.

"Zach, are you okay? Don't move unless you feel okay. They taught us that in school. Oh, Zach, I'm so sorry." Allison's usual sparkle had disappeared. She looked close to tears. "It was my fault. I shouldn't have chased—"

"Hey, Al. No, it wasn't. And I'm fine. See?" He started to push himself up from the ground when a searing pain in his right wrist made him grimace and sit back down with a groan.

"No, you're not!"

"Allison, Zach—what in God's name—" Diana tore across the yard and dropped to her knees next to them.

Zach managed a weak grin. "Pretty good running for an old lady, Diana."

"Very funny. Where do you hurt?"

He held up his wrist, which was already beginning to swell. "Something's broken or sprained in there, I think."

"Have you tried to walk?"

"No. I've only eliminated crawling so far."

"You're a real riot. Help me lift him up, Allison."

"Diana, I can—"

"Be quiet, Zach. Take his other arm, Allison."

As Diana crouched beside Zach and put one arm around his lean torso, Zach stopped objecting to her help. Her violet scent wafted around him, while the softness of her breast pressed against his rib cage as she and Allison guided him upright. He automatically tightened his grip on Diana then gasped as another pain shot through his right wrist.

"Do your legs hurt?" Diana asked quickly.

"No. Still just my wrist." *But the rest of me feels wonderful, snuggled next to you like this. Doesn't Allison have somewhere else to go?*

"Hold him up on your side, Allison. Let's walk him up and down the yard."

Allison giggled. "Mom, you make Zach sound like Beethoven."

"That's okay," Zach said, as he relished the lush ripeness of Diana's body brushing against his side. "Beethoven has a pretty good life. Plenty of food and lots of fondling."

Diana glanced up at him from beneath her dark lashes. "He's also penned up in the yard a lot."

"Yes, but where does he sleep?"

"He sleeps in Mom's room," Allison answered. "He's a terrific watchdog."

"Then I'd better make friends with Beethoven," Zach commented dryly.

"Oh, he likes you already," Allison said.

"That's good." Zach chuckled. Was he imagining it, or could he feel Diana's accelerated heartbeat? The points where their bodies touched were becoming exceedingly warm, and he didn't think that was all due to the Illinois weather.

Gradually, to his regret, she eased away from him. "Okay, I'm convinced you can walk, so let's drive to Emergency and have your wrist X-rayed."

"Diana, I can't afford to—"

"I have insurance to cover it. And even if I didn't, I wouldn't let you take chances with a possible broken wrist."

"Can I go, Mom? I want to make sure Zach's all right."

"I'd rather you stayed here, so you can explain things to Laurie when she comes home. If nobody's here, and the note says we're at the clinic...well, you know."

"Yeah. I guess you're right."

"Wait here, Zach. I'll get some ice in a bag and my keys.

And I'd better tell Susie that's the end of her piano lesson for today."

"I'll get the ice, Mom. It'll make your wrist feel so much better, Zach." Allison ran after her mother into the kitchen.

Zach stood alone in the middle of the yard. His wrist hurt like hell, but he felt wonderful. The warmth of Diana and Allison's concern surrounded him with a kind of comfort he hadn't felt in years, maybe not since he had been a little kid, before his mother and father had divorced. He liked the feeling.

Allison burst through the screen door with Diana right behind her. "I wrapped a towel around the bag of ice," Allison explained as she ran toward him. "That way it won't be quite so lumpy and cold. Hold it around your arm like this." Carefully she placed the ice pack over his swollen wrist, and he smiled at her tender ministrations. "Better?" Her blue eyes begged him for reassurance.

"Much better, Al. You're terrific."

"Next time I'll tie Beethoven up while you're on the ladder."

"Okay. But the accident was mostly my fault, Al. The ladder was too close to the house, like you said." He glanced at Diana and saw her puzzled look. Was she beginning to suspect he was all thumbs when it came to maintenance work? Still, he couldn't let Allison continue to blame herself for the mishap.

Later, as Diana drove down the tree-lined street toward the medical center, she gave him the same puzzled glance. "About the accident, Zach—"

"By the way, I meant to ask you something, too," he interrupted. Not now. This was not the proper time to have to admit his handyman inadequacies. When he would finally tell her, he wanted to be kissing her in between confessions. "What was all that about Allison staying home? Why couldn't we leave Laurie a note?"

Diana pressed her lips together and stared straight ahead. "Allison and I left a note for Laurie when Jim had his heart attack and we took him to the hospital. I had no choice, and Allison begged to go with me. But Laurie was all alone, and...a note even slightly similar wouldn't be a good idea."

"I understand. You three had quite a rough time of it. You've adjusted remarkably well."

Diana's silver gaze slid sideways then back to the road. "Have we? Sometimes I wonder. The girls have reacted to you like lost puppies." *And so have I, perhaps.* "I'm becoming a little alarmed by their instant attachment to you. Especially Allison's."

"Well, I think it's terrific. If I can fill a gap in their lives, that's great." He studied her profile, the deep-set eyes, straight nose, rosebud mouth. A mouth that hadn't tasted a man's lips in a long time. If only she would let him fill the emptiness that he knew lurked in her heart.

"So I've hired a man who can fix people's troubles, as well as the kitchen sink?" Diana arched one slender eyebrow.

"I can try," he said quietly.

She pulled into the medical center parking lot and shut off the motor. "How wonderful. You breeze into our lives, fill our days with sunshine and then take off for the beaches of California to work your magic with someone else. What more could we want?"

"Diana—"

She laughed mirthlessly. "I've gotten myself into a no-win situation. If I tell you to leave now, the girls will want to know why, and they'll never agree that they could become too attached to you. We'd have a huge fight, I'm sure. But if you stay, I'm afraid they'll be devastated when you go home." *And will I be?* "I can pay now or pay later."

Zach didn't answer. Perhaps she was right. He sighed. "I don't want to hurt those girls, Diana. Tell me what you want and I'll do it."

She stared at him for a long moment. "I don't know what I want. But as soon as I find out, you'll be the first person I tell. Right now you've got a wrist that needs attention." She flipped open the car door and stepped onto the asphalt.

An hour later they walked together toward the car. Zach held his forearm, wrapped securely in a professional ice pack, away from his body. Diana carried the elastic bandage they were instructed to apply when the swelling receded.

"Two weeks," Zach muttered. "Can you believe a lousy sprain will put me out of commission for two weeks? How am I supposed to take notes? How am I supposed to type?"

Diana's gaze flicked over Zach's scowling face and injured wrist. She began to laugh.

"You think it's funny? I don't appreciate the joke."

"That's because you are the joke," she said, laughing harder. "I hired you as a handyman. How much work do you expect to get done now?"

5

ZACH WORKED at sounding disappointed. "I guess that makes me pretty useless, huh?"

"For two weeks, it sure does." She slid behind the wheel, and Zach settled himself on the passenger side of the front seat. "So much for my plan of keeping everyone busy."

"I'll take notes left-handed," he decided.

"Can you paint left-handed?"

Zach chuckled. He wasn't sure he could paint right-handed. "I doubt it."

"Isn't this wonderful." She started the engine with unnecessary abruptness. "What good are you to me?"

"I'd love to answer that, but I'd probably get slapped."

Diana glared at him, but her body had already begun to tingle. "You certainly would. You'd better find another way to justify your existence, Zach, and fast."

"Maybe I could find some little jobs. I noticed the hinges on my door squeak. How about yours?"

"They squeak, which is the way I like them. Don't you dare oil the hinges, Zachary Wainwright. It doesn't take much imagination to figure out why you'd want quiet bedroom doors." She glanced over to catch him grinning mischievously. "Cut it out! Not five minutes after you're on the disabled list, all you can think of is—"

"Can I help it I've got the sexiest landlady east of the Mississippi? I don't know what that perfume is you're wearing, but you smell exactly like a bouquet of violets. They're becoming my favorite flowers."

"I'll throw away the bottle." She veered into the traffic.

"Then while you're at it, you'd better get rid of your soft silky hair. I've been dying to touch it ever since I saw you."

"I'll shave my head."

"And that neat little figure beckons to me every time you walk in the room."

"I'll gain twenty pounds. Oh, Zach, this isn't going to work! I think you'll have to leave."

"Will you tell the girls, or shall I?" he challenged.

"God, I can see their faces now. They've been so happy recently that they practically dance around the house. I can't tell them you're moving out."

"Then don't," he said quietly. "Let me oil the hinges."

Her heart began to race. He was suggesting an affair. And she couldn't pretend she hadn't considered the possibility ever since he'd first stood on her front porch. But she wasn't the sort of liberated woman he was used to in California; he'd have to understand that. "No," she said softly.

"We'll be discreet. No one will ever suspect."

"I don't believe that, Zach. Children, especially this age, have sensors like you wouldn't believe. They'd pick up on an affair between us in a minute."

"So?"

"They're at a very delicate age, just discovering their own sexuality. Knowing their mother had a lover would embarrass them more than you could ever guess."

"Funny, but that didn't stop my mother."

Diana's head whipped around at his muttered comment, and her heart wrenched at what he'd revealed. "Oh, Zach." She returned her gaze to the road, but she could still see in her mind the aching vulnerability in his blue eyes. "I'm sorry," she said gently.

"It was a long time ago."

"Yet you still remember how you felt."

"I walked in on them, Diana. I wouldn't allow that to happen with the girls."

"You couldn't guarantee it wouldn't happen. I won't risk it. They need predictable behavior from me right now. The answer is still no."

They were both silent for several minutes.

"Okay," Zach said at last. "But tell me, Diana of the violets, if the girls weren't in the picture, would your answer be the same?"

She flushed.

"Your cheeks are the most delicious shade of pink. I bet you taste like strawberry ice cream."

"Zach, really. This is an outrageous conversation we're having."

"But fun. Come on, Diana. I want to know where I stand. I bet you've never told a man point-blank that you wanted him, have you?"

"Zach, this is getting us nowhere. The girls are very much in the picture. They will be for several years."

"All right. But say those years have flown away. Would you still refuse me?"

She remembered the way he'd looked stretched out half-naked on his bed the afternoon she'd brought him the electric fan, and her body began to hum with the same sweet longing she'd felt then. Her hands trembled on the steering wheel. "I don't know, Zach. I'm a small-town girl with small-town morals."

"Okay. Suppose no one would ever find out?"

"Then," she said, her voice barely audible, "I wouldn't refuse you."

He shut his eyes and leaned his head back against the seat as he fought down the desire gripping him. "I don't think I've ever been so close to a woman I wanted, who wanted me back, without taking her in my arms, Diana. I think we've painted ourselves into a corner."

"Was that supposed to be funny?"

"No."

"So what will we do, Zach? We're back at square one. If you leave, the girls will be unsettled, which I don't want. If you stay..."

"We'll both be candidates for sainthood, and I make a lousy saint."

"Then you're going to leave."

He raised his head and looked directly at her. "Not unless you tell me to, Diana."

"I have to be the villain."

"Somebody does. You're elected."

"Whatever happened to chivalry?"

"Don't you know your history? It died."

"Great." Diana found herself laughing in spite of her dilemma. Zach *was* fun. "Tell you what. Let's see how we do for a few more days. If the strain is too great, we'll reconsider the matter then."

"Will we look at the problem from all angles?"

"Probably not."

"Then by reconsider you mean reconsider my leaving, not reconsider oiling the hinges."

"That's right."

"Too bad." He sighed. "But I'm not dealing the cards. I'll accept your plan, Widow Thatcher. Want to kiss on it?"

"Definitely not."

"Damn."

FOR THE FIRST THREE DAYS of their trial period, Diana experienced the glow of a schoolgirl with a new crush. The atmosphere in the house was charged with an electric excitement that gave her more ambition than she could remember having in years. Zach was right—a lot of work could be accomplished with rechanneled sexual energy.

Even the oppressive heat lifted temporarily from Springfield, and Diana sang her way through her daily chores. Zach laboriously took notes left-handed during the morning hours then spent his afternoons chauffeuring the girls around in between trips to the library. The summer evenings found all four members of the household gathered around a card table for an ongoing game of Monopoly.

Diana watched the girls blossom in the steady glow of Zach's attention. At times she was almost jealous of the camaraderie they enjoyed, the spontaneous hugs, the cheerful banter. Zach went out of his way to avoid touching her, and she did the same. At times their eyes would meet, and warmth would spread through her body at the message he sent her. But his outward behavior was beyond reproach.

By the sixth day, as the family gathered for Sunday breakfast, Diana admitted the tension of unfulfilled needs was getting to her. Her dreams at night had become increasingly erotic, and the man in every dream was Zachary Wainwright. Sitting across the kitchen table from him made it very difficult for her to concentrate on a feature story in the Sunday paper, but she kept trying.

Finally she glanced covertly in his direction. Apparently the subject of her fantasies was handling celibacy far better than she was. He lounged easily on the kitchen chair with his ankle propped across his bare knee and the sports page spread open on his lap. He seemed completely absorbed in the baseball standings, oblivious to her hungry gaze. And then he looked up.

"Hi," he said softly, and his blue eyes touched the secrets of her soul.

"I just wondered how the Giants were doing," she fibbed, ducking her head.

"They've had an extremely frustrating few days—ah— I mean games."

"Oh."

"Mom, will you make Al give me the funnies? I think she's memorizing them." Laurie stomped around the table and grabbed for the sheet of comics in her sister's hand.

Allison snatched the paper out of reach. "I got here first, so you can wait. If you hadn't spent twenty minutes on your precious hair, you might have gotten to the table before I did."

"Well, at least I don't look like a punk rocker, with hair sticking out everywhere."

"At least I don't swim like a dog."

"That's enough, girls," Diana remonstrated.

"Yeah," Zach interjected. "If you two don't clean up your act, you might not get invited to the state fair next weekend."

Allison whooped and dropped the comics. "The fair? Freaky! Oh, Mom, can we go?"

"Well, I..." She paused in confusion. If Zach was planning an activity a week away, he was automatically extending his stay at least that long. "Maybe Zach and I should discuss—"

"Please, Mom," Laurie echoed. "We...we didn't go last year."

"No, we didn't." Diana could feel Zach watching her, waiting for her reaction. She looked at the eager faces of her daughters. Of course they'd go to the fair. Of course Zach would stay on, regardless of her dreams, of his frustrations. They were both civilized adults, not primitive creatures driven by lust.

"Zach would love the fair, Mom," Allison said, her eyes shining. "We'll take him to Happy Hollow and ride everything and go through the livestock barn and—"

"Forget the livestock barn," Laurie interrupted. "It smells worse than your sneakers."

"Listen, Supernose," Allison shot back, "*nothing* smells as bad as your gross hair spray. Barf me out the door!"

"For two young ladies who want to be invited to the fair, neither of you is doing very well," Diana commented mildly.

"Then we can go?" Allison cried.

"Why not?" Diana glanced across the table and met Zach's wide smile. "Should be fun. Of course, any girls who can't be friendly and courteous to each other this week may have to stay home."

"Would you like the funnies now, Laurie?" Allison said with exaggerated politeness.

"It's about ti—ah—yes, thank you," her sister replied with a tight smile.

"I need you to help me rewind my bandage, anyway, Al," Zach said, folding the paper and stretching. "It came loose again in the night."

Diana averted her eyes from the play of muscles under Zach's shirt as he moved. *I am the mother of two adolescents and a full three years older than this man*, she reminded herself sternly. *He's never been married, never had children. He's just an inexperienced kid, really.* The lecture wasn't working. Diana had a feeling Zach was experienced in all ways that mattered.

"There," Allison pronounced with satisfaction as she

secured the metal clip on the elastic bandage. "Is your wrist getting better?"

"I think the bandage can come off for the fair. How about that?"

"Perfect," Allison said with a big smile. "I bet you're real good at throwing baseballs and darts and stuff, huh."

"I don't know, Al. Those midway games are tough."

"They're hard for me, but not for you, Zach. You could win something for each of us, even Mom."

"How about that, Diana?" Zach glanced across the table, his smile teasing. "Want a big stuffed animal for your bed?"

Diana rolled her eyes and stood up. He knew damn well what she wanted for her bed, and she couldn't have it. "No, Zach. You can keep your prize in your own room."

Zach's hearty laughter echoed through the kitchen, and Diana hid a smile behind her hand.

Allison giggled as she watched Zach wipe the tears from his eyes. "What's so funny?"

"Your mother, Al."

"She didn't say anything funny."

"Never mind, Al. It's kind of a secret joke."

"It is?" Her eyes bright with interest, Allison looked from Zach to her mother. "You guys like each other, don't you?"

Diana swallowed hard then glanced at Zach.

"Yes, we do," Zach said soberly.

"That's good," Allison proclaimed, then dashed out of the kitchen. Laurie followed grudgingly.

Zach and Diana stared at each other for several long seconds.

At last Zach spoke in a low voice. "Still think the girls

would mind if we...?" He stopped and raised his eye-brows questioningly.

"Yes, I do. What Allison wants is friendship between us, Zach."

"What I have in mind is very friendly."

"Look, there's a difference and you know it. I'm not taking chances with these girls' psychological development by throwing their mother's sexuality in their faces."

Zach groaned. "God, Diana. This is more difficult than I thought it would be."

"Want to forget the whole thing?"

"No. I may be miserable now, but I'd be more miserable by leaving and depriving myself of being around those little squirts." He captured her gaze. "And you," he added. "I like living here, Diana, even if we can't..."

She regarded him steadily, realizing how important his presence had become to her, too. "But you'll have to go sometime, when your work is done."

"True. But sometime is a long ways away from immediately. I don't have all the answers, Diana. I only know that next weekend I'd like to take you to the fair."

"Okay, Zach. We'll try another week." She turned and began running water into the sink. Zach stood and took a step toward her then thought better of tempting himself with her violet scent and walked out of the kitchen.

Except for a few forgivable exceptions, both girls showed remarkable restraint with each other during the days that separated them from their adventure at the fair. Diana couldn't deny the salutory effect Zach's presence had on her daughters, but she found herself walking a never-ending tightrope of emotion. Wherever she looked, Zach was there, his blue eyes beckoning her.

THE AUGUST HEAT AND HUMIDITY RETURNED with a vengeance, and Diana gave the only working fan to the girls, who traded every other night. On Friday both Laurie and Allison chattered like little girls waiting for Santa Claus as they planned what would happen the next day.

Darkness came slowly that evening, but at last the house was quiet except for the steady dripping of the kitchen faucet. Diana lay with the sheets thrown back and listened to the steady chirp of crickets and katydids. The room above hers was quiet. No pacing tonight.

The almost sheer cotton nightgown stuck to Diana's damp body. She rolled to one side and lifted the hair away from her neck. Maybe she should cut it. Or shave it off completely. She chuckled in the dark gray silence that surrounded her.

What good would it do to shave her head or throw away the perfume or gain weight? Maybe Zach wouldn't find her attractive, but she'd still want to mold herself to his sun-bronzed body. Did that make her some sort of hussy? Her nipples tightened, and she pressed both hands against her breasts in an attempt to suppress the desire that welled up from her heart at the thought of him. Damn, it was hot!

Impatiently she swung her legs over the edge of the mattress and placed her bare feet on the oval shag rug next to her bed. Beethoven raised his head. "Stay, Beethoven," she whispered, and the spaniel dropped to his paws with a sigh.

Diana opened her door and crept noiselessly into the kitchen. A glass of lemonade would cool her down a little. She longed for a shower, but water running through the old pipes would wake up everyone in the house. Working with extreme care, she got ice and the lemonade pitcher out of the refrigerator with a minimum of noise and poured herself a tall glass of the chilled liquid.

Before taking a drink, she ran the icy tumbler across her forehead and down each cheek then placed it for a shivery moment in the moist valley between her breasts. Ahhh! She leaned against the counter and sipped the tart lemonade while she thought about the outing planned for the next day. Zach may have asked the girls along, but Diana felt very much as if she was going out on a date with a man. A sexy man.

Above her on the second floor, Zach heard the creak of her bedroom door. Straining to make out every noise, he identified the hum of the refrigerator when she opened it and the muffled clink of ice. She was trying to be very quiet, which meant she didn't want company.

And if he knew what was good for him, he wouldn't give her any. What was she drinking? Surely not liquor. He suspected there wasn't a drop in the house. Probably lemonade. He pictured her rosebud mouth at the rim of the glass, her slender fingers curved around the welcome chill of it.

He even knew what she was wearing, because he'd helped to fold the laundry one day. The cotton garment was damn near transparent, but he could hardly blame her for wanting to be cool. Didn't he sleep with nothing on? His mouth grew dry, and sweat beaded his forehead. A glass of lemonade would taste pretty good right now.

He didn't remember making the decision to go down, but he was suddenly pulling on nylon running shorts. Dammit, he was paying rent! If he wanted a glass of lemonade in the middle of this sweltering night, he would get himself a glass of lemonade. If Diana didn't like it, she could hustle her little behind back to bed, with her guard dog, Beethoven.

Diana heard the bedroom door squeak; she froze. Maybe he was headed for the bathroom. Then a stair groaned under his weight, and she knew he was on his way. She could run back to her room and hide with her half-full glass, or she could stay and brave it out. She stood her ground. Whose house was this, anyway?

"Any left for me?" His shadowy figure loomed in the kitchen doorway.

"Help yourself." As he walked past her, Diana heard the rustle of his nylon running shorts, but she could tell from the vague outline of his body that he wore nothing else. His broad back gleamed, looking smooth and powerful in the faint light from the stars outside the window.

"Couldn't sleep. Too hot. And there's a damn mosquito that keeps whining in my ear."

"You ought to turn on the light and kill it, or you'll be covered with bites in the morning."

He laughed. "I think I've already got one on my rear end." He took a glass from the cupboard.

"That's what you get for sleeping in the altogether."

She wondered if he deliberately turned to look at her when he opened the refrigerator door. She was standing right in the middle of the shaft of light, and she blinked at the glare.

"Not much difference between that and what you've got on."

"It's hot," she said defensively.

"You're telling me." He took out the lemonade pitcher and closed the door. "Need a refill?"

"No, thank you. In fact—" she paused to drain her glass "—I think I'll toddle on to bed now."

"Uh, Diana?" He poured the lemonade then glanced in her direction.

"Yes?"

"I forgot to ask Al to rewind my bandages. Could you possibly...?"

"I thought you were taking it off tomorrow," she hedged, reluctant to move closer and touch him. "Does it matter?"

"Maybe not. I just thought—"

She decided her cowardice was silly. "Okay. Sit down at the table."

He obeyed. "Do you need the light?"

"No. My eyes are adjusted to the dark."

He placed his bandaged arm on the table, and she pulled up a chair and sat down. "I guess after the fair you'll be able to start painting again." She unfastened the metal clip, and he lifted his arm so that she could unwind the bandage.

"Should be able to." His fingers were within five inches of the thin material covering her breasts. He concentrated on keeping his hand from shaking. She smelled moist and fragrant, like a watered pot of violets, and he decided he was a masochist to be down here, so near to her.

"Do you think your wrist is healed?" Diana unwound the last of the bandage, and he lowered his hand, palm up, fingers curled slightly, in front of her. She stared at it in fascination as her imagination placed those quiet fingers against her skin, stroking, arousing...

"I think it's healed."

"Good." She placed the end of the bandage in his palm, held it there and began rewinding the elasticized strip over his thumb and back up his wrist. It took all the control she had to keep her hands steady. She thought his breathing became more rapid, and then he leaned back nonchalantly in the chair, as if her touch meant nothing to him.

"Diana, stop me if you'd rather not discuss this, but why didn't you and the girls go to the fair last year? I can imagine the reason, but I need to know if any time bombs will go off while we're there. Does it have to do with Jim?''

"Yes. His death was only a few weeks before the fair. He was a tractor salesman, and the fair was a big deal for his company. They always have a large display and the annual tractor pull. I—we—thought it would be too much for us." She finished winding the bandage and picked up the metal clip.

"I figured that, and I've been a little concerned. The girls seem to be looking forward to tomorrow, but I wondered if you'll be all right." His soft murmuring voice seemed to caress her bare skin, and her heart began to thump crazily.

She began fastening the clip over the bandage. "I think so."

His free hand, cool from grasping the lemonade glass, covered hers as he leaned forward again. "Are you sure? I really want you to go, but I'll be glad to take the girls, if you'd rather stay home."

"Thank you, but I'll be fine." Her hand tingled under his, but she chose not to pull it away. The pressure of his hand on hers felt so right, so good.

"I'm glad to hear it." His thumb caressed the back of her hand. "I don't want to step on memories, Diana."

"You're not." She heard the breathless note in her voice. *Leave, Diana. Leave now.*

"We made it through another week." His hand lifted and brushed lightly up and down her forearm. She watched its path in trembling fascination. She should make him stop. She really should. "How're you holding up?"

"I—okay."

"I'm going crazy."

She glanced up at his shadowed face, and even in the

dim light she could see the intensity there. "Me, too," she admitted in a whisper.

"Diana—" He rose from his chair and pulled her up with him.

"Zach, we mustn't—"

One step brought him around the corner of the table, and his arms folded her against his lean body. "For God's sake, Diana," he muttered, just before his lips crushed down on hers.

6

DIANA'S GASP was swallowed by Zach's forceful kiss, and then there was no turning back. He'd made the decision for both of them, and with a grateful moan Diana wrapped her arms around his strong neck and opened her mouth to his determined invasion.

She reveled in the restrained strength of the muscular arms that held her tight, but not so tight that she couldn't move. And to move was ecstasy, as the hard muscles of his strong body imprinted themselves against her. The thin cotton of her nightgown and the sleek nylon of his running shorts might have been nothing at all, so aware was she of every inch of his lean torso, of the desire thrusting toward her.

Boldly Zach slipped both hands beneath the cotton hem of her nightgown and stroked up her rib cage. Beyond rational thought, she leaned back to allow his fevered touch on her aching breasts, and the bandage across his right palm grazed her nipple as he caressed her. She began to shiver uncontrollably as the sensuous massage continued.

Zach lifted his head, and his breath came in ragged spurts. "Now, Diana? Can we stop this nonsense and enjoy each other? Have we suffered enough?"

Through a haze of passion she gazed at the dim contours of his face. Her body waited, damp and ready. She couldn't remember ever wanting anything as much as she wanted this man to fill her, to take away the horrible ache of emptiness deep inside. But her throat closed over the words.

"You aren't going to say it, are you?" he accused hoarsely. "Dammit!" He dropped his arms and backed away. "Damn that prudish Midwestern mentality of yours. You wouldn't stop me if I made love to you in that bedroom, but you'd sure as hell blame me afterward."

Her voice shook. "Do you care?"

He walked away from her and gripped the back of a kitchen chair. Even in the dim light she could see the whitening of his knuckles. "I wish to hell I didn't. I wish I could go into that bedroom with you right now and get rid of all my frustrations—yours, too, by the way—and then turn a deaf ear to your recriminations."

Diana swallowed hard, and tears misted her eyes. "I wouldn't let you shoulder all the blame."

"Blame?" He whirled back toward her. "There shouldn't be any blame. What kind of word is that? I'll tell you what kind. Blame is a judgmental word that implies wrongdoing. I don't happen to think our making love would be wrong, but obviously you do."

She wrapped her arms closely around her body as alternate waves of hot and cold washed over her. "In these circumstances, yes."

"If it weren't for those girls, I'd pack my bags tonight."

"Go ahead. I'll take care of the girls. I always have."

"No. I promised them the fair, and they'll have their wonderful day." He ran trembling fingers through his sandy-colored hair. "After that, I don't know." He glanced over at her. "Life could be so easy, Diana, if you'd turn loose from that outdated thinking."

"Outdated by whose standards?" she challenged in an unsteady voice. "Let's suppose we became lovers. At first perhaps we'd be careful to return to our separate beds before morning. But one night both of us would fall asleep."

"No."

"It's bound to happen, Zach. And then we'd come out of the room together, in front of Allison and Laurie."

"Let's suppose you're right. Are you sure they couldn't handle it?"

"You've been around those girls enough, Zach. Think about their level of sophistication. Think about them, for a change, instead of our needs. They're not ready for a mother with lovers."

"Lover," he corrected automatically.

"Oh? After you leave town you'll demand that I go back to my celibate state? Why should I? The girls will be properly broken in, and I can carry on like *The Merry Widow!*"

"Stop it, Diana." The idea of a string of men in her life following his departure put him into an unreasonable rage, but he couldn't help how he felt.

"Stop what?" she said, perversely goading him further. "I don't think you're following this situation to its inevitable conclusion, Zach. Once you take me to bed, you can't control the chain of events that will be set in motion. You won't be here, anyway, so why be upset?"

His hands curled into fists that desperately wanted to punch someone. Making love to Diana was one thing. Being first in a parade, starting some sort of chain reaction, was something else again. What had begun as straightforward lust had turned into a jumble of confusing emotions.

His voice came out in a frustrated growl. "Well, I'm not taking you to bed, so we can drop the subject. Good night."

Zach stomped past her and up the stairs with such vehemence that she worried the girls might wake up. But the house was quiet as she sank back against the clammy sheets in her lonely bedroom. She lay staring at the ceiling as if her eyes could bore a hole through the old wood and provide a view of what Zach was doing. Eventually his steady tread back and forth told her. He was pacing away his thwarted desire. Diana tossed restlessly and wondered much later, when the pacing had stopped, if she'd have been wiser to follow his example.

With the first glow of dawn came pulsing drumbeats from both the girls' radios. Diana groaned and pulled the pillow over her head. She didn't remember sleeping at all, but she must have drifted off in the early morning hours after Zach had stopped pacing above her head. How could she face him this morning, let alone spend the day with him?

She lay listening to the girls scurrying around upstairs to the beat of their music. Their excited giggling filled her with remorse. Why hadn't she left the kitchen last night before the inevitable had happened? She'd tempted fate and Zach, and only she could be blamed for what had followed. Blame. There was that word again.

But she felt responsible for the kiss. More than a kiss, she admitted, flushing at the memory of Zach's strong hands kneading the heated skin of her breasts. She'd let down the barriers to passion, and because she had, she dreaded the day that was to have been such a treat for all of them.

Above her Allison pounded on Zach's door. "Wake up, sleepyhead. Today's fair day!" she chortled before bounding down the stairs.

Diana sat up and threw the pillow to the far side of the room. Last night wouldn't ruin Allison and Laurie's outing, she vowed, swinging her legs over the edge of the bed. She'd paste a smile on her face and make sure the girls had the time of their lives. With renewed determination she marched into her bathroom to get ready for the day ahead.

"WHERE TO FIRST?" Zach asked as they stood inside the admission gate.

Allison and Laurie began chattering at once.

"Hold it," Zach said, raising both hands. "One at a time."

Diana stood slightly apart from the threesome and watched Zach. To his credit, he appeared as relaxed and carefree in front of the girls as before. She could almost believe she had imagined last night's kitchen scene, except for the look in his blue eyes when he had first seen her that morning. His gaze had swept over her flowered sundress hungrily, touching the swell of her breasts and the curve of her hips under the summery material.

"Better wear sunscreen on those shoulders," he had said casually, but his eyes had been bright with the recently gained knowledge of her body. Innocence was gone forever.

But here amid the sun-splashed color of the fairgrounds, the dark secrets of last night lost some of their potency. Diana smiled at her daughters' enthusiasm.

"Happy Hollow! Happy Hollow!" Allison chanted, jumping up and down.

"Not yet, bimbo," Laurie said. "We're on a budget, don't forget. If you blow your money on rides first thing, what will you do tonight?"

"I dunno."

"Laurie's right," Zach said, putting an arm around Allison and hugging away her scowl as Laurie preened in triumph. "Besides, I've been on carnival rides before. I want to see the other stuff—the animals and handmade quilts, huge tomatoes—all that."

"Laurie and I know some kids in 4-H," Allison offered. "Let's go over there."

"Sounds good," Zach said. "Okay with you, Diana?"

"Fine." She gave him a grateful smile. He really was terrific with the girls. He'd make a wonderful fa—Good God, what was she thinking? Oh, sure, Zach would be glad to give up his dream of a professorship at Stanford to live in dull little Springfield with a ready-made family. He'd turn in his surfboard and swinging life-style in a minute. Hah!

"Wait!" Laurie called as they began walking in the direction of the building where the 4-H exhibits were housed. "Let me comb my hair, if we're going to see people we know."

"Laurie Thatcher, I'm going to stick your head in a threshing machine!" Allison put her hands on her hips and glared as her sister took a long-handled comb from the back pocket of her shorts and ran it methodically through her dark hair.

"Hey, Al," Zach teased, "don't forget what I said about changes. You may have a comb stuck in your back pocket one of these days."

"Never." Allison made a face and bounded several paces ahead of them, while Laurie hung behind to check her hair-combing job in the reflection of a refreshment-stand window.

Zach reached over and took Diana's hand as they walked. "'Never,'" he said with a chuckle. "How easily kids say that word."

She couldn't decide how to react to his matter-of-fact gesture. Pulling her hand away would focus unwanted attention on what he'd done, but his touch was bringing back all the tumultuous emotions of the night before. She glanced up at him, a question in her silver eyes.

He gave her a quizzical smile. "I think hand-holding's allowed, don't you?" he said in a low voice only she could hear.

"I guess so."

"You look wonderful today, even with those little purple smudges under your eyes."

"You're not still angry?"

"I tried to be, but then I realized you're only doing what you think is best for your children. How can I be angry about that?"

"I shouldn't have stayed in the kitchen last night."

"I shouldn't have come down." He laced his fingers more firmly through hers. "Let's try to put last night aside and have fun today. We'll pretend we're high school kids on our first date."

Diana smiled at the whimsy of his idea. "Okay."

"That's my girl." He squeezed her hand. "Chickens, pigs and cows, here we come!"

Diana enjoyed this year's livestock displays more than she could remember enjoying any other year's, simply because Zach was so fascinated with everything. They watched milking contests and sheep judging, walked along endless rows of rabbit cages and goat pens. Laurie forgot to complain about the smell, and Allison laughed with delight every time Zach exclaimed over a new wonder.

"Little chicks are coming out those eggs!" he pronounced as they passed a large incubator. "Come here, Diana. Just look at this."

"Mom, they're selling the chicks," Allison said eagerly. "Only fifty cents. Look at those ones with the curly feathers!"

"Aw, Mom. They're darling," cooed Laurie. "Couldn't we each have one?"

"Chickens?" Diana raised her eyebrows. "They're cute now, but they'll grow into big birds in no time. Where would we keep them?"

"Zach will build us a pen," Allison announced confidently. "Won't you, Zach? And I'll help."

"Uh, I don't know if chickens are a good idea, Al. Beethoven would go crazy."

"Then you put the pen up on stilts," Laurie said, warming to the idea. "The chickens will pay for themselves, Mom. They'll lay eggs. You won't have to buy eggs anymore."

"No, we'll have to buy whatever it is they eat." Diana looked skeptical.

"Chicken feed?" Zach contributed helpfully.

Diana glared at him. "Right."

"Please, Mom," Allison begged. "Laurie and I have never had a pet of our very own. Beethoven belongs to the whole family, but Laurie and I have never had a goldfish or a turtle or anything that was just ours. Couldn't we have these cute little chicks?"

Diana glanced questioningly at Zach, and he shrugged. "Well…"

"Allison and I will take complete care of them, Mom," Laurie said.

"Sure you will." Diana looked heavenward.

"Really! You won't have to do a thing. We'll even pay you back whatever the wire and boards for the pen cost from our allowance."

"Yeah," Allison agreed. "And Zach and I will build the pen, right, Zach?"

"If you say so, Al." He studied the structures around

him more carefully. Looked simple enough. A little chicken wire, a little lumber, a few nails—what the heck?

"Well...okay," Diana said reluctantly, and the girls cheered loudly. "But we can't carry two baby chicks around for the rest of the day. We'll have to come back for them before we go home."

"That's okay!" Allison said immediately, grinning at her sister. "Thanks, guys."

"Yeah, thanks," Laurie said, breaking her usual reserve to hug first Diana and then Zach. Allison followed suit. Quickly they picked the two chicks they wanted, and the woman supervising the incubator separated them from the others.

"They're called frizzled Cochins, girls," the woman told them.

"And frizzled they'll be if Beethoven gets ahold of them," Diana said as they walked away from the incubator.

"He won't," Allison insisted. "Zach and I will build the greatest cage in the world. What shall we name them?"

Laurie took her comb from her back pocket and ran it through her hair. "We've got Beethoven. How about Mozart and Chopin?"

"Freaky idea, Laurie," Allison said.

Diana stared at her younger daughter. *Freaky idea?* Allison had actually complimented her sister and hadn't even mentioned the fact that Laurie was combing her hair again.

"Thanks." Laurie smiled at Allison. "Those chicks will be fun. I'm going to teach mine to eat out of my hand."

"Me, too. Say, wanna go hear that rock band that's supposed to be playing now?"

"Sure, why not?" Laurie replied then turned to Zach and Diana. "You guys want to come?"

"We'll take a rain check," Zach said. "Meet you back at this spot in an hour, okay?"

"Okay!" The girls exchanged a look of delight and hurried toward the sound of rhythmic drums.

"I think I may faint dead away," Diana remarked as they disappeared into the crowd. "They acted as if they liked each other."

"It's going to get better. Allison may not realize it, but she's growing up."

"I noticed the other day she's almost as tall as Laurie."

"Who is almost as tall as her mother."

"Tell me about it." Diana laughed. "She borrows my clothes all the time. Although it seems like yesterday that Allison and Laurie were like those little girls over there, holding on to my hand for dear life." Diana watched the toddlers wistfully.

"And this morning they were squabbling over who got the eye shadow first."

"Allison has on eye shadow today? You're kidding." Diana's uneasiness increased. Her girls were growing up faster than she'd thought.

"Would I kid about an important development like that? She put it on real light. I don't think she wanted us to see it."

Diana looked into his blue eyes, warm with a combination of understanding and amusement, and she realized how nice it was to have him around. "Thanks for today," she said simply.

"You're most welcome."

"I'm having a great time."

"Me, too." He gazed down at her smiling face and thought that he'd never had a better time in his life. He seemed to have known Diana forever, and tonight it would be as natural as rain to drive home, say good-night to the girls and walk arm in arm with Diana into their shared bedroom. If only the situation were that uncomplicated. "Come on," he said, grabbing her hand. "Let's have our fortunes told."

Diana laughed. "Don't tell me you believe those things. Now they tell fortunes by computer."

"Sure, I believe them. Haven't you ever noticed that everything they say about you is positive? I figure we need all the good news we can get."

"That's one way to look at it." She walked jauntily beside him, feeling freer than she had since Jim had died. Jim. He hadn't crossed her mind until now. Carefully she probed the memory, gauging how much the thought of Jim bothered her right now. The sadness was still there, would always be there, but the sharp pain that that plagued her for many months was gone. And she knew why. Zachary Wainwright.

"Okay, here we are. Stick your hand in there, and the mysterious El Computero will read your palm," Zach directed.

"What a riot." Diana followed his directions; the machine buzzed, then her fortune came rolling out of a dot matrix printer. "The modern age."

Zach handed the required amount of money to the turbaned woman behind the machine. "What's it say?" he asked, leaning over Diana's shoulder.

She folded the paper to conceal the message. "That I'll live a long and happy life."

"That's it?"

"Just about."

"What do you mean by 'just about,' Diana?" He made a playful grab for the paper, and she held it out of reach.

"You get yours done, then I'll decide whether you can read mine."

"Fair enough." He held his wide palm under the machine, and seconds later his fortune spewed from the printer. "Okay. Mine says—" he paused to clear his throat dramatically "'—Your scholarly ambition is great and you will succeed in matters of intellect. However, practical tasks are not your—'"

"Not your what?" Diana urged, catching his arm.

"Never mind."

"Never mind? You practically dragged my fortune away from me, and you have the nerve to say never mind?" Diana flashed him a devilish grin. "Give it here!"

He held the paper over his head. "You promise to trade?"

Diana thought of the words typed on her printout. Dangerous words. But her curiosity got the best of her. "I promise."

"Okay. Here." He handed her the piece of paper.

"Let me see. 'Practical tasks are not your strong suit.' Zach, shame on you. You're a fraud."

Her smile twinkled at him, and he knew she was kidding, but he couldn't let her go on thinking he was a true maintenance man. She meant too much to him now.

"That's right, Diana. I am."

Her expression became puzzled. "What?"

"I am a fraud. I'm not an accomplished handyman."

"I never said you had to be a professional. Someone to do little odd jobs, that's all."

"I know, and I thought odd jobs would be no problem. But the truth is, I've never painted a house or fixed a sink or rebuilt a fence."

She stared at him in disbelief. "Just what can you do?" A wry smile twisted his mouth, and she colored. "I mean, besides that!"

"I'm a very good teacher and an excellent researcher."

"But you repaired that fan!"

"No. I paid to have it done."

"You paid someone? Then let me believe that you—" She faced him, hands on her hips. "Zachary Wainwright, that's sneaky and despicable and dishonest and—"

"Hold it." He raised one hand. "I never said I'd personally fix that fan. I've taken on the responsibility for whatever jobs you have, and they will be done. Furthermore, I have been a help to you, perhaps in ways you might not realize at the moment."

Diana stood in the middle of the milling crowd, under the bright lights of the commercial exhibits, and stared at him. Had she always suspected he wasn't quite the handyman she had hired him to be? "I should put you out on your ear. I gave you a break on the rent because I thought you could be of some real use."

"I think I have been," he said softly.

Her gaze took in his ocean-blue eyes, his muscled chest under a faded blue T-shirt, the cutoff shorts that showed off his tanned thighs. She never tired of looking at him. Then she thought of the happiness that now pervaded a household that had once struggled to escape the gloom of tragedy. True, he presented a problem to her sense of virtue, but even that made her feel more alive than she had felt in months. Maybe in years.

"Yes," she said slowly, "I guess you have been."

"I want to stay, Diana."

"But what about all the work that needs to be done around the house? Despite what you say, I don't see how you'll manage."

"Let me worry about it. I'll read books, talk to the guys at the hardware store. I'm willing to learn."

"This is ridiculous. A handyman who isn't handy. I should have my head examined."

His smile was contagious. "I think I'm handy, in my own way. Fixing the sink isn't everything."

She chuckled. "No, it certainly isn't. But when I placed the ad in the paper, that's what I wanted, a fix-it man for the house."

"Maybe."

"What do you mean by that?"

"I have a theory about that ad, but we'll save it for later. I want to read your fortune."

Silently she handed him the folded printout.

Zach opened the paper and began to read. "'You will have a long life filled with creativity and happiness, provided you choose a mate who understands the basic sensuality of your nature.'" He looked up and found she'd wandered to a display several yards away. In four quick strides, he was beside her. "Didn't want to face the music, huh?"

"That's right."

"I had to deal with my fortune; you can take yours like the trooper I know you are."

She picked up a brochure on water softeners and flipped through it. "It's just a silly gimmick, Zach. Those printouts don't mean anything."

"It came pretty close with me."

"Your fortune could apply to a million people."

"And probably does," he assented mildly. "And yours could apply to a million people, too. It also fits Diana Thatcher perfectly." He took her by the shoulders and turned her to face him. "Don't you agree?"

The color rose to her cheeks at his knowing smile. "Just because of last night, you think—"

"Correction. Just because of last night I'm positive. But there are restrictions on us, and I'm not going to argue with them on this special day. Besides, we're on our first date, and a gentleman does not discuss making love on a first date. Instead he buys his sweetheart some cotton candy. Let's go." He tucked Diana's fortune in the pocket of his shorts and steered her toward the cotton candy machine.

"How do you know I want cotton candy?"

"Girls at carnivals always want cotton candy. There is something very feminine and sexy about nibbling pink globs of spun sugar, and girls know it."

She laughed, and the mood became one of fun again. By the time they met Allison and Laurie, both of them were sticky with cotton candy and laughing over a shared joke.

After a lunch of hot dogs the four of them toured the rest of the fair, except for the midway. Everything received rapt attention, everything but—by unspoken agreement—the tractor display. Zach thought to himself that in another year Diana and the girls might not be bothered by that, either. But of course he wouldn't be here to know. The realization didn't add much to his enjoyment of the day, and he pushed it aside.

Afternoon became soft evening. Colored lights blinked invitingly from Happy Hollow, where loud music competed with the screams of fair-goers whirling on the rides.

"At last, the really exciting part," Allison breathed as the four of them headed for the row of carnival games. At both girls' urging, Zach threw softballs at milk bottles until Allison and Laurie were holding button-eyed teddy bears.

"How about one for Mom?" Zach asked the girls. "Shall we try for one more?"

"Yes, yes!" they chorused.

"No," Diana said quietly. "I'm worried about your wrist, Zach."

"Oh, yeah," Allison said, a shadow of concern crossing

her young face. "Gee, I hope you didn't hurt it again with all that throwing."

"Nope. Feels great." Zach grinned and flexed his muscles then winked at Diana. "But your mother's right. I'd better take it easy this first day without the bandage. I've got houses to paint and chicken coops to build."

Allison gave him a big hug. "I'm so glad you're here, Zach."

Laurie added a shy "Me, too," and Zach reached over and rumpled her hair. "Hey, watch that!" she cried, but she was laughing.

Zach glanced over Allison's blond head and caught Diana's eye. "I'm glad I'm here, too," he said, gazing intently at her. "Very glad."

"Let's go on the roller coaster," Allison suggested, pulling at Zach's hand.

Zach reached for Diana. "Only if I can get this pretty lady to go along."

"The roller coaster?" Diana echoed in a protesting voice. "You can take the girls."

"That's what I plan to do—all three of them. Come on, Diana. Put some adventure in your life."

She chuckled and allowed herself to be pulled toward the ticket booth. "I do believe I have."

Through the daredevil thrills of the roller coaster and the giant octopus ride and the rocket ships, Zach held her tight as they both screamed with the abandon of children. Diana couldn't decide if her heart was racing more from the spinning rides or the intoxicating feel of Zach's strong arm around her. At times she felt as though she were seventeen again, just as he had suggested they pretend they were, but at the end of each ride, when she looked into the darkened depths of his blue eyes, a woman's desire rose in her.

"And last but not least, the Ferris wheel," he announced, once their string of tickets had dwindled.

"Naw, Allison and I want to ride the roller coaster again," Laurie said.

"That's okay," Zach said. "Which do you want, Diana?"

"Ferris wheel," she decided. "When I was younger, I loved the view."

Zach rolled his eyes. "Do you think someone as old as you might still like it?"

Allison sighed. "There she goes again, sounding like she's over the hill."

"I do not. I realize I'm no kid, that's all." Diana folded her arms defensively.

"We'll work on her attitude, Al," Zach promised. "She'll be thinking young in no time. Why don't you and Laurie take off for the roller coaster and meet us back here? I'll help your tottering mother on to the Ferris wheel."

"Great!" Laurie said. "Let's go, Al."

Diana turned to Zach. "*Al?*"

He shrugged. "Maybe Laurie's losing some of her prim and proper ways."

"Meaning I should, too?"

"I didn't say that."

"No, but you were thinking it. Somebody's got to be the responsible one around here, Zach."

"Then let's trade off. Right now I'm responsible for giving you a lovely ride on the Ferris wheel. So relax." They stepped to an open car, and the attendant locked them into the swaying seat. Zach curved his arm around her smooth shoulders and pulled her close.

Her body sang at his now-familiar touch, but her mind

wouldn't let go of their problems. "Zach, you insist on making complicated situations seem simple."

"And you insist on making simple situations complicated." The huge wheel turned, sending them up a few feet off the ground. "Let's get back to being high school kids on a first date. By this point in the evening, you should be putting your head on my shoulder."

"That's protocol?"

"You bet."

"If you say so." She tucked her head into the hollow at his neck. "I can hear your heart beating."

"It's a wonder the noise isn't driving you crazy." He turned his head, and his lips brushed her forehead. "Your hair is incredibly soft. Do you wash it in rainwater or something?"

She chuckled. "No. In the shower. Another romantic fantasy bites the dust." The wheel carried them higher and higher as passengers loaded below them.

"Only to be replaced by a new fantasy—you washing your hair in the shower."

"I don't think a high school boy would say that on a first date."

"Probably not. And if he did, your proper response would be to slap him and move away."

"Do you want me to do that?"

His arm tightened around her. "Nope."

The wheel turned once more, and they were swaying at the top of the wheel. "Oh, Zach. How beautiful."

His free hand tipped her chin up, and he gazed deeply into her silver eyes. "Yes. The most beautiful thing I've ever seen."

"Is this protocol, too?" she murmured, knowing what he intended.

"Absolutely." His lips brushed gently against hers, and

her sigh of assent mingled with his soft groan of desire. But the kiss remained sweet, while the passion they both held in check made them tremble with longing.

ZACH DIPPED HIS PAINTBRUSH into the can of creamy liquid suspended beside him and applied a wavering line of white to the windowsill. He welcomed this intensely physical work that left him exhausted at the end of the day. After mornings spent in his room or the library, he set up the ladder and painted with the dedication of Michelangelo. And with the skill of Dumbo, he thought with a grimace as a glob of paint landed on his sneaker.

But at least by evening he barely had the strength to hold his fork at the dinner table, and sleep came early and easily now that the humid summer heat was relaxing its hold on Springfield. His dreams weren't as easily controlled, but he couldn't be thrown out of the house for those.

Through the half-open window he heard the loud bleats of the Bad News Brass, and he smiled as he pictured Diana patiently directing the trio of boys. She had on a lacy white blouse today, an ultrafeminine sexy-looking concoction. Watching her drove him wild—her delicacy and refinement combined with an inner fire to create the most irresistible creature he'd ever known.

Like Zach she worked frantically these days, and they rarely talked. Whenever she wasn't teaching music, she was compulsively cleaning house or shopping for Allison and Laurie's school clothes.

School. It was to start tomorrow, and how in heaven

would he and Diana manage to keep away from each other with the girls out of the house every day for several hours? He was no saint—she'd been warned about that already. The logical answer was for him to move out, but he resisted taking such a drastic step.

Zach knew rationally that he and Diana could not live forever with the arrangement they had, but other than moving, no easy answers occurred to him. Diana was right about the girls. An obvious sexual liaison would embarrass them, and he didn't want to hurt Laurie and Allison any more than Diana did. But God, how her silver eyes haunted him, how her ripe woman's body beckoned whenever they were in the same room. He'd known the mindless delirium of touching her milk-white skin, and he couldn't forget.

The paintbrush trembled in his hand as he relived for the hundredth time their brief moment in the darkened kitchen, and he smeared his line of paint onto the pane of glass. Swearing with restrained fury in case either of the girls were within earshot, he reached for the paint rag. Tomorrow he'd spend the entire day in the library. Maybe he'd have to spend every day in the library or risk being alone in a quiet house with his lovely Diana—a situation neither of them was strong enough to handle.

With a heartfelt sigh Zach dipped his brush into the white paint once more.

AT BREAKFAST THE NEXT DAY, the girls gulped their food and fiddled with their new clothes.

"I'm finally going to Washington Middle School," Allison said with a triumphant sigh.

"Best middle school in town," Laurie boasted. "Maybe in the whole state. The whole country, probably."

"Yeah. I wouldn't go to another school for anything.

Tammy's parents told her they might be moving. Boy, is she unlucky."

"I wouldn't go," Laurie declared darkly. "I'd run away or something."

Diana listened with understanding. Since Jim's death the girls had clung to the things in their life that hadn't changed—school and friends. In many ways she envied them their scheduled activities. Especially today.

To avoid being alone with Zach, Diana had planned a shopping trip, lunch with a friend and an appointment with the hairdresser after that. Zach cooperated by announcing he'd be at the library until late in the afternoon. Silently they communicated across the breakfast table: one day at a time.

Diana coordinated her return home with the end of school. Listening to Allison and Laurie's accounts of the first day was timeworn tradition, and once the girls were back in the house, the danger of being alone with Zach would be gone. Gone, that is, until the next day.

Allison breezed through the front door first. "Hi, Mom. What can I eat?"

"Fruit. How was your first day?"

"Freaky. No cookies?"

"Fruit."

"I'll just have milk. I've got all good teachers except Mr. Dudley, and does he have the right name. A real dud." Allison opened the refrigerator.

"Maybe he'll improve."

"No chance. He sat us alphabetically, which put me right behind that doofo-brain George. All the good kids are on the other side of the room. Why does my last name have to start with *T*?"

"Lousy luck of the draw, I guess. Who sits across the room?"

"Oh, Sharon, and Lesli." Allison poured her milk. "And Ted," she added, talking into the open refrigerator as she replaced the milk carton.

"Ted?" Diana struggled to keep a straight face. Allison had never included a boy in her list of "the good kids."

"Yeah. He's new. Mom, do you think I'd look better with a different haircut?"

"I don't know. Maybe," Diana replied casually. To register shock would not be appropriate.

"Tonight I might look at some of Laurie's magazines. Get some ideas. Is Zach home?"

"Not yet. Did you see Laurie on the bus?"

"Yeah." Wariness flickered in her eyes, and she abruptly changed the subject. "Gotta put on my old clothes," she said, rising. "And get out the tools. Zach said we'd build the cage for Mozart and Chopin this afternoon. They can't stay in that cardboard box much longer." She finished her milk and ran up the stairs. In no time she bounded back through the kitchen, dressed in shorts and a T-shirt.

"Allison, your glass."

"Oh. Right." She snatched it from the table, gave it a cursory rinsing and disappeared out the back door.

Diana sat at the kitchen table, musing about Allison's remarks. Zach had been right. She was growing up. And what was the deal with Laurie and the bus? Had Allison been snubbed by Laurie's crowd? Diana hoped not. Then she pictured Allison and Zach struggling with their project this afternoon, and she almost laughed out loud. What sort of strange monstrosity of a chicken coop would she have in her backyard by nightfall?

The front door creaked open, and Laurie trudged through the living room and into the kitchen. She plopped her books on the table, and avoiding her mother's eyes, went to the cupboard for a glass.

"Laurie? Is something wrong?"

"No."

"Have a good first day?"

"It was fine." She opened the refrigerator and took out the milk.

"Any bad teachers?" Diana eyed her daughter with concern. Laurie was quieter than Allison, but usually not this much quieter, especially on the first day of school.

"No." She poured the milk with studious concentration then stood at the counter with her back to Diana.

Diana waited for a full minute, and when no more conversation seemed forthcoming, she voiced her primary fear. "Did Allison embarrass you on the bus?"

"No."

Diana gritted her teeth in frustration. She should give up this stupid parent's game of twenty questions, but she decided to venture one last sally. "Are you coming down with something?"

"I feel fine, Mom."

"You don't act fine, Laurie," Diana said, her exasperation showing in her voice. "Are we in some teenager mode where you refuse to talk to me?"

Laurie turned slowly and looked at her mother. "Jenny Caruthers is a bitch, that's all."

"Laurie!" Diana's eyes widened. "I've never heard you use that kind of language."

"It's the only word that fits." Laurie's eyes grew glassy with tears. "I wish I could punch her lights out!"

Diana was on her feet in an instant. "Laurie, my goodness!" She pried the glass from her daughter's clenched fingers. "What is it?"

Laurie brought both hands to her face and began to sob.

"I wasn't going to tell you!" she cried. "I promised myself I wouldn't, and now—"

Diana gathered her daughter close and rocked her back and forth as a thousand horrible possibilities flashed through her mind. "It's okay," she crooned mindlessly. "Everything's going to be fine, darling."

"It's only that I didn't know what to say," Laurie choked against her shoulder. "She made me so mad that I couldn't talk."

"Say about what?"

"You and Zach!"

Diana felt a cold fist close around her heart. "What—do you mean?"

"Jenny was asking all these questions." Laurie sniffed. "Asking if you two were married or just living together. In front of my other friends, too. She asked how I liked my mother's new boyfriend. She even wanted to know where he slept!"

"Laurie, I'm so sorry." Diana swallowed hard and held her daughter tighter.

"So am I, Laurie," said a deep baritone.

They broke apart and turned to see Zach standing in the kitchen doorway, his eyes filled with pain.

"The last thing I want is to hurt you, any of you," he continued, walking toward them. "If my presence is doing that, I'll have to leave."

"Oh, no, Zach." Laurie wiped her nose with the back of one hand. "I don't want you to leave."

The back door banged shut. "Leave?" cried Allison. "Did someone say Zach is going to leave? What's wrong with Laurie?"

"Someone said a few hurtful things to Laurie after school today," Diana explained.

"So what? What does dumb old Jenny have to do with

Zach leaving?" Allison said, the pitch of her voice rising rapidly.

Laurie looked at her sister. "You heard her, didn't you? That means the whole bus heard her!"

"It seems I'm causing you all embarrassment," Zach said quietly.

"No! That's stupid." Allison grabbed his arm frantically. "You can't leave, because I need you to help me with the chickens and my homework and everything, and I—oh! I just knew this would happen!" She burst into tears.

"Allison." Zach drew her against him. "Don't cry. Nobody's going anywhere yet."

"Al! My name is Al, and don't you forget it," she said between choking sobs.

Diana took a deep breath, afraid that she, too, might break down at any moment. "Let's all sit down with a plate of cookies and talk this over."

Allison lifted her tearstained face. "We can have some? You said before we couldn't."

Diana smiled tremulously. "I know. Some situations call for cookies." She gave Laurie one last hug and walked to the ceramic cookie jar, where she filled a large plate with the batch she'd made during her frenzied attempts to keep busy.

"I'll get the milk," Zach offered.

They all sat down at their normal places, Zach and Diana across from each other and the girls at each end of the table.

Fortified with a large supply of her favorite peanut-butter treat, Allison began, "Okay, what's this business about Zach leaving?"

Diana searched for the right words. "Jenny—"

"Who is a complete nerd," Laurie added.

"Maybe so," Diana agreed. "Anyway, she made re-marks to Laurie suggesting that Zach and I were...that we..."

"That we were acting like married people, without be-ing married," Zach supplied gently.

"I know. She thinks you're sleeping together," Allison blurted out, her mouth full of cookie.

"Allison!" Laurie said sternly.

"But you're not!" Allison protested. "Why didn't you say that, Laurie? And while you were at it, why didn't you tell Supernerd Jenny to stick her big fat head in a—"

"Why didn't you? If you heard it, why weren't you the brave one to tell Jenny off?"

"You know I'm just a seventh grader," Allison pro-claimed hotly. "Seventh graders don't go around telling off eighth graders, now do they?"

"Take it easy, girls," Zach said gently, quelling their ar-gument with one glance. "The point is, Laurie's friends may not believe anything she says, especially if she gets mad about it. Looks like I've put all three of you in an awkward position, and it's time for me to move out."

"Not on your life," Allison said staunchly, reaching for another cookie. "You're staying. Laurie doesn't want you to leave, either. Didn't you say that, Laurie?"

"Yes."

"Besides," Allison continued, "if you move out, it'll look like those stupid girls were right, like you've got something to hide."

Zach smiled apologetically at Diana. "No-win situa-tion, huh? What do you think?"

"Allison has a point, but that doesn't mean you should stay if you're the least bit uncomfortable about the gossip. Jenny and her friends may have gotten the idea from their parents."

Zach shook his head. "I'm from out of town. Gossip doesn't bother me." He looked straight at Diana. "I'm more worried about you."

Silence descended over the table for several moments, and then Allison spoke again. "I don't know about Mom, but I want you to stay."

"So do I," added Laurie.

Diana met his concerned gaze with an uncertain expression. What if she and Zach had been sitting here today with guilty consciences? Jenny's accusations were false now, but how much longer would they remain that way?

"Diana?" Zach said softly, his blue eyes intent.

She clenched her hands together on the table. Now was her chance to remove the temptation of Zachary Wainwright forever. Regardless of what the girls said, if she asked him to leave, he would go. And she knew he would back the decision and keep the girls from blaming her.

She held his gaze unflinchingly, but her voice quavered. "I want you to stay."

A flame leapt to life in his blue eyes. "Thank you."

"Way to go, Mom," Allison said approvingly.

"And I'm going to tell that Jenny a thing or two about her dirty mind!" Laurie vowed. "Wait till I get through with her."

"Then it's settled," Allison proclaimed. "Come on, Zach. We've got a chicken coop to build."

After they left Diana stood at the kitchen sink, peeling potatoes and watching the Laurel and Hardy act that was Zach and Allison trying to build a cage for the chickens.

"Mom?" Laurie said, her mouth full of cookies.

"Yes?" Diana put down the peeler and turned toward the table. She'd forgotten Laurie was still sitting there.

"It's probably none of my business, but has Zach ever talked about—that is, do you think he would ever..."

"What, Laurie?"

"I wondered if he ever mentioned living in Springfield. Permanently."

"No."

Laurie sighed.

Diana picked up the potato peeler again. "He'll only be here until his research on Lincoln is finished, Laurie."

"I know that's the way it was planned, but I think he likes you a lot, Mom."

"Oh?"

"You should see the way he looks at you. Like Michael Douglas in *Romancing the Stone*. Hungry eyes."

"You're seeing far too many movies, young lady."

"Not compared to Jenny. She gets to see all the R-rated ones on their VCR."

"And how many have you watched at her house?"

"What am I supposed to do, Mom? Hide my eyes when I'm over there? Anyway, I probably won't go over to stupid Jenny's house anymore, anyway. And you're changing the subject. I say Zach likes you. *Really* likes you."

"I like him, too."

"Well, then, why don't you get married? That would solve everything!"

Diana concentrated on her potatoes and tried for the matter-of-fact tone of the anchorwoman on the six o'clock news. "For one thing, we may like each other, but we're not in love."

"I'm not so sure about that."

"Well, I am." *Lust, maybe, but not love. And you'll have to watch more than R-rated movies before you understand the distinction between the two.* "But there's another major reason we're not getting married."

"What's that?"

"He hasn't asked me."

"Give him time, Mom. I wouldn't be surprised if one day he popped the old question."

"And how would you feel about that?"

"Great! I think he's a neat guy. The four of us could be really happy here."

"Laurie, Zach will be living in California," Diana said with quiet emphasis, "and he'd expect his family to live there, too."

Laurie looked puzzled. "California?"

"That's right. Zach's dream is to become a professor at Stanford. That's why he's earning his doctorate." *Might as well squash this idea early*, Diana thought. "I take it you wouldn't want to live in California?"

"No way! I'm going to Lanphier High School, no matter what."

"Then I guess that takes care of all the questions, doesn't it?"

When Laurie didn't answer, Diana glanced over her shoulder at her daughter. Laurie sat staring morosely at her half-eaten cookie. Putting down the peeler for the second time, Diana walked to the table and put her arms around Laurie's slumped shoulders. "I'm sorry. I know how much you like Zach and wish he could stay around forever. But you can't get your hopes up. I probably need to have a talk with Allison, too."

"That's okay, Mom. I'll talk to her."

Diana was silent for a moment as she considered that Laurie probably could do a better job of explaining everything to Allison. The time had come when a wise mother stepped back and encouraged the alliance between her children to strengthen, as it seemed to be doing every day. When Zach left, the girls would need each other more than ever. "I'd appreciate your talking to her, Laurie. Thanks." She gave her daughter a smile and a hug.

In the backyard Zach sawed and pounded with a vengeance. If he'd doubted the true lay of the land before, he had a Triple A roadmap now. If their mother indulged in a sexual relationship without the benefit of marriage and lived blatantly in the same house with the man, Laurie and Allison would become social outcasts in their crowd at school. A distance of more than miles existed between Springfield and California.

Therefore, he could put up with the lure of Diana, knowing he couldn't have her, or he could remove himself from temptation by leaving the house. Was the tiger behind door number one or door number two? He swung the hammer viciously against the wood, and it split.

"Da—uh—doggone it," he said, glancing guiltily at Allison.

"That's okay, Zach," she said with a smile, adjusting her hold on the split board. "I've heard swear words before."

"Oh?"

"Yeah. You should have heard Mom the other day when the toilet broke down, and we had to hire a plumber."

Zach chuckled. "Turned the air blue, did she?"

Allison looked puzzled. "No, I don't think so. She doesn't like those bathroom sprays."

"It's an expression," Zach explained gently. "It means she swore a lot."

"Oh. Then I guess she turned the air dark blue."

"Your mother?" Zach grinned. "Such a lady, yet such a surprise sometimes."

"Yeah. That was the day she decided to advertise for a handyman. Boy, am I glad she did."

Zach looked away from the worship in Allison's eyes. How could he ever leave? When Allison got that puppy-dog look on her face, his heart melted. And Laurie, quiet sensitive Laurie, desperately needed the little words of encouragement he gave her every day. And his unwittingly provocative Diana. Whether she admitted the fact or not, she had come to depend on his presence to balance the family, even if he wasn't allowed to satisfy her inner cravings.

But what about him? Was he staying because of the needs of three people, regardless of his own preference? No, he answered honestly. The warmth of this family group gave him something he hadn't known he'd missed until now. He loved the sharing, the confusion, even the squabbles. Somehow he'd tolerate the restrictions on his sex life. Somehow.

WITHOUT DISCUSSING THE NEED TO DO SO, Diana and Zach concentrated with even more fervor on their work and chores around the house. On the day following the incident with Jenny, Laurie cornered her classmate and delivered her rebuttal. In the days that followed, the Thatcher dinner table became the scene for regular updates on the tentative rebuilding of Jenny and Laurie's friendship. Within a week Laurie came to the table with a big smile, obviously bursting with good new.

"You'll never guess what Jenny's having," she said with a grin of triumph.

"Here comes the Jenny report," Allison droned, winking at Zach.

"Be nice or I won't tell. And you'll shrivel up and die of curiosity. Then you won't be able to go, either."

"Go where?" Allison's expression became animated.

"Well..." Laurie paused for effect. "Jenny said today that she is having—"

Laurie's announcement was cut short by loud barking and squawking from the backyard.

"Mozart!" cried Allison, leaping up from her chair.

"Chopin!" Laurie echoed, racing after her sister.

Zach and Diana exchanged a look of alarm and followed the girls out the back door. The yard was strewn with enough frizzled feathers to stuff a good-sized pillow, and more were rapidly accumulating as the chickens alternately escaped and were pounced upon by Beethoven. The birds ran in crazed circles, while the cocker spaniel barked joyfully at finally getting to play with the creatures that until now had lived frustratingly out of reach. The chicken coop lay on its side, the door sprung open by the impact of its fall.

"Beethoven, no!" Allison lunged for the dog and managed to wrap her arms around his squirming body. "Bad dog!"

Laurie chased one chicken, while Zach and Diana tried to corner the other. Any progress the girls had made in taming the birds was lost as they fluttered and dodged away from the hands that reached for them.

"Al, take Beethoven into the house and bring us two bath towels," Zach directed. "Don't get pecked, Diana."

"Chopin's gone completely nutso!" Laurie wailed, making another grab for her pet.

"Wait, Laurie," Zach said. "Okay, here comes Al with the towels. You take one, and I'll take the other. Diana, you and Al herd them in our direction, and when they're within reach, we'll each throw towels over their bodies and pick them up."

"Okay," Diana agreed, circling behind the squawking chickens. "I don't know if I'll be much good at this."

"Just remember how Lassie did it in those old movies on TV, Mom," Allison suggested, creeping cautiously around in the other direction.

"Do I have to bark?" Diana said dryly, and Allison giggled.

After several attempts Laurie and Zach managed to blanket the chickens with the towels and carry the birds back to their cage. The door was refastened and the coop righted.

"That was a great trick," Allison said. "I thought you didn't know anything about chickens, Zach."

"I don't," he admitted. "One of my friends had a parrot, and that's how he caught it."

"I'm going to wring Beethoven's neck," Laurie said.

Zach studied the chicken coop. "Don't blame Beethoven. The supports for the cage weren't strong enough."

"Sure they were," Allison defended them both. "We did a super job, Zach."

"I'm afraid not." Zach sighed. "Look, you two may as well know something I've already confessed to your mother. I'm not very accomplished as a handyman."

Allison and Laurie exchanged glances, and then Laurie spoke. "We know that."

"You do?" He faced Diana. "You told them?"

"No, I didn't."

"Mom didn't have to tell us," Allison said. "We figured it out." She shrugged. "But we don't care."

"You don't?" Zach stared at them incredulously. "But if I'm not any good as a handyman, what use am I around here?"

Allison scraped the toe of her sneaker across the grass then glanced at him shyly. "We just like you. You're...you're fun. I mean, Laurie and I aren't really of any use, either, but I know Mom likes having us around. It's the same thing."

"No, it's not," Zach argued. "Your mother loves you. You're her children. I'm..." He trailed off in confusion and appealed silently to Diana for help. She just smiled mysteriously. He glanced again at the girls, and a funny lump rose in his throat. "Thanks, kids," he said gruffly and opened his arms.

Allison and Laurie ran to Zach and hugged him enthusiastically. Over the tops of their heads he looked at Diana, and the glow on her face reached something deep in his soul. If the girls hadn't been there, he would have wrapped his arms around her and kissed her senseless. He couldn't have prevented himself.

"Well," he said, releasing the girls, "what was the great announcement you had, Laurie?"

"Oh! I almost forgot. Jenny's invited both me and Allison to a slumber party this Friday night. Isn't that neat?"

8

DIANA GULPED. "That's—that's wonderful," she said, sneaking a glance in Zach's direction. He looked as if he'd been struck by lightning. They'd never considered the possibility that both girls might be gone overnight. Diana racked her brain for a similar circumstance and decided this hadn't ever happened before. Laurie's friends hadn't included Allison or vice versa.

Allison gazed at her sister in disbelief. "Jenny wants *me* to come?"

"Sure. Besides, I asked her if you could."

Allison's mouth dropped open. "You did?"

"Why not?"

"Uh, I dunno," Allison hedged, obviously afraid she might ruin the entire miracle.

"So then you're coming, right? That is, if Mom says we can go. Can we, Mom?"

Diana's mind whirled. "Next weekend? Let me see. I don't think we have any plans."

"Of course we don't have any plans, Mom," Laurie said dryly. "I mean, we don't exactly have an active social life."

Diana smiled distractedly. "True." And it was. After the first flurry of invitations following Jim's death, the calls came less and less frequently. She and the girls kept to themselves. Diana occasionally had lunch with some of the wives of the couples she and Jim had known, but that was about it. The world was not designed for single people, especially single parents.

"So we can go?" Laurie persisted.

"Yes, you can." Diana dared not look at Zach as a mixture of excitement and fear coursed through her. How would she handle this unexpected turn of events? Could she handle it?

"Wow! That's freaky!" Allison exclaimed, racing for the house. "Come on, Laurie," she called over her shoulder. "What's Jenny's number? We have to tell her right away we'll be there."

"I'll dial it," Laurie answered, running to catch up with her sister.

"Are we supposed to take sleeping bags or will a pillow be enough?" Allison's excited voice grew dimmer as the girls disappeared into the house. "I hope everybody brings tapes, and then we can..." The sound of her animated chatter faded away, leaving Zach and Diana alone in a deep well of silence.

Zach cleared his throat. "Allison sure is happy about being included."

Diana stared at the screen door that had banged shut behind the two girls. "Yes."

"Diana." His voice compelled her to turn and face him. "I'm not made of steel, and neither are you. How in hell will we—"

"We just will, that's all," she interrupted, not wanting to hear their dilemma stated out loud.

"You're going to stay in your room, and I'll stay in mine, for the entire night? Diana, I have enough trouble keeping my hands off you when the girls are here. My God, sometimes I imagine I can hear you breathing down there below me, and I think of that thin nightgown you wear and that ripe body under- neath——" He clenched his fists. "The girls are the only reason I've held back. If I know they're gone..." His blue eyes blazed with frustration.

"We can't sleep together, Zach, and chance ruining everything," Diana said, her shoulders tense.

"Or gaining everything," Zach said with deliberate emphasis. "Is this slumber party a gift to us? The girls would never have to suspect what had gone on while they were away."

"No, Zach, no!" Diana threw up both hands as if he'd physically threatened her and shook her head. "We can't risk it."

"Translate that to you won't risk it, Widow Thatcher. You'll play it safe, like you have all your life."

"We'd better get inside." She looked away from him. "Dinner is probably stone-cold."

"It's not the only thing that's stone-cold around here. How can you be worried about dinner instead of whether or not we'll make love?"

"Zach! The girls might hear you. Or Mrs. Eckstrom."

"And we certainly can't risk that, either," he said bitterly. "You're devoid of any sense of adventure, Diana. I'm amazed you hired me in the first place." He spun on his heels and strode into the house. The slamming screen door echoed like a shot through the quiet evening.

"So am I," Diana whispered.

WITH EACH DAY that brought them closer to Friday, Diana's inner conflict grew. A subtle change had taken place in Zach's behavior toward her. His previous frustration had been tempered by understanding, but Diana sensed that understanding was now in short supply. Zach would never force her into anything, she knew. But if he appeared in her bedroom, if he touched her even once, she'd be consumed by the passion that gripped her as surely as it did Zach. He wasn't the only one who listened for breathing in the night.

Still, Diana couldn't rid herself of the belief that one night of lovemaking, even if they could keep it secret from the girls, would be dangerous and volatile. A sexual union between her and Zach had the power to upset the delicate fabric of the relationships in the house. He was right. She was afraid to risk it. Perhaps she'd simply lock herself in her bedroom.

On Friday afternoon Diana heard Laurie and Allison bustling in the front door, and she waited for them to burst into the kitchen to look for her. Instead they headed immediately upstairs, murmuring intently.

Diana smiled to herself as she finished scrubbing the sink and dried her hands in preparation for her first music student. But her heart wrenched a little. The girls had been so absorbed in each other that neither of them had bothered to greet her. Diana welcomed the new sisterly closeness, but she couldn't escape the uneasy feeling that soon they wouldn't need her at all.

As she set up the music stands for the Bad News Brass, Diana considered for the first time the shape of her days once Allison and Laurie left home. In less than six years they both might be living in college dorms or sharing apartments with friends. And she would be...alone in this big house.

"Mom?" Laurie stood at the foot of the stairs. "Could you come here for a minute?"

Diana crossed the room. "Can't you find the other overnight case?"

"No, it's not that. We found both cases. It's Al. She's got the cramps."

"Allison?"

"Had to happen sometime, Mom," Laurie said with a little smile. "I was about this age, if you remember."

"But Allison's still so..." Diana clutched the newel post. Her baby? Her last baby?

"I think you'd better talk to her, Mom. She's furious."

At that news Diana's initial shock gave way to amusement. "I bet she is. Right before the big slumber party. It *is* rotten luck." She started up the stairs. "Is she in her room?"

"Uh-huh. I gave her the necessities, and I told her to take aspirin. The cramps will probably be gone by tonight, but she's still complaining that life's unfair."

Diana mounted the stairs and walked down the hall to Allison's room. She tapped on the door. "It's Mom."

"Door's open."

Allison lay on her bed curled into a ball with her face toward the wall. Diana stepped over the books and clothes littering the floor and sat on the edge of the unmade bed. "Laurie tells me you're not entirely happy with the turn of events."

"Who would be?" Allison continued to stare at the wall.

"In some families they throw a party when this happens. After all, today is very important to you. You're growing up." Diana stroked Allison's bright hair and felt a lump rising in her throat. Allison would become a beautiful woman, probably marry some terrific guy and have her own children, but she would never again be Diana's little girl.

"Phooey on growing up," Allison mumbled. "I only wanted to get my hair cut. Try out some of Laurie's makeup. I didn't want *this*."

"Well, Allison," Diana said with a smile in her voice, "some things can't be controlled in this world, and you've just discovered one of them. Besides, now you'll really fit in with Laurie's friends. I remember last year they had a big contest to see who would be first."

"They did? That's dumb."

Diana put her hand on her daughter's hunched shoulder. "Allison, it's not so bad," she said softly. "You're very lucky to be a woman. Women can have children. And if you do, I hope he or she brings you as much joy as you've brought me."

Allison lay very still and then in one wild motion she flopped over and threw herself into her mother's arms and held on tight. "I love you, Mom."

"I love you, too, honey." Diana rested her cheek against Allison's hair and prayed for the strength not to cry.

"I just don't feel ready to grow up."

"I know. But everything doesn't have to change. You're still allowed to watch cartoons on Saturday morning and play Monopoly until you drop."

She glanced up, a mischievous gleam in her blue eyes. "And tease Laurie?"

Diana laughed. "I assume from that crack that you're feeling better."

"Yeah. Thanks." Allison smiled and wriggled out of her mother's arms. "Think I'll practice my drums until it's time to go."

"And *I* think I'll close your door," Diana said, rising and walking out of the room. An energetic beat followed her down the hall, and she knew Allison had decided to accept her fate with typical bouncy optimism. Diana smiled. Allison's sunny outlook on life did bring joy to the house. But Allison wouldn't always live here.

For the next half hour Allison's drum practice, Laurie's radio and the Bad News Brass filled the air with noise. For the first time Diana realized how much she cherished the racket and how empty her life would be without it. Before, she'd been so immersed in raising the girls that she'd taken one year at a time, like a hurdler in a race. Today, unexpectedly, the finish line had appeared on the horizon.

One of these days she'd be middle-aged, a quiet music teacher living alone in an old house in a respectable community. She'd fix Sunday dinner for her daughters and their families. She'd work on charity drives. She'd—

"Excuse me, boys," Diana blurted out, right in the middle of a measure. "I'll be back in a second." She raced into her bedroom while three pairs of eyes peered after her. The boys glanced at each other then grinned and passed around a pack of bubble gum.

Diana flipped on her bedroom light and studied herself in the dresser mirror. Tiny lines that had definite ambitions to become crow's feet spread faintly from the outer corners of the silvery eyes Zach had praised so much. She parted her hair, the dark cloudy mass that supposedly drove him crazy. There, just above her right temple, she found it. A gray hair.

Fumbling in a drawer for tweezers, Diana yanked the gray hair out by the root. "I'm not ready for this," she mumbled to her reflection, then made a face as she realized Allison had said the same thing not long ago. And what had been her wise and wonderful reply? "Some things can't be controlled in this world, and you've just discovered one of them."

"Bull," she muttered now, then returned to finish the boys' lesson.

Later, as she drove home from Jenny's house, Diana reached automatically to switch off the girls' rock station. Her hand stopped halfway to the knob then returned to the steering wheel. The music had a pounding beat and a suggestive lyric sung by a deep male voice. Diana wondered what Zach would think of the song. Zach. He hadn't come home by the time she'd left with the girls. Would he be there now?

He wasn't, and her crazy rock-music mood deflated immediately. Perhaps he'd decided to make life easier for both of them and found other quarters for the night. After what she'd said, could anyone blame him for avoiding the situation entirely?

The house was achingly quiet, and she tuned the aging stereo in the living room to the same rock station she'd heard in the car. Twisting the volume knob upward, she tried a few tentative dance steps. Jim had been strictly a ballroom-type dancer, and once Diana had met him she gave up the wild sensuous movements of the more modern steps. But she hadn't forgotten them.

The skirt of her lavender-print dress swirled around her knees as she swung her hips in time to the beat and clapped her hands. "I'll show you middle-aged," she announced to the blaring stereo as her movements became more abandoned. "You can keep your charity drives, too," she cried, whirling around the room. "And I may not be home for Sunday dinner!" The music stopped, and the jovial voice of a disc jockey advertised a special at a fast-food restaurant.

Breathing rapidly, Diana walked to the stereo and turned down the volume. She straightened, pushed the damp hair away from her face and smiled to herself. She felt better. Thirsty from all the exertion, but better. She started toward the kitchen for a drink of water and froze. Zach was leaning against the door frame, his arms crossed over his chest.

"How—long have have you..." she stammered.

"Long enough to know I'll have to fix my own Sunday dinner."

"I'm so embarrassed."

"Why? You're a good dancer."

"I used to be, when I was younger."

He looked up at the ceiling. "Here we go again." He pitched his voice into a quavering near-falsetto. "Fetch my cane, sonny."

Diana put her hands on her hips. "Go ahead. Make fun of me. I bet you can't imagine what it's like to find your first gray hair or the first stage of wrinkles."

"Not true. The barber told me last week that I have lots of gray hair, but it doesn't show much in blondes. My family is prone to early gray. And all that California sun has taken its toll, in case you hadn't noticed. The clock ticks for me, too, Diana."

"I hadn't noticed. To me you look young and vibrant. Gray? Really?"

"Want to see?" He took a step forward, and their aloneness suddenly imprinted itself forcibly on her.

"I believe you," she said hastily, and he paused, his blue eyes speculative.

"Young and vibrant?" he said with a half smile.

Diana dropped her gaze. "Now you're fishing."

"Damn right. California surfers need compliments, too." His tone was deceptively light, but Diana sensed the tension in him from across the room.

"How about some dinner?" she chirped nervously. "You must be starved."

His grin widened. "I'll pretend you didn't say that."

"Zach, I didn't mean to—"

"Easy, Diana. I know you didn't. You're the model of propriety, as long as someone's watching, that is."

"You're teasing me about the dancing."

"Very gently." He sensed her hesitation, her fear of the possibilities ahead of them in the next few hours. But her rock-hard core of determined virtue seemed to be melting. He decided not to push the issue of what would, or would not, happen between them tonight. "Let's toss some sandwiches together and eat them on the back porch."

"Instead of dinner? I had some pork chops ready to fry, and I—"

"Too much work." He walked into the kitchen, talking as he went. "We'll use that leftover ham, and I'll help you throw them together. Don't you get tired of the same old cooking routine?"

"Sometimes," Diana admitted, trailing after him. "But routines can be...comforting."

"I agree," he said, taking bread and lettuce from the refrigerator, "and I understand why you've maintained them. But when the time is right, routines should be broken, or they become ruts."

"You might be right." Diana pulled the cutting board from under the counter.

Zach winked at her. "California surfer philosophy. And speaking of California, is there any chance that somewhere in this house you've got a bottle of wine?"

"Wine? With sandwiches?"

"Is there an Illinois law against it?" He loaded his arms with ham, mustard, mayonnaise and cheese from the refrigerator.

"Don't be a smart aleck. As a matter of fact, I might have a bottle or two stored in the basement. Jim used to give wine as Christmas presents to some of his best customers."

"But you don't drink it."

Diana glanced at him archly. "You think I'm a real prude, don't you?"

"Let's say I think you're conservative. It has a nicer ring to it. You must admit you haven't been guzzling booze in my presence. No beer or wine in the refrigerator, no bourbon in the side cupboard. I assumed you don't drink."

"I used to have a glass of wine occasionally, when—"

"If you say 'when I was younger' I'm going to smear you with mustard."

Diana laughed. "You sound like Allison."

"Al and I have a lot in common."

Yes, you do, Diana thought. *You both approach life with a gusto that I envy.*

"I interrupted you," Zach continued. "You were saying?"

"I was trying to explain that I don't like to drink alone," Diana said quietly.

"Oh." He was silent for a moment. "Sorry about that."

"It's okay."

He glanced up from tearing the lettuce. "You're not alone now."

"No, not at the present moment," she clarified, underlining the transitory nature of their relationship.

"I think living in the present is a pretty good idea," he countered mildly. The invitation in his blue eyes made her heart thump loudly in her chest.

She was afraid that if she didn't find something to do immediately, he would take her in his arms. "I'll get the wine," she said quickly and fled down the basement steps.

Within a few minutes they were settled on the porch swing with a bottle of Chablis on a side table, paper plates in their laps and brimming wineglasses. Zach had even remembered to fill Beethoven's dish with dog food, and the spaniel munched happily beside them.

Zach raised his glass then thought better of it and took a healthy swallow of wine. A toast could spoil everything, if Diana read an implication into it that he didn't intend, an assumption of the evening's outcome. Yesterday he would have sworn they'd be sleeping apart tonight, just as she had vowed earlier in the week. Now he wasn't so sure. Something about her was different.

Diana sipped her wine and smiled at Zach. "This is nice, although Mrs. Eckstrom may keep the grapevine humming for days if she sees us. A picnic on the porch, wine, no kids..."

"Diana, we are the only two people on the block who know we have an empty house in there. Unless Mrs. Eckstrom's information sources are better than I thought."

"She seems to know everything, but you're right. I'm acting paranoid." Beethoven finished his meal and came to curl up at Diana's feet.

Zach swallowed a bite of sandwich then gazed at her thoughtfully. "But not as much as I'd expected," he said, tentatively voicing his confusion. "I expected to come home and find you hiding away in your bedroom under a ton of face cream with rollers in your hair. Instead you're bebopping in the living room, and looking pretty damn sexy, as a matter of fact."

Diana flushed, but his praise felt good. Very good. "That was a whim. Maybe because of Allison."

"Allison?"

"She..." Diana paused and glanced at Zach. She needed to confide in someone, someone who cared.

"What about Allison?" Zach prompted, his eyes kind.

"Today she officially became a woman."

"Really?"

Diana nodded then smiled wryly. "And she wasn't happy, believe me. Thought it was a great inconvenience before the big slumber party."

Zach chuckled in understanding, and Diana was very glad she'd told him. "I bet." He glanced sideways at Diana. "So you got a sudden urge to dance?"

She gazed into her half-full wineglass and sighed. "Trying to forget my age, I guess. As of today, I no longer have a little girl." She swirled the white wine and took another sip to disguise the fact that she was dangerously close to tears.

Zach watched her silently then touched her hand. "You're beautiful," he murmured.

Diana gave him a tremulous smile. "Thanks."

"Thank you."

"For what?"

"For sharing the news about Allison."

Diana wiped gathering moisture from the corner of her eye. "I'm glad to have someone to tell. Someone who gives a damn."

"I'm glad you realize that, Diana." His thumb stroked gently against the back of her hand.

"It's obvious you care about those girls, Zach."

"Not just the girls."

Her heart pounded, and she looked away from the intent expression on his face. "Zach, I—"

Immediately he withdrew his hand. "More wine?" he asked conversationally.

Diana took a deep breath. "I'd better not. I've become maudlin enough as it is."

"Are you kidding? You ought to attend a California encounter group if you want to see maudlin."

"No, thanks."

"Loosen up, Diana. Have some more wine," he urged, picking up the bottle.

"I don't think so. How does that limerick go? 'Candy is dandy but liquor is quicker.'"

Zach's blond eyebrows rose a notch, and he replaced the wine bottle on the table. "That was uncalled for."

"Oh, don't get upset. I was only teasing."

"I'm not amused."

"Now who's being touchy? A few days ago you accused me of lacking a spirit of adventure." Her silver eyes blazed. "What do you want?"

"You know perfectly well." His blue eyes bored like augers into her soul. "But I didn't plan to get you drunk to accomplish it. I suggested the wine because I thought we needed to relax a little to relieve the tension of this crazy situation. I don't want a bottle of wine to be an excuse for the decision you—we—make, any more than you do."

Diana didn't have to ask what decision he was talking about. She began to tremble, and she clutched her paper plate as it started to slide from her lap. "I'm sorry," she whispered.

Zach glanced at her shaking hand and laid his gently over it. "Let's go inside. The porch swing is too public a spot for what I have to say."

Diana felt the heat of his skin touching hers, which made her leap up as if she'd been burned. Beethoven jumped up with her, his tail wagging. "Beethoven wants to play," she babbled, anxious to focus attention on another topic.

"Tomorrow I'll throw sticks for him until his little legs fall off," Zach promised, taking the paper plate and wineglass from her. "But tonight he stays outside."

Diana swallowed hard. "All right."

Zach stacked her plate on top of his, and holding the

two wineglasses by their stems, motioned her inside. Silently they walked into the kitchen where Zach deposited the plates and glasses then turned to her.

"I'd like to hold you while I'm saying this."

She took a hesitant step toward him, and he met her halfway. Gently he pulled her into his arms and guided her head to a resting place in the curve of his shoulder.

"You're quivering like a leaf, Diana."

"I should have accepted another glass of Dutch courage. I'm scared."

Gently he stroked her back. "Don't be, Diana. You know how much I need you, but I won't force anything. Neither of us wants to compromise our situation or embarrass the girls."

"No." Her voice sounded small in the silence.

"Diana, if we make love tonight, they'll never know. We'll make sure of it."

Warmth spread through Diana's body, warmth that would soon become raging desire. She didn't have much time to make her decision. Soon passion would make it for her. "What about after tonight?" she asked softly. "Have you thought of that, Zach?"

"Yes," he admitted. "It won't be easy, but life is becoming damn near impossible now. The girls will be gone at other times, and I'm willing to wait until then."

Despite his deceptively easy touch on her back, Zach was thoroughly aroused. Diana felt the first wave of desire wash over her as she felt his warm pulsing maleness against her. "Not while they're in school, Zach." She was weakening, and her voice was breathless with emotion. "I won't have us scrambling to make the bed and get dressed before they get home."

"All right." His breathing quickened, and he lowered

his lips to the side of her neck. "God, that perfume, Diana."

She closed her eyes and savored the damp heat of his mouth trailing kisses up her neck to the curve of her jaw. Delirium was close. Soon he would take her lips, and then nothing else would matter but mindless surrender.

"Diana," he murmured close to her ear. "I know your body's answer." His hand moved down to cradle her hips and crush her tightly to him. She moaned softly. "But you have to tell me that I can love you. I won't let you melt against me and abandon all responsibility, much as I want to. Commit yourself, Diana. Say you want me to love you tonight."

"Zach," she pleaded, "you know."

"No, I don't." His warm lips left her throat. "Look at me."

Reluctantly she raised her head from the haven of his shoulder and gazed languorously into the fiery blue of his eyes.

He drew a shuddering breath. "Say it. Say it, Diana, or so help me, I'll leave this house tonight and sleep on a park bench rather than have you claim tomorrow that making love was a mistake."

Diana's dazed mind fought to sort out her feelings. Zach wanted her to come to him guilt free. Could she do that? Would she be able to look her daughters in the eye tomorrow if she lay in a passionate embrace with Zach tonight?

9

DIANA GAZED into Zach's rugged sun-bronzed face. In a matter of months he would be gone. And then, in slower stages, the girls would leave. Life, youth, excitement were slipping away from her. But now, in this moment, she held all three in her arms.

She tried to speak, gulped and tried again. "I—want you tonight, Zach," she said haltingly. "Please love me."

His breath caught in his throat. "Gladly," he whispered. "Gladly, Diana."

At last she felt the promise of his lips, the arousing flick of his tongue against hers. After weeks of watching him move through the house, his virility calling to her deepest feminine instincts, she knew the rush of warmth as he pressed her to him. Her body shook with anticipation.

As her heart raced out of control, she felt his hand mold to her waist then skim up the thin material of her bodice and cup her full breasts. She wanted those hands against her bare skin, wanted to touch him in return. Boldly she tugged his T-shirt from the waistband of his shorts and slid her palms up the smooth length of his torso to the bunched muscles of his shoulders. He groaned and stroked her taut nipples with the pads of his thumbs.

Breathing hard, he lifted his mouth from hers. "Let's go upstairs."

"Upstairs?"

"Yes. This time, yes."

Diana understood. The upstairs bedroom held no memories of married love. Zach's choice was the right one, until they established their own style, their own pattern. "I'll meet you there," she said, withdrawing reluctantly from his warmth. "I wasn't exactly prepared, and I need to—"

"If you like, I'll take care of—"

"No." She smiled at their polite exchange. "I will."

"I'll wait here."

"No, go on up. Please. You might even—" she took a breath and rushed on "—take your clothes off." Before he could respond, she ran from the kitchen into her bedroom. Then she listened for his tread on the stairs and the creak of the old wooden floor above her head that told her he was in his room.

Her hands, made clumsy with passion, jabbed at the buttons of her shirtwaist, and she wondered if he was stripping off his T-shirt without a quiver. After tossing her dress on the bed, she stepped out of her shoes and pulled her slip over her head. Was he unzipping his shorts? She licked her dry lips.

Diana pushed the straps of her bra over her ivory shoulders, reached behind her back and unhooked the fasteners. Her creamy breasts fell free, and she touched them wonderingly. The skin felt taut, stretched firm and tight with desire. She slipped the damp fabric of her panties over her hips then stood in the middle of her bedroom, her eyes lifted to the room above. She heard the bedsprings squeak under him. He was waiting.

ZACH STRETCHED OUT on the mattress of the four-poster and draped the white sheet over his aroused body. He left the bedside lamp on. Below him, he heard a drawer open and close. Would she come to him fully dressed, or had she, too, removed her clothes? Never in his life had he lain like this, waiting for a woman. Seduction had always involved the gradual undressing ritual, the slow discovery of his partner's body, the thrill as each level of inhibition faded away.

But this unusual preliminary had driven him to a fever pitch of desire, until he doubted his ability to hold back with Diana, to make sure her own response equaled his before he buried himself in her softness. God, how he ached for her! If she hadn't said yes tonight, he probably would have considered leaving the house forever. A guy had only so much control, and in the past week his primitive urges had nearly overpowered him.

The wooden stairs announced her approach, and his heart beat faster. He watched the doorway; suddenly, she was there, a hesitant smile on her rosebud mouth. A pale blue silken robe was belted loosely around her small waist, and her pert nipples thrust against the material, announcing to him that she wore nothing underneath.

"May I come in?"

He propped himself up on one arm and held the other out to her while he devoured her with a hungry gaze. The robe made little whispering noises as she crossed to him on bare feet, and when her fingers entwined with his, he closed his eyes briefly and hoped for the strength to take it slowly.

Her voice was low, husky. He'd never heard it like that. "You followed my instructions," she said.

"Of course." He drew her toward him, and she perched on the edge of the mattress. He released her hand and rubbed his knuckles gently across the pucker of her nipple under the blue material. Her silvery eyes darkened. "You haven't changed your mind." He meant it as a statement, not as a question.

"No."

Deliberately slowing his movements, he reached for the belt of her robe. His fingers slid under the loose tie and pulled it free. "I've never seen you," he said. "Only imagined..." His hand slipped beneath the lapel of the garment and gently pushed it aside. "God." His gaze lifted to her face. "You're like porcelain, Diana."

"But I'm not," she said. "Porcelain is easily broken."

His sun-browned hand drifted from her collarbone down the slope of one breast, and he trembled at the silken perfection of her pale skin. "And I know you're not. You're a strong woman, Diana, but you're made so delicately." He pushed the other side of the garment away and took a quivering breath. "So delicately."

She shivered as his feather-soft touch outlined the curve of each breast.

"Take off the robe," he murmured.

She stood and allowed the pale blue covering to slide from her shoulders to a shimmering puddle on the wooden floor.

"My lovely moon goddess," Zach breathed. "How I want you."

Her silver gaze flickered over his prone body. "I want you, too," she said softly. "Pull back the sheet, Zach."

Wordlessly he complied, and her eyes glowed with approval as she took in the bronzed skin of his chest and the sun-lightened hair covering it, beckoning her to caress him. She glanced lower, to the strip that was not tanned by the California sun, and to the proud thrust of his manhood, surrounded by dark blond whorls of hair.

"You're beautiful," she said, her voice catching in her throat."

"Men aren't beautiful," he said with a crooked smile.

"You are."

"Come here, Diana."

With a sigh of longing she lowered herself beside him, then tentatively brushed her hand over his chest and down to his flat stomach. "I've wanted to touch you for so long," she confessed.

"Diana..." His blue eyes begged for more, and her hand dipped lower. When her slender fingers closed around him, he moaned and reached for her. "I've dreamed about this—you touching me, me touching you. It's better than my wildest fantasies. Oh, God, Diana." He stilled the erotic movements of her hand and brought it up to his chest. "Can you feel that? You're driving me crazy."

She nibbled on his lower lip. "You've been driving me crazy ever since you arrived on my doorstep."

"And ever since I saw you standing there, looking so cool and collected in that horrendous heat, I've wanted to find out if I could get beyond that cool exterior and make you moan, make you whimper and call my name." His tongue dipped into the hollow at the base of her throat, then began a slow journey to the tip of her breast. "Heat up for me, Diana," he whispered, circling the erect nipple with tiny licking kisses.

"Oh!" she gasped, arching her back as he took her into his mouth. She writhed against him, needing everything his hands and lips gave her as weeks of repressed desire burst forth in a cascade of emotion. His hand slid between her thighs, and he groaned at her moist readiness. But he wanted more, and he stroked her intimately until her breath came in short panting cries that fell on his ears like the sweetest music.

She twisted against the pressure of his fingers, and he knew she was close. But he wanted the last moment of ecstasy to belong to both of them, and he took his hand away. "Tell me," he whispered in her ear. "Tell me what you want."

"I want—I want you inside me," she panted. "Fill me, Zach, please!"

He moved over her, gazed into her flushed face for a heartbeat and drove home. "Diana!" He hardly recognized his own choked cry as her rich satin warmth received him. Never had a woman excited him as this one did. Never.

Diana rose to meet him, craving the union that she'd denied herself, denied him. She sensed that in that moment of joining he surrendered himself completely to her, to the primitive need that carried him beyond all pretense of control into a world of pure sensation. Then she, too, forgot everything but the glorious pressure building within her as his relentless rhythm carried her higher and higher.

The world narrowed to only this, and she thought she might scream with exquisite pleasure as they trembled on the verge of cataclysmic release. She called his name, and with one sure thrust he tumbled both of them over the edge and catapulted them down, down into oblivion.

For long moments she lay in the aftershock, unable to move or speak. Zach's blond head rested on her shoulder, his face turned away from her. Gradually his breathing returned to normal.

"Zach?"

He stirred. "Zach who?" he mumbled lazily, kissing her shoulder.

"Is that how they do things in California?"

He lifted his head and propped his cheek on his fist so he could look at her. "Funny, but I was about to ask if that's how they do things in Illinois. You pack quite a wallop."

"Thank you."

"Oh, you're welcome, Diana. You're very welcome."

He combed his fingers through her dark hair. "This fatal attraction is all your fault, you know. You promised to shave your head."

"That would have taken care of your problem, but not mine."

"That's what you think. Even bald you'd have me running after you."

"I'm glad." She smiled up at him. "We were terrific, weren't we?"

"I'm not sure that's a strong enough word."

"Maybe because we denied ourselves for so long."

"You think so?" He shook his head. "I don't quite buy that, but in a little while we can test your theory. If the second time is a total washout, you've got a case."

"The second time?"

"Hmm-mmm." He traced the delicate curve of her eyebrow with one finger. "Of course, I'd be more than willing to continue the testing for, say, a third time. Maybe even a fourth, or a fifth, or—"

"Zach!"

"Is there a legal limit in Illinois?" His palm brushed in a circular motion over her breast, and Diana felt the ache growing deep inside her. Was it possible for her to want him again so soon?

"I heard the number ten somewhere," she said as her breathing accelerated under his touch.

"What a shame to have a quota," Zach murmured as his light caress changed to a sensuous massage. "But then, who's counting?" He accepted the invitation in her silver eyes and lowered his lips to hers.

THE LAMP GLOWED ALL NIGHT on the bedside table. Once Diana reached to turn it off, but Zach stopped her, saying he loved waking up from his catnaps and looking at her, then watching as he roused her with kisses until they were entwined in a passionate embrace once more.

Dawn found them staring dreamily into each other's eyes.

"It's morning," Diana announced softly.

"Can't be. Someone's shining their headlights in the window, and you only think it's morning."

"And I suppose that's a particularly melodious cricket, and not a sparrow chirping outside the window."

"Now I know how Cinderella felt at midnight. I don't want our time to be over, Diana."

"Neither do I." She sighed longingly. "It's been a wonderful night, Zach. I'll never forget it."

"What do you think Jenny would take to have a slumber party on a regular basis, say, three or four times a week?"

Diana laughed. "Jenny would do it for nothing. It's her mother you'd have to bribe."

"Oh? Is she pretty?"

Diana pushed up on one elbow. "How dare you say such a thing, Zach Wainwright, after all we've—"

"Shush, Diana." He pulled her hard against him. "Just testing your jealousy reflex. It works great. And to silence your fears, I haven't the slightest interest in another woman."

"Not even if she could provide regular sex?"

"To coin a phrase, I seek quality, not quantity. Somehow I'll survive until the next slumber party. What time do you have to pick up the girls?"

"Ten."

Zach glanced at the clock by the bed. "Then there's time."

"For what?" Diana asked, batting her eyelashes innocently.

"For this," he growled in mock ferocity, rolling on top of her. "I must have my way with you."

"And I with you, gorgeous man." Diana lifted her lips for his kiss, and they began their familiar sensuous journey once more.

Later they agreed that Diana would shower downstairs and Zach upstairs, in order to accomplish the task without luring each other back into bed. Zach finished first, and rubbing his damp hair with a towel, he strolled casually into Diana's room while she was putting on her underwear.

She glanced at him and fought the tug of desire that would be very dangerous to succumb to, considering the short time they had left before the girls had to be picked up. "Where's your shirt?" she teased. "No fair flaunting your muscles."

"What about you, parading around in those little lacy items?"

"I am not parading. You didn't have to come waltzing in here, you know."

"Yes, I did. I wanted to see what I missed." He hung the towel around his neck and held on to it with both hands to keep from reaching for her. "I didn't have the experience of seeing that stuff on you last night."

Diana straightened her bra strap and glanced at him, one eyebrow raised. "Do I pass muster?"

"How come you look sexy, no matter what you wear? You could probably put on a gunnysack and my hands would itch to touch what's underneath. Yes, dammit, you pass muster, so well I'm all hot and bothered again."

Diana laughed and walked to her closet. "You're wonderful for the ego. But I'll put on some slacks, so we can both control ourselves."

"How about shorts?"

"Oh, I don't—"

"Why not? The paper says it will warm up again today. I think they're wrong, though. The heat wave came through last night."

"Perhaps they're referring to the weather?" she suggested mildly.

"Oh. Weather." He grinned at her.

"I have half a mind to wear shorts, now that you mention it." She looked at his cutoffs then back at the slacks in her hand. "They would be cooler, wouldn't they?"

"Cooler for you, warmer for me. I'm an idiot to suggest this, because I'll probably spend the day staring at your beautiful legs and imagining them wrapped around—"

"Zach, you'd better not."

"I won't. I promise. Have you got some shorts?"

"No. I'd have to borrow a pair of Laurie's, but I'm sure she wouldn't mind. And they should fit. I'm really tempted."

"Then do it. I'm a real fan of yielding to temptation."

"No kidding." Diana rolled her eyes. "Well, okay." She hung her slacks back in her closet and reached for her robe.

"What's that for?"

"I can't run around the house in my underwear."

"Why not, Diana? No one's here but me."

She looked at him for a minute. "You're right. Excuse me." She brushed past him and ran lightly up the stairs.

Zach watched her go, her full ivory breasts quivering despite the restraint of her bra, and shook his head. "Why is it that the more I loosen her up the more I suffer?" he muttered to himself.

Breakfast was a lighthearted meal as they shared the cooking and clean-up chores amid jokes and laughter. Diana's body felt tingly and alive. No doubt about it, Zach was good for her. In spite of her former resolve, she began considering that they might, if they were very careful, enjoy each other occasionally while the girls were in school. Who would know?

She decided not to tell Zach just yet. Better to surprise him once the girls were home again and she felt satisfied that her daughters didn't suspect what had happened in their absence.

"If you'll feed Beethoven, I'll pick up Allison and Laurie," she said, twisting the faucet knob hard to the right.

"Still drips, I see."

"I have it on a list of chores for my handyman."

"I'll be honest with you, Diana. I don't know how much I'll have to learn before I can fix that faucet."

She walked to him and wound her arms around his neck. "Ask me if I care if you fix it or not," she said, nuzzling his cheek.

He gathered her into his arms. "Are you suggesting that as long as I keep you satisfied in bed you'll overlook a little dripping faucet?"

"Something like that."

"You've got a deal." He captured her lips in a searing kiss that soon had them breathing hard. With a deep sigh, he pushed her away from him. "You'd better go."

"Yes."

They still clung to each other, reluctant to finally end their wonderful interlude.

Diana gazed into Zach's clear blue eyes and gave up her plan to surprise him. "I wasn't going to say this yet, but if everything seems to be normal around here and we-'ve succeeded in keeping our relationship a secret from the girls, I think once in a while, when the two of them are at school..."

His wide smile made her heart sing. "You read my

thoughts. Now I won't have to be devious and seduce you into that decision."

"You would have done that?"

"Absolutely. I'm not about to wait for Jenny to plan another slumber party before I make love to you again."

She smiled at him. "I'm shocked."

"No, you're not. You're excited. I can see it in your eyes. You wouldn't want a trained lapdog you could order around, even if you think you would."

"You're right."

"So go get those little twerps, and we'll cope with the rest of the weekend. But on Monday morning..."

"Yes," she said breathlessly.

"Mmm." His gaze swept over her. "You'd better leave, pronto."

"Okay." She stepped out of his arms and walked unsteadily to the door. "See you soon," she said, pushing open the screen. An excited bark greeted her. "And speaking of trained lapdogs, Beethoven looks hungry."

"I'll try to come out of my fog long enough to feed the little sucker. And the chickens, right?"

"If you don't mind." She blew him a kiss from the door and skipped out to the garage. Once she was in the car, she flipped on the radio to the rock station and sang loudly all the way to Jenny's house.

Allison and Laurie piled into the car, bleary-eyed from lack of sleep, and slumped in the back seat.

"Did you have a good time?" Diana asked brightly.

"Great," the girls said in unison and closed their eyes.

"I still don't understand why they call these gatherings slumber parties," Diana commented. "Obviously nobody sleeps."

"You're not supposed to sleep at a slumber party," Allison explained.

"I see." Diana's thoughts returned to Zach and their night together. Adults had the same sort of language contradiction as teenagers, after all. She and Zach hadn't exactly slept together, had they? A thrill of excitement coursed through her as she dreamed about Monday, when the girls would be in school. Was the excitement tinged with guilt? Maybe a little. "How're you feeling, Allison?" she asked, concentrating on her mother role.

"Fine."

"No more cramps?"

"Nope."

Laurie stirred from her daze. "How come you turned on our station without us even asking?"

"I find the music cheerful."

"Cheerful? You always said it sounded like two tomcats in a barrel."

"Maybe I've changed my mind."

"Oh." Laurie gave her mother a puzzled look then curled back against the seat.

When they pulled into the drive, the girls straggled out then stopped to stare when Diana opened the door.

"Mom, you've got on shorts," Allison said in amazement.

"And they look vaguely familiar," Laurie added.

"You're right, Laurie. I heard today would be very warm, and I thought you wouldn't mind."

"Of course I don't. I told you once a long time ago you should borrow a pair. You said they were undignified for a widow with two nearly grown daughters."

"Maybe I changed my mind about that, too."

Allison shook her head. "Weird."

"You said it," Laurie agreed. "Leave for one night, and she freaks out on you."

"Girls, I really don't think this is such a drastic—"

Beethoven leaped down the porch steps, barking his greeting and drowning out whatever protest or explanation Diana had planned to make.

"Hey, Beethoven!" Allison called, putting down her overnight case and pillow and crouching to hug the wriggling dog. "Did you miss us, boy?" She glanced up at Diana. "Did he wander through the house last night, looking for me? Laurie says he usually does that when I'm gone."

"No." Diana swallowed nervously.

"Really?" asked Laurie, bending to pet the dog. "He stayed curled up on your rug all night?"

Diana's palms began to feel damp. "No, as a matter of fact, we—I—decided to let Beethoven sleep outside last night."

"Outside?" the girls chorused.

"You don't have to look at me as if I'm some ax murderer. Beethoven's a dog. It was warm last night, and I'm sure he enjoyed the fresh air."

"Oh, poor Beethoven," Allison crooned, scratching the dog's floppy ears. "I bet you were lonesome, all alone in the dark."

"Yeah, Mom," Laurie added. "I don't think that's such a great idea. Beethoven's not used to sleeping outside. He might get sick, or maybe a bigger dog would get into the yard, or—"

"For heaven's sake!" Diana tried to hide her growing dismay with anger. Had she seriously expected to conceal anything from two inquisitive adolescents? "Sleeping out here didn't hurt him a bit. Look at him. He's perky as ever."

"Because now he knows we're home to take good care of him," Allison said, her blue eyes accusatory.

"That's enough, girls," Diana warned.

With a sigh Allison stood and picked up her pillow and overnight case.

Laurie started up the porch steps then glanced with curiosity at the table beside the porch swing. "What's that?"

Diana followed the direction of Laurie's gaze and saw the half-full wine bottle still sitting on the table. Her heart began to race. "I guess I left it out there."

"When?" Allison said, picking up the scent of something interesting. "Did you have a party or something?"

"No. Zach and I sat in the swing and drank a glass of wine with our sandwiches, that's all."

"For dinner?" Laurie's gray eyes widened. "Sandwiches for dinner?"

"Why not?"

Allison took up the cry. "We've *never* had sandwiches for dinner."

"And then you didn't even finish cleaning up," Laurie said, looking at her mother in amazement.

"Yeah," Allison piped up. "And you always tell *us* to clean everything up, or we'll get ants."

Laurie shook her head and made a clucking sound with her teeth, and in that moment Diana thought her daughter sounded at least forty years old. "Rock music, shorts, Beethoven out all night, wine bottles left on the porch." She gave her mother a strange smile. "What in the world went on here last night, Mom?"

DIANA FELT THE BLOOD RUSH from her face. They knew. Good God, they knew. "I—"

"Hey, Al, Laurie! How's it going?" Zach, looking like a blond Adonis in his snug T-shirt and white cutoffs, stepped out onto the porch.

"Fine," answered Allison, but Diana could have sworn her daughter gave Zach a strange look.

"I guess we can't leave you two alone anymore," Laurie said, and Diana thought her heart had stopped beating. "We come home and find wine on the porch, Mom in shorts, Beethoven out all night...."

Zach glanced quickly at Diana. "Guess we need you girls around to keep us in line," he said with a grin that Diana could tell was forced. Had the girls noticed, she wondered.

"That's for sure," Allison agreed, glancing from Zach to Diana. She turned to her sister. "Well, I don't know about you, Laurie, but I'm taking a nap."

"Sounds good," Laurie replied with an exaggerated yawn. "See everybody later." She climbed the remaining steps and crossed the porch, passing Zach without a glance in his direction.

Allison hurried after her. "Wait up!" she called, heading for the screen door Laurie held open. Diana heard them speak to each other in muted tones once they'd escaped inside the house. She strained to hear what they were saying, although she dreaded knowing what it might be. Were they discussing their mother's betrayal? Were they trying to decide what to tell Jenny, now that all her suspicions had come true?

Zach sauntered down the steps, and his hair gleamed brown and gold in the sunshine. He appeared relaxed, but one look in his blue eyes and Diana knew he was nervous.

"What was that all about?" he asked casually.

"You know damn well what it was about," Diana said, her voice low and intense. "They suspect something. I fielded their questions pretty well until Laurie spotted the wine bottle. Why didn't you take it in last night?"

"Why didn't you? I seem to remember having my hands full of plates and glasses."

"But the wine bottle was the most—" Diana caught herself and sighed. After all, she hadn't carried anything into the house last night. She'd been too emotionally involved in their situation. "You're right. I should have picked it up. But you fed Beethoven on the porch this morning. Didn't you see the bottle? God, it was like a red flag to those girls. They know I never drink wine anymore."

"No, I didn't see the bottle. My mind was occupied with something else," Zach said edgily. "Perhaps you'd rather I adopted an 'out of sight, out of mind' philosophy toward you?"

"I wish you'd been thinking about the fact that the girls were coming home, and that we don't want to advertise our little arrangement!" Diana said angrily.

"Is it my responsibility, then?" His blue eyes grew icy. "You're allowed to float around in a romantic haze, but I'm supposed to make sure all the telltale signs are erased? Sorry, but you didn't make that clear."

"I thought I made it very clear! Obviously you don't

understand how perceptive those girls are. The shorts you suggested I wear caught their attention immediately, and then they complained because Beethoven was out all night, which was also your idea, and then you leave wine bottles sitting around, so—"

"Diana." He gripped her shoulders and gave her a little shake. "Cut it out. You're very close to ruining the beautiful thing we've been building so carefully the past few hours."

She looked at him mutinously; then slowly her rebellion crumbled, and her eyes filled with tears. "I'm sorry," she whispered. "All of a sudden I'm consumed with guilt, and I'm heaping it on you, just like you once said I would."

"That about sums it up." He smiled gently. "But I accept your apology."

"Oh, Zach, I think we blew it. We got carried away with our emotions and forgot we've got to be on guard every moment."

"You're blowing the girls' reaction out of proportion, imagining they know more than they do."

"No, they sense changes around here. All of them were small—insignificant—until they put everything together. First off, I met them with rock music blaring from the radio."

Zach's eyes sparkled with amusement. "You did?"

"I felt so good, so happy, and the music fit my mood perfectly."

"I can relate to that." He rubbed his hands up and down her upper arms.

"You'd better let go of me, Zach. One of them could come out here."

"Are you kidding? Those girls were walking zombies. They're out cold by now."

"Please."

He sighed and dropped his hands. "Okay."

"Anyway, Laurie wanted to know why I was playing their music without being asked. That surprised both of them. Then they noticed my—Laurie's—shorts."

"And then you opened your mouth about Beethoven."

"No, I didn't," Diana protested. "Allison asked me if he'd wandered around the house looking for her last night."

"And you couldn't have said yes?"

She regarded him steadily. "No, I couldn't."

"It's a little white lie, Diana. You wouldn't be drummed out of Springfield for telling a little white lie. I bet even Abraham Lincoln told at least one in his life."

"I'm sorry. I couldn't do it, that's all."

Zach groaned. "Because you feel guilty. Keeping our relationship a secret from them will be harder than I thought."

"No, it won't." She stared at a point past his shoulder.

"Diana, carrying on a love affair and keeping it secret from two smart girls will almost surely involve a few white lies."

She swallowed hard. "That's why we won't have a love affair," she said, not looking at him.

He stared at her for a long moment, and when he spoke his voice was emotionless. "We won't." It wasn't a question.

"No. They may think something happened last night, but we'll give them no more reason to believe it, and the whole incident will be forgotten."

"Oh, will it?"

Her head jerked around, and her eyes were moist. "I don't mean by me. By them."

"That's a relief. I was beginning to wonder how cold

and cruel you could be." He had somehow managed to wipe all expression from his face.

"I don't intend to be cruel, Zach." Her lower lip quivered. "You think this is an easy decision for me?"

"I don't know. You came to it awfully fast. Was I a disappointment to you last night, Diana?"

"That's a ridiculous thing to say."

"I wonder. What we shared must mean less to you than it does to me. Otherwise you'd be more willing to find ways around our problems."

"There are no ways around our problems," Diana said, her voice shaking with emotion. "The difference between us is that I care about the feelings of those girls, and you're only interested in satisfying your sexual urges!"

"That's a rotten thing to say."

"As of now I feel like a rotten person, so I guess it figures. And right now this rotten person has a load of laundry to do and music students coming this afternoon. For some reason I seem to be behind in my work."

"And with you, that's probably an unforgivable sin," Zach said sarcastically. "Don't let me keep you from your duty."

"I almost did, but now I understand what must be done," Diana said quietly. "If you're unhappy, you're free to move out at any time."

He looked as if she'd slapped him, and then the dazed expression left his face. "The hell I will," he said, hunching his shoulders. "I'm staying right here, Diana. I want to see if you can stand up under your own edict."

Her silver eyes blazed. "I could order you to leave. After all, you're not a handyman."

"You could do that." He crossed his arms over his chest. "But you won't, because Allison and Laurie would never forgive you. When I move out of my own free will, they'll have to accept it. But if you throw me out, you'll be one unpopular lady."

"You're very sure of yourself."

"No, I'm very hurt. But I'm willing to wage guerrilla warfare to win back what I've lost."

She faced him resolutely. "It won't work, Zach."

"We'll see."

They stood, gazes locked in silent combat, until inevitably the fire in Zach's eyes ignited a warmth in Diana's body. Her cheeks flushed, and his lips curved in satisfaction. Dropping her gaze, she fled quickly, sure that there was a triumphant gleam in his blue eyes as he watched her race for the house. She would have been surprised had she turned and discovered that the suspicious brightness in his eyes was not inspired by triumph at all. He blinked angrily and crouched to pet Beethoven, who bounded up to him with a stick in his mouth, ready to play.

MONDAY AFTERNOON Laurie and Allison brought Diana the announcement of a band trip scheduled for the following month. Diana glanced over the letter, and the paper trembled in her hand. The girls would be gone two nights this time. She tucked the announcement in a desk drawer and vowed to keep the news from Zach for as long as possible.

On Tuesday the girls started picking arguments with each other. Diana tried to ignore their behavior, but at last, on Friday afternoon, with the Bad News Brass due soon, she decided enough was enough. The tension of living in the same house with Zach, combined with the girls' constant bickering, drove her to take action. She stood at the bottom of the stairs and listened, trying to understand the problem. What had happened to the lovely comradeship that had been developing between her daughters?

"Beating a drum is easy!" Laurie shouted. "Any bimbo can do it. Try playing the flute and see if you'll be chosen."

"Try practicing your flute once in a while, Puckerlips, and maybe you'll have a chance in the tryouts," Allison sneered. "I work on these drums every day."

"Yeah, and disturb the whole neighborhood. At least my flute plays a real song, not some banging and crashing like garbage cans tipping over in the alley."

Her mouth set in a grim line, Diana started up the stairs. Zach was supposed to be working in his room, but she doubted anyone could concentrate with both girls in full voice. And she wanted Zach to finish his dissertation. The sooner he did, the sooner he'd be gone. When he left, her house and her heart would be cold and empty, but at least she wouldn't have the constant tug-of-war between her desires and her concern for her daughters' welfare.

"You don't like drums because you have no sense of rhythm," Allison taunted.

"Speak for yourself, bimbo. Every time the band gets off the beat, it's because of the drums. And guess who's on the dru-ums."

Diana arrived in the doorway of Allison's room in time to see Laurie stick out her tongue and Allison pick up a shoe. She aimed too high, and the brown loafer sailed over Laurie and Diana's heads to land smack against a solid object. Diana spun around and saw Zach standing in the hall, rubbing his forehead.

"Didn't know I was in the line of fire," he said bemusedly.

Laurie's face grew red with embarrassment; she raced

back to Allison's room. "You bimbo! Guess what you've done now."

Diana hurried toward Zach. "I'm terribly sorry."

His gaze roamed over her. "Are you?"

She grew uncomfortable under his thorough appraisal. "Of course." She started down the hall toward the stairs. "I'll get some ice from the kitchen so you won't have a lump. I'm sure if we put ice on it right away, we can—"

His fingers encircled her wrist. "I'm fine, Diana. Don't worry about the ice."

"I think it would be a good idea, so if you don't mind, I'll—"

His thumb caressed the inside of her wrist. "You have a very strong pulse," he said softly. "Why, Diana?"

"Are you okay, Zach?" Allison asked, appearing hesitantly from the depths of her room. "Laurie, uh, mentioned my shoe accidentally, that is, sort of..."

"Typical bimbo stunt," Laurie muttered, trailing after Allison.

"I'll live," Zach said, releasing Diana's wrist. "Which is more than I can guarantee for you two, the way you're blasting each other. What's the problem?"

"Yes, for heaven's sake, girls. Zach's trying to work on his dissertation, I'm sure."

"Actually, I was composing a poem to the moon goddess."

Allison seized on his statement as a way to change the subject. "You write poetry? Freaky!"

Diana refused to look at Zach. Guerrilla warfare was right. He hadn't missed an opportunity all week to make a veiled reference to their night together or accidentally touch her and hold the contact a moment longer than necessary. Her nerves were wearing very thin.

"I write when I'm inspired," Zach commented, glancing at Diana's taut face. "It's been a little slow the past few days, what with the noise and all."

Allison scrubbed the toe of her sneaker across the wooden floor. "Oh."

"So why are you two throwing things?"

"I *didn't* throw anything," Laurie announced loft- ily.

Allison bristled. "Oh, of course not, Miss Perfect Pants. You only stuck your tongue out at me."

"I asked why, not who," Zach said evenly. "You don't each have to tell me everything you know about the other. It's none of my business."

Both girls' eyes rounded as they absorbed this new phi- losophy.

"It's our instruments," Allison said. "Laurie says drums are a cinch."

"They are," Laurie insisted, "compared to the intrica- cies of a flute."

"*Intricacies?*" Allison hooted. "I bet you pulled that word out of last week's vocabulary quiz. What a stuck-up word."

Diana could be silent no longer. "You girls didn't used to make fun of each other's instruments," she interjected. "After all these years you should both realize each one is important to the band."

"Tell that to our band director," Laurie muttered. "He says we have too many flutes to take them all on the band trip to Champaign now that the trip budget has been cut, so he's having tryouts for the flute section."

The band trip, Diana thought in dismay. They were go- ing to discuss it in front of Zach.

He glanced at Diana and raised his eyebrows then re- turned his attention to Laurie. "This outing must be a big deal."

"Big deal is right," Allison chortled. "Greyhound bus,

staying Friday and Saturday night in a motel, playing in a competition. It'll be freaky!''

"Sounds like it," Zach said, gazing steadily at Diana. She avoided the challenge of his eyes. "When is it?" he asked casually.

"Three weeks from Friday," Allison said. "I can hardly wait!"

Laurie made a face. "I can. It'll be a dumb trip."

"You're just saying that because I'll get to go for sure, and you might not."

"It's not fair! You're a seventh grader, and I'm an eighth grader. I should automatically get to go instead of you."

"Let me guess," Zach said. "The same band that's long on flutes is short on drummers."

"Can I help it if I picked drums?" Allison said. "I wish all the flutes could go, too. At least I did, until Laurie started acting so mean."

"Laurie, you may do fine in the tryouts," Diana urged. *But if you don't, you can be a chaperone for your mother at home.*

"Mom, you know how I freeze up when I have to play solos. I'm better than I used to be, but still…"

Yes, Diana knew. She had one daughter who threw herself into performing as if made for the spotlight and another who wanted nothing more than to be lost in the crowd. Laurie's love of music was tempered by the fear that if she became too proficient, she'd stand out. Now her reluctance to shine was catching up with her.

"I hope you make it, Laurie," Zach said evenly.

I bet you do, Diana thought. And so did she, for Laurie's sake. For her own peace of mind, she'd rather have Laurie stay at home.

"But in case you don't," Zach continued, "how about an alternate plan?"

"Like what?" Laurie didn't look interested.

"Seems to me that's the same weekend Huey Lewis and the News are in town."

Laurie's eyes widened in wonder. "You mean go to the rock concert?"

"Why not?"

"I've never been to a rock concert," Laurie breathed.

"Neither have I," Allison said, looking suddenly uncertain about her privileged drummer's status. "But I'd still rather go on the band trip," she added staunchly.

"To tell the truth, so would I," Laurie admitted. "And I'm going to practice hard for those tryouts. But if I don't make it, the concert idea sounds super." She hesitated. "Who will buy the tickets?"

"I will," Zach and Diana said at once.

"Zach," Diana protested. "It's a great idea, but you can't afford—"

"Yes, I can, thanks to living here instead of in a hotel. Besides, I have a guilty conscience because I haven't fixed the kitchen sink." He gave Diana a lopsided smile.

Her stomach churned. Last Saturday morning he'd promised to keep her satisfied in bed so that she wouldn't notice the dripping faucet. "Okay," she said slowly. "When are the tryouts, Laurie?"

"Monday, and I plan to spend the weekend practicing. Tuesday the band director will announce who made it. Can we still get tickets then?"

"Maybe not front row," Zach said. "But I'm not quite that rich, anyway. A few seats will be available, I'm sure."

"I'll sit anywhere," Laurie said, smiling. "Thanks, Zach." She reached up and kissed him lightly on the cheek. "You're great."

"So are you, Laurie." He gave her a quick hug. "Think you two can hold it down now?"

"Sure, Zach," Allison promised. "Sorry we bothered you." She looked at him slyly. "If I break my finger or something like that, can I go to the concert?"

Diana glanced sharply at her daughter. "Allison, don't you dare—"

"Oh, I won't. I really want to go on the trip. Just covering all the angles, Mom."

"Okay, Al," Zach said, chuckling. "The concert will be considered compensation for all minor disasters that might keep you from going on the trip. Does that satisfy you?"

Allison nodded happily. "Yep. Guess I'll do some homework now. See you two later."

"Yeah, me, too," Laurie said, heading for her room. "Plus I've gotta practice." Both bedroom doors closed, and the hall was silent.

"The Bad News Brass will be here any minute," Diana mumbled, turning toward the stairway.

"How long have you known about this trip?"

She paused on the landing. "The letter came home yesterday."

"You deliberately didn't mention it to me."

She glanced at him over her shoulder. "That's right."

"Scared?" he asked softly.

The familiar ache began as she saw desire flare in his eyes. "Why should I be? All I have to do is tell you I'm not interested."

"That's all you have to do," he agreed, leaning against the wall and crossing his arms over his muscular chest. "But I know how terrible you are at lying, Diana."

Her silver eyes flashed. "You're so damn sure of yourself."

"I have reason to be." He cocked his head toward the open door of his bedroom. "Remember?"

"Why don't you leave me alone?"

He gazed at her, his blue eyes dark with leashed passion. "Sometimes I wish I could." He shook his head. "Sometimes I wish I could."

Diana tore her gaze from his and ran down the stairs before her trembling arms would reach for him and her traitorous voice begged him to love her.

FLUTE MUSIC ECHOED through the house all weekend, but Tuesday afternoon brought the news that Diana had almost expected—Laurie was not chosen for the trip. Zach whisked her up immediately and drove her to the ticket office before she had time to sink into depression. As Diana watched him drive away, contradictory emotions tugged at her.

She felt Laurie's disappointment keenly, but it was leavened with relief that her resolve to stay away from Zach would not be tested. And she was glad, wasn't she? Diana chewed on her lower lip and tried to convince herself of the wisdom of never again making love to Zach. Succumbing to desire could only bring more heartache.

In the days that followed she repeated that sentiment over and over, hoping that eventually it would become so much a part of her that the incessant yearning for Zach would lessen. But her body was no longer ignorant of the pleasures Zachary Wainwright could bring, and it clamored for his touch.

Diana kept busy away from the house on school days, for fear that a look, a chance brush of fingertips, would destroy all her resolutions. All that kept her from falling apart was the growing affection between Zach and the girls. They idolized him, and Diana realized that he had been right when he said she couldn't throw him out. Allison and Laurie would never forgive her.

On the Thursday afternoon before the band trip, Diana heard the girls even before they got inside the house, but their loud voices seemed to be pitched high in excitement, not anger.

"Mom! You'll never guess what!" Laurie cried, her cheeks flushed and her gray eyes sparkling.

Diana stared at her, knowing without any explanation what had happened. For some last-minute reason, her oldest daughter was going on the band trip.

THE GIRLS' BOISTEROUS CHATTER during dinner provided a convenient screen behind which Zach studied Diana and tried to gauge her reaction to the turn of events. He could tell she was nervous from the way her fork trembled in her hand. She ate little.

He knew that if matters were allowed to take their course he and Diana would make love when Allison and Laurie were in Champaign. He wanted her so much he could taste her lips on his, feel her taut ripeness under his fingertips. And she wanted him. In the past weeks he'd often caught her looking in his direction with hunger darkening her silver eyes. She fought against her emotions, but she couldn't entirely suppress them.

Lovemaking between them would be full and good. In one weekend they could blot out the yearning, pleasure each other in ways so long denied them. Once Diana took the girls to school the next morning, suitcases in hand, they would be gone until Sunday afternoon. Two nights and nearly three days. He knew the joy she would bring him. So why was he even questioning his next step? After dinner he should stock up on wine, tidy up his room and anticipate the weekend.

As he helped her clear away the dishes, she spoke in a low voice. "I want to pay you for the concert tickets, Zach. Laurie's forgotten about them, but I haven't. I doubt you can get a refund at this late date."

He stacked the plates and smiled at her. "You don't want to go?" Silly question. Weighing a rock concert against Saturday night alone with Diana, he didn't want to go, either.

"Not really. That was for Laurie."

Then how do you want to spend the evening, sweet Diana? He didn't dare ask. "I may be able to get a refund first thing in the morning. Don't worry about it." *I'll clear my calendar, on the chance that you'll let me hold you all night in my arms.*

"Zach, this development presents—"

"Let's talk about it later," he said hastily, not wanting to hear what she had to say. "We both need some time to think." He walked into the kitchen and deposited the plates on the counter. "I'll call the girls down to do the dishes, and then I have a few errands to run."

"Zach, we've got to have an understanding about—"

"Later, Diana. I'll be back."

But he deliberately stayed out past the time when he thought she'd be in bed, and when he returned to the house everything was quiet. He put the bottle of wine in the back of the refrigerator behind several cartons of milk so the girls wouldn't spy it then climbed the stairs to his room.

As he lay in bed, he tried to focus on the look in Diana's eyes when he had been loving her, touching her in all the places that made her moan with desire. Instead all he could see was the fear in her eyes when he'd walked out on the porch and discovered the girls staring at the half-empty wine bottle.

Dammit! Would he fall victim to an attack of nobility? What kind of a spell had Diana woven, that he'd seriously entertain the notion of denying himself? Hell, he'd be denying her, too! They'd both be fools not to take this second opportunity to be together, wouldn't they?

Below him Diana lay awake and listened to Zach toss in his bed. She had to arrive at a decision before the girls left. Last time she had allowed herself to drift toward the idea of sleeping with Zach...until the emotion he inspired propelled her into his bed. How easily that could happen again. Her hands clenched at her sides. How easily, indeed, considering the weakness that consumed her whenever she thought of his virile body, the magic of his hands.

Now Diana knew the incredible joy to be found in his arms, and she yearned for him. Strangely, she didn't feel guilty any longer about betraying Jim. No, memories of her late husband were no obstacle, but her misgivings about Allison and Laurie still plagued her. Tomorrow morning, after driving them to the school for the trip, she would return and face Zach. By then her decision would have to be made.

IT WAS. Diana walked into the kitchen and found Zach at the table, sipping a cup of coffee.

"Diana, we've got to talk."

"Yes." She sat down at the Formica table.

He pushed his cup away as if he'd only used it as a prop, an excuse to be sitting there when she came home. "I'm probably a damn fool for suggesting this, but why don't I stay in a motel this weekend? That would solve everything."

Her mouth dropped open. "What?"

He smiled self-consciously. "I know. You expected the fast rush, didn't you? Don't think I'm not sorely tempted." He gazed deeply into her eyes. "But it seems I've got a conscience that won't let me make both of us temporarily happy and you miserable with guilt by Sunday."

Diana's heart wrenched. She hadn't expected such compassion, and his understanding made what she was about to say a thousand times more difficult. "Thank you, Zach."

He pushed his chair back. "I'll throw a few things in a suitcase and be off."

"Zach, wait a minute."

He paused and sat back down, hope flickering in his eyes. Diana looked away, knowing that in another moment the hope would be dashed forever.

"One weekend apart isn't going to solve this problem," she said, staring at a spot of dried milk on the linoleum. "We both know it." She forced the next words out. "I've—I've decided you'll have to leave."

He drew in his breath sharply. "You mean permanently, don't you?"

She twisted her hands in front of her and nodded. "By the time I pick up the girls on Sunday, you can be moved out. That would save them some trauma. I'd appreciate it if you'd let me tell them it was a mutual decision, but if you want me to take all the blame, I will."

"Diana, you don't have to resort to this." His voice was strained. "I've put the pressure on you recently, but that's over. My ego wanted you to snap and come to me. The fact that you didn't proved how much you want to protect those girls, and I'm ready to accept that."

Somewhere she found the courage to look at him. "You don't know how many times I've nearly 'snapped,' as you put it. You may think we can go on this way for the rest of your stay here, but I don't."

He pounded the table with his fist. "Dammit!"

"I'm sorry Zach. We've made a mess of this."

"Have you thought of how the girls will feel when they come home and I've disappeared without even saying goodbye?"

"Yes. And it won't be easy. But I'm afraid if they're here when you leave, you won't be able to go, and I won't be able to force the issue."

He fiddled with his coffee cup. "You're probably right."

"I'll help you look for a place, if you like," she ventured. "I know the area. I can probably find something not much more expensive than—"

"I don't give a damn about the money!" He leaped up and began pacing the kitchen floor. "I don't want to be cut off from you, from the girls."

"You have no choice," she said, struggling to keep calm. "This is my house."

He paced silently, and Diana fought the urge to reach out to him. She wanted him so much.

At last he spoke. "You're right, of course. I can't live here unless you allow it. If you're willing to risk the girls' disappointment, I have no more arguments." He stopped pacing and faced her. "I'll begin looking this morning."

"Would you like me to help?"

"No, I'll take care of it, Diana."

She swallowed the lump in her throat. "All right."

"I'll be in touch." He strode to the front door and thumped down the steps. He was gone.

Diana listened until she heard his car pull away from the curb; only then did she put her head in her arms and let the tears come. She cried hard, berating herself the whole time for her emotionalism. What was wrong with her? Zach was only a hired handyman, and not much of a one, at that. She'd known him for a matter of weeks. An adult woman didn't cry over someone she'd met so recently. That was for a silly schoolgirl who fancied herself in love.

Abruptly the tears stopped, and she slowly raised her head. Was she falling in love with Zach? Propping her chin in both hands, she stared with bloodshot eyes at the chair he had recently occupied. Zach of the sun-bleached hair and ocean-blue eyes. True, his lean bronzed body made her ache with longing, but he could also make her laugh. When a problem arose with the girls, he was quick to soothe hurt feelings, offer solutions. He was kind, generous and loving, even if he dripped paint everywhere and couldn't repair the kitchen faucet. God, how she'd miss him!

"Diana Thatcher, you're a complete idiot!" she ranted, smacking the table with both palms. "Not only do you lust after his body, you've fallen in love with him! Of all the dumb stunts you've pulled, this is the dumbest."

She paced frantically up and down the kitchen, until she realized Zach had done the same thing. "Now you even act like him," she muttered to herself. She stomped into the living room and vented her frustration with crashing piano chords.

The day was empty and difficult until after school when the Bad News Brass arrived for their lesson. For the first time Diana rejoiced in the rambunctious behavior of the three boys who distracted her from endless thoughts of Zach.

All day she'd wondered what he was doing and whether he'd been successful in his search for living quarters. He'd have to come back sometime, if only to gather his belongings. Could she face him, knowing the extent of her feelings?

After the boys left Diana grabbed her purse and a light jacket from her bedroom closet. Then she heard the front door open and close. Footsteps approached her room; he stood in the doorway, blocking her escape.

"Going somewhere?"

I love you, she wanted to cry out at the sight of him. Today his T-shirt was tucked into faded jeans instead of shorts, in deference to the cooler fall weather, but his arms and face still glowed with healthy color. "I—yes, as a matter of fact."

"Must have made some quick plans."

Her heart pounded in her chest. Should she insist on moving past him and leaving? "Did you find a place?" she asked, hoping to distract him into stepping aside.

"Yes."

Why did his answer plunge her into despair? This was what she wanted, had demanded. Speaking became difficult as her throat constricted. "Then you're here to pick up your things."

"No. I move in Sunday." His blue eyes focused intently on her.

"Oh," she said weakly.

"So where are you off to?" He leaned against the door frame.

Diana lifted her chin and took a deep breath. "Dinner and a movie."

His expression hardened. "A date?"

"No. By myself."

The look on his face softened to one of understanding. "Diana, you don't have to do that. I won't bother you."

"It's not you I'm worried about." She could have bitten her tongue out as desire leaped in his blue eyes.

"That's nice to hear," he said gently, moving into the bedroom.

"Zach..." She backed away a step. "Perhaps I shouldn't have been so honest."

"Perhaps you shouldn't." He watched her carefully. "And I won't play cat and mouse, Diana. However, the thought occurred to me that on Sunday you and I are making the noble sacrifice of separating. I wonder if we don't deserve something for ourselves in the meantime?"

Diana stood in the middle of her bedroom, transfixed by his bold suggestion.

"Think about it," he said. "I'll be in the kitchen, pouring myself a glass of the wine I bought last night."

She raised her eyebrows in surprise.

"Oh, yes," he said. "I was preparing for the big seduction number, tried to talk myself into it until the wee small hours of the morning. But I couldn't go through with the plan. At first I figured that for long-term gain I'd give up a short-term pleasure." He shrugged. "But now that I've accepted that the long-term gain is out the window, I'm ready to find that pleasure. But only if the lady is willing." He turned and sauntered into the kitchen.

Diana licked dry lips. Already her body clamored in answer to Zach's proposition. Try as she might, Diana couldn't find a more glamorous word for it. A proposition for pleasure. Love didn't figure in it, nor did commitment, nor even friendship. On Sunday Zach would leave her house, never to return, and people didn't become emotionally involved when they were about to end a relationship.

Unfortunately for her, she was already emotionally involved. And now she had a choice—to throw away her last chance to be with Zach, perhaps minimizing the pain on Sunday, or crowd the remaining hours with memories that held the power to hurt or comfort her for years to come.

As Diana stood, torn by indecision, the telephone rang in the kitchen. She heard Zach's baritone then his measured tread toward the bedroom.

"Mrs. Eckstrom wants to know if one of the girls would like to come over this evening and pick a few of her chrysanthemums for our Sunday dinner table."

Diana and Zach exchanged a long look.

"I'll talk to her," Diana said and walked by him into the kitchen. Her hand trembled slightly as she picked up the receiver from the kitchen counter. "Mrs. Eckstrom? Zach told me you're offering some of your flowers to us. That's really nice."

Zach walked into the kitchen and leaned against the counter, where he could see Diana's face. She gazed unflinchingly into his blue eyes as Mrs. Eckstrom explained her overabundance of chrysanthemums.

"We'd love to have them, Mrs. Eckstrom," she said evenly, "but all of us are glued to the television set right now, and the program will be on very late. The girls will be quite busy tomorrow, too, but I could do it then."

A soft light glowed in Zach's eyes. He straightened and walked to the cupboard containing the wine goblets.

"You won't? Then perhaps Sunday," Diana said. She watched Zach set an empty wineglass next to his full one. Wine splashed ruby-red into the second goblet and arched up its sides, until Zach lifted the bottle away and the wine quivered an inch or two below the rim. His strong fingers curved around each delicate stem as he lifted both glasses from the table and walked toward her.

"Thank you for thinking of us, Mrs. Eckstrom. Have fun at the bazaar tomorrow, and I'll send the girls over on Sunday." The click of the receiver sounded incredibly loud to Diana as she hung up the telephone and turned to Zach. Silently he handed her the goblet of wine then touched the rim of her glass with his in a wordless salute. As they each brought the wine to their lips, their eyes spoke a primitive message that needed no words.

Slowly Diana lowered her glass and smiled provocatively. "My place this time," she murmured, turning toward her bedroom. "And bring the wine," she said over her shoulder.

Zach's gaze lingered on the sway of her hips under her tailored forest-green slacks. Why did her body, always demurely covered, excite him more than those of all the bikini-clad beauties of the California shore? Would he spend the rest of his life longing for the sight of her lustrous alabaster skin?

He feared he might, and that Sunday would begin a stretch of hell unknown before. Most of all, he feared he was in love—in love with a lady who wanted nothing more than one short weekend of fun and games before she sent him on his way.

She'd even told a white lie in order to have this time with him. He couldn't have predicted that, wasn't sure how deep her passions ran. But she was all woman, and at least for now, she was all his. He picked up the wine bottle and followed her into the bedroom.

The shades were lowered to the sill, and Diana's bedside lamp cast a circle of light on snow-white sheets scattered with a pattern of tiny violets. Still fully clothed, Diana sat just outside the circle of light and sipped her wine.

Zach walked to the bedside table and set down his glass and the bottle then reached for her goblet. She took another sip of the ruby liquid before handing the glass to him. He placed it beside his then turned to look at her.

"You're constantly amazing, Diana," he said quietly.

"Am I?"

"My suggestion was a shot in the dark. I didn't think—"

"Let's not think," Diana said, lifting her face and exposing the ivory column of her neck to the light.

"If that's what you want." He searched the luminous depths of her eyes. Passion lurked just under the surface, but was there another emotion, less fierce, yet more compelling? He couldn't be sure.

"Yes, that's what I want."

"All right." Zach reached out and curved his bronzed hand around the white satin of her throat then bent to taste the lips she parted in welcome. His knee found the edge of the bed, and he guided her gently backward until she lay across the smooth flowered sheets and he half covered her with his muscular torso.

Her lips, flavored with red wine, moved sensuously against his, and her tongue teased and withdrew in a coquettish way he'd never known her to have. He lifted his head and gazed at her. "You do know how to play, after all, you wanton minx," he said, his breathing labored.

"You're helping me remember how," she replied, her silver eyes sparkling with desire. "You've shown me how to enjoy myself again, Zach." She slipped her delicate hand under his shirt and circled his nipple with the smooth edge of her fingernail, tickling him softly.

"And I thought you were a proper Midwestern girl."

"Not tonight." She felt his nipple tighten.

"Then seduce me, Diana."

"That won't be difficult."

"Are you implying I'm easy?"

She chuckled. "Yes."

"Them's strong words, lady. Prove it."

"Okay."

His blue eyes darkened as her hand moved down and unsnapped his jeans. Unerringly she found the zipper, and then her soft fingers insinuated themselves under the elastic of his briefs and curled possessively around the throbbing evidence of his arousal. He gasped as she stroked him.

"Give?" she murmured.

"Anything you want," he groaned.

"You know what I want," she whispered.

"I think so," he said, half laughing, half moaning. "Diana, if you don't stop—"

With tantalizing slowness she released him. "I want to undress you, Zach."

"You've already done half the job."

"Not really. I want to feel powerful, Zach. I want you in my power. Lie back and let me take off your clothes."

"As long as I can return the favor."

"Eventually."

"Eventually?" he protested. "Diana, how long is this—"

"Be quiet and lie back."

"Yes, ma'am." He relaxed against the violet-patterned sheets.

"Lift your arms up."

He did as she ordered, and she slid his shirt slowly up

over his wide chest, pausing to kiss and nibble his still-tanned skin. "Oh, Zach," she sighed. "You're so beautiful and brown."

"And you're so beautiful and white. I love that about you."

Her nibbling stopped as the magic word "love" tumbled from his lips almost carelessly. "Do you?"

"Among other things."

"Well, I love this light-colored fur all over your chest," she said, forcing herself to use the word as nonchalantly as he had. "I love running my fingers through it."

"That tickles."

"I thought maybe you weren't ticklish." Wickedness gleamed in her eyes.

"I'm not."

"Hmm." She pulled the shirt over his head and up his arms, kissing and tickling as she went, while he clamped his lips together to keep from laughing. "Now," she said, holding his wrists bound with the shirt, "I have you captured." With a mischievous grin she glanced down at his face, but she was mesmerized by the sudden intensity in his blue eyes. Her smile faded.

"Yes, you do," he said simply.

"But I'll let you go," she murmured, disengaging the shirt and looking away.

"What if I don't want to escape?" he asked softly.

"Then," she said, her hands moving gradually over his chest and down to his waist, "then..." With lighting swiftness she pounced on him and sat astride his body. "Then I'll tickle you until you cry out for mercy!" She made good her threat, until at last, laughing and breathless, he caught both her hands in one of his.

"You're a devil. Whatever happened to that sedate Widow Thatcher?"

"I gave her the night off. Do you miss her?"

"Not a bit, Diana. Come here." He pulled her forward and kissed her hard on the lips. "Are you going to finish your job?" he mumbled against her mouth.

"Right away," she breathed. Pushing herself up, she grasped his jeans at the waist and worked them over his hips. When his jeans, shoes and socks were gone, she looked up to find him watching her. Only his cotton briefs, bulging with the evidence of his desire, remained.

He raised one tawny eyebrow. "Well?"

"I never believed in doing a job halfway."

"Good girl."

She slipped her fingers inside the wide elastic waistband and lovingly removed the last barrier to her view of him. He lay before her, fully aroused and magnificent. She would never forget what he looked like, lying there in her bed. No matter what would happen after Sunday.

"My turn," he said gently, reaching for her hand and drawing her down next to him.

"I could look at you forever," she said, gazing into his blue eyes as he began unbuttoning her blouse.

"Fine with me." Zach pushed the material aside and rubbed his palm in circles over her flat stomach. Forever. Was that the word he'd been searching for, every time he thought of her? He watched her eyes as his fingers moved upward and unfastened the front clasp of her bra. Forever.

Excitement glowed bright in her silver gaze as his hand moved under the wispy material and stroked across the silken mound of her breast. Forever. She arched upward, pressing the hard bud of her nipple against his palm, and he bent to take her moist eager mouth with ravenous lips. The taste of her satisfied his deepest hunger, and he slipped his arm behind her back and pulled her hard against his heated body. In that moment he knew he would not give her up so easily.

12

DIANA FELT THE CHANGE in mood from playful teasing to fierce desire, and she moaned deep in her throat as the rhythmic thrust of Zach's tongue told her what he wanted. Breathing heavily, he lifted his mouth from hers while he fumbled with the button and zipper of her slacks and shoved the material impatiently over her hips.

She wriggled out of the slacks and kicked off her shoes as he reached for the delicate lace of her panties. Soon those joined the pile of clothing in a heap on the floor. He slipped one arm under her knees and another behind her shoulders to lift her higher onto the bed. Then, not seeming to care that her blouse and unfastened bra still clung to her body, he moved over her, bracing himself on outstretched arms propped on either side of her head.

The fire in his blue eyes was a more powerful aphrodisiac than any orchestrated prelude to love, and she opened herself willingly, eager to satisfy his unspoken demand. Then he was there, filling her, wiping away the emptiness of the past. His gaze, dark with possessive intensity, held hers captive as their movements increased in tempo. The silken material of her blouse twisted under her back as she grasped his shoulders and writhed under him.

Her lips formed his name, and she saw his mouth curve gently, knowingly, before passion blurred her vision and her fingers dug into the rock-hard muscles of his shoulders; violent spasms shook her body. Faintly she heard his voice above her, murmuring soft words as he continued his sensual movements, prolonging the sensations that spun through her.

Before the coil of tension could relax, she felt it tightening again, and she gasped out her surprise. With a delighted chuckle he lowered his body close to hers and nuzzled her throat.

"Yes, Diana," Zach whispered as her breathing accelerated with the persistent rocking of his hips against hers. "And this time I'll be with you."

His breath was hot against her neck. She licked the salty film covering his shoulder then nipped the bronzed skin as he pushed her closer, closer. Her body grew as malleable as soft clay, and she lost the distinction between his flesh and hers. Faster and faster they blended, one with the other, driving toward an inevitable fusion. At last it arrived—a mind-shattering explosion that burst triumphantly through the barriers each had created. With cries of joy they clung together in the whirlpool of sensation, holding tightly to the person who had become a part of the other—forever.

They lay in silence for long moments. Finally Zach started to speak, cleared his throat and tried again. The husky timbre of his voice revealed more than his words.

"The game's changing, Diana."

Her eyes fluttered open. She stared at the ceiling, and her words were almost too soft for him to hear. "I know."

He raised himself up on one arm. "Diana—"

She turned her head and laid a finger across his lips. "Later, Zach," she whispered. "Let's enjoy every moment of our time together. We'll sort out the problems later."

"Maybe there won't be problems."

Her lips curved in a sad smile, but she said nothing.

"All right, Diana. Later." He kissed her briefly. "I'm thirsty. Let's have some more wine."

Diana fluffed the pillows, and they propped themselves up in bed to drink the wine from a single goblet. He watched her over the rim of the glass while she laughingly rid herself of the rumpled garments he hadn't bothered to remove earlier. As she threw them with a flourish on the pile of clothes on the floor, her unfettered breasts swayed seductively, and Zach felt desire pulsing through him again.

He handed her the wineglass, and once she had swallowed the last of the red liquid, he took the goblet from her and bent close to lick a tiny drop from the corner of her mouth. Her breath quivered around his tongue as it flicked teasingly over her wine-drenched lips. His hand, still holding the goblet, reached blindly for the bedside table, and then he toppled her under him, his whole being crazy with wanting.

A new richness wove itself into their lovemaking throughout the night. Self-consciousness disappeared, and when their stomachs began to growl with hunger, they spread a picnic supper in the middle of Diana's bed and ate without bothering to put on clothes. They showered together, shared jokes and pieces of their past. And most of all, they loved, without naming the emotion that replaced the need for sleep with the need to submerge themselves in each other.

WHEN MORNING CAME, Zach leaped out of bed. "Let's go somewhere today."

"Together? I don't think that would look—"

"Out of town, then. How about New Salem? I should

see the place, anyway, get the feel of Lincoln's earlier years, before he moved to Springfield."

"I don't know, Zach."

"Come on. You won't meet anyone you know. I bet everyone there will be from Wyoming or someplace like that."

Diana laughed. "Okay. I haven't driven to New Salem in ages."

"And don't take any money. You're on a date with me today."

"Pretty free with your spending, aren't you?"

Zach's expression sobered. "That's not your concern anymore, Diana."

The pain they'd tried to submerge surfaced in her eyes. "No, I guess not."

He forced a smile. "Besides, in a few short months I'll be in the chips."

"Oh?"

"But that's a secret I'll save for later. Get dressed, moon goddess. We're spending an entire day together, with no girls, no neighbors, no worries. Right?"

"Right." She smiled, resolving not to spoil the promise of a last golden day with the man she loved by thinking of their impending separation.

Zach was in his element, touring New Salem with its reconstructed log cabins and rustic flavor. He steeped Diana in historical lore with as much authority as she had once initiated him into the wonders of a state fair. They drove home at dusk, passionately debating the merits and disadvantages of pioneer living.

Their night together, colored with the joy of a day in each other's company, held the warmth of friendship as well as the heat of desire. And while darkness still lay beyond the lowered blinds, they avoided discussing what would happen at daybreak.

At last a crack of dull gray appeared between the sill and the shade, as they both had known it would, and they gazed into each other's eyes in recognition. Their charmed hours, wrested out of time, were gone.

Gently Zach reached out and traced Diana's kiss-swollen lips, which only moments before had been smiling at a childhood memory she'd revealed. Now her face was solemn, waiting. "You're so beautiful, Diana," he whispered.

"No more than you."

"You know what I have to say." His gaze roved her face, searching for reassurance. "I can't let you go, Diana. You mean too much to me. We mean too much to each other."

She shook her head and swallowed hard. "It won't work."

"Some good news came in the mail on Wednesday," he said, pushing past her objections. "That's the secret I was saving. I've been invited to interview at Stanford next month. I'm a serious candidate, Diana."

She hated to watch his enthusiasm build, knowing it would lead nowhere. "I'm happy for you, but—"

"Don't you understand? I'm going to land that job, and then—"

"No, Zach."

"Diana, please. Marry me."

Her eyes filled with tears. A moment that should have been filled with joy was bathed in pain. Right now, no matter how much she desired it, marriage to Zach was impossible.

He took her silence as hesitation. "Not this minute, Diana. We can wait until the job is certain, and I understand we can't live together until then, but maybe by Christmas...I could face the separation if I had that to keep me going."

"What about the girls?"

"What about them? I love them; you know that. We'd be a happy family—you, me and the girls. I recognize now that a family is very important to me. A professorship at Stanford should support us, especially if you teach music."

"Zach, you don't understand." Her gray eyes reflected her misery. "I couldn't move the girls to California."

"Why not? Allison said she'd love to see the ocean and movie stars."

"Yes, but did you ask her if she wanted to leave Springfield permanently, say goodbye to friends she's known since first grade and start over in a brand-new school?"

Zach studied her face, not answering. Then he looked away. "No, I didn't." He swung his muscular legs over the edge of the bed and stood up. "But kids can adapt to change, usually better than adults."

Diana watched as he began to pace the room. "Sometimes they can, Zach," she said gently. "Allison and Laurie aren't like the kids you're used to in California. They were born and raised here. They're not world travelers. Their security is here, especially now that they have no father. They've got their hands full adapting to that change."

"Dammit, I can help! You've said yourself I provide a needed male influence for them."

Her heart ached for him, for them. "I know, and they care for you, but not enough to be uprooted from everything they've ever known."

"How can you be so sure?"

"I asked Laurie."

"When?"

"Remember the incident with Jenny? After that blowup, Laurie stayed in the kitchen while you and Allison worked on the chicken coop. She hinted that you and I should get married."

"Smart girl, that Laurie."

"But when I explained that your future would be in California and marriage would mean all of us moving there, she dropped the idea like a hot potato, Zach. She's determined to attend Lanphier High School. I'm sure Allison would answer the same way."

"I'd like to talk with them."

"No."

He wheeled and walked back toward her. "Why not, Diana? Afraid I could change their minds?"

She propped herself on one elbow. "As a matter of fact, yes. If they both believed we wanted to get married, and their wishes stood in the way of our happiness, they'd give in. And possibly resent it the rest of their lives."

"But *their* wishes are standing in the way of *our* happiness. Don't you care about that?"

"At this moment our wishes are not as important as theirs."

"The hell they're not! I happen to love you, Diana Thatcher!"

"Oh, Zach!"

"And I happen to believe you love me."

His golden image swam before her as tears filled her eyes. "Of course I do," she whispered.

He lowered himself beside her and bent to cup her face in both hands. "That's all I have to know," he said, brushing at her damp cheeks with his thumbs. "The girls will understand, Diana. All right, so Christmas is too soon. They can finish out the school year, and then all three of you will come to California." He buried his fingers in her soft hair. "I can have a house waiting, if you like, or wait until you—"

"No, Zach."

His fingers tightened against her scalp. "Diana, you just admitted you love me."

"I also love the girls, and I won't drag them out to California next summer."

"The girls will be fine!"

She wrenched away from him and slid out of bed. "I don't believe that. I have to be able to live with myself, Zach. The answer is no." She walked around the bed to the closet and pulled out her robe.

He stood up and faced her across the room. "What is your suggestion, then? All my study has been directed toward a professorship at Stanford. Do you expect me to give that up?"

"Of course not," Diana said, tying the robe's belt securely around her waist.

"Diana, we love each other!"

She looked at him bleakly. "Don't you see? That's irrelevant."

"Irrelevant?" His expression was incredulous.

"Yes. Our love doesn't change the fact that I must stay here with the girls and you must pursue your opportunities in California. It's over, Zach."

"No. I won't accept that."

"You have no choice." She turned away from the pain in his eyes. Why did their beautiful weekend have to end this way? Yet she had known it would from the moment when she had sensed in the heat of their passion that he loved her. Zach must have thought proposing would solve everything, but instead they were more miserable than before.

"My God, Diana. I can't believe you would give up everything we could have together, just because neither you nor the girls are willing to leave the security of this town. What do you want to do, shrivel up and die here rather than risk making a mistake or inviting someone's moral judgment on you?"

"Excuse me. I have to feed the dog," she murmured, hurrying toward the bedroom door before Zach could glimpse a fresh outburst of tears.

"Damn the dog! Damn your duties and obligations! You don't know how to live, Diana!" he called after her.

For the next few hours they treated each other like polite strangers. Diana kept busy, laundering every item that could conceivably be cleaned, including curtains and small throw rugs, while Zach made trip after trip from his room to the Corvair with armloads of disorganized belongings.

By midmorning the Corvair was piled high, and above the creaking scraping noises of the washing machine, Diana heard the sound of Zach's pacing in his bedroom. He was packed, but he couldn't bring himself to leave. Diana listened to his even tread across the wooden floor as the washer whirled into its spin cycle. Then suddenly she couldn't hear Zach's footsteps over the clanking buzzing noises coming from the washer, and the machine began rocking violently.

"Don't you dare!" Diana cried as the noise became deafening. "Don't you dare break now!"

The clanking grew louder and more ominous, until with one final groan the washer stopped.

"Dammit!" Diana kicked the machine with all her might and beat on the closed lid with clenched fists while she used every swear word she knew; then she made up some more as tears poured down her cheeks.

She didn't realize Zach was behind her until his strong arms wrapped around her flailing arms and drew her back against him.

"Take it easy," he crooned. "Stop, Diana. Turn around here and let me hold you."

Wordlessly she obeyed, crumpling against him like a paper doll. "The w-washing machine," she choked. "The washing machine broke."

"I heard the noise." His mouth twisted sardonically. "I came down to see if I could do anything."

Abruptly her sobs changed to almost hysterical laughter. "Do anything? You? You can't fix anything, Zachary Wainwright."

"That's where you're wrong," he murmured against her hair. "I can fix all the important things, if you'll give me a chance."

"Is that right?" She raised a tear-stained face. "Well, right now this washing machine is extremely important. Can you fix that?"

"No."

"And how about the dripping kitchen faucet? Can you fix that?"

"No." His smile was sad as his gaze roved over her rebellious face.

"Then what kind of handyman are you?"

"The wrong kind for you, apparently." He released her and stepped away. "Tell the girls goodbye for me. And tell them...tell them I left of my own accord." Wearily he turned and walked through the living room and out the front door.

The door closed with a click, and silence reigned in the big old house. Gradually, as she stood ramrod straight as if before a firing squad, Diana became aware that the silence was not total. From the kitchen sink behind her came the steady plop of water from the dripping faucet, the rhythm as constant as a clock ticking away the seconds, the minutes, the hours, the long days that stretched endlessly in front of her.

"GONE?" ALLISON CRIED, racing in the kitchen door and dropping her overnight case in the middle of the floor. "What do you mean, *gone*?" She took the stairs two at a time and flung open the door to Zach's room.

"Mother, you can't be serious," Laurie said, walking to the foot of the stairs and peering up at Allison. "His stuff's there, right, Al? Mom's kidding."

Allison turned slowly from her inspection of the room and looked down the stairs at Laurie. "She's not kidding."

"What?" Laurie spun toward her mother. "Where is he?"

"I'm not sure. He got another place, that's all."

"Where?" Laurie persisted. "You must know where."

"No, Laurie, I don't."

Allison walked halfway down the stairs. "You had a fight, didn't you?"

"Not exactly," Diana answered. "Look, girls, you don't have to understand all the details. Zach and I decided we weren't...getting along very well. And he certainly wasn't much of a handyman."

"What difference does that make?" Allison protested, close to tears. "He tried real hard, and I—I want him to come back!" Her chin quivered.

"Me, too, Mom," Laurie said quietly.

Diana took a deep breath. She had known this moment would be bad, but in the best interests of everyone, she had to get through it. "Zach would have left around Christmas, anyway. You would be more attached to him by then and miss him even more."

"Why does he have to go at all?" Allison wailed, slumping down on the steps. "Doesn't he like it here?"

"Not as a permanent home," Diana answered. "His home is in California, just like yours is here. He's hoping to get a special job at Stanford University."

"Well, I wish I could go to California with him!" Allison declared.

Diana glanced up in speechless shock.

"No, you don't, Al," Laurie interjected with a sigh. "You'd go to a different school, have to make all new friends."

Allison dropped her head into her hands. "I didn't think of that. I sure wouldn't want to really *live* there. Lanphier's better'n any old California high school. But I want Zach!"

Diana listened quietly. The girls had confirmed exactly what she'd told Zach. They wished he'd stay, but they were hardly willing to follow him anywhere. And why should they? Zach wasn't the cornerstone of their existence, only a welcome addition. Eventually their flurry of activities would fade the memories of his stay in the house.

If he'd become a cornerstone of *her* existence, she had only herself to blame for falling in love with the wrong man. But intense as the pain was, she didn't regret any of the time spent with Zach. He'd taught her that she was still a passionate, vibrant woman, and her life was richer because he'd been part of it. How she'd miss him!

"Mom, are you all right?" Laurie peered anxiously into her face.

With an effort Diana smiled. "I'm fine, honey. A little tired, that's all."

"Didn't you get enough sleep last night?" Allison asked innocently.

Diana stared at Allison, dumbfounded. Such a simple logical question, yet how should she answer? Once she had told Zach that she couldn't lie to her children, yet the truth at this point would reveal everything she'd been working so hard to keep from her daughters.

Laurie touched her mother's shoulder. "Never mind, Mom," she said calmly. "It's really none of our business." She glanced significantly at her sister. "Is it, Al?"

Allison's head swung back and forth from Diana to Laurie. "No," she said at last. "Not really. Want us to pick those flowers at Mrs. Eckstrom's now, Mom?"

Diana gripped the newel post and tried to control her whirling thoughts. What was happening? Who was shielding whom? "That would be fine," she murmured.

"We'll put our stuff in our rooms," Laurie said, running up the stairs, "and then we'll go over. And I promise not to use the good scissors this time."

"Okay," Diana said weakly, wandering toward the kitchen.

"And Mom," Laurie added, calling over the banister, "let's have sandwiches for dinner. Al and I will make them, and you take it easy."

Diana turned in the kitchen doorway to tell Laurie

she'd make the sandwiches, but her daughter was already in her room. Would Laurie have made such an offer before Zach had come to live with them? Probably not. Chalk up another one for the fix-it man. And Laurie's incredible grown-up handling of an awkward situation. Zach's example of diplomacy and loving kindness had saved face for all three of them, even after he was gone. Suddenly Diana was sure. Her daughters would never mention it, but both of them knew she and Zach had been lovers.

UNABLE TO TOLERATE THE SILENCE of his small impersonal apartment, Zach spent the afternoon walking. He directed his footsteps, knowing aimless wandering would take him right back to where he wasn't wanted. Were the girls home yet?

Home. He'd have to give up referring to Diana's house that way. The lovely old two-story dwelling was home to Allison and Laurie and to the woman he loved, but not to him. Not anymore.

He gazed upward through frost-blushed red maples to the crisp blue October sky. In a few weeks Springfield could expect its first snowfall. So much for the giant snowman he'd dreamed of building with Allison and Laurie, and the warm Christmas he had planned. Might as well work sixteen hours a day on his research and get the hell out of town.

Zach turned the corner at Edwards Street and walked down Eighth, past the restored homes of families who had been Abraham Lincoln's neighbors one hundred thirty years ago. Their names flitted through Zach's mind—George Shutt, Henson Robinson, Allen Miller,

Sarah Cook. Zach envied the sense of community suggested by the reconstructed neighborhood.

He reached his destination and leaned against the white picket fence across the street from the tan house with leaf-green shutters framing its windows. He liked the side view of Lincoln's home better than the imposing formal front. The side entrance led to a lattice-covered porch and a backyard where children might have played. From the front of the house Zach could imagine Lincoln the politician, but from the side he glimpsed Lincoln the family man.

The house was the only one Lincoln had ever owned, the only place he'd put down roots. Then, after twenty years, he had allowed duty and ambition to take him away forever. His farewell speech, as he had stood at the depot before leaving to accept the presidency, had haunted Zach all afternoon.

My friends, no one not in my situation can appreciate my feelings of sadness at this parting. To this place and the kindness of these people I owe everything.

13

THE REALIZATION THAT ALLISON and Laurie knew about her alliance with Zach had a curiously liberating effect on Diana. The passing days found her laughing and talking with the girls in a more relaxed fashion than ever before. Gradually her relationship with them became less that of a parent-child and more of a partnership.

She depended on them as companions, too, and they acquiesced in an almost protective fashion. Diana knew that soon she must stop leaning on Allison and Laurie for emotional support. After all, they wouldn't be around forever. But in the first weeks after Zach had left, she took unabashed advantage of their company to ward off the demons of loneliness.

One cool Saturday afternoon, after the last music student had gone, Diana walked into her bedroom to record a payment in her ledger. But suddenly she was sitting on the edge of the bed, close to tears as memories of Zach closed in around her. While she was teaching or when she was with the girls, she kept her equilibrium, but moments like this caught her by surprise.

Jumping up impatiently, she wiped her eyes and marched into the living room, where Allison lay on the floor in front of the television and Laurie sprawled on the sofa reading a book.

"Let's have a leaf-raking party," she said.

Allison gave Diana a suspicious look. "What do you mean, a party? Sounds like work to me."

"Don't be so lazy, Al," Laurie said, glancing up from her book. "You want us to clean up the leaves, Mom?"

"All of us will clean up the leaves...eventually," Diana replied, smiling with fond understanding. Her oldest daughter was developing quite a conscientious attitude, but if Laurie didn't watch out, she'd become as stuffy about her responsibilities as her mother had once been. "But first we can rake them into a big pile and jump in them, like you used to when you were little."

"Freaky!" Allison said with a grin. "Let's go."

"Aw, Mom. That stuff's for kids," Laurie protested.

"It is not," Allison cried, pulling on a jacket.

"So what if it is?" Diana rummaged through the coat closet and found a hooded orange sweatshirt. "I'm going to do it."

Laurie's eyes widened. "You are?"

"Sure." Diana tugged the sweatshirt over her head and fluffed out her hair with her fingers. "Come on, Al."

Allison stopped dead in her tracks. "Mom, you called me Al."

"Isn't that what you're going by these days?"

"Yes, but I thought you didn't like it."

"Well, I've changed my mind. Al is sort of cute and perky, and it goes with your new haircut. Coming, Laurie?"

Laurie sighed. "I guess so. If you two plan to make fools of yourselves in the backyard, my reputation's shot, anyway."

As they trooped into the garage to go after rakes and plastic garbage bags, Allison turned to her mother. "You know, this is the kind of thing Zach would do."

Diana fought down the lump of emotion that rose inevitably in her throat. "Yes, I know." She reached blindly for a rake. "Last one outside is a rotten egg."

They staged a contest to see who could rake the biggest pile of the yellow maple leaves in ten minutes, and the cool autumn air was filled with their taunts and shouts of triumph. Beethoven incurred the wrath of all three contestants as he scampered through each pile and sent leaves flying.

"Mine's the biggest!" Allison proclaimed.

"Is not," Laurie argued. "Look at my pile from this angle, and you'll see it's much bigger than yours."

"You're both wrong," Diana chortled. *"Mine's* the biggest."

Allison and Laurie glanced at her then at each other. "Not anymore!" they shouted in unison and dove for her pile, scattering the crunchy leaves everywhere.

"No fair!" Diana cried. "All right, you asked for this." She ran toward Laurie's pile and leaped into the middle of the dried leaves.

"I get Allison's!" Laurie yelled, and soon all three of them were jumping from one bed of leaves to another, with Beethoven running and barking at their heels and the caged chickens adding their squawking to the bedlam.

"Hey," called a deep baritone. "Can I play, too?"

All three stopped in midmotion, like children in a game of statues.

Allison found her voice first. "Zach!" She scrambled to her feet and ran to open the back gate. Catching hold of the sleeve of Zach's corduroy coat, she pulled him inside the fence. "We're—" she stopped to get her breath "—we're raking up the leaves."

"I can see that." He grasped her by the shoulders and

turned her slowly around while he studied her short bouncy haircut. "Very nice, Al. Makes you look older."

"Thank you," she replied primly.

"Too bad you weren't here for our contest," Laurie added, walking toward him.

"Yeah, or for the part when we jumped in the leaves," Allison said, giggling. "You know whose idea it was in the first place?"

Zach grinned at her. "Yours."

"Mom's," Allison said, her blue eyes sparkling.

Zach finally allowed his gaze to linger on Diana. Self-consciously she got to her feet and ran nervous fingers through her tousled cloud of dark hair. Her silver eyes sparkled in surprised greeting before she glanced away uncertainly, and his heart almost stopped beating. How could she have become more beautiful in a matter of weeks? His memory hadn't done her justice.

"Your mother thought of all this? That's great," he said, his voice husky with what he didn't want to feel. "By next summer you'll be spraying her with the garden hose."

"Can you stay for supper, Zach?" Laurie asked, touching his arm.

Zach raised an eyebrow. "Don't you mean dinner?"

"Nope, because we're eating in the kitchen tonight. That's more like supper, isn't it? Dinner's when we eat in the dining room. We don't do that much anymore."

"My, my." Zach shook his head. "I leave you women for a few weeks and look what happens. Your mother's cavorting in the backyard, with leaves all over her sweat-shirt, and you've stopped serving in the dining room, and Al's cut her hair—what else?"

His teasing blue eyes held a question as he looked at Diana, but instead of meeting his gaze she looked down at her sweatshirt and began brushing the leaves away with shaking hands. What was he doing here? And could she stop herself from running across the yard and throwing herself into his arms?

"Not much else," Allison said. "But we sure miss you, Zach. Can you stay and eat with us?"

Zach glanced appraisingly in Diana's direction. "That's up to your mother. After all, it is Saturday night, and she might have a date or something."

"She doesn't go on dates," Allison said, and Laurie reached over and nudged her with an elbow. "I mean, she *could* go on dates if someone—cut it out, Laurie!"

"Al's trying to say that Mom's very discriminating," Laurie remarked, glaring at her sister.

Allison snorted. "There she goes again, Miss Dippy Dictionary. When did you learn that one?"

"Eighth graders learn lots of things, bimbo. Like when to keep their mouths shut."

"Oh, yeah? I haven't noticed that you—"

Zach cleared his throat, and Allison sneaked a guilty glance upward.

"Excuse us, Zach," she said in a tiny voice. "We'd like you to stay for supper."

"It's your mother's decision," Zach repeated.

Allison turned pleading eyes on her mother. "Can he, Mom?"

Diana gulped. Like hell it was her decision. Zach knew she wouldn't say no, with Allison and Laurie staring at him like lost puppies. Again the question pounded through her brain. Why was he here? "If the girls would like you to stay, it's fine with me."

Laurie eyed her mother then studied Zach. "We would," she said firmly. "If you don't mind soup and toasted cheese sandwiches, that is. I'm fixing it." She pinioned Allison with a baleful stare, daring her to insult the cook.

"Sounds terrific," Zach replied.

"Sure does," Allison agreed, giving her sister a sunny smile. "All this running around is making me hungry."

"Want me to get started, Mom, or help rake?"

"Go ahead and start supper, Laurie," Diana said. "Allison and I will clean up the leaves." Now that the shared meal would be a reality, they might as well get through it as quickly as possible. Did Zach imagine he could just drop by on a casual basis once in a while? Her nerves wouldn't stand it, and she'd tell him so the first chance she got.

"I'll help, too," Zach offered cheerfully, picking up one of the rakes.

"Great!" Allison said and grabbed her own rake. "Did you notice the fence is still holding up, Zach? Beethoven hasn't gotten out once. And the chicken cage is okay, too, only rocks a little bit. Maybe while you're here, you can help me move it into the garage, where it's warmer. I wanted to put them in the basement, but Mom's not too crazy about—"

"Allison, my goodness," Diana interrupted. "You'll talk Zach's ear off."

Her daughter's blue eyes narrowed. "That's twice now, Mom. I thought you were calling me 'Al' as of today?"

Diana felt Zach's curious gaze on her. "Uh, sorry. I forgot."

"Mom says 'Al' goes with my new haircut," Allison confided to Zach.

"She does?" Zach leaned on his rake and watched Diana as she continued to work with feverish intensity. A smile played across his lips.

"I'll hold a garbage bag, if you'll rake the leaves into it," Allison suggested. Zach continued to stare at Diana. "Or you can hold the bag, and I'll rake into it." No answer. Allison threw up both hands. "Guess I'll do it by myself, since no one's paying any attention to me."

"What?" Zach's head swiveled in Allison's direction. "You say something, Al?"

Allison grinned. "Yeah. Wanna hold the bag while I rake leaves into it?"

"Good idea."

She shook her head and grinned some more. "Grown-ups."

"Careful, Al," Zach said, shaking open the bag. "You'll be one of those someday, too."

"If I am, I hope to have more sense than some people I know."

He lowered his voice. "You wouldn't be talking about present company, would you?"

"I might." Allison regarded him slyly and spoke in a whisper. "Running off and leaving Mom like that. She's so miserable that Laurie and I have our hands full keeping her even halfway happy."

Zach exercised an iron will to keep from dropping the bag and crossing the yard to take Diana in his arms. His sweet lonely Diana. And hadn't he been through the same hell? "Is that right?"

"Yep. You should come back."

"Hmm."

"We won't fight if you do."

"Oh, Al, sweetheart. I didn't leave because of you two. I've missed you like crazy."

"Really?" Allison's smile lit up the pale autumn afternoon.

"Really."

"Then Laurie was right."

"About what?"

Allison raked harder. "Nothing." She stopped raking and glanced up at him. "But we don't care what Jenny says anymore," she blurted out hurriedly then resumed her raking.

Zach almost dropped the bag of leaves. The girls weren't so naive, after all. They'd figured out his and Diana's problem, and they wanted to solve it, regardless of the consequences to themselves. Diana had been right. He could have convinced them to move to California, or even the moon, if he'd tried. But he couldn't take advantage of devotion like that.

"You can close this one up," Allison announced. "Why don't you get another bag for Mom's pile?"

"Good idea."

"I have lots of good ideas. Here's another one. I'm going in to help Laurie." She dashed across the yard, with Beethoven scampering after her.

Zach picked up a black plastic bag and walked across the dry brown grass toward Diana. He clenched the bag, praying for the willpower to keep his hands to himself. A few matters had to be settled before he touched her again. But dammit, they would have to be settled soon, or he'd go nuts.

"Like some help?"

She glanced up from the pile of brown and gold leaves.

"I'll hold the bag while you rake," he explained while she continued to study him.

"Why are you here?" she asked softly.

"I couldn't stay away."

Her lashes fluttered over her eyes, concealing her reaction. "You can't drop in like this, like some casual friend. I'm—you make me nervous."

"Good."

Her silver eyes flashed. "We are not going to start up again, Zach," she said in an urgent undertone. "I will not pursue a relationship with someone who's here today and gone tomorrow. The girls deserve more than that, and so do I."

"I agree. Does your faucet still drip?"

"What?" She looked at him as if he'd gone crazy.

"The kitchen faucet. Does it still drip?"

"Of course it does. After I had paid to have the washing machine fixed, I couldn't very well afford another repair bill."

"I thought you might have hired another handyman. No more ads in the paper?"

She stared at him in surprise. In the weeks that he'd been gone, never had she considered advertising for another handyman. She realized that didn't make much sense, unless...

"I once told you I had a theory about that ad," he said, as if reading her thoughts. "Want to hear it?"

"Not particularly."

"I'll tell you, anyway. You wanted someone to fix the sink and paint the windowsills, but more than that, you wanted a friend."

She gripped the rake with both hands, and he wondered if she might swing it at him. "I did not advertise for a romantic partner!"

"I didn't say that. The sexual electricity between us was a bonus—but the friendship was essential."

"Nonsense. I have the girls."

Zach nodded. "I think now you do, but you didn't then, and you won't have them forever. Have you considered that?"

"Yes!" she hissed and began raking furiously.

"Good." He shook open the bag.

They worked in silence for a few minutes, while Diana fumed at his impertinent questions. What was this, a fact-finding mission to soothe his battered ego? Well, she might as well get a few questions answered, too. "How was your interview at Stanford?"

"Very nice."

"Did they offer you a job?"

"Not yet, but I think there's a good chance."

"I'm sure you're pleased." In spite of her immediate anger with him, she experienced a jab of anguish that his departure was almost assured. Even though he hadn't been living in her house for the past few weeks, he'd been in the same town. Soon half a continent would separate them. Logically the difference shouldn't matter, but it did.

"You've stopped raking," Zach chided softly. "Something bothering you?"

"Of course not," she snapped, resuming her task with a vengeance. "Everything's dandy."

Zach watched the determined set of her jaw, and a smile flickered across his face. Unless he didn't know her at all, she still cared a hell of a lot. Thank God for that.

Supper was noisy as both girls filled Zach in on their recent activities. After they had eaten, he helped Allison and Laurie with the dishes, and Diana, feeling almost as though she was in the way, wandered into the living room and switched on the television set. A short while later the girls walked Zach to the front door.

"So long, Diana!" he called from the doorway.

Diana couldn't find a suitable reply. *So long?* He breezed in this afternoon, told her he'd been compelled to come back then left at seven-thirty in the evening? She'd expected him to invite her to a movie or for a cup of coffee or even a drive in the hopes of luring her back to his apartment for a roll in the hay. She'd had it all figured out, and now he was leaving?

Laurie and Allison waved goodbye then shut the door on the chill autumn night.

Her hands stuffed in her jeans pockets, Allison strolled toward the sofa, where Diana sat pretending to watch the images on the television screen. "Gee, wasn't it freaky to see Zach again?"

That about sums it up, Diana thought. "I—I guess so."

"I'd say he looked terrific," Laurie added, plopping into the easy chair. "A little thin, and his tan's faded, but he's really a hunk, don't you agree, Mom?"

Diana swallowed. "He's okay, if you go for that type."

Allison peered at her mother. "What type?"

"Oh, you know. The California surfer type with muscles, sun-bleached hair—you know." Diana affected complete lack of interest.

Allison grinned. "Oh, *that* type. Did you know you stared at him all through dinner?"

Laurie darted a reproachful look across the room at Allison.

"Well, she did," Allison insisted. "But I can see why. He's pretty nice scenery."

"Listen, girls. I don't know why Zach dropped over today, or if he plans to come back, but you'd better realize that in a few short weeks he'll leave Springfield. He's only a temporary friend."

The girls exchanged glances; then Allison shrugged with exaggerated nonchalance. "That's the way it goes."

"Yeah, Mom," Laurie added. "Win a few, lose a few." Allison had a sudden fit of coughing, and Laurie jumped up to pound her sister on the back. "Come on, Al," she said, dragging her sister by the arm into the kitchen. "You need a glass of water."

Slowly Diana began to piece everything together. Only one explanation made sense. Zach had disregarded her wishes and convinced the girls that they'd love moving to California. He'd had the chance, while they were all doing dishes and the sound from the television blocked out their conversation.

She considered confronting the girls with her suspicions but decided against it. Why should they become further embroiled in a controversy that was really between her and Zach? If she was right, he'd come back over to present his case, and when he did, she'd be ready for him. The Thatcher women were not going to trail halfway across the country after Zachary Wainwright!

THE NEXT MORNING Laurie arrived at the breakfast table, wailing that her underwear was in tatters.

"Please, Mom, take me over to White Oaks. Every time I get undressed in PE, the girls will make fun of me. Look at this." She held up a ripped pair of underpants.

"I wish you would, Mom," Allison said. "I don't want to be known as the sister of someone whose underwear self-destructs."

Diana examined the garment. "That's exactly what it looks like, Laurie. We bought these in August. Where'd we get them?"

"Some discount store, and see how they held up? Let's go to some nice place in White Oaks. Today."

"Okay, but what about yours, Al? We must have bought them together."

"Different batch, I guess," Allison said airily. "My undies are in A-number-one shape."

Diana frowned. "Strange. Well, after lunch is fine with me. You probably want to go, anyway, don't you, Al? You could get some ideas for your birthday presents."

"Can't. Too much homework."

"Oh?" Diana glanced at her younger daughter in surprise. Allison, allowing homework to come between her and a trip to the mall? Perhaps she was growing up faster than Diana had suspected. Still...she sipped her coffee thoughtfully. Something strange was going on. But what?

After lunch Allison spread her math on the kitchen table with a great show of industry, barely looking up when Laurie and Diana left.

"I've never known Al to have so much dedication to homework," Diana remarked to Laurie as they drove across town.

"I guess she's finally realizing the value of studying," Laurie said primly then deliberately changed the subject.

The shopping trip took longer than Diana had expected. Laurie dawdled over the underwear selection then insisted on browsing through several clothing stores to point out potential Christmas gifts. Finally Diana insisted her feet were tired, and Laurie reluctantly agreed to go home.

From a block away Diana spotted the orange Corvair parked in front of the house. "Laurie?"

"Gee, Mom, Zach must have dropped by while we were gone."

"I may be getting older, but I'm not senile yet. You planned this mall trip, didn't you? And Allison's homework was an excuse to be here when Zach arrived."

"Uh, yeah."

"What on earth is going on?"

"I, um, it's a surprise, Mom! Don't make me tell you."

Diana gripped the steering wheel tighter. A surprise? What did he have in mind, a banner announcing the move to California? Suntan lotion and beach towels for everyone? Well, she'd just see about that!

"Mom, you look mad," Laurie said nervously.

"I am not mad," Diana said through clenched teeth. "But I intend to teach Zachary Wainwright a lesson."

"Mom, please don't be—"

"Never mind, Laurie. I'll handle this." She parked the car in the driveway, jumped out and slammed the door.

Allison burst through the back door. "Wait, Mom. You can't go in yet."

"Oh, yes, I can."

"But, Mom, you'll ruin the surprise!" Allison turned to Laurie. "Couldn't you keep her away longer?"

"I tried, but you guys should be done by now. It's been three hours!"

"Well, we're not. Zach had an eensy bit of trouble. Mom, wait," she begged, but Diana brushed past her and pulled open the back door.

"Come on, Al," Laurie advised, tugging on her sister's arm. "Let's make ourselves scarce. No telling what will happen now."

Diana stormed through the door. "Zachary Wainwright, I don't know what you're up to, but I—my God, what is this mess?" She almost tripped over a large plumber's wrench lying beside Zach's prone body. His head and shoulders were wedged under the sink, and the kitchen floor was strewn with an assortment of tools, nuts and bolts.

"Hi, sweetheart," came his muffled greeting. "Would you hand me that wrench?"

"Which one? We have enough here to start our own hardware store. And what's this sweetheart stuff? We are not sweethearts, nor are we likely to be. I demand to know what—"

"Don't be hasty with the conclusions, Diana. Let me finish this first. I need the big wrench, somewhere near my foot, I think."

"Oh, all right. Here." She picked up the wrench and placed it none too gently in his outstretched palm.

"Thanks. Al and I thought we'd be done by now, but we ran into a few complications. I think I've almost got it, though. I couldn't afford a diamond ring, Diana, so this will have to do."

"Diamond ring? Zach, we've been through this before, and there's no way."

"The faucet sparkles almost as much as a diamond, don't you think?" Zach commented from under the sink, as if she hadn't spoken. "It's washerless so it won't drip. Take a look."

With a sigh Diana stood up and gazed at the shiny object perched on the sink. Zach, who didn't know a plumber's helper from a socket wrench, was replacing her dripping faucet. Or attempting to replace it. She didn't know whether to laugh or cry.

"The instructions said if I just tighten—dammit!"

"What? What happened?" Diana peered under the sink.

"Nothing."

"What do you mean 'nothing'? I know you, Zach, and you don't swear over nothing."

"Oh, hell. Now it's bleeding."

"Bleeding? Zach, what have you done? Come out from there this minute and let me see."

"But I'm almost done! Damn, it's dripping on the cabinet."

"Zach!" Diana reached under the cabinet with both hands and pulled. "Get out from under there this minute. You don't know the first thing about this, and you could easily lose a finger or maybe even a hand or—"

All at once he wiggled out and was face-to-face with her. "I don't care," he murmured. "I just don't want to lose you."

"Zach, it's—it's no use," she stammered. Oh, his eyes were so blue! She struggled to remember the speech she'd rehearsed for this moment, the moment when he'd announce that the girls favored the move to California.

"I've applied for a job at Springfield Community College."

"No matter what the girls said, we're not—" She stopped and stared at him. "Repeat that, please?"

"I'm no longer a candidate for the job at Stanford."

"Wait a minute, Zach. Everything you've done up to now was geared toward landing that job. Stanford is your dream."

"Wrong." He took her arm and pulled her down to sit beside him then glanced in dismay at her blouse. "I got blood on you. Have you got a small bandage?"

She leaped up. "Your wound! I completely forgot. Hold out your hand."

He obeyed silently, and she inspected the cut across his palm.

"Doesn't look too bad. Just messy. I'll be right back." In a moment she returned from her bathroom with a small box of bandages, cotton swabs and antiseptic. "Let me have your hand again," she said, sitting next to him.

Zach rested his palm in her lap. "How about taking the rest of me, too?" he asked gently. "Think you could fall for a guy who teaches history at Springfield Community College? I know this fellow pretty well. He's lousy at fixing things around the house, but he's crazy about you, and he'll even take night classes in home maintenance, if that would help."

"Oh, Zach." Diana's vision blurred, and she struggled to see the wound she was dabbing with antiseptic. "You shouldn't have taken yourself out of the running for the Stanford job. Maybe if you write to them immediately, they'll reconsider hiring—"

"No, Diana."

She placed the bandage over the cut with trembling hands. "Zach, I can no more expect you to give up Stanford than you can expect us to move."

"Dear, sweet Diana. Don't the folks in Illinois understand compromise? Abraham Lincoln was a master at it."

She chanced a look into his eyes, and her breath caught in her throat. "What sort of compromise?" she whispered.

"Oh, Diana," he groaned. "How those eyes have haunted me. I want you so much." His lips drifted toward hers, but he caught himself. "We have to get this settled, once and for all."

Diana took a shaky breath. "Okay."

A cool autumn breeze blew through the screen door, and Zach heard the creak of the porch swing. The girls were out there, listening. What if Diana said no? He focused on the screen door, afraid he might see the refusal on her face and lose the courage to say his piece.

"The compromise I propose is this. I'll work in Springfield until the girls graduate from high school, and then you and I will move to California as soon as Stanford will have me. In the meantime I'll become the damnedest expert on Lincoln they've ever seen."

Her mouth formed the word "yes," but no sound came out.

"I realize you may not want to leave here, even after the girls graduate, but that seems only fair, if I—"

"Zach," she whispered hoarsely. "Yes."

His blue gaze swung to her radiant face. "Yes?"

She nodded, love glowing in her eyes.

"*Yes?*" he fairly shouted.

"Why not? I love you, my fix-it man."

"Why, Widow Thatcher," he breathed, "I believe you do." And he kissed her, gathering her against him despite the grease covering his shirt and the presence of two smiling girls standing with their arms around each other's shoulders, their noses pressed against the screen door.

LOOK FOR OUR FOUR FABULOUS MEN!

Each month some of today's bestselling authors bring
four new fabulous men to Harlequin American Romance.
Whether they're rebel ranchers, millionaire power brokers
or sexy single dads, they're all gallant princes—and
they're all ready to sweep you into lighthearted fantasies
and contemporary fairy tales where anything is possible
and where all your dreams come true!

You don't even have to make a wish...
Harlequin American Romance will grant your every desire!

Look for Harlequin American Romance
wherever Harlequin books are sold!

Harlequin Romance®

Delightful

Affectionate

Romantic

Emotional

Tender

Original

Daring

Riveting

Enchanting

Adventurous

Moving

Harlequin Romance—the
series that has it all!

HROM-G

HARLEQUIN SUPERROMANCE®

...there's more to the story!

Superromance. A *big* satisfying read about unforgettable characters. Each month we offer *four* very different stories that range from family drama to adventure and mystery, from highly emotional stories to romantic comedies—and much more! Stories about people you'll believe in and care about. Stories too compelling to put down....

Our authors are among today's *best* romance writers. You'll find familiar names and talented newcomers. Many of them are award winners—and you'll see why!

If you want the biggest and best in romance fiction, you'll get it from Superromance!

Available wherever Harlequin books are sold.

Harlequin® Historical

From rugged lawmen and
valiant knights to defiant heiresses
and spirited frontierswomen,
Harlequin Historicals will
capture your imagination with
their dramatic scope, passion
and adventure.

Harlequin Historicals...
they're too good to miss!

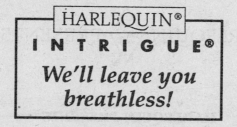

HARLEQUIN  PRESENTS®

HARLEQUIN PRESENTS
men you won't be able to resist
falling in love with...

HARLEQUIN PRESENTS
women who have feelings
just like your own...

HARLEQUIN PRESENTS
powerful passion in
exotic international settings...

HARLEQUIN PRESENTS
intense, dramatic stories that will keep you
turning to the very last page...

HARLEQUIN PRESENTS
The world's bestselling romance series!

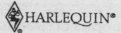

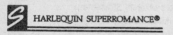